W9-BMP-243

Amsterdam Trilogy, Book Two

The New Worlds of
Isabela
Calderón

Sequel to The Seventh Etching

Judith K. White

Judith K. White

iUniverse LLC
Bloomington

The New Worlds of Isabela Calderón
Sequel to The Seventh Etching

Copyright © 2014 by Judith K. White

All rights reserved. No part of this book may be used or reproduced by any means, graphic, electronic, or mechanical, including photocopying, recording, taping or by any information storage retrieval system without the written permission of the publisher except in the case of brief quotations embodied in critical articles and reviews.

Certain characters in this work are historical figures, and certain events portrayed did take place. However, this is a work of fiction. All of the other characters, names, and events as well as all places, incidents, organizations, and dialogue in this novel are either the products of the author's imagination or are used fictitiously.

iUniverse books may be ordered through booksellers or by contacting:

iUniverse LLC
1663 Liberty Drive
Bloomington, IN 47403
www.iuniverse.com
1-800-Authors (1-800-288-4677)

Because of the dynamic nature of the Internet, any web addresses or links contained in this book may have changed since publication and may no longer be valid. The views expressed in this work are solely those of the author and do not necessarily reflect the views of the publisher, and the publisher hereby disclaims any responsibility for them.

Any people depicted in stock imagery provided by Thinkstock are models, and such images are being used for illustrative purposes only.

Certain stock imagery © Thinkstock.

ISBN: 978-1-4917-3232-8 (sc)
ISBN: 978-1-4917-3231-1 (hc)
ISBN: 978-1-4917-3230-4 (e)

Library of Congress Control Number: 2014908097

Printed in the United States of America

iUniverse rev. date: 05/06/2014

Dedication

FOR ALLEN

Prologue
Unearthed Mystery

July 23, 2002
St. Augustine.com
"Spanish cross from 1600s found"
Peter Guinta, Senior Writer

An exquisite bronze cross, dating back to the early 1600s Spanish settlement in St. Augustine, Florida, has been unearthed at an archaeological dig downtown.

Preliminary opinion says it's a "Caravaca Cross," which reportedly carried papal indulgences attached to it and was used in Spain as protection against lightning and rabies and as an aid to childbirth.

The Caravaca Cross is similar to the French "Cross of Lorraine," which also has two horizontal arms. The Latin Cross has only one arm.

City Archeologist, Carl Halbirt, said he was surprised by the intricate workmanship of this object, the fused front and back plates, the hinge at the top and the engraved wheat on its face.

"I've never seen a cross like this one," Halbirt said. "They have been found in the Southeast, the Caribbean, and in Canada, but not here—not until now."

Pressed for an estimate of its monetary value, he said, "The value is in the significance we want to place on it. It's part of St. Augustine's history. You really can't put a price on that sort of thing."

His excavation turned up other objects—buttons, bones, pottery, spoons, and seeds—in a barrel well and trash pit that date the artifacts to the mid 1600s.

"This crucifix is an absolutely outstanding find," says John T. Powell, a college professor, museum curator, and consultant. "Whoever had this was a person of some means. This is in the top 10 or 20 percent of rarity. You just don't find something that intricately made."

Halbirt said that when the cross was lost, St. Augustine had 600 to 700 residents.

According to Leslee Keys, Executive Director of the Ximenez-Fatio House, the cross will be included in an exhibit at their visitor's center.

"This is the 10th dig on the property," Keys said. "We didn't expect to find anything that unusual. The greatest value to all of us is that it's so rare and so early. It's a one-of-a-kind artifact."

* * *

But we are left with an unsolved mystery: Why was the cross buried in that trash pit? Who put it there?

PART I
Spain

Chapter One
Sea, Sand, and Memories

1650
Village of Santos Gemelos
Department of Asturias

A haven—that is what Isabela sought. Here on this strip of beach. A brief escape from her longings and fears, from a dreary household, from an uncaring husband. The steady sound of gentle waves offered solace from the horrors she had experienced just beyond in the open sea.

She reached down, curled her wrist and came up with a fistful of ocean water. In order to steady her hand, she kept her elbow tight against her body. Before it all dripped through her fingers, she lifted the water to her nose and sniffed its brine, its fishiness, secrets, and mysteries. She licked the drops that remained, along with the tiny, chewy bits of seaweed. Resisting the urge to swallow, she savored the salty taste on her tongue until it faded.

One moment the sea was a calm, stately beauty, the sunlight or moonlight plunging its depths and reflecting off its surface. A composed, flirtatious lady bedecked in layers of green and blue flecked with diamonds and rubies. But she could never trust this *grand dame*. The next moment, clouds might hide her loveliness. A wind could excite her. She may turn into a holy devil reaching up with all her force to pull down, capture, surround, kill.

1

All her life Isabela had observed this deceptive monster and once she nearly succumbed to its rages. During a confused moment, she wished fervently to lose herself in its blackness, to disappear in its depths. She wanted to join her father there. And the wounded sailor, Jules, who gave her a desperate kiss—her first kiss ever—before diving from her father's sinking ship and disappearing. But it was Cornelius who pulled her back into the rowboat and into reality. Cornelius handed her a bucket. "Bail," he bellowed. And bail she did while Cornelius pulled the oars and rowed. Hours later Isabela—a sodden creature in a tattered silk nightgown twisted around her limp body—arrived at the shore of a strange city. Guttural sounds of its language approached and receded as she regained consciousness. She came to love that city. Amsterdam. The city where she met Pieter.

"Mama, Mama, give me the cup, please. Pedro's made a castle. I want to fill up the moat."

"Not yet, Nelita," Pedro said with older brother irritation. "I'm not finished. Mama. Come see. Here's where the horsemen approach. They're still far away, these soldiers. See, Mama?" Pedro placed his carved wooden toy figures on a sand path some distance from his miniature castle's entrance. "You can tell how far away they are. When they look ahead, the path looks narrow. I made it that way. That's perspective. Like you taught me, Mama."

"Per . . . pec . . . tif," Nelita struggled to repeat. She reached up to her mother. "Cup please, Mama?"

With their dark hair and eyes and their olive skin, her children looked thoroughly Spanish. They spoke no Dutch. They had never visited Amsterdam. Yet every day something in her life with them in this coastal village where she was born reminded Isabela of the eighteen months she spent in that city. Nearly a decade ago. So far north. So far away. So much a part of her.

Perspective. That one word sent her back in time to Pieter who placed a piece of charcoal between her fingers. She felt the warmth of his hand as he guided her drawing. The only art lesson she ever received.

"You can do it, Isabela. See how the canal gradually narrows the farther away from us it flows? Just below us it's wide. If you draw the canal's path as it moves away from you, it will become a trickle. Eventually, it will nearly disappear."

But she must not dawdle in the past. Diego has stated that he will take Pedro on his first voyage—a celebration of his tenth birthday. There is no persuading him otherwise.

2

"He will follow the path of his grandfathers and father, Isabela. You think he's still your little baby?"

Nightmares of the shipwreck pursued Isabela. The terror of losing her precious son to the sea overwhelmed her. She must find a way to protect her child.

"Time for the evening meal soon, my lovely children," Isabela coaxed in her lilting way as she began to gather up toys. But Pedro was wading in the surf away from her.

"Mama, come see what I found," he yelled.

"Show me another time, Pedro. We have to climb back up for the evening meal."

"No, Mama, come here. I want to show you this."

Isabela took Nelita's hand and walked toward her son's voice. He had gone much farther than she thought, to an area of the beach she wasn't even aware of. She panicked when she couldn't see him, although she had just heard him calling her a moment earlier. She began running.

At high tide, the cliff reached into the sea blocking off a section of a secluded cove. Isabela picked up Nelita and waded through the surf calling her son's name. Her damp skirts and petticoats slowed her down. She spotted him waving, sitting in a small abandoned rowboat, tucked up against the bluff. Pedro had grabbed one of the oars and was pretending to row.

"Leave the boat as you found it, Pedro. Come on now," she called to him.

Once they had sloshed their way back to their play area and were tidying up, Pedro warned,

"Careful, Mama. Don't destroy my castle. See how I built it? It has a moat all around. Five floors. Lookout towers on all sides. A flag made out of seaweed on top. A Spanish flag. My soldiers protect the castle, Mama."

Pedro picked up two of the three-inch tall wooden soldiers. He gave voice to their increasingly threatening words as they warded off an unseen enemy.

"Don't you come any closer. We will maim you. We will torture you. We will kill you. This castle belongs to OUR King."

Isabela recoiled from her son's violent utterances, but she understood that in part he was trying to fulfill the role of his often absent father, that he felt vulnerable growing up without a steady, male presence in his life. Already he was quite proficient with a sword.

"I'll beat you to the top," Pedro yelled down to his mother and sister.

Built into the cliff fifty years ago under the supervision of Isabela's grandfather, the stone stairs had nearly been taken over by weeds that encroached from both sides. With one hand, Isabela guided Nelita. In the other she held a wooden bucket that contained the sandy soldiers and the few digging utensils she had borrowed from Cook's kitchen.

"How many more steps, Mama?"

"Let's count them together."

"*Uno. Dos. Tres.*"

"Only three more, Nelita. Three. That's a special number to you, isn't it?"

"Three? Of course, Mama. I know that. I am THREE YEARS OLD!"

Nelita took a step upward and slipped on a patch of uneven moss dampened by yesterday's downpour. As she felt a rivulet run down her leg and caught sight of a redness seeping through her ankle-length frock, she began to howl. Isabela dropped the bucket, which clanged down the stairs spilling soldiers. Scattered now they looked as if they had been injured or killed in battle. She half expected the miniatures to begin writhing in pain.

"OH, NO!" Pedro cried out when he turned to see what had happened.

He squeezed by his distressed sister and gathered up his soldiers.

"I'll take charge of these," he pronounced.

When Isabela and her children arrived at the top step, her mother-in-law, having heard Nelita's wailing, stood looking down on them, hands on hips, lips pursed.

"What has happened now? I don't know why you insist on taking the children down there, Isabela. They come back filthy, smelling of fish . . . and now hurt as well?"

Isabela had learned not to respond to every critical, scolding, unhelpful comment. She brushed by Doña Juana and took the children directly to Cook's cottage where she knew Nelita would be soothed and coddled. Cook came running out to investigate and led Nelita to her shelf of remedies. She cleared Nelita's chubby toddler knee of sand and pebbles, then gently rubbed salve onto the small wound. Although the scratch did not require it, Cook made a big show of painting a smiling little girl face on a clean piece of cloth and affixing it to Nelita's knee.

On the path back to the big house, Isabela cheered her daughter with the same song she sang to the orphan Nelleke years ago, the night

4

Nelleke arrived at the Amsterdam City Orphanage and burned her hand with hot wax.

"*Sana, sana, colita de rana.*
Si no sanas hoy, sanarás mañana."

Heal, heal little tadpole.
If you don't heal today, tomorrow you will.

* * *

Once the simple, tense meal was over, Isabela retreated to the room she shared with her son and daughter. After she read them a Bible story, all three kneeled in prayer beneath the crucifix. She tucked them into bed and lulled them to sleep with a Dutch lullaby she herself had learned in the orphanage.

Slaap, kindje, slaap.	Sleep, little child, sleep.
Daar buiten lopt een schaap!	Outside strolls a sheep.
Een schaap met vier witte voetjes,	A sheep with four little white feet,
Dat drinkt zijn melk zo zoetjes.	That drinks its milk so very sweet.
Schaapje met zijn witte wol.	Little sheep with its white wool.
Kindje drinkt zin buikje vol.	Little child drinks its belly full.

* * *

At last came the time of day she enjoyed most.

Isabela moved the candle to her writing desk tucked into a nook, a corner of the room she shared with her children. Thanks to the warning from Cook just before her wedding, she was able to salvage this piece of furniture—one of the last of the many gifts her Captain father brought her throughout her childhood. A young lady of fourteen then, she was enchanted with its carvings, the three levels of narrow, deep drawers, the secret cabinet attached below the desk. After confirming that her children had fallen asleep, she reached on tiptoe for the cabinet's key placed high on a stone ledge.

From the cabinet she removed three wooden boxes—also gifts from her father. Knowing of her interest in collections—shells, buttons, bits of fabric—he often searched during his travels abroad and found these for her. All with lids, they originated from three different countries—England, France, and Italy—places he visited before war interfered.

One lid had a simple painting of Mary, holding the baby Jesus. Mary's face was not visible, but Isabela was sure she was smiling her mild, gentle smile. She was bent over her infant, feeding him perhaps, soothing him, wondering at his beauty, or pondering his future, knowing that he was God's son sent to earth. The ends of Mary's head scarf enveloped the baby, connecting mother and child forever.

The second lid was randomly scattered with cherry-sized red stones surrounded by small shiny clear ones. At fourteen, she admired them for their brightness. She wondered who had selected the jewels and arranged them like flowers. Did a man make the box and a woman design the pattern perhaps? Did they work together to create this miniature masterpiece? She didn't think then about whether they were real rubies or diamonds. Recently, she had begun to wonder what their worth might be and if she could ever part with them. The third lid made of a lighter wood than the others was plain, smooth and varnished.

The boxes contained every letter she had received since arriving back in her village. She regarded each one as a treasure, even though it was delivered months after being written and always left her wanting more recent news.

The Mary box overflowed with letters from the loquacious Nelleke. The jeweled one held her friend Anneliese's amusing descriptions of daily Amsterdam life as the daughter and then the wife of wealthy merchants. The plain one had only a few letters—business letters she called them—from The Orphanage's Housemother or from Mr. Broekhof. Isabela had never been able to break the habit of scanning each letter before reading it, searching for Pieter's name, for any mention of him, no matter how brief, no matter how many times she had read the letter before.

Although Nelleke was a neighbor of Pieter's, she was much younger than he, involved in her own, new family's activities, and rarely mentioned him. As his sister, Anneliese, wrote of Pieter occasionally, mostly with concern.

"Once my brother's life path was so clear to him. Study with Rembrandt. Become a member of the artist guild. Establish himself. Marry. He continues to paint, but it's travel that consumes him. Florence. Rome. Antwerp. Brussels. He is a devoted uncle to my children. He never seems to tire of inventing games to amuse them. They adore him and miss him. Yet he seems so restless."

Isabela did not need to read those words. She had memorized them. She too worried about Pieter, but to contact him, to correspond with him, would be unseemly, highly improper, and perhaps not helpful for either of them. Actually it would be impossible. By now she's learned that one of the reasons Diego came for her was because her aunts, Tía Anacleta and Tía Lucia, shared Isabela's Amsterdam letters with the de Vega family. Apparently both her aunts and her future in-laws became concerned by Isabela's increasingly enthusiastic descriptions of Pieter. They feared she would never return to Santos Gemelos to fulfill the marriage arrangement her father made for her at her birth. Even after all these years, Doña Juana sorted Isabela's mail before giving it to her, suspiciously turning over envelopes, perhaps searching for clues of unfaithfulness.

As part of her nightly ritual of letter reading and writing, some evenings Isabela chose a letter at random from one of the three boxes. She closed her eyes, removed a lid, and ruffled through the contents, knowing that whatever letter she chose would surprise and delight her as much as it did the day it arrived. Other times, she took weeks to go through one box at a time, reading the letters in order.

This time she chose the latter approach. She removed the painted lid and lifted out the letter on top—the first letter she ever received from Nelleke—eleven months after Isabela was awakened in the middle of the night by Diego and Cornelius and brought from Amsterdam back to her home village. Isabela remembers staring at the seal, puzzled by the initials N.B., and wondering who it could possibly be from. The letter began in Nelleke's large-lettered, labored scrawl and continued in the elegant handwriting of Nelleke's new mother, Myriam Broekhof.

16 May 1642
Dear my darling, my friend, my Big Sister Isabela,

> *Mama says that greeting was too long, but I will make it shorter next time. I promise.*
> *You are alive! You are in Spain! You are home! Your letter arrived today. A courier (Mama had to help me spell that word) brought it from the orphanage (that word too). A letter addressed to me, Miss Nelleke Stradwijk. Except I have a new name now. Nelleke Broekhof. They even baptized me again in the church. I have a new home, new parents, and two*

new brothers. Big brothers, not a younger one like Jacob. Mama and Papa take me to the farm to visit Jacob sometimes.

I could not finish the midday meal. I was so squirmy that finally Mama and Papa excused me from the table. Mama and I went to Anneliese's house so she could translate your letter. It took a long time. I was jumping in my chair waiting for Anneliese. Mama tried to hold my hands still.

First Anneliese read your English in silence. I remember how jealous Anneliese was that you had spent six weeks in England before you landed in Amsterdam and how the two of you used to chatter away in that language. Then it was my turn to be jealous, since I could not understand a word.

Next Anneliese said your words out loud to us in Dutch. Pieter was there. I think he was impatient too. He walked around a lot.

This is taking too long. I have so much to tell you. Mama will write now. But she will write MY words. I miss you, Isabela. I was so scared when we woke up and you were not there. I threw myself on your bed and hid my face in your pillow. I would not get up for breakfast or school. The police came and looked for clues. Mrs. Heijn (oh how happy I am that I don't have to call her Mother anymore) told them that you must still be wearing your nightdress. That was because Mrs. Heijn found your uniform in the wardrobe.

Your day clogs were still under the bed. I worried that you were wandering somewhere in bare feet. I was the one who noticed that your rosary was not where you always kept it—under your pillow. I know how you cherished it. At least, we hoped the rosary was with you. Although we are not Catholics, we hoped the rosary would protect you.

Then we learned today exactly what happened to you. You are married. You will have a baby soon. I wish I could see you, Isabela. I do so wish it. I wish it so, so much.

I help Mama a lot. I have my own shopping basket. You should see my new bonnet. It has a broad strip of yellow ribbon.

Right now I am sitting at my desk. It's just my size. I have my own ink, my feather pens, my rose petals, and my notebook—just like Mama. We sit side by side. We read and we write. Mama teaches me.

I am still seven. I haven't gotten any older. I'll always know how old you are, Isabela. I just add ten like this. 7 + 10 = 17. You are seventeen. Every day Mama does number work with me.

Mama says I should ask you about yourself, Isabela. You will be a wonderful mama. You got to practice with all us little girls. I know you will sing to your baby—those lullabies in French and Spanish. I can hear you in my head. *The funny way you say Dutch words. Oh, I am starting to cry a little. Mama hugs me. She knows how I miss you, Isabela. I didn't know where you were. I didn't know why you left without saying good-bye.*

But Isabela, can I call you just Bela when I write my next letter? It's shorter. It takes less time. Besides, Mama says if we add an "l" it will be "Bella" and that means "beautiful" in your language. You see, Isabela? Bella? It's perfect because you yourself are so, so beautiful.

Papa says letters take a long time to arrive at their destination. (A new word for me. Destination. I like it). Sometimes they don't ever get there. Your country and mine are in a war. I sometimes see soldiers here. I think war is silly, even ridiculous (another word I learned recently). Ridiculous. The fighting makes it harder for letters to get through, Papa says. I do so, so, SO hope you get this letter, Isabela Bella.

Mama says we must now arrange for this letter to be sent. That means I don't have time to tell you that Daniel lets me play with his toy ship now. Also that I hoist up my skirts and run with the kite Samuel gave me . . . and I almost never fall. Did you know I can read and write now? I can count almost to infinity too. Do you know how many numbers that is? If you were here, I would show you.

Your friend and "little sister" forever,
N..E..L..L..E..K..E B..R..O..E..K..H..O..F

In Isabela's handwriting: "Received 22 August 1642, three months after Nelleke wrote it."

* * *

Reading Nelleke's first letter always took Isabela's mind back to the shock of waking up to see Diego and Cornelius dressed as Dutch soldiers, tapping her on the shoulder, peering down at her, motioning for her to get out of bed.

"Quickly. Now," they hissed.

Chapter Two
Fall 1641 Amsterdam City Orphanage

hey motioned for her to be silent. She knew what was happening. She knew she would never again see the orphan girls sleeping soundly only a few feet away. Those twenty little girls she had been caring for those past eighteen months. She did not want to frighten them. She felt terrible knowing they would awaken in a few hours and find her gone. How it pained her that she would never be able to explain or say good-bye.

The men wrapped her in a blanket and swooped her up out of bed. Diego put her down and indicated she should walk ahead of him. Pulling the blanket around herself, she felt the cold tiles through her thin stockings. When she squirmed around for a last glance of Nelleke in the dark, Diego pushed her forward. Cornelius led the way. Diego picked her up again. He carried her down the stairs and out the door all the way to the harbor. A city watchman accompanied them through the streets. Apparently they had bribed him.

Once on the fishing boat they had rented, the men gave her clothes that belonged to the fisherman's wife. At dawn when the mast-like tree trunks closing off the harbor were unlocked, they sailed out to where Diego's ship, temporarily and illegally flying a Dutch flag, waited for them. With a small crew of four men, they set sail for her village in Spain. Isabela soon learned the answer to two of the puzzling questions about this entire incident: Where was the orphanage night guard? How did Diego and Cornelius break into the orphanage? She overheard Diego and Cornelius recalling the night's adventure in mocking, amused, bragging tones.

"Hope that guard got a good night's sleep."

"Nice soft bed, eh? Probably still tied up on the floor of that little guard house."

"His mouth stuffed with his own glove."

"That'll teach him."

Strutting the deck with inflated self importance, the two men imitated the guard.

"'Officers, I am the night guard for The City Orphanage. How may I be of service?'"

"Oh yeh! Big strong fella."

"Frightened old man is more like it."

Between sentences, they stopped to guffaw.

"Ready to hand over the key wasn't he?"

"With the point of a dagger at his throat."

The two men removed swords from their sheaths and gestured toward each other with mocking threats.

"And what about your . . . betrothed . . . that cook who expects to marry you?"

More raucous laughing, slapping of thighs.

"Good job. Fooled her. Told me everything."

Now imitating a woman's voice in exaggerated high pitch:

"Isabela? That gal from England or Spain maybe? You know her? She's a love. Children adore her. Where does she sleep? In the room with her little girls—about twenty of them. Where is that room? Oh. Second floor. See, if you enter from the courtyard, you pass through reception. The stairs are on the left. At the top of the stairs, that's Isabela's room on the right side. Say, you're not smitten with her are you?"

"So much for her. Didn't even have to pay her a single stuiver for spilling out all that information."

"Didn't have to marry her either."

* * *

After a few days on the ship, after the shock of being ripped away from her present life with no warning, as the distance between her and Amsterdam became greater, Isabela began to study her surroundings. Diego must have left Santos Gemelos in a hurry. He did not seem to be well prepared for this trip. The only food she had been given was dried fish. Eventually, crew members threw out shallow nets, but catching fresh fish in deep rolling water was challenging apparently. Whatever the nets did turn up kept them all alive. Diego could have docked for a few hours and picked up supplies, but he pressed on.

Her father's vessel had been completely different—well ordered, scrubbed daily. He had his own cabin. Yes the Captain's room was tiny with little more than a desk leaning up against a cot, but it was all wood-lined, clean, and private. During the time she was with him, her father turned over to her his large bed in a room adjoining the cot and desk. That mattress was set deep inside a frame so she didn't feel the constant rocking so much. Not until the deadly storm hit.

On Diego's ship there were no Captain's quarters. The men took turns sleeping below on any cot or hammock that happened to be empty. They hung a short curtain for her, but it was right next to whoever else was down there. She must do her business there just like they did, carry it upstairs to the deck and throw it overboard.

After one week of wearing the clothes of the unseen fisherman's wife—petticoat, bonnet, blouse, skirt, apron, and stockings that were not clean in the first place—she could smell every part of herself. Especially because she was leaning over the railing sick with nausea. The wind sometimes blew her own vomit back at her.

Her father, on the other hand, had managed to appear clean at all times. He wore his brushed jacket with the gold braid and his tidy cap that fit so snugly even the most determined gust could never blow it away. She watched him trim his beard and wash his face each morning. No matter how long the journey, whenever he left his ship at Santos Gemelos, he arrived home smelling of soap. This crew did not wash. They had brought little water for either washing or cooking.

There was another major difference between the two Captains—her father and her betrothed. Her father took his Captain role very seriously and, as such, commanded the respect of his crew. There was no question who was in charge, who was making the major decisions, yet he did not bully or disparage or mock anyone. He also felt the weight of a leader's responsibility, the importance of caring for his men and returning them safely to their families. Perhaps it was just a matter of style, perhaps her father would appear old-fashioned to Diego, but she found Diego lowered himself by hobnobbing with his crew. Rather than projecting leadership, he was more like one of them. They were a team perhaps, but a team of equals. It worried her. In a crisis, who would give the commands and who would obey them? Most of the time someone other than Diego was steering. He passed his time drinking wine, sleeping, and playing cards. On the fifth day, Diego came to her with a wooden container.

"I forgot to give you this," he said.

It was the first time he had spoken to her since telling her on the first day that they would be married soon after they arrived and she would move into his family home.

She borrowed a knife from a crew member to pry open the container. After days of nothing but gray water and sky, the first thing she noticed were the colors inside. There was something about seeing blue and green again and, yes, splashes of red that cheered her. Even if she closed the box and never looked inside again, she believed she would feel more confident about surviving this trip. All along there had been that nagging thought that she might perish as she almost did the last time she sailed. She hadn't let herself dwell on that fear. Now suddenly she acknowledged how that thought had occupied her mind ever since Diego pulled her up into his ship and set sail. These colors were like a beacon leading her to the glory of solid land with all its radiant hues.

Tenderly and thoughtfully arranged by her two aunts, these were gifts from Heaven. On top was a tin box. Carefully prying it open with the borrowed knife, she found her favorite cakes—almond with a touch of honey. When she took a bite, her mouth filled with dry crumbs, but she still gobbled them hungrily. Under any other circumstances, her next gesture would have been to share the cakes with others, but her shipmates had behaved in such a distant manner, barely acknowledging her presence, often using rough and bawdy language near her, she felt justified in keeping the rest of the box's stale contents for herself.

She plucked a handful of black olives from a jar, unwrapped a dozen hardened figs, nibbled on some moldy cheese. Her well-meaning aunts had no sense of how long a journey this would be. Even though the food was far from fresh, the varied textures touching her lips and tongue and sliding down her throat brought tears to her eyes. This was nourishment from two people who had known her since birth, who were like her second and third mothers. She examined the packed sausages, and determined they had turned green and were inedible—at least for a human. A pair of adventurous seagulls appeared above her. Perhaps the coast of France was just out of sight? When she held up a greasy sausage, both seagulls dove for it. The winner plucked it from her fingers. The second squealed a demand for a sausage of its own. Within minutes, gulls had devoured the entire batch.

Looking back at her successful efforts to convince her father to allow her to accompany him on that voyage right after her mother's death, she realized that her aunts had lost both a sister—their dear Rosa—and a niece—herself, Isabela—within a short time. She imagined her arrival back in Santos Gemelos—the aunts slightly older but brightening, relieved, no, overjoyed to see her.

'I am certain Tía Anacleta will come to meet me,' Isabela thought. 'She'll wave a white scarf over her head so that I can find her immediately. We'll cling to each other and walk arm in arm up the cliff to our home. We'll talk and talk. We'll sing. She'll play the harpsichord, show me her latest needlework and embroidery, serve me wine, ask about the wedding plans.'

Anacleta was the only one of the three sisters who ever left the house.

'Tía Lucia will NOT come to the pier—even to greet me.' After her betrothed was killed in battle when she was twenty, Lucia never recovered. She was withdrawn, but content to live with her sisters, provided for, as they all were, by her sister's husband, the Captain. Only Isabela could occasionally draw Tía Luisa out of her sad shell, amuse her, and even sometimes make her laugh.

The days on the ship passed with tortuous slowness. She had hoped to help with cooking perhaps or with mending but, in fact, the men did not want her involved in any task. Attempts at conversation with any of them, including Diego, had been met with stares or scorn. They wanted her to sit quietly on deck or disappear altogether behind the small curtain below. They had turned her into a ghost.

Isabela took her time exploring the remaining contents of the carton. Each item felt like a treasure. She imagined her two aunts, accustomed to some guidance from their now deceased sister, Isabela's mother, Rosa, trying to work together to make decisions—and under pressure to make them quickly.

"What foods would our girl enjoy most, do you think?"

"A leg of lamb perhaps?"

"We don't have time to roast anything. What do we have on hand?"

"She'll need fresh garments."

"Yes, of course. It's important for a bride-to-be to remain beautiful and radiant at all times."

Beneath the tin were several layers of wrapped fabric. As she unfolded the top layer, she found herself looking at the pale-blue damask dress with the white-lace bodice that her aunts had made as her Confirmation dress. Then the light-green silk one she wore for her Saint's Day one year. The third garment was a pale yellow with gold daisies that she wore on the hottest summer days. They had even included the matching bonnet.

Neither aunt had ever been on a ship. That was obvious. What were they picturing? Isabela treated royally? A mug of steaming water with lemon and honey brought to her on a tray while she gazed into the horizon and imagined her pending wedding, marriage, and motherhood? Strolling the deck on the arm of her betrothed in one of these fancy garments sheltered by a parasol—oh, and here was one of those too in the carton, white, multi-ruffled and impossibly delicate in the face of the constant wind. A reminder of the intriguing imports her father always brought home to the women in his family. If they could only see and smell her now, they would be horrified. Her once dark, shining curls had become gummy and limpid, their color difficult to determine. Even if she had a comb, she would not have been able to move it through the salt and filth embedded in her scalp. Yet so desperate was she for a change of clothing, she descended with the dresses below and tried them on one by one behind her feeble curtain.

Amsterdam's City Orphanage was governed by the wealthiest and most upstanding men in town—the Regents. As part of their duty to support the orphanage, they wisely invested the money they raised and the orphans' inheritance too if there was any. Every fall the proceeds from a highly anticipated and well attended theater performance were dedicated to the orphanage. The rules were clear and strictly enforced. To be accepted at the orphanage, a child's parents must have registered as Amsterdam citizens. They must have offered proof of their marriage in one of the local Calvinist churches. They must have registered the birth of their child. All this while hoping never to need the orphanage's services. The Regents supervised every aspect of the orphans' lives: clothing, learning, health, training for independence, and diet.

When Isabela stepped into the first dress—the Confirmation one—she realized that the slim, girlish figure others had often admired had disappeared. There were no mirrors in the orphanage. She had no time to dwell on her appearance there. She could not pull this blue dress over her bosom. The green silk did stretch enough to cover her, but she split a seam trying to button it up. She held the yellow daisy one against the others and realized it would fit her no better. The rich foods the orphanage provided its staff and residents had added girth without her realizing it.

There was a shawl, however—a knitted woolen one with dark-red flowers. A shawl that clashed with every dress, but of all the people on the ship, only she would notice that. Perhaps she could wear one of the dresses open in the back, but covered by the shawl. If she held the shawl tight or tied it somehow, the shawl might not blow out to sea. She also found a fresh petticoat and stockings. No shoes, unfortunately. The fisherwomen's old shoes were quickly becoming even more worn and torn. They were often soaked.

When Isabela appeared on deck in her fresh clothes, the shawl wrapped tight to cover the gaps, the men noticed the change. They did not hide their amusement.

"Would ya look at her?"

"What's she doin' tonight? Off to a ball with the King of France?"

Isabela had to admit that the dresses were highly inappropriate, that they too would quickly become sodden and soiled. Given the dearth of water for scrubbing the only other set of clothes she had, however, these were her sole options. She returned below deck and unwrapped one more garment—a night dress with a delicate embroidered collar. Until now she had worn the fisherman's wife's clothes all day and all night. Now she could change before sleeping. She felt vulnerable with the men so close by and repulsed by the uninhibited sounds they made while they slept, but possibly out of respect for her betrothed status or because some of them knew her father, they did not approach her. Or were they feigning a modicum of respect until they were paid? She heard snippets of conversation among the crew when Diego was not close by. Something about their pay hinging on returning her safely, about promises from Diego involving his future wife's worldly goods.

* * *

Unable to read, do needlework, or embroider, and without conversation of any sort, Isabela was becoming despondent. The voyage seemed interminable. She was weary of facing forward, constantly hoping to catch sight of her village in the distance. She positioned her wooden bench so that it faced the rear of the ship instead. Better to be surprised when they actually arrived. And surprised she was! At first she was confused, even frightened by the men's sudden outburst of shouting. When she realized the source of their excitement, she stood, turned, and looked. Barely discernible at first were the familiar cliffs of her childhood. She had never seen them from this direction. Some rose straight up from the sea, fortress-like, daring invaders to come closer. Others curved backwards as if trying to escape the sea altogether. Some appeared to be of solid gray slate. Some consisted of bare rock all the way to the top. Others had mossy sections with a few trees. The most beautiful were striated with pink horizontal stripes as if a giant, while walking along the beach, casually scraped them with his heavy sword and left them bleeding from shallow wounds.

She quickly descended below and rummaged among her dresses, searching for the least soiled. The golden daisies had faded, the damask was ripped. The fit was no longer a problem, though. She had consumed all of the edible packed foods from her aunts two weeks ago. The dried fish diet had sucked her back into her girlish shape. She chose the blue, the Confirmation dress even though the lace bodice had turned gray.

The twin bluffs for which the village was named became visible, and on top of each bluff the matching homes of the village's two wealthiest families. As the vessel approached its destination and the bluffs became clearer, Isabela's father's voice came back to her. It was as if he were standing next to her.

"Santos Gemelos. Blessed twins. Twins, Isabela. Imagine if you had a sister who looked exactly like you, had your dark curls and brown eyes, your mother's olive skin. You share the same birthday. You're the same height. The same weight. You even dress alike. Every day you wake up and the first thing you see is that look-alike girl beside you. She's your twin.

"That's what it's like for the bluffs," Captain Calderón continued. "But they've been up there looking at each other for thousands of years, maybe tens of thousands or hundreds of thousands. They're great pals like Captain de Vega and I are."

When she was ten, Isabela learned another reason for the town's name. Greek twins, Cosmas and Damián, were the patron saints of surgeons, doctors, and dentists. Indistinguishable one from the other, the brothers, devoted Christians, practiced medicine among the poor, but always refused payment. Supposedly they were born in the fourth century in Arabia, but lived in Cicilia. In spite of their goodness and deep demonstration of faith, after being accused of promoting a cult and falsely claiming to have performed miracles, they were both tortured and beheaded. Every year on September 26, the town celebrated a feast in honor of their martyrdom.

High up, overlooking the sea, ancestors of the Calderóns and the de Vegas built identical homes on the twin bluffs from where mothers, wives, and children could look out and watch for the return of their men. Once when a savage storm destroyed the de Vega home, they rebuilt it to match the original exactly. Although the upper part of the homes were wooden, unlike any other home in the village, the lower halves were stone—stone brought from a distant quarry on donkeys, some of whom collapsed from a week of carrying their heavy burden.

With two maiden sisters and a married couple already filling the home's two bedrooms, Isabela's father built a second story—just for his daughter. Therefore the home on the right bluff was higher and roomier than the one on the left. A cluster of cottages at the foot of the bluffs began a few yards from the beach and stretched backwards into the valley. The village ended at a formidable mountain range.

As she got closer she could see cows, sheep, and goats grazing on a lower plateau. Just as the ship entered the narrow harbor with its gentle curve like an arm reaching out to embrace them, the men lowered all the sails and the ship came to an abrupt halt. It could go no further without running aground. From that point the seawater quickly became more and more shallow—so shallow, and for such a long stretch that, as a child, Isabela alarmed her mother by lifting her skirts and wading through the clear green water farther and farther away from shore. The sand felt both solid and squishy between her toes.

Today though, she would try to muster some dignity. She was returning to Santos Gemelos as a lady, as a woman about to marry. Soon she would be a mother herself perhaps. Cornelius lowered a boat and helped her step into it. Diego and the remaining crew followed in a second boat. They rowed toward shore. With each motion of the oars through water, the waves became calmer, comforting Isabela's soul.

As Isabela prepared to disembark, she looked out over the beach. Villagers, none of whom she knew personally, welcomed back their fathers and sons with fresh oranges as was the custom. Other greeters may have hoped for fresh goods to purchase or barter. She did not expect to see her reclusive Tía Lucia, of course, so she scanned the beach for the beloved, cheerful face of Tía Anacleta. When Diego noticed her searching, he said,

"You know one of your aunts was quite ill when I left to fetch you."

"Which aunt?" she inquired with alarm.

"Oh, I don't know. They look alike to me. I can't tell them apart."

Neither aunt was in the crowd. She hoped that at this very moment they were preparing a feast for her. At the thought of approaching her home, her mouth began to water with the thought of succulent, sweet, solid food—anything but salted dry fish.

Diego and Cornelius were occupied with the boat—placing cargo on carts, gathering mail to deliver, securing mounds of rope, and tossing debris overboard. Cornelius offered to walk her up the cliff to her home. She could see that the main door was shut. Had they not heard the shouting? Sensed the excitement? Were they not watching out for her? Were they not curious when the family dogs whelped and barked their joy?

When Isabela burst inside she gasped with delight at the familiar sight of all the gifts her father had brought his family through the years. As if nothing had been touched during her absence, each piece of furniture, each painting, each sculpture was in exactly the same position. Every item brought forth a specific memory. But the odors had changed. She breathed in heavy air, mustiness, neglect. When she lovingly caressed the cupboard with its display of copper pots from France on the lower shelves, a large porcelain bowl from China and a plate from Delft above, the tip of her fingers became covered with dust. The glass on the paintings was smeared so badly she could barely discern the art.

"Tía Anacleta!" she called. "Tía Lucia! It's Isabela. I'm back. I'm home."

There was no answer. No movement. 'Perhaps the ship's arrival found them unprepared. Tía Anacleta must be in the village making purchases for supper,' Isabela thought. Then she noticed on the rear veranda which the Captain had built to protect his family from cold winds, Tía Lucia, sitting in her favorite chair, her hands folded in her lap—not knitting, not reading. Isabela regarded her aunt for a moment. Her usual solemn expression, more gray hairs, more flesh hanging beneath her chin. But also something new. A vacant stare.

Isabela stepped onto the veranda and knelt down beside her aunt, who did not seem to notice her approach. She did look up, though, and smile her rare and slow smile. She reached out to pat Isabela's face. She tucked a loose hair into Isabela's bonnet.

"Are you not cold out here, Tía Lucia? Shall I bring a blanket for your knees? Where is Tía Anacleta?"

At the mention of Anacleta's name, Lucia's lips began to tremble. She looked confused, lost. She tried to remember. She hesitated.

"Gone," she finally said. "My sister, Anacleta. Gone. And my sister, Rosa. Gone. The Captain has not returned either. But *you* are here, Isabela. Now YOU are here."

Tía Lucia leaned over and embraced her weeping niece.

Chapter Three
Wedding Preparations

Isabela's presence revived Lucia somewhat. With only two of her family of five left, the home seemed desolate. Their former cook showed up even though, as she told Isabela, she had not been paid for lo these many weeks. Isabela's first meal home was not the feast she had hoped for, but for the first time since her final meal in the orphanage, she felt the comfort of a full belly. Lucia too ate every morsel put before her. Although she still often lapsed into that vacant look, gradually Lucia was able to talk about her sisters without closing her eyes and whimpering.

But why had the cook not been given her wages? Isabela had never listened much on those rare occasions when the subject of family finances was discussed. There always seemed to be plenty of money for whatever they wanted. How were the bills paid, though, during her father's long voyage? Who had been paying them since his drowning death nearly two years ago? Tía Anacleta would have taken charge, she's sure of it. She, among the three sisters, was the most sensible, the only one with a sense of numbers. In fact, she began to remember that before his trips, her father sat down with Anacleta and went over household expenses. Although his trips lasted three-to-six months, she believed she once overheard one of those pre-voyage conversations. Always the careful provider, she heard him say—she could hear his voice now—that he had put aside enough to cover an entire year in case he was delayed.

He would never have entrusted Lucia with that responsibility. When Anacleta died, everything must have fallen apart. It wasn't just the garden, then, and the lack of food in the kitchen. Lucia was not only depressed, she had no idea how to run a household.

Isabela ran to her father's large oak desk and began rummaging. Almost immediately she found an envelope marked "Household Expenses." Inside was a ledger much like the one her father used for his business. Isabela would study that information later. Right now she needed to determine if there was enough money to pay the cook. Indeed there was and there was a small amount left over.

After her wedding, Isabela would take her meals in her new home, but what about Lucia's ongoing needs? She continued to look through her father's drawers, reaching all the way to the back, pulling out maps, mementoes, and ledgers that dated back a decade. When she came upon a stash of jars full of coins, she was stunned. She counted ten jars full, three partially full. Through the glass, she saw that most of the jars contained Spanish currency. Another French. Another Italian. Still another held miscellaneous coins—a collection perhaps. She poured some of these into her palm. One appeared to be ancient. Holding it up to the lamp, she saw that it was nicked in two places. The worn engraving was in Latin. She could not make out what was printed on one side of the coin, but the other appeared to be a likeness of Caesar. Such a coin must be worth an enormous sum.

'What if a thief, upon learning that an old woman lives in this large house alone, breaks in? Where is the first place he would go to look for something valuable, easy to pack up and take away, quick to sell?' Isabela asked herself. 'Right where I found it. Here in my father's desk. Am I being unnecessarily afraid? No. Better to be cautious, to think ahead, to plan, like my father.'

Attempting to think like a robber, Isabela left a generous number of coins in her father's desk. 'The thief might assume this is all there is. It IS quite a bit.' She hid the other jars in various places. In Anacleta's writing desk. In the back of her wardrobe. Standing on a kitchen chair, she pushed several jars as far as she could reach behind some heavy, seldom-used pots. She moved the chair away. The current cook had returned home for the night. She was not particularly energetic or ambitious. It was doubtful she would ever climb up to look in that cupboard.

* * *

Diego had said they would be married soon after arriving. Isabela had not heard from him so she did not know if a date had been set. Of course, the ceremony would take place in the church, but where would they celebrate afterwards? She was fatigued from the trip and from caring for Tía Lucia, from hiring a housekeeper and directing the cleanup of her neglected home. She waited to hear from the de Vegas, assuming they were making all the arrangements, extending invitations, hiring musicians, supervising the preparation of a celebration meal. If those tasks were usually part of the bride's family's contribution, well she simply did not know where to begin.

She also hoped that once in his own home with his own parents, away from his duties as ship Captain, Diego would become more conversant and would show some interest in her. Their two Captain fathers grew up together and were both friends and sometimes rivals. After they married, they met only in the town's tavern where they occasionally shared a smoke and a tankard. It was in that noisy establishment that they celebrated Isabela's birth and decided her fate. When Isabela's mother learned of the betrothal—a decision made without consulting her—she was uncharacteristically enraged. The Calderón and de Vega wives could not abide each other. There was no visiting, no sharing on saints' days, no contact. Isabela had seen Diego only twice before he showed up by her bed in Amsterdam.

When was she was seven, her father took her to a lavish party at the de Vega home to celebrate their only son's first decade of life. Stiffly dressed in a full-length, multi-layered gown and uncomfortable new shoes and overwhelmed by the number of people, the music, and the platters piled high with meats and sweets, Isabela clung to her father and asked when she could return home to the quiet of her calm, studious, poetry-writing, crocheting household.

The second time was when her father insisted on taking her to join the de Vega family when Diego set off on his first sea voyage at age fourteen. A crowd gathered waving banners, cheering, and applauding as the slender young man mounted the ship's plank and stood on deck. Although Isabela suspected he was really frightened, he raised his chin up, saluted the onlookers unsmilingly, and appeared cocky and quite certain he could conquer any challenge. Diego did not acknowledge his mother who wept profusely and insisted on staying until the ship was out of sight.

Having been utterly shaken by Jules's kiss before he plunged into the sea and drowned with her father's ship, and months later charmed and delighted with Pieter's kisses on the night of Saskia's wedding celebration, she wondered what Diego's kisses would be like. Hard, wet, cold, insistent and desperate like Jules' or slow, tender, teasing like Pieter's? Would Diego ever study her face the way Pieter did both when he was painting her portrait in the reception area of the orphanage and when they were sitting next to each other that evening? Even when they were dancing, he did not stop contemplating her, engaging her, amusing her. His rapt attention enveloped her in sweet warmth. The wedding may have been Saskia's, but Isabela felt she herself was dancing at the center of the world that evening.

And her own wedding celebration? Would it resemble Saskia's? Varieties of jams and biscuits, cheese and breads were set beside bowls of creamy yellow butter waiting for the official blessing of the newlyweds that would signal the beginning of the feast and the music. The guests all sat, but no one touched a morsel. After saying grace, Saskia's father held above the heads of his daughter and new son-in-law thick bunches of juicy, succulent purple grapes.

"May God bless this newly married couple," he began.

"May they always remain the proud, productive Christian citizens of our city which their families raised them to be; may their devotion remain true and their fidelity live long; may their union be fruitful and joyful."

When Mr. Comfrij presented the bride and groom each with a bunch of grapes and spread his arms to encompass them, to the great amusement of the hundred or so guests, Mrs. Comfrij stood and yelled,

"That's right. Mr. Confrij and I want grandchildren. Lots of them."

The ensemble played. A parade of women and men entered the rooms with steaming platters. The servants continually refilled casks of wine and pitchers of ale.

When the orchestra took a break, songbooks were distributed. The guests, satiated after the three-hour feast, but still anticipating sweets, joined in one rousing chorus after the other.

'Will I look as happy and thrilled at my wedding as Saskia did?' Isabela asked herself. She did not think so. Saskia had chosen Philip to be her husband or, rather, they had decided together. Isabela's father chose Diego for her. Besides, how could she enjoy kisses from such a stern, unsmiling young man? A resentment, approaching a feeling of betrayal, began to creep into her consciousness—her father whom she so adored and trusted—how could he have done this to her?

She was becoming increasingly anxious about the wedding night. She had heard talk among the orphanage's Big Sisters—all of it hearsay.

"My sister says it hurt, but it was quite pleasing."

"You want to know the truth? I want it all the time. Is that a sin?"

"My mother told me when my time comes, I should look for ways to avoid it as often as possible, that it's a dreadful business."

Isabela had never discussed "the dreadful business" with her mother. Her maiden aunts would not have been any help. She had occasionally seen animals mating and she understood something about the mechanics, but she could not imagine participating in anything like that. The little she knew made it sound so strange. She thought of the few married couples with whom she was acquainted. Her parents seemed delighted with one another. During her father's long trips, her mother often remained in her room and left the care of her child and home to her sisters. She seemed to miss the Captain terribly, but returned to a happy energetic state while he was there. Her father treated her tenderly—reminding her to wear her shawl on their evening walks, holding out her chair for her at meals, sharing amusing anecdotes from his trips. So how bad could that marital business have been for her mother? The Broekhofs too—Nelleke's new parents. Nelleke once referred to their bed raised and surrounded by a heavy velvet drape. The couple slept there together every night.

'It isn't just to produce children, then, is it?' She thought. 'There's something more to it . . . but what?' If she were marrying Pieter, he would explain it to her. She could never ask Diego. They talked about nothing and certainly not about that.

The one decision Isabela felt she had to make herself was about her wedding dress. Diego had said the wedding was imminent, so there probably wasn't time to make a dress. The three dresses ruined on the recent trip were her best dresses and they were unsalvageable. When she tried to talk to Tía Lucia about her dilemma, that blank stare came over Lucia's face. Yet the next day, Lucia presented her with an idea. All of Isabela's mother's clothes were still in her wardrobe. Lucia remembered her sister Rosa's wedding day and she believed Rosa kept the wedding dress.

Isabela had not entered her parents' bedroom since her mother died there two years ago. She tiptoed in and just stood for a moment. Her eyes landed on her mother's personal table under the window. Her hairbrush with remnants of the dark hair that had never changed color. An open box of decorative combs to hold up her heavy locks. Earrings. Necklaces. Bows. Ribbons. Isabela sniffed one perfume bottle after another—all of them gifts from her father, most of them from France—and tried to capture her mother's scent. She thought she identified her mother's favorite—*Femme Charmante.* She sat on the bed and caressed its thick quilt and then gingerly, as if she were intruding, lay down on the bed shared for twenty years by her parents—her first and primary models of a married couple.

Tía Lucia refused to enter the room, so once Isabela forced herself to open and look through her mother's wardrobe, she brought dresses to her aunt in the sitting room where she repeatedly read outloud the same line in the same book and then stared out at the veranda. Finally Lucia identified the wedding dress, but seeing it sent her off to another dreamy place.

Isabela tried it on. Not only did it fit perfectly, it flattered her slenderness. The gown lifted her breasts, cinched her waist, and spread out over her hips. However, Isabela, though small, was less petite than her mother. The dress stopped half way down her calf. The church would not marry any woman whose ankles were visible. In fact if such a woman attempted to enter the church for any purpose, she might be chased out or even accused of being a harlot or a witch. The dress must reach the floor.

Aunt and niece searched through all their scrap fabric. They considered cutting a piece of an existing dress. Nothing matched. Finally they found a thick ball of wide imported white lace. From France perhaps. If they made a five-layer ruffle for the bottom of the dress, they hoped no one could see through it. It looked a little odd with the dress's style, but it would have to do. They set aside a bit of leftover lace to decorate the veil her mother had worn.

While they were cutting out the long lengths of lace which stretched from one side of the sitting room to the other, a knock on the door surprised them. Isabela heard the familiar voices of her recent fellow travelers and the mocking sound of Diego's and Cornelius's laughter.

Isabela invited the two men to sit. She offered them tea and pomegranate juice which they declined, then wine which they accepted. Tía Lucia moved the lace aside.

Pleased that Diego was at last paying them a call, Isabela suggested they sip their wine on the veranda.

"No," he said, "I prefer to be inside."

Diego did not look at his hostesses or engage them in conversation. With his usual expressionless face and slightly raised left eyebrow the young man instead gazed critically around the room. Holding his wine glass in one hand, with the other he rubbed the fabric of the divan on which he was sitting.

"Where did this piece originate?" he asked.

The awkwardness that had filled the room since the men arrived lifted somewhat. At last there was something he was interested in, something to talk about. Sharing stories about the many objects in the room delighted Isabela. She led the men on a tour.

"'The divan and matching chair were the latest fashion among the wealthy in Paris,' my father told us. Nobles were constructing what they called 'apartments' within their castles. In contrast to the formal spaces used for entertaining on a large scale, the private spaces were used for dressing and relaxing, but also for receiving small numbers of visitors."

Isabela invited them to feel the smooth wood of the harpsichord, to explore the collection of toys: a windmill, dolls, a miniature dollhouse, a foot-tall, carved wooden soldier.

On every surface, in every cabinet, she pointed out an object from France, Sweden, Denmark, England, Italy—all of them infused with memories. Diego did not admire the beauty of the objects, and he seemed impatient with the anecdotes. He asked,

"How much did your father pay for this?" Or "How much is that worth?" Isabela and her aunt had no idea. These were gifts.

Isabela stepped to the harpsichord and slid gracefully onto its matching stool.

"Shall I play for you?" she asked sweetly.

"That's not necessary," Diego answered dismissively.

After he had peered at several paintings, Isabela shared with the men a favorite but sad story.

"Twice, before war made it too dangerous, my father visited Amsterdam. He brought me a painting from there of a man whom I later met—Rembrandt. When I saw the artist for the first time, I felt instantly that I had met him before, yet I knew that was impossible. Then I realized that Rembrandt was the man in the portrait, that it was actually a self portrait. He painted his own face with all its flaws. He is a brilliant man and so . . ."

Diego interrupted.

"Rembrandt? I've heard of him. His work draws a high price. Where is that painting? I want to see it."

"Sadly, it went down with my father's ship."

"That's too bad," Diego responded sternly. "You should have been more careful about what you selected to take on that trip. Of course, you should never have left Santos Gemelos in the first place. Do you realize the risk I took entering that city to bring you safely back home?"

Diego nodded at his companion and the two men left the house, leaving behind a totally bewildered and stunned young woman.

Isabela was an only daughter raised by two doting parents and two indulgent aunts. The few times she descended the bluff and entered the village, usually to attend Mass, children jumped up and down at the sight of her. She heard women say, "Oh, it's the little princess." She always smiled and waved. It did not occur to her as a child that "the little princess" might be for some a sarcastic way of describing her.

Never had anyone addressed such harsh words to her as the ones Diego spoke before leaving abruptly. Even the Housemother at the orphanage, who was strict and whose speech was often unnecessarily firm, never spoke to Isabela in that manner. She recognized Isabela's importance to the children, but also that Isabela's skill, intelligence and bearing reflected well on the Housemother herself. Diego's tone shook her. She saw herself in a new way. Was she unappreciative? Spoiled? Hopelessly naïve?

Chapter four
Married Lady

⌒

Two days later Tía Lucia and Isabela had sewn the last layer of ruffle on the wedding dress. They were going through the jewelry of all the women in the house—their own plus the two deceased sisters', Rosa's and Anacleta's. As they held selected pairs up to the dress looking for a good match, they reminisced about the source of the jewelry.

Tía Lucia: "Oh look. How tiny and sweet. These were my very first pair of earrings. I'm sure of it. I haven't looked at them for years. I was seven."

Isabela: "My father brought me these from Madrid when I was that same age, Tía Lucia. Tiny gold crosses for my small ears."

Tía Lucia: "These were Anacleta's, but she would never wear them. I believe they belonged to my mother, your grandmother. Anacleta found them too garish. From Italy maybe. Anacleta dressed simply. She rarely wore any jewelry at all."

Isabela: "Can you remember which earrings my mother wore with this dress, Tía Lucia?"

As Tía Lucia searched her memory and looked through the jewelry that had belonged to her sister, Rosa, they heard another knock on the door. Both women stiffened, fearful that it was Diego. They dreaded a second awkward and unpleasant visit.

A plump woman with a sweet, serene smile stood alone on the doorstep. Wearing a fresh apron that Isabela suspected she had chosen specifically for this visit, she carried a basket on one arm. Even with a heavy black shawl around her shoulders, she shivered.

"Good evening. Please forgive my intrusion. I work for the de Vega family. They and everyone else call me 'Cook.'"

Isabela was so relieved that the caller was anyone other than her future husband, she immediately invited the woman into the house.

"Please sit down. May I offer you a hot cider?"

"Yes, that would be lovely, but I can't stay long."

"First tell me if you would," Isabela inquired, "how is it that people use the English word 'Cook' to address you?"

"It was the Captain—Captain de Vega. He suggested it when I began working for them. 'Aurelia?' he said referring to my Christian name. 'That's too fancy. Too long too. In my travels to England, I've learned that the gentry call their servants by their function. A lot easier than remembering all their names. You're going to cook for us . . . so that's it. We'll just call you 'Cook,' he said.'"

Reaching into the basket, Cook handed Isabela a package.

"I baked these for you," she said. "Honey buns. I wrapped them as soon as I took them from the oven. I had hoped they would still be warm, but the wind on the bluff is quite strong tonight."

Cook continued to speak urgently.

"Please forgive me. I . . . I've come with a suggestion. You will be married the day after tomorrow and you will move immediately into the de Vega home. You will have a good-size room of your own—large enough for you and your future children. May I . . . I think you might . . . Well, I'm sure there are some personal items you'll want with you. I think you should select and send to your new home as many as you can and soon . . . in the next two days."

Cook's expression was kind and caring, but also tense and concerned.

"I must be going," she said. "If you have any favorite foods, I would be pleased to prepare them for you."

Isabela had imagined that she would have weeks, even months to go through all her belongings. She would visit Tía Lucia every day. Together they would reminisce and tell stories about each item just as they did with the jewelry. She would divide her time between both homes, carefully packing each delicate item like the dollhouse from England, for example, for her first daughter, and her father's swords and Captain jackets for her sons. The process might take years.

From the way Cook delivered the information, it seemed that she was not acting as a messenger from her future in-laws. She had come on an errand of her own. Isabela felt afraid. Cook's words and her manner—were they a warning of some kind?

That very evening, she went upstairs to her room and began grabbing dresses, petticoats, shoes, boots, bonnets, stockings, shawls. Then bed coverings. A favorite quilt. What else? What of all the items her room held—her entire life really—was most important? Her writing desk. Letters—from her father during his travels, letters she wrote from Amsterdam that her aunts had saved. Her writing quills and ink. Books. Each one precious. She read a few lines from a French children's book, *Pour l'Enfant Qui ne Rit Jamais*, but forced herself to stop, to continue her task. Needlework and embroidery tools. An easel, paints, brushes.

Driven by a nagging fear of loss, of emptiness, hour after hour, she packed. Ever mindful of the children she longed for—bright, inquisitive, amusing children like her adored Nelleke—she packed some toys from her childhood—a China doll the size of a real newborn with its own set of dishes, caps, and aprons. A game of marbles. Even a slingshot. Her father had tried to teach her how to use it, but she was not interested. Perhaps she would one day have a son who would enjoy it.

At midnight she turned to the decorative items—a delicate blue and green porcelain bowl with matching pitcher. A collection of fans from Japan—hand painted her father had said. Isabela had imagined delicate Asian women dressed in kimonos chatting, alternately taking sips from tiny teacups and stroking a line on the bare fan canvas with delicate thin brushes. Sharing their handiwork for the others to admire. She wondered as a child if she might ever travel that distance—to meet those women in person.

'Do I have only one more day to make selections?' she asked herself. 'Or am I just panicking? Maybe I am just behaving like a nervous, silly young bride.'

Then she remembered all the coins stashed around the house. The jars were glass. They were heavy. How could she pack them and send them to a house whose owners she barely knew? Even if they were her future-in-laws, they had been cruelly distant and uncommunicative. Would they go through all her belongings?

Isabela grabbed scissors, needle and thread. For the rest of the night she ripped open all the cushions in the house—some from far away, many designed and embroidered by her mother and aunts and by herself. She shook out fistfuls of coins from the jars and arranged them deep into the stuffing of the pillows, then shook each one to make sure the coins did not make clinking sounds. Next she set about re-sewing every pillow. The thread did not always match. Her stitches became jagged. By morning half the jars were empty.

She hired a large cart and sent off the pillows along with all her selected items—perhaps one-tenth of what she hoped to keep. And those were only her personal items. She would leave the downstairs rooms as they were . . . for Lucia . . . and hope that Lucia could eventually move with her into her new home. In the afternoon she received a terse message:

"Dear Isabela. You will be married in the village church at noon tomorrow after the morning Mass. You will then move immediately into our home. We welcome you into our family." It was signed in a man's handwriting: "*from Captain de Vega and his wife, Doña Juana.*"

* * *

Tía Lucia had not left the house for twenty years. She had not greeted her niece at the pier upon her return from Amsterdam. She did not attend her niece's wedding. Cornelius came to the home and accompanied Isabela down the bluff on foot to the church in the village center.

"I'm surprised you're still in Santos Gemelos, Cornelius. Are you leaving for Amsterdam soon?"

"I can never go home, Isabela."

"Never return to Amsterdam? What do you mean?"

"I was the one who arranged for the fishing boat and the Dutch flag on Diego's ship in the harbor, you know. I threatened the orphanage security guard, tied him up, tossed him on the floor of his cubicle and threw away the key. It was me who bribed the city's night watchman to accompany us to the harbor. All those actions could land me in prison. When we came for you, you must have noticed we were dressed like Dutch soldiers? Impersonating a Dutch soldier is against the law, of course. What I had to do to get my hands on an outfit befitting a Dutch soldier . . . well you don't want to know. Were I ever to return to the city, I would be punished severely. Possibly executed."

"But Cornelius, why did you do all that then?"

"For the adventure, Isabela. And for the money."

"How much money?"

"Diego promised me a hefty payment. Our understanding was that I would receive that payment after your wedding."

They were almost at the bottom of the bluff. The village would soon come into view. Isabela wanted to know more.

"Cornelius, during the shipwreck when my father drowned with his crew . . . you saved me. You rowed all night and took me to live with your family. You and your mother and father and sister—you all saved my life."

"For coin, Isabela. Lots of it. At the beginning of that voyage when your father asked me—or perhaps ordered me—to save you in that hidden boat should we run into trouble near my homeland, he also told me there was a satchel under the seat inside a water-proof container. That was my payment. That was why I saved you."

"I suppose you could have rowed yourself, left me behind to die, and taken the money anyway," Isabela said bitterly.

"No, I couldn't do that. The storm was heavy. The boat kept filling up with water. You bailed and you bailed. I could not have bailed and rowed at the same time. You kept us both alive, Isabela. Neither of us would have made it without the other."

* * *

The villagers seemed to be better informed than Isabela about the wedding. They had apparently been anticipating it for days. Dressed in their only set of good clothes, a crowd of fifty people gave a cry when they spotted her. Isabela held tight to Cornelius's arm as they pressed toward her.

"Look at that dress."

"Her earrings. The sun shines on them. See how they sparkle!"

A few women, remembering her as a small child, shed tears.

"She's all grown up now."

"Still so beautiful."

"The same dark eyes and black hair."

"Delicate, isn't she?"

By the time she reached the church door, Isabela's arms were filled with the flowers many children held out to her. Diego and Friar Fernando waited on the top step of the entrance to the church. Although Diego did not acknowledge her arrival, Isabela did think Diego looked handsome in his dark-blue, formal vest and jacket, his boots cleaned, his sable in its scabbard. She took note of a missing brass button, though, and decided that offering to sew it back on might be her first wifely gesture.

Friar Fernando placed her arm through Diego's, opened the church door and led the couple down the aisle. Although she had not seen them for eight years when they bid Diego good-bye down by the dock on his first voyage, she recognized the couple in whose home she would live beginning immediately after the ceremony. Captain de Vega, wearing the blowsy faded shirt and gray woolen vest she remembered seeing him in years ago, leaned on his cane and raised up stiffly to stand and greet her with a nod. The once proud, strutting, commanding Captain had aged considerably. He was obviously suffering from the leg injury he endured some five years ago. 'Perhaps,' Isabela thought, 'I can find a way to relieve his pain.' Doña Juana, unsmiling beneath the long veil that covered her head, remained seated, but also nodded. Villagers, none of whom she knew by name, filled the church, made the sign of the cross, genuflected, kneeled on the stone floor, and said a brief prayer before arranging themselves on wooden benches. Some stood.

Friar Fernando arrived in Santos Gemelos as a twenty-year-old nearly a quarter of a century ago. He served his flock by becoming one of them—not just baptizing, listening to confessions, performing weddings, holding Mass, and speaking at funerals—but also by joining them for drinks in the taverns, gorging on feast days, and joining in their laughter. He held Isabela when she was just a few days old, sprinkled her still scaly scalp with holy water, and welcomed her into the Catholic Church. At her First Communion when she was ten, he placed a wafer on her delicate tongue, held the communal goblet from which she sipped, and promised her everlasting life.

Seeing her now safely returned to her birth place, a seventeen-year-old bride, orphaned, more lovely and sweet than ever, moved him so that he could barely speak the words he had repeated hundreds of times for so many other village couples. The villagers took note of his distress and sniffled along with him. Isabela was touched, but also fearful. Did the friar and perhaps the villagers too know something she, in her isolated, pampered life, did not know? Were they happy for her or were they concerned?

"Do you, Isabela Maria Lucia Calderón . . . ," the friar asked.

When he finished the question, Isabela looked up at her betrothed and said sweetly,

"Yes, I do."

Diego looked straight ahead.

"Do you, Diego Carlos Blandón de Vega . . . ," the friar then asked.

"Yes, I do." answered Diego, still looking straight ahead.

The bride and groom along with the guests exited into a bright afternoon on the town plaza. Lute and guitar music greeted them. The villagers did not hold back. They ran to the refreshment tables and began grabbing the free treats. The guests of honor—Isabela and her new family—took their seats on the highest step of the church. Cook brought them each a plate of delicacies and a goblet of wine.

As the crowds continued to gorge on food and drink, the musicians took a break. A girl of perhaps six years stood in front of the newlyweds and tentatively began to serenade them in a pure, lilting voice. The villagers gathered behind her and fell silent. Shy at first, the child gained confidence. Isabela was captivated by the melody, joyful at moments, but with a wave of melancholy flowing through it. The words were not easily deciphered, but they seemed to tell the story of a bird in flight. As the child neared the end of her performance, she took a deep breath, lifted her chin and held out the final high note until her voice began to waiver. Listening to that last note was like watching a bird flyer higher and higher and disappear. The girl curtsied quickly and ran off. The crowd applauded and cheered.

Isabela was seized by a longing to know this mysterious and gifted singer, to hear her sing over and over, to learn the song and sing with her. She asked Cook to bring the child to her so that she could learn her name and thank her. Cook searched, but the young performer could not be found. Cook apologized and said she would try to learn the child's identity.

Having devoured all the treats quickly, but continuing to drink, the crowd began to dance. First they all held hands and danced in a large circle. When they had exhausted themselves momentarily, individuals and small groups performed. As men and women began pairing off to dance, Isabela felt a sudden staggering loneliness. Whereas dancing with Pieter at Saskia's wedding was so exuberant and continued for hours, her new husband had made no effort to engage her in the merriment. Cornelius certainly was enjoying himself, though. After several attempts, Isabela made eye contact with him and motioned for him to approach her. What did this situation call for? Should she ask Diego's permission before she stood up to dance with another man? 'No,' she thought defiantly. 'It is my wedding, my groom is ignoring me, and I will do as I wish.'

The villagers cheered when Isabela joined them. The music became faster and livelier. Cornelius swirled her around and around. Several times he held her tight to keep her from falling when her foot got caught on a stone or brick. Other young men approached them wanting to dance with the bride, but Cornelius motioned them away. When the music slowed, Isabela whispered,

"Cornelius, I understand that you cannot return to Amsterdam yourself, but if I give you a letter, do you think you could manage somehow to get it delivered?"

Before heading to their cottages for evening milking followed by a simple evening meal of olives, oranges, and dry bread, each family nodded or curtsied their good wishes and their good-bye's in front of Isabela and her new family. When few people remained in the plaza, the five members of the de Vega household began the climb up the bluff. Led by the older Captain de Vega and his ever-present cane, they paraded slowly. Juana leaned on her son, followed by Isabela and Cook. Diego and the Captain shared the same broad shoulders, the left lower than the right as if it needed to balance out the weight of their swords. Just behind Juana, Isabela saw now that she too was frail and slightly bent. Immediately after the wedding, Isabela was absorbed in watching all the activity. When she turned to share an observation with Doña Juana, who had by then lowered her veil, she was shocked by the change in this once handsome woman. Her hair was gray and thin, her cheeks sunken, her nose prominent and beaked. She wore cracked but serviceable boots.

'Perhaps I can take a lesson from my mother-in-law there,' thought Isabela who was still wearing her mother's dressiest shoes—the ones with white bows. Now covered with dust and filling with sand, they were too small for her. She hadn't noticed when she was dancing that they were pinching her toes, but now she was beginning to feel the pain.

Although the de Vega house was not far in distance, the path to reach it was arduous and long. Isabela felt some apprehension, of course, but also some excitement. She was looking forward to a tour of this other Captain's home which she anticipated would be filled with objects from afar just as hers was. Cook had said, "You will have your own room." That apparently meant that Diego and she would not share a bed—a thought she found puzzling, but also comforting. She would enjoy the privacy of her own space and her own possessions.

It was late afternoon when they arrived at the front door of Isabela's new home. When Doña Juana turned to allow Isabela to enter ahead of her, she noticed the flowers that both Isabela and Cook held.

"Throw those away in the bushes, Isabela."

"But, Doña Juana, these were a gift from the village children. Nearly every child brought me a flower."

"Those are wild flowers gathered from who knows where. They're probably full of bugs and nettles. I don't abide flowers in my home. They make me sneeze. They irritate my throat. Dispose of them now."

"I'll take care of them, Doña," Cook said reaching for the violets, daisies, and hollyhocks in Isabela's arms. Cook gave Isabela a brief reassuring look as if to say, "Don't worry about the flowers . . . or about HER, for that matter," then walked in the direction of her cottage, her arms full of the colorful bouquets.

When the Captain opened the front door of his home, Isabela experienced disappointment and shock. The room was large. A fire burned in the fireplace, but the space was barren, severe, colorless. The only furniture was a worn wooden table surrounded by benches on each of its four sides, two wooden chairs by the fire with a low table in between, and in the corner a simple desk with its own bench. There were no objects to explore. There was no fabric. There were no cushions, no paintings, no décor of any kind. She saw no books. Next to the desk, there was a globe similar to the one that still sat on its stand in the main room of her own home. Her mother and aunts studied the globe during her father's travels hoping to identify his location. Now she supposed she and her children would do the same with this globe, while Diego was away. She vowed to ask Diego to arrange to move her harpsichord. Both the beauty of the instrument and the music coming from it would help fill up this unpleasant space. She would teach her children how to play. They would invent songs together.

The older and younger captains sat in the chairs by the fire, lit their pipes and smoked. They did not speak. Juana explained that there was no kitchen in the house.

"Behind the fireplace is a pantry and small food-warming space. Cook prepares our meals in her cottage and brings them to us. But I believe we have all feasted enough for today."

Juana beckoned for Isabela to follow her.

"The Captain and I sleep in that room," Juana said pointing to the left side of the large middle room.

"Your room is on the other side, on the right. It was Diego's room when he was small. The Captain and I hoped to fill it with other children, but that did not happen. Now that room will be for you and your children. When he's here, Diego sleeps in the small room at the end of the hall just beyond yours."

Doña Juana opened the door to Isabela's room. What a relief it was to see her own possessions—everything she had feverishly packed and sent off after Cook's visit. The bright quilt from her childhood painstakingly and lovingly sewn for her by her aunts during her mother's only pregnancy. Her desk and matching carved chair. Cartons with her clothes lay open. On one of several small tables she had put in the cart, someone—probably Cook—placed the matching bowl and pitcher her father brought her from England. Its familiar glazed pale blue and green pastoral scenes cheered her somewhat.

"It has been an exhausting day for all of us," Juana told her. "Good night, Isabela." Juana shut the door.

Isabela moved among her things and made some effort to organize her letters, quills, and inks. She wandered to the window and was relieved that although she could not see her home—her former, childhood home—from this side, she could look down on the harbor and to the open sea beyond. It was almost dusk now, but she could make out stone stairs that led to a small beach. She would have the desk moved over to the window tomorrow, she thought. And she would send for her wardrobe. There was no place to store her clothes here. She planned to spend most of her daylight hours with Tía Lucia. At night this room would become her sanctuary. She could not imagine sitting silently by the fire with the home's other inhabitants in that large, empty room.

"An exhausting day for all of us," Doña Juana had said, apparently indicating that it was time for Isabela to retire. Fatigued, but not ready to sleep, Isabela stepped out of her wedding dress, laid it on top of one of the clothes cartons and rummaged in another carton for her night dress—the silk one she and Aunt Lucia had designed and embroidered for this night. After lighting a candle, she straightened the crucifix that was hanging crookedly on the wall, kneeled to pray, rose, and chose a book of poems. Once in bed she reveled in the warmth of the quilt covering her and in the luxury of the gown's gentle fabric against her skin.

She blew out the candle and had begun to doze when she was awakened by rustling and whispering in the hallway outside her door. Diego, carrying a lamp, entered her room with no warning and no greeting. He placed the lamp on her desk, removed his boots, pulled the quilt off the bed and tossed it on the floor. Standing over her he motioned for her to raise her nightdress. In a desperate attempt both to engage this man in conversation and delay what she dreaded and feared, she asked,

"What is it you want?"

"You know what I want. You know why I am here. Raise your gown."

She sat up, reached down and pulled the gown up to her knees. Exposing her stockings and her legs to this man—this rough stranger who was her husband—made her tremble with humiliation.

"Higher," Diego ordered. "And lift up your hips."

When she obeyed, he slipped a cloth under her, lay on top of her, yanked the gown up above her waist, unbuttoned his pants, and entered her. She cried out in shock and pain. She wanted him out. She wanted him off. She wanted to run out of this house all the way along the path—even in the dark—to her home on the opposite bluff and never return here. She never wanted to set eyes on this man again.

Diego placed his hands on her shoulders and held her down as he moved in and out of her. She felt imprisoned. The motion seemed to go on and on as if she would have to endure this forever. Finally he groaned and slumped with his full weight on her. Then he rose and motioned for her to raise her hips again.

"What are going to do to me now?" she cried indignantly.

"It's finished," he said. "It's done."

He pulled away the cloth he had placed under her and rose from the bed. She pulled her gown down toward her feet, reached for her quilt, and covered herself.

Diego showed her the white cloth with the blood stain.

"This is good," he said. He took the cloth to the door. She saw by the lamplight that his mother and father had apparently been standing in the hallway throughout her ordeal.

Upon viewing the cloth, Isabela heard Juana say,

"Well, thanks be to God. Who knows what she was up to in that heathen city? With that painter? We will watch her carefully though, Diego, while you're away. We must be assured that any child she bears is our own."

Chapter Five
Soul-Saving Music

Isabela lay in her new bed trembling from humiliation, alienation, and the fear that Diego might return. In the dark, she reached for the book of poems and held it tight, although she did not light the candle. She could not focus enough to read. As the hours passed with no sleep, she began to acknowledge an anger unlike anything she had before experienced. She was livid with the heartless de Vega family for treating her like an object, a vehicle to produce the children they themselves had failed to create. "With that painter?" Doña Juana said. Was she referring to Rembrandt? Pieter? How did she even know about them? Though it pained her further, she was also furious with the father she had always adored and trusted for deciding her future when she was a mere helpless babe. By morning, she came close to cursing God. "Is this what you saved me for? Why did you not let me drown with my father?"

As light began to reach her through the window at the far side of the room, she rose and removed the painted lid of Mary and Jesus from one of the small boxes she had sent here. She stood clutching to her chest the depiction of mother and son and looked down at the water below. At this early hour the harbor was covered with mist that reflected the orange of the rising sun along with sunrise streams of pink and blue. Gazing at the serene and dedicated mother holding her doomed infant, Isabela prayed,

"Oh Blessed Mary, Mother of Our Lord, my torment cannot compare to the agony you suffered. Send me solace. Remove from my heart this mounting hate. Forgive me."

* * *

Isabela jumped when she heard a quiet knock on the door. Diego had simply opened the door and burst in last night without knocking. Was he feeling contrite? Did this gentle knock indicate that he was capable of treating her with respect, that he might even apologize? When she heard a light tapping a second time, she returned the box's lid to its place, wrapped herself in the quilt and tentatively opened the door. Cook stood in the hallway with a tray.

"I've brought you a bit of breakfast, Señora," Cook whispered. "The Captain and Doña Juana take the first meal of the day in their room. I thought you might like that too."

Señora! Isabela heard the word, but recoiled from the form of address and its implications. Nevertheless she had to resist throwing her arms around this generous woman. Did Cook suspect that she had suffered last evening and throughout the night? Or was she just doing her duty? Her mild reassuring smile indicated that perhaps she understood or at least suspected. And where was Diego? Had Cook already served him in his room next to hers?

"How kind of you . . . Cook." Isabela found "Cook" demeaning, especially for such a dignified and caring woman, but she followed the lead of the de Vegas. "Please come in."

Cook set the tray down on one of Isabela's tables and moved toward the door. Then she turned and walked back to Isabela. In a low voice—'does she always whisper?' Isabela thought—Cook said,

"You'll visit your former home today?"

"Yes, I plan to go every day to see Tía Lucia. She is not well."

"Well, you may want to prepare yourself for some unpleasant surprises."

"Has something happened to my aunt?"

"No, I don't believe so."

Cook turned to leave but again walked back to where Isabela still stood by the window, puzzled and alarmed.

"You know you can visit me any time in my cottage. From here, you wouldn't even know it's there. It's hidden by a row of trees. Exit the front door of the house, turn right and follow the path. You'll see the chimney smoke."

With a slight pat on Isabela's arm before taking her leave, Cook said, "I'll show you my herb garden."

Isabela had not eaten since Cook brought her the plate of treats yesterday at the wedding. She took the wooden plate back to her desk to sit in the room's only chair, and quickly devoured half the still-warm bread wrapped in a cloth, slices of cheese, and an orange. She rewrapped the rest of the bread for her aunt. She dressed and moved down the hall toward the front door, so eager to leave this house she did not see her mother-in-law sitting in one of the chairs facing the fire.

"Where are you going, Isabela?" Doña Juana called accusingly. "You must always tell me of your intentions. Otherwise, I will be concerned about you."

"I am going to visit with my aunt, Doña Juana. She is not well."

"She will need you today. Go then. I should tell you that Cook brings the midday meal at noon and a light evening one before dark. Please join us for meals. We retire early."

"And Diego?" Isabela asked.

"Diego is rarely here."

Once outside, as the fresh, cool, salty air filled her lungs, Isabela felt as if she were learning to breathe all over again, as if she had stopped breathing yesterday when she took her first step inside the bare, dark house. She said a silent thank you to the builders of the two houses for their foresight. Thanks to them, it was not necessary to climb down the bluff from one house, pass through the village and climb up the bluff to reach the twin house on the other side of the harbor. There was a path along the bluff that connected the two houses. Here and there, she could see the boot prints from Diego and Cornelius and smaller prints in both directions, probably from Cook.

She stopped several times to look down at the harbor on one side and the village on the other. It was early, but she saw fishermen preparing their boats and heading out for the day's catch. She was too high up to hear, but she could imagine the shouts and grunts, the scraping of the heavy nets, buckets, and pots. In the village people were milking the cows behind their modest homes, feeding chickens, pulling up water from their wells and lugging it to wherever it was needed. Isabela had never been to the theater, but she felt as if she were looking down on a play performed by busy little dwarfs. Women were starting to gather by the communal well in the center of town. Older children helped with chores. Small ones ran around chasing each other and knocking each other down. She imagined their squeals.

Isabela was unfamiliar with this path. She enjoyed the way it followed the sharp turns and curves of the cliffs, going straight for awhile and then suddenly turning so that she could not always be sure what she might see just ahead. A rabbit? A fallen limb? A burst of flowers? It became a game of surprise. She began to notice the different rock formations. One like half a face with a prominent nose. One like an animal with horns. When she came upon a hornet's nest, she veered off the path to avoid it and stepped up her pace.

She heard the shouts and sensed the movement before she saw them. Rounding the last bend in the path, she came upon a scene that so stunned her, she stood motionless, rejecting what her eyes told her. 'Did I go in the wrong direction?' she wondered. It was like arriving mistakenly at the home of strangers. But no, this was her home and it was being raided. She saw several large carts—six of them arranged haphazardly in front of her door. Three of the carts were already filled. Finding that her legs could still move, she ran from cart to cart. She saw her parents' bed, her own bed, both her parents' wardrobes and her own.

Men exited her home in two's and three's, emptying the house of ornate lamps, the matching French divan and stuffed chair, decorative mirrors, even her mother's dresses and petticoats. Isabela was frantic. Where was Tía Lucia? Was she safe? She pushed by one man who was leaving with a painting under each arm. Isabela caught a glimpse of it as he passed her. She was ten when her father slowly, teasingly unveiled this work of art to reveal an English girl perched on a swing hung from the branch of a tree. The little girl's shoes did not quite touch the ground. The deep-blue ribbon on her bonnet floated up behind her. Looking at that painting always infused Isabela with a feeling of freedom and delight. She thought she understood what it would be like to somehow turn into a lark, to fly up to the top of the cliffs and down again, barely skimming the water, singing the entire time. But that beloved painting was joining others already in the carts.

Just inside the door she saw placed on its side her elaborate dollhouse from Denmark. It looked so forlorn with its curtains hanging sideways, its chimney horizontal, the rooms topsy turvy, living spaces on top and sleeping rooms below. When she was eight, she delighted in tidying up every miniature room. She even removed the drapes, washed them and rehung them so that her little house remained fresh and clean. Now the house looked as if it had been blown over by a hurricane. At least she had salvaged its contents . . . or was someone scavenging and emptying out her room at the de Vega's this very moment?

When a second man scooped up the dollhouse and began taking it out the door, Isabela blocked his way.

"What are you doing?" she demanded. This is MY HOME. Everything here has belonged to my family for decades. Put down that dollhouse."

"Just followin' orders, Miss. Move aside."

At that moment Isabela spotted Diego on the far side of the room, leaning against the harpsichord.

"What is happening?" she demanded as she approached him. "Are you the one who is responsible for the removal of all my possessions?"

"YOUR possessions, Isabela," he sneered? "When a woman marries, everything she owns becomes the property of her husband. Your father knew that when he arranged our betrothal seventeen years ago."

"But what are you going to do with it all?"

"Ship it to Madrid."

"For what?

Diego had lowered the harpsichord's lid. Although quite small, it had always looked rather majestic. Now it had a deflated appearance. In need of a hard surface for writing what appeared to be lists of every object in the house, he had turned the instrument into an impromptu desk.

"What do you think I'm taking it to Madrid for? Do you believe anyone in this village has the means to purchase this stuff?"

"You're selling it all then?"

"That is my plan."

Isabela was startled by a voice rising from underneath the instrument.

"We could dismantle it. Take it down the bluff in pieces and reassemble it."

The man was apparently looking for ways to take it apart.

"Let me keep this instrument, Diego," she pleaded. "We can move it to your house. It would look beautiful in the corner near the fireplace. Our children could learn to play it."

"For what? My children will have more important things to do with their time."

Diego poked at a few keys with one finger. Besides, my mother would never tolerate this tinny irritating sound."

"What MORE IMPORTANT THINGS, Diego?" Isabela asked in a mocking tone. "Will you train them to steal other people's goods perhaps?"

He looked as if he might strike her. Would he? Here in her home? In front of these men?

He regained some composure. Turning his back to her, he said,

"Go back to my parents' home, Isabela. That is where you belong now."

She realized that she had not yet seen her father's massive desk in any of the carts. Was it too heavy to move? She walked into her parents' room which by now she hardly recognized. After stuffing her pockets with some of the coins she had left there only two nights before—her ridiculous attempt to fool an imagined thief when the real thief was her husband—she grabbed whatever else her arms could hold and stuffed it into one of her mother's decorative bags. She returned with the bag to where Diego was still leaning against the instrument, taking inventory, perhaps estimating the worth of each object.

Isabela knew that this instrument, which her father referred to as a virginal, could in fact be taken apart and moved. It arrived in carefully wrapped pieces. Shipped from Italy with instructions, it took days of careful, delicate work to unite the sections into a whole. For that task her father hired a master craftsman from far-away Padua. Serious and focused, Don Romero stayed in their home until the project was finished.

Compact with simple lines and no décor, made with unvarnished medium-brown wood, it sat on two legs with large comical feet supporting the keyboard in front, a single leg and foot holding up the tapered back. In a triumphant celebration of his completed work, the craftsman sat down and played for them. The women were entranced. He stayed and gave them lessons. The instrument came with a pile of sheet music. While they waited for more to arrive—from their native country but also from France, England, and Germany, they made up their own tunes. In spite of their delight with the music, Tía Anacleta and Tía Lucia were sad to see Don Romero leave.

Now all these years later a frustrated, furious, and defiant Isabela sat down on the leather-covered bench which Don Romero had also assembled. The orphanage in Amsterdam had no harpsichord. She had not played for almost two years. But the music she knew by heart returned to her. The crisp sound filled the room. Small-scale motets by Henri Dumont. Sacred tunes by Johann Rosenmüller. A dancing zarzuela by Juan Hidalgo. The more objects the burly men removed, the faster she played.

When she began her favorite duet cantata by Barbara Strozzi, Tía Lucia opened the door to her bedroom where she had apparently taken refuge. Ignoring the chaos around her, she walked straight to the instrument, sat next to Isabela and launched into her part of the duet. When aunt and niece had exhausted their repertoire and themselves, there was little left inside the house. The harpsichord was still standing on its sturdy feet. It was still intact, alone in the empty room.

Isabela went to the kitchen where there was no sign of the cook. And no wonder. Every pot, pan, and cooking utensil had been taken away. The fire was out. She could not even make a pomegranate tea for Lucia. She gave her the leftover bread from her breakfast.

She found Diego outside, throwing protective tarps over the carts.

"What is to become of my aunt? I want to bring her to live with me."

"That's impossible. We have neither the space nor the means to feed another mouth."

"Are you leaving her to die alone in this empty house?"

"She will be fine with the nuns."

"Nuns? What nuns? You can't send her away to a strange place. This has been her home for nearly forty years. She is fragile."

"Calm yourself, Isabela," Diego said as he tightened the heavy ropes that held the tarps in place.

"Everything is arranged. Everything will be fine. It's the nuns in this house I'm referring to. The Church has purchased it. They're turning it into a convent."

Chapter Six
Sanctuary

I sabela's days fell into a pattern that lasted for the next eight weeks. Breakfast in her room. A brief stop by Cook's cottage for food scraps—something she and Aunt Lucia could eat for their midday meal. Down the path to her old home where she visited with her aunt most of the day. Return up the path for a mostly silent meal with Captain and Doña Juana. Reading or needlepoint in her room. Sleep. She did not see or hear from Diego during that time. His parents did not mention him either.

After a few days of pondering the many questions she had about all that had befallen her, she said to Lucia,

"I overheard Doña Juana refer in a pejorative tone to 'that painter.' What was her meaning? I met a well-known artist, Rembrandt, once when he and his pupils were painting up on a wall surrounding the city. Was she talking about him? His student, Pieter Hals, was kind enough to accompany me and my little orphan friend, Nelleke, back to the orphanage after an errand one day.

"Pieter then made an offer to paint my portrait and donate it to the orphanage. I saw Pieter on two other occasions—one evening when along with Nelleke and perhaps sixty other guests we attended the same wedding celebration. A second time the Sunday before Diego came for me. Each week from Sunday evening until the following Sunday morning, my duties were to care for twenty orphans in my charge. Sunday during the day was the only free time I had. Sunday mornings I attended church. On that last Sunday afternoon I stepped out for a few hours with Mr. Hals. Along with dozens of others, mostly families, we walked along the canals. Mr. Hals gave me a painting lesson.

"The way she pronounced 'that artist' so suspiciously has made me wonder how Doña Juana even knew about Mr. Hals. I can assure you there was nothing unsavory about my brief contact with Rembrandt or my friendship with Pieter. What I don't understand is how the de Vegas became aware that I had met them."

Lucia buried her head in her hands. Isabela waited. Finally, Lucia confessed.

"We showed them your letters."

"My letters? All of them? But they were meant for your eyes only, Tía Lucia—yours and Tía Anacleta's. Why would you do that?"

"The words you chose to describe Mr. Hals alarmed us. Posing for him did not seem, well, ladylike. We were concerned that you would marry Mr. Hals. We knew he was not of our faith. We both wanted to see you married in the Church as your father intended and to the man he had chosen for you. We both wanted so very much to see you again, Isabela, before we died. You cannot imagine how lonely we were without you."

Through new tears she said,

"I realize now that what we did may not be making you happy. At least, not yet. I am so sorry, my darling child. We had the best of intentions. Anacleta and I had no power to bring you back. We were dependent on the de Vega family to do that for us."

"I don't know what everyone has imagined, but I was wearing my modest orphan uniform when I posed, Tía Lucia. There were people in and out of the room constantly—maids, orphans on their way to school, the housemother. I was never alone with the man.

"May I ask you another question? Cornelius was a crew member of the ship that went down with my father. Nearly two years ago he saved my life. In order to find me and bring me back here, Diego needed a Dutchman willing to risk his life. Cornelius has since told me that he was promised a large sum for smoothing the way for Diego, safeguarding our passage through the city and our exit out of the harbor. But even if they read his name in my letters how did the de Vegas know how to contact Cornelius, Tía Lucia?"

Lucia swallowed. She looked to the side, avoiding Isabela's confused, pleading eyes. Her lips trembled as she said, "Your father kept careful records. For every hire, he made notes in a black ledger. In that large oak desk of his. Name. Nationality. Age. Address of kin. When Diego asked us if we had any knowledge of the Dutchman—the one who saved you . . . . well, we gave him access to that ledger."

Isabela was distressed that first her private correspondence and then her father's business documents were shared with the de Vegas. She felt totally violated, helpless. She had always thought that love protected and supported, that love was a gift. Now she felt that love and betrayal were somehow linked. Would she ever trust anyone again?

* * *

By the end of the two months after her wedding day, the Church had transformed her former home. The large central room was now a combination chapel, meeting and dining area. In the three bedrooms partitions were raised to form four cells. That meant a total of twelve identical sleeping spaces each equipped with a rosary, a simple wooden bed with a thin mattress, a stand to hang one of the two habits nuns were allowed, and a bedside table with Bible and candle. Some of the cells had no window. The partitions did not reach the ceiling. That meant that although the women could not see each other, they could hear each other praying, reading out loud, snoring, weeping, and everything else.

Tía Lucia's personal items were not taken away. By the time Diego discovered that she had been hiding in her room, the carts were full and he was impatient to leave. She was a resident, not a nun, but she was assigned to one of the cells. Isabela helped her arrange some items under the low bed. She asked one of the carpenters to build shelves. Even so, Lucia could barely turn around in her reduced space.

Yet as the nuns began moving in, Lucia became, if not exactly lively, more alert. She behaved somewhat like a hostess welcoming overnight guests. Having lived among women all her life, she enjoyed the nuns' company. When they discovered how well she played the virginal, they encouraged her to play. Even though she was allowed to play sacred tunes only—no zarzuelas, no motets, nothing that might excite the emotions or hint at sensuality—she found pleasure in creating music for them. When the stricter nuns were outside, she sometimes even teased the younger ones with a few bars of dance music.

A twelfth nun—a very young woman, whose parents sent her away after she gave birth to a child fathered by a married neighbor—slept in the kitchen. Sister Mari did most of the cooking for the group of thirteen. Although the food was deliberately plain, Lucia kept busy helping with the preparation and serving. Secretly, she attempted to liven up the meals' bland taste by sprinkling them with spices and other secret ingredients. She was almost caught once when Sister Agathe recognized the taste of garlic.

"Where on earth did that come from?"

Mari said nothing. She continued chopping almonds. At least those were permitted.

The nuns were required to partially support themselves. They weeded and planted the neglected garden. They pruned the orchard's fruit trees. Soon sheep grazed nearby providing wool for the nuns themselves, but also for weaving into saleable garments.

As Lucia began participating in all these activities, Isabela cut back on daily visits. She needed to redefine her days. She also found that the long walk to and fro tired her and she was experiencing an urgent need to speak with Cook. Until now their contact was brief, their conversation centered on meals.

Whenever Isabela stopped by there were always people inside the cottage and out. Men, women, and children lounging on the grass, sitting on the step, standing alone or chatting in small groups. Upon learning the source of her midday meal, Tía Lucia had said,

"Oh, Cook! Yes! She's the woman who visited Heaven. At least that's what they say."

Visit to Heaven or not, Isabela felt Cook was the only woman she could ask about a serious and private matter that worried her. Choosing a time of day when she hoped all those lingering people would be too busy to visit, she tapped on and walked through Cook's door that was always open. She nodded at a woman who was just leaving. Cook was now alone. Motioning for Isabela to sit down, Cook smiled at Isabela with a welcoming confidence as if she always knew Isabela would seek her companionship sooner or later. Humming to herself she placed a ball of dough on a white floured surface, divided the dough into four sections, then pressed, folded, and stretched each piece.

Isabela focused on Cook's hands. She had noticed them before, but now she could study them. She guessed that Cook was about forty-five years old. The kneading motions were slow and gentle, but required strength. Cook used her hands every day for more demanding work as well—gardening, baking, frying, lifting. One might think that hands so occupied might appear abused and worn, that they might bare scars from burns and cuts. Cook's hands resembled those of a woman twenty years younger. No wrinkles or veins were visible. Her long white fingers burrowed into the dough, pushed and pulled. The backs of her hands were surprisingly smooth. Cook waited for Isabela to reveal the purpose of the visit.

"Four loaves, Cook? Who are the fortunate people they are destined for?"

"One for your breakfast tomorrow. One for the Captain and Doña Juana's breakfast. One for me. The fourth for anyone who visits and seems in need of nourishment," Cook answered brightly.

"I'm noticing your hands. How do you keep them so young looking and silky?"

"I rub them with lanolin twice a day."

Cook stopped kneading and covered the dough. She washed and dried her hands and reached for a small bottle—one of many on a shelf on the far wall near her bed. She brought over a basin, slowly washed Isabela's hands, and squeezed a few drops of the bottle's white liquid into her own palm. Then she rubbed the liquid on each of Isabela's hands taking care to touch the entire palm, back, and between the fingers as well as Isabela's wrists and lower arms.

Cook kept her herbs and balms across the room from the fire, but the lanolin had absorbed some of the flames' warmth. For the first time perhaps since that final night when she fell into her orphanage bed after reading and singing to her little girls, Isabela felt her whole body relax. She closed her eyes and gave herself over to creaminess and gentle caresses. In that humble one-room cottage, she felt God's presence. She felt His love envelop her. Finally, she brought her sweet-smelling fingertips to her cheeks and wiped away tears.

Cook had learned not to ask the first question. Sometimes a visitor just needed to get away from a difficult situation for a short time. Others went into great detail about a mistreatment they had experienced, a loss they suffered, a recurring nightmare, a physical pain.

Cook sat across the table from Isabela and waited silently, calmly, her lovely hands folded on the table in front of her. When after several minutes Isabela had said nothing, Cook rose quietly, stretched the four piles of dough into four different pans and placed them in her clay oven. The smell of baking bread filled the little house.

"Did you have a husband?" Isabela asked, feeling herself begin to tense up again.

"Yes, I did."

"What was he like?"

"He was a simple man. A farmer. A dear man. He was a hard worker, but as he worked in the fields, he must have made an effort to be alert to something he might share with me, something he thought would interest me."

"What sorts of stories did he tell you?"

"Oh, let me think. He died long ago.

"One time he helped a mare during a difficult birth. Her calf was born with only three legs. Without dwelling on it, knowing instantly that it would be useless on the farm, possibly even in pain, and would die young, he shot and buried it. But it bothered him for days. 'Why would God do that?' he pondered. 'Why would God create an innocent but deformed creature like that colt?'

"He knew I loved birds. I wondered at them. I admired them, especially with the way they fed and protected their young. They spent so much time encouraging their offspring to fly, even knowing that once they learned, the parents would no longer be needed. Their babies would fly away forever."

For a moment, Cook lost her usual air of quiet serenity and calm watchfulness. 'How did it happen,' Cook wondered, 'that with this young woman, the roles had become reversed? Now it was SHE who was talking about HER life.'

Isabela grasped immediately the implication of one's young leaving forever.

"So you had children?" she asked quietly.

"A girl who died in early infancy. Two strong boys. My husband and I wanted them to stay on the farm. God knows we could have used their help. But they were restless. They promised. 'Just one trip, Mama. Just one trip to see what's beyond that harbor. We'll come back with so many stories to tell you. Then we'll settle here. We'll marry.'"

Isabela waited.

"That was almost ten years ago. I never heard from either of them. Lost at sea, probably. When my husband died, I sold the farm. I couldn't do all the work. That's when I came here. I had heard the de Vega's were letting servants go. I knew about this gardener's cottage. I liked that it was hidden from the main house by those magnificent tall trees.

"I approached them with an offer to cook for them for free if they would allow me to live in the cottage and grow vegetables in the garden beside it. I grow much of the food consumed here. Friends bring me more than I can use. They climb the bluff. They stay awhile. The next time they come they might bring a bolt of cloth for a new apron and bonnet. A slab of beef. Decorative candles. A dozen oranges. I share it all with others. Those trees give me privacy, but they also block the winter wind. From high up here I see the sunrise on one side, the sunset on the other. I can see the water below. Except for missing my husband and my boys, I am never lonely."

Cook was somewhat stunned to find herself sharing so much. She was an intent listener. She almost never talked about herself. It returned her to a time when she was a girl. Together she and a friend from the neighboring farm stole time to run through the pasture down to the pond, dip their toes, roll in the grass, and chatter.

Cook stopped talking. She removed the breads from the oven, cut two slices, slathered them with butter and crushed blueberries and poured warm wine into two goblets—her best ones that she rarely used, given to her as a wedding present. She served. She waited. Finally, Isabela spoke. But she was not ready to share her angst. It was still she who continued to do the asking.

"Cook, your first night with your husband. Was it difficult?"

Cook was not surprised. She expected this might be the topic, the motive for this visit.

"My husband was not educated. He didn't read. He had limited skills. He was poor. But he loved me. He never forced himself on me. I looked forward to our nights together."

Isabela sighed. She hung her head. She looked as if she might cry.

"Child, I can give you something—a special oil—to smooth the path. He may object at first, but he'll learn to enjoy it himself."

"Thank you, Cook. I've been with him only one time—on our wedding night. I cried out in pain. He's been away now for two months. I'm so frightened about his returning, never knowing when he may throw open my door.

"I don't want to have a child with Diego. I think he would be a horrible father. The Captain will not live much longer. His mother is . . ."

Isabela hesitated. After all, Doña Juana was Cook's employer. Could she trust Cook to keep her confidences? Of course she could. Her trustworthiness was evident in all the people who visited.

"His mother is hateful."

Cook stepped to the door and beckoned.

"Step outside, Doña Isabela. Look over there on the far side of the garden under the fir tree? What do you see?"

"I think I see crosses."

"Yes. Count them."

"Five?"

"Yes. Five small crosses—one for each child Doña Juana lost. Two before they were born. Two at birth—boy twins. An only daughter when she was four. Diego is the only child she has left.

"How can you be certain you don't want children, Isabela? I can see that with your sweetness, your sensitivity, your grace, you would be a wonderful mother. You had lots of practice with . . . how many children were in your care at the Amsterdam orphanage?"

"Twenty."

"If you're certain you don't want any, I'll give you strong vinegar to put inside you. But vinegar is pungent. You don't want Diego to smell it. Men don't like it when you mess with their seed. You must follow it with orange essence. I'll give you some of that too."

'Oil, vinegar, essence of orange, a man's organ. How much can fit into my little space?' Isabela wondered.

"Oh, and vinegar also helps kill the disease."

"Disease? What disease?"

"They call it *mal francés*. You don't think the men on the ships go without women all those months, do you? They stop at ports. Women are waiting to greet them, to lure them. They pay the women. Those women have been with many, many men. They are unclean. Some of the men end up pocked and blind. They give the disease to their wives."

"*Mal francés*? I can't worry about that now. As for avoiding a child, I think it may be too late. Does God create a life from one encounter? The woman's first? A violent painful experience? Where the woman feels attacked and discarded? I fear such a child would suffer from some abnormality."

"Nature does not care how or where or by what man a woman bears a child. Each child is born innocent. It has no memory of the moment of conception. It just wants to draw that first breath, sip that first drop of milk . . . and live. It wants fiercely to live. Do you mind my asking . . . when did you last bleed?"

"Not since my wedding night. I've been nauseous too and tired."

"Do not fear this experience, Isabela. Your body is made for giving birth. I will help. You will rejoice when you first hold that baby. For years he will give you great pleasure."

After contemplating Cook's words, Isabela memorized them. The words became a promise, a prayer.

"You will rejoice. The child will give you great pleasure."

"Cook, how can I thank you? I feel so grateful."

Isabela stepped outside, then turned back. Cook was watching her.

"Cook, people say you visited Heaven. Is that true? How did it happen? Did you die and return to earth?"

"I will tell you the story when you visit next."

Chapter Seven
Stories from Cook's Youth

Three days after that first visit, Isabela again sat at Cook's long food-preparation table and watched Cook as she rinsed and chopped vegetables for the day's midday stew. Fresh from her garden, beets, squash, and parsley made a colorful mosaic floating in a savory sauce.

"I told them, Cook. Doña Juana and Captain Vicente. They were in their chairs by the fire as they often are—just kind of staring ahead. They've never added a chair for me or invited me to join them. I stood over them. I told them I had something to tell them. They turned to face me.

"'I am with child,'" I said. "Saying the words out loud made my situation more real somehow. I did not want to cry in front of them. I hurried on. 'I have not lain with Diego since our wedding night. That must be when it happened. Your grandchild will be born in seven months—a June baby.'

"Two things happened, Cook. Two things that I've never seen before in that house. Doña Juana smiled. Not a big smile, but a smile that for a moment transformed her usual sour expression. She also reached over and squeezed Captain Vicente's hand. I had done my duty. I didn't linger, standing there. That was the extent of the rejoicing. I have no idea where Diego is. Has he returned from Madrid? Left on a voyage on another ship? His ship is still moored beyond the harbor. I can see it from my window. I felt I should tell them first. I will tell Tía Lucia when I visit her next."

Cook listened, nodded.

"And how are you feeling, Doña Isabela? The morning sickness? The fatigue?"

"Fine now, Cook. I'm sure our visits have something to do with my improvement. No wonder you have so many visitors. "Can you tell me? About your visit to Heaven? Your visit has become a legend in Santos Gemelos, hasn't it? I realize that now. You must have told the story many times."

"My story begins, as so many do," Cook said, as she stopped to pour cider into the goblets she reserved for Isabela's visits. "With a story that precedes mine."

Cook had noted that for all Isabela's learning, her knowledge of languages, of poetry, of music, of art, and given she was one of the few women in Santos Gemelos who had travelled and returned, there was still much she did not know about the world. In her home high on the bluff and later in the Amsterdam orphanage, she had been sheltered, Cook concluded. At seventeen Isabela was a full-grown woman soon to be a mother herself, but she was still an innocent in some ways. So Cook began the story within the story by asking a question,

"Are you familiar with the pilgrimage route to Santiago de Compostela?"

But Cook underestimated Isabela. Using the elevated, almost erudite language Isabela sometimes slipped into as if she were reading, she answered, "Of course. The martyred apostle, St. James The Greater, the brother of Jesus. He helped drive the Muslims out of Spain. For centuries Christians have come from throughout the world to worship at his tomb. I can remember two occasions when my father told us excitedly about meeting pilgrims in our very village. They had strayed off the path somehow. One was from far-away Denmark. Another was French. France borders Spain, of course, but to walk the path from there to the coast must be arduous."

"That is exactly right," Cook said. In preparation for continuing the story, she took several sips from her drink.

"My story involves a French pilgrim, in fact. From Limoges. Centuries earlier, Gérard's ancestor, Aymeric Picaud, wrote one of the earliest known guidebooks on the pilgrimage. Since then many of the following Picaud generations undertook the long, demanding journey. Gérard was accompanying his grandfather whose dying wish was to follow the path through France and Spain and to leave a relic at the famous tomb—a certain relic that held special meaning for him.

"They entered Spain through Roncesvalles and walked through our cities of Pamplona, Logrono, and Burgos. The grandfather was devout and determined. As a sign of repentance and atonement, he began the journey wearing a *cilice*, a scratchy undergarment made of stiff goat hair. He also insisted on dragging a heavy wooden cross. But the *cilice* and cross so exhausted him that they were making little progress. Reluctantly the grandfather abandoned both. For a while, they were able to move at a somewhat faster pace. It had taken months, but they had covered 85 percent of the path. They had probably three more weeks to travel before reaching their destination.

"Our village does not grow like some villages, you know. Part of the reason, I think, is because of space. We are tucked in between the sea and the mountains. Another reason is that young people often leave to live along the route. They make a living servicing the pilgrims who need food, water, and medical help. They become guides. The poorest pilgrims sleep on the ground, but others are wealthy. Housing them requires many workers.

"As your father learned, occasionally a pilgrim passes through our village. Well not exactly passes through. It's usually a young, lone pilgrim who wearies of the route and wants to explore the valleys on either side of it. Sometimes it's someone seeking out a distant relative.

"Gérard Picaud ended up here for a different reason. His grandfather had been very clear that should he fall deathly ill along the route, he wanted a friar, not a priest, to give him the last rites. If he could not return to his native farm village outside the city of Limoges, he wanted to die in a similar village, not in a city, even if the people spoke no French.

"As they approached the last large city before Santiago—León— Gérard's grandfather became delusional. He insisted on continuing the route on his knees. It was his penance, he said—a penance for what, Gérard never learned. The path was worn smooth in some places, but in others it was strewn with pebbles and sharp stones. Bloody knees did not deter the grandfather. Because Gérard could hardly continue on foot alongside his elderly, bent grandfather, he too began travelling the path on his knees. Obviously, they made almost no progress. Gérard began to despair.

"Gérard loved his grandfather. He did all he could to help his grandfather realize his dream, something the old man had longed for since boyhood. His grandfather spoke often, Gérard told me, of the moment he would return home to Limoges to show off the award given to those who complete the entire journey. Both his older brother and his uncle had the award. Gérard had seen it and described it to me. It's a diploma bordered in sturdy Gothic imagery with an array of rococo ribbons at the top. The words are in Latin and confirm that the pilgrim completed the trail and visited the cathedral *pietatis causa*—for spiritual reasons. Neither Gérard nor his grandfather ever earned that coveted diploma.

"Gérard cleaned his grandfather's wounds as best he could—his own too with the help of the occasional aide along the route. His grandfather collapsed as they were passing near León. He could go no further. Gérard, by now weakened himself, purchased a wheelbarrow and pushed his grandfather into the city. The grandfather was horrified by the city's noise, smells, and crowds, by the hawkers lined up trying to sell their cheaply-made wares. Every quarter hour, bells from the cathedral and smaller churches clanged and competed for attention. The grandfather covered his ears."

"'I want to die in peace!'" he demanded in a still strong voice. "'Take me to a small village. Find me a friar.'

"After inquiring about where one might locate a village with a friar, a small village, a tranquil one, Gérard pushed his grandfather to Santos Gemelos. It felt right, Gérard told me, given that the city was named for twin brothers who were doctors. That meant going up and down several paths at the bottom of the mountains. Along the way, people helped push and pull the wheelbarrow, they covered the grandfather with a blanket, they provided food and drink. Still, shortly before they arrived here, the grandfather died. Gérard sought out Friar Fernando. A forgiving man who did not always follow the strictest rules of the Church, Friar Fernando said that since the grandfather had nearly completed the pilgrimage and had collapsed on his way to a shrine, he would perform the last rites over his body, thus ensuring his everlasting life.

"Locating a suitable final resting place was an urgent matter. The burial ground beside the church was reserved for residents of the village. Gérard was near collapse himself. The entire ordeal had so weakened him that he could barely stand. My father happened to be in the center of the village at that time. He had taken our two horses to the blacksmith.

He joined the crowd that had gathered in the square. My father offered a generous solution. He would bring the two men—one dead, the other ill—to his farm, bury the old man and care for the younger one until he was well enough to return to France.

"Others helped my father mount the two men on our horses. My father led the horses back to our farm and buried the grandfather. In our shed, he set up a simple wooden frame and covered it with straw to serve as Gérard's bed. I was a girl of fifteen. We owned one of the three largest farms in the valley at the time. My parents were illiterate, but they hired a tutor to teach my brothers to read. I was the youngest child and only girl. I protested loudly when they excluded me from the lessons. I cried and cried. The tutor asked if I could join and my parents relented. There was much work to do on the farm. The tutor came only once a week for two hours, but we all three learned quickly. We helped each other with our lessons.

"At first it was my mother who washed Gérard's wounds and spoon-fed him. They did not want me alone with a strange man, even a debilitated one. By the third morning Gérard was more feverish and weak than when he arrived. Not wanting him to die too quickly as his grandfather had, we called for Friar Fernando to give him the last rites. My mother had given up on Gérard. She was convinced he wouldn't be alive when the friar arrived. She returned to her many chores. I hurried through my duties that morning. I gathered eggs so quickly I feared I would break them all. I milked the cow. I churned the butter with all my strength. I swept the floor of our two-room dwelling. I abandoned the mending, the washing, even the preparation for the midday meal.

"I warmed some water, prepared a hot drink with some of the water and carried the rest to the shed in a large bowl. Gérard was curled up like a baby in the womb and breathing laboriously. I almost left, not wanting to witness his death. Once I had watched my father attempt to heal the badly scraped foot of a lamb. The lamb had been bleating in pain all day, begging for relief. The mother offered her milk, of course, but it did not pacify the poor critter. My father rubbed the torn flesh with a sticky substance from a plant that grew wild in our meadow. By the end of the day, the lamb nursed contentedly. The next day she stood and walked. By the second day, she was frolicking.

"I had never seen that green sap used on a human body, but I felt I had nothing to lose. How could it make the situation worse? I washed Gérard's face and hands and placed a cool cloth on his forehead. He was so light, it was easy to pull him up. He couldn't sit entirely upright, but raising him took pressure off his lungs. His breathing became less labored. I broke off a thick stalk of the rubbery plant. The inside of the stalk was lined with the thick substance. Cautiously, I took a clean cloth and rubbed a little in the least raw parts of Gérard's damaged knees. When nothing terrible happened, I continued patting on the sap until the wounds were covered. I cracked open a smaller stalk and rubbed sap on Gérard's palms, which had tiny pebbles from the Compostela path embedded in them.

"I had never touched a man like that. I didn't want to let go. I held his hand in both of mine while I sang every hymn I could think of. By the time the friar arrived, Gérard had opened his eyes. He had spoken. Since most of his words were in French, I didn't grasp their meaning, but I did understand, 'Merci' and I did appreciate his look of gratitude.

"After what seemed to my family like a miracle, I was released from a few of my chores and given the responsibility of caring for Gérard. I learned he was about thirty years old. He had a wife and two children. He was impatient to return to them, knowing they must be terribly worried about him. He was too weak to write, but he dictated a note to me, laboriously spelling out each letter. Given my limited ability to write even in my own language at the time and my unfamiliarity with the French alphabet, I can only imagine how such a note might appear to his relatives. The important thing, I realized, was that he was thinking and communicating and, of course, if the note arrived, that his family would learn that he was alive. It took a long time to write the brief communication and the effort tired us both.

"Each day I pressed sap to his wounds and hands. I began rubbing each finger, in between the fingers, in part I had to confess because I loved his warmth. I loved sitting near him. I held each of his hands between mine. That was how we ended each visit.

"After two weeks, I helped Gérard stand, although he leaned on me heavily. Scabs were forming over his knee wounds. In another two weeks he was limping tentatively around the shed. I could see he was getting impatient to leave. The thought that he might soon be gone upset me. I still held his hands every day, but toward the end of his stay with us, he was holding mine too. We laughed at ourselves trying to communicate in our different languages. We discovered many words that were similar in both Spanish and French.

"He was also talking a lot then about his family and I found I could grasp more and more. Like me he had two brothers, but no sisters. His son was nine years old, his daughter three. His wife's name was Bernadette. He called her Bijou. Somehow he conveyed to me that Bijou means 'jewel.' I brought the family Bible to the shed and read to him. It was in Latin. Since we were both Catholic, reading the familiar stories was a bond. Then one evening he said he had three gifts for me. 'Gifts?' I wondered. He had arrived with nothing."

Chapter Eight
A Pilgrim's Gifts

All this time while Cook told about Gérard, Isabela sipped her cider and listened. She did not want to miss a word of Cook's story. She realized that, although one might think that Cook had told this story many times, it probably wasn't so. People visited her often—sometimes as many as a dozen villagers and farmers a day, both wealthy and poor. But they came with cares of their own. They did the talking. She listened. She gave them an herb or a salve or an elixir. She finished each visit by looking in their eyes, wishing them speedy healing and holding their hands in hers—men, women, and children.

That Cook had once visited Heaven made sense to them. She had a celestial aura, calmness, and an infectious confidence.

A youth of perhaps fourteen years tapped on Cook's door. Cook beckoned him to enter. She held his hands and looked in his eyes.

"You are much improved, Antonio. I can see that."

She removed his cap and parted a section of his thick, black, wiry hair.

"Yes, it's almost healed."

She broke off a stem from one of the many plants she kept in the windows of her room—thick, sturdy, graceful, slightly curved stems reaching toward the sun. Except for their deep-green color, the stalks resembled Cook's long smooth fingers. She dabbed some of the sap onto a section of the boy's scalp, re-covered it with the protective locks and then with the cap.

"Mama said to tell you thank you and to give you this," Antonio said, handing Cook a package. Cook unwrapped it while the boy watched proudly.

"Mama made it," he said. "Just for you."

Cook caressed the fabric of the bright scarf and beheld its beauty 'Silk?' she asked herself. 'Could this poor family have purchased silk?' She felt guilty accepting the gift, but she knew this boy's mother would sacrifice anything for the joy and relief of seeing her child return to normalcy after a disorienting blow to the head. Indeed Cook's home overflowed with gifts. She felt she gave so little yet she received so much in return.

The young man stepped outside, but turned around and walked back inside again. Like others before him, he asked,

"Cook, when you visited Heaven, did you see God?"

"I did not see Him with my eyes, Antonio," she answered. "I did not see our Lord or our Blessed Mother."

The youth seemed disappointed until she explained.

"Perhaps my visit to Heaven was too brief to see them in the same way I'm looking at you right now. But I felt them. I felt them all around me. I knew they were there. I still sense their presence—every moment. What I experienced was a love so powerful . . . well, it's hard to explain in earthly terms. It's a love that was there before us. It's here now in this humble cottage. It's above us. It's below us. It's everywhere. It surrounds us. It has always been there. It will always be there. It's a forever love. It's eternal. Since that visit, I've never doubted God's love—not for a moment."

Cook placed the scarf over her head and tied it at her throat. The gesture pleased the young man. As she always did with all her departing visitors, she again looked into his eyes and held his hands in hers for a moment. As the boy stepped through the door, he turned to smile at Cook. He lifted his hat jauntily and lightly patted the healing gash that once threatened to take his young life.

* * *

Cook was aware that Isabela sat waiting patiently for her to continue her story. Sometimes after such a visit, she needed to be alone for a short while. It felt as if her soul needed replenishment. Isabela noticed Cook's distracted look.

"Shall I return another time, Cook? Do you need time to rest?"

Cook shook her head. She reached for one of the ten pairs of gloves she kept on pegs hanging in a corner. In the crowded room which contained the totality of Cook's possessions, cooking utensils, and healing tools, Isabela had not noticed the gloves before. These gloves were obviously made with thought and care. 'Made by cook herself?' Isabela wondered. Using bits of cloth from various cast-off fabrics, she must have stitched the gloves to fit her hands precisely. Cook picked up a log and placed it in the low-burning fire. The flames brightened. Warmth filled the room.

As if she could read Isabela's mind, she explained,

"Years ago I began wearing gloves to protect my hands. Now people make them for me. They knit them or patch them together or crochet them. Some are dainty with embroidered flowers. Some are weighty and inflexible. The ones you see are only the ones I'm using now. I have dozens more. I'll show you the collection some day.

"Please stay, Isabela. I'll finish my story if you like. You are a dear to listen so attentively."

"Your storytelling is a gift in itself, Cook."

"So . . . to continue," Cook began, "Gérard told me he had three gifts for me."

"'Before I show them to you, though,'" he said, "'let me give you a little demonstration.'

"Placing his hands on my shoulders, he sat me down on his bed. I was able to visit with him an hour a day at the most. Apparently he had been exercising in secret—loosening and strengthening his legs, preparing for his return to France. His knees would remain badly scarred, but he proceeded to walk in place. He picked up speed until he was running, but still without moving forward or backward. He switched to hopping and no longer just in place, but from one end of the little shed to the other, first on the left leg, then the right. He moved sideways. He twirled in a circle.

"Watching his performance, I began to giggle with amusement. It was a one-man show that reminded me of a travelling troupe I had seen in the village square when I was a little girl. The wilder their antics and tricks became, the more coins people threw at them. My laughter encouraged him. He jumped up and down and once landed so hard, my delight turned to concern.

"'Don't worry,' he said, 'I'm nearly all healed . . . so much so that I'm feeling quite guilty that I haven't lent a hand here to your generous family. I know the work on a farm never ends, but it is also strenuous. I'm so close to building up to full strength, I do not want to jeopardize my recovery.'

"He asked me to close my eyes and reach out my hand. I knew immediately what the object was. It was the scallop shell that all pilgrims sew onto their cloaks during their walk on the *camino*. He had shown it to me before and explained its meaning. Pilgrims arrive from all over the world. The shell's points symbolize the places where each comes from, from where each pilgrim begins the journey—the doorstep from their own homes. The grooves represent the paths they follow. All successful pilgrim journeys converge at the same place—at Santiago de Compostela symbolized by the shell's point at its base. All along the route pilgrims see shells on sign posts and on buildings. These act as guidelines, but also as encouragement. 'You are nearing your destination,' they seem to say. 'Take heart. You will get there.'

"I objected strenuously to the gift. 'No,' I told Gérard. 'You must keep this. It is a remembrance of all you suffered, of everything you've seen and experienced, of your loyalty to your grandfather. Show it to your children.'

"'I have my grandfather's scallop shell,' Gérard told me. 'I want YOU to have this one. You've shared this journey with me. You've made it possible for me to return home. You can show it to YOUR children some day.'

"He folded my hand around this 'gift number one' as he had called it. He held my hand in both of his firmly and looked in my eyes until I nodded in agreement. I knew he would leave soon—probably in a few days. I wanted to sit on that makeshift bed in that small shed forever with my hand sheltered in both of his.

"He then did something that completely surprised me. He bent over and removed my boots.

"His voice became softer. Almost in a whisper, he said sweetly, 'For gift number two, you must be prone.' 'I must be prone?' I asked him, understanding neither his words nor his direction. '*Oui, étendue, prolongée,*' Gérard repeated. This time, he made a sweeping gesture with his arm. He wanted me to lie down on his bed. All those weeks it was he who lay on that bed. I certainly never had.

"'I am giving you a glimpse of Heaven,' Gérard continued in his coaxing way. 'Some men know how to give a woman such a gift. I am one of those men. But you must be totally relaxed.' He made the sweeping gesture again, playfully, as if we were children and he were inviting me into his play castle. But he had promised a glimpse of Heaven. I was curious. I trusted him.

"We had loaned Gérard two pillows. He placed one pillow on the floor and kneeled on top of it, still protecting those knees, I'm sure. He arranged the second one under my head so that my neck was also supported. 'How is that?' he asked still in hushed tones."

Every time Cook quoted Gérard, she imitated him. Isabela scooted closer to Cook on the bench they shared. She wanted to hear every muted utterance. To visit Heaven? To be there even for a moment? She wanted to remember it all.

"He noticed that I was tense. Expectant," Cook nearly whispered.

"Gérard said, 'In France we call that Heavenly moment *un petit mort*—a little death. You're moved to a different place—a wonderful place, but you return.'

"I must have been holding my fists tight against my chest. Gérard took my fists in his hands and placed my arms at my sides. He began caressing the hand nearest him.

"'This is what you do for me, isn't it? You taught me this. This is part of my gift—returned to you.'

"I understood then. He wanted to return a favor. But his massage was more thorough than mine. He caressed between my fingers, the whole length of each finger. He concentrated on the palms, caressing with his fingertips, but also pressing with his thumbs.

"When he stopped momentarily, I opened my eyes to smile and thank him. I made a gesture to sit up. I assumed that I had already received the second gift. But no. Gérard motioned that I should remain in place—there—stretched out on his narrow bed. Gently, as a reminder to keep my eyes shut, he pressed his hand over them. He caressed my scalp. I thought he might remove my bonnet. I was relieved when he made no attempt to do so. I relaxed as he lingered over each of my features—eyes, nose, cheeks, even my mouth.

"When he reached my chin, I again assumed the gift was complete. I stirred. Gérard closed my eyes once more. He gently pressed down on my shoulders indicating, I assumed, that I should remain in that position.

"'Why would I sit up anyway?' I thought. It felt wonderful. It was late afternoon. The sun was falling on the other side of the house, but there was still light seeping into the shed. I could feel it through my eyelids. One candle burned on the low table beside me. I began to doze.

"I don't know how long I slept, but I know it was a deep sleep. I was aware of or I remembered later Gérard caressing my body. The sensations I experienced were tantalizing. I wanted to stay there forever in that tiny space with Gérard hovered over me. The caresses became more insistent, not rough, but with more pressure.

"That's when it happened, Isabela—what Gérard had promised me. I thought the sensation of the caresses was the gift—my glimpse of Heaven. But this was so much more. I understood what he meant by 'a little death.' It was as if I left my body. It was like rolling up a hill, up and up to a summit. With my whole body and soul I wanted to reach the top, yet I didn't want the rolling to ever stop either. I flew into the clouds. Toward Heaven. To God. My head had no more thoughts. I was pure spirit, pure joy.

"The experience was so intense, I slept on. The feeling of being lifted lingered. My mother came to call me home for evening prayer and meal. She found me on Gérard's bed with my boots off, but, 'Thank God,' she said—fully clothed, with my skirt and petticoat in place around my ankles. I always changed into a clean apron when I visited Gérard. The apron appeared as clean and unmussed as when I arrived. But I had visited Heaven. I knew it. And that visit changed me.

"The candle was out. Gérard was gone."

Chapter Nine
A Third Gift

"The next day my parents sent me to clean out the shed. They needed it for storage. That's when I found..." Cook hesitated. "The messages. In French, of course, but I understood them more or less. At our midday meal that day I translated the note addressed to my parents. He thanked them for their generosity. He apologized for not being well enough to help out on the farm and for leaving without saying good-bye. He said he was suddenly seized with longing to see his family and he wanted to start out before dark. He hoped they understood. They would remain forever in his heart and prayers.

"I never showed them the second note addressed to me. Not quite a love letter, it praised me for my spirit and my healing touch. Gérard implied that I had a rare gift, one that saved his life and might benefit others.

"He also left me . . ." Cook reached into her bosom, pulled out a chain and lifted it over her head.

"This," she said placing in Isabela's hand a light-weight object—a delicate and unusual cross unlike any cross Isabela had ever seen.

"It's made of white bronze I learned. Few people know I have it. I've kept it all this time."

Isabela looked down at the cross that reached from one side of her palm to the other. It seemed to be two thin crosses held together with tiny pins. The object was made with two horizontal crosses actually. The upper one was a shorter imitation of the one below it. A reddish fabric

69

showed through its round holes—three holes on each horizontal cross, three on the vertical base. Isabela walked with it to the open door where the light caught its shine. Images of wheat stalks etched in its surface made it shimmer. The cross seemed to tremble.

Cook explained that this was a relic—an extremely rare one.

"It's a Caravaca Cross—an imitation of the original double cross that was carved centuries ago from a splinter of wood which came from the very cross where Christ died. That first double cross is kept in a small chapel in a church in Vera Cruz. People who have been there and seen it all give the same report. The chapel gives off a unique aura of calm. As soon as they step inside the chapel, they are overwhelmed with a sense of peace. They feel surrounded by love emanating from that cross.

"Through the centuries, those who are fortunate to wear a Caravaca Cross believe it protects them—from plague, from shipwreck, and from evil."

Isabela pressed her lips to the cross and returned it to Cook who tucked it back into her blouse. Recently married and struggling to keep the secret contents of her pillows from her husband, Isabela asked,

"Cook, did your husband know of the cross?"

"I always wore it. He noticed it first on our wedding night. I told him that Gérard had given it to me because I had helped bring him back to life. I don't think he ever understood its worth. There are so few of these crosses. Some say they are worth so much that even all the gold in the King's coffers isn't enough to purchase one.

"I'd like to think that Gérard gave it to me not just out of gratitude, but because he cared for me. He wanted me to feel protected. I didn't say that to my husband, though. He was somewhat jealous and suspicious for awhile about my feelings for Gérard. After a few months he didn't mention Gérard anymore. Neither did I."

"And what about your visit to Heaven? Gérard said some men know how to take a woman there. Was your husband one of those men?"

"I looked forward with immense anticipation to my wedding night. I assumed that as a married woman, I would experience the rolling out-of-control delights for the rest of my life. I was disappointed. My man was sweet, but inept. He really didn't understand what a woman is capable of. I tried to make suggestions. I hinted. I guided him. He seemed horrified. 'Who spoke of that? I know you were chaste. I know you don't hang around taverns eavesdropping. It certainly wasn't your mother who told you things like that. Where do these ideas come from?

They are ungodly. It was that Frenchman wasn't it? I don't want to hear of such things again.'

"I suspected that my husband was jealous that Gérard may have known ways to please a woman that my husband did not know. Comparing himself to what I had told him about Gérard may have made him question his own manhood. He showed his love for me in other ways."

* * *

After Cook put the finishing touches on the midday meal, Isabela accompanied her to the de Vega's back door. As they stepped into the warming kitchen, Isabela kissed Cook good-bye in the way she might kiss her Tía Lucia. She returned to the main house and took her place at the dining table with her mother- and father-in-law.

When Isabela first moved here, her attempts at conversation were met with clipped answers or even silence. Since her announcement, the weighty silence had lifted somewhat. It was as if the couple had no memories of being young parents. Now with Isabela's encouragement, they began to relive Diego's babyhood, even to tell stories. Although Isabela loathed the adult Diego, the child in her belly came from him. She was anxious to learn all she could about Diego as an infant, as a little boy.

"What was his first word?" she asked them.

"What was the first word he ever said?" Doña Juana repeated.

The couple looked at each other and shrugged their shoulders.

"Fire maybe? No. Sword, I think. Although we couldn't decipher the word at first. Diego lost his temper trying to make us understand. He yelled 'Sode. Sode.' and pounded on the door to the bedroom. That was where the Captain kept his. Diego was drawn to the shiny steel probably."

"I told him he had to wait until he was eight years old to hold it," the Captain chimed in. "He didn't like that. Even as a tot, he could really get angry. I showed him how to hold the handle. That wasn't enough to please him. He screamed. I knew what he wanted. I refused to remove it from its scabbard. Eventually his mother diverted him with a toy monkey. But he always wanted to return to the sword hidden from him in our room."

As Isabela took leave of Captain Vicente and Doña Juana, on her way to her room she noticed that a third chair had been placed by the fire. 'Was Diego home?' she wondered. The thought made her whole body tense. She closed her bedroom door and kneeled in prayer.

Diego did not come barging in on her. In fact she rarely saw him during the next two years. That night, as she fell asleep, she pondered Cook's story. She was fascinated, but also frustrated. Her experience with Diego couldn't have been more different. 'Would she ever get a glimpse of Heaven? Experience a *petit mort*? Did you really need a man to lead you there or could you get there and return on your own?' She couldn't help believing that of the few men she'd known only Pieter could treat her so tenderly that she would experience a *petit mort* that would lift her to another world.

In Isabela's dream she saw Cook ascending into Heaven led by Gérard who held her hand. God held out his arms to Cook. It was hard to see Him clearly in the distance, but Isabela knew God was there. Just as Cook felt His Heavenly embrace and the exhilaration and joy she had described. An invisible force pulled Cook backward. Cook and Gérard returned to earth, to the little shed.

As Isabela slept on, the scene changed completely. Cook was in her cottage adding eggs to cake batter. Four eggs. She cracked each one separately and stirred its goo into the flour mix. Watching her, Isabela began to feel the tingling Cook has described, the feeling of being lifted out of her body. Delicious waves gripped her and urged her upward. Her insides seized in anticipation. Cook stirred the third egg into the stiff mix. Slowly and deliberately, she turned the thickening dough over and over until the egg was absorbed. With deliberate and sure gestures, Cook used a large wooden spoon to lift and lower the batter, to turn it over, twist and stir it. Isabela was certain then. 'When Cook finishes mixing in the fourth egg, I will have reached Heaven.'

Throughout her pregnancy, Isabela continued to have similar dreams. She began to suspect she didn't need a man to produce these feelings, yet vague thoughts of Pieter were often intertwined with the specifics of the dreams. She began to think of him as the Compostela lover she would never know.

In one repeating dream she watched a tulip swaying in the wind. A breeze blew away the delicate outer petals. One by one the soft colorful petals gently flew off. The tighter inner petals followed. Finally, just when the last petal lifted away leaving only a swaying slender stalk, the wave would seize her. She soared into the air with the tulip.

Although Isabela visited with Cook every few days, she kept these dreams to herself. Cook was busy with her orchard, garden, food preparation, and visitors, but she always took time for a little conversation. One day she had news.

"I found the little girl who sang at your wedding."

Chapter Ten
Same Song—New Version

Isabela placed several skirts and dresses in a bag for the walk down the path into the village. Her clothes had become too tight and had begun to press against her growing belly. On top of the garments she placed an almond cake baked by Cook who would accompany her. Not wanting to attract the attention of Diego or his parents and the questions that would surely follow any purchases she might make, Isabela had left all her family coins tucked into the six cushions. She lived as they did with simple meals and spartan surroundings. So smitten was she by the child's music, though, she made an exception. She tore out a few stitches from one of the cushions and shook out a coin. She would arrive at the child's home with thank-you gifts as well as work for her tailor parents.

"Two streets behind the church," Cook said. "I've walked by it many times, but for the first time I saw the child playing marbles in front of the house with her older brother. I was sure it was she and I stopped to ask her. 'Hello. Wasn't that you who sang at Doña Isabela's wedding?'

"The child is quite shy. She nodded, twirled her skirts for a moment, and ran inside. Her brother followed her. Neither child spoke to me. I confirmed with a neighbor and learned her name—Briana Valverde."

As Cook and Isabela walked carefully, avoiding rocks and slippery stones, Doña Juana's warning nagged at her somewhat.

"Just be careful. Conduct your business and leave. Those people are foreigners. You should not associate with them. There are other tailors in the village. Why that tailor?"

Isabela had learned to pay little attention to Doña Juana's negative attitudes. She could not name a single person her mother-in-law seemed fond of.

The house was located in a row of wooden dwellings that served both as shelter for families and shops for business. In most of the shops the front room was used for selling goods or services and also doubled as the family's kitchen. Some had a back room for sleeping. Others had only that one room that served every purpose. When Isabela stepped into the shop with Cook behind her, she saw that a large curtain separated the modest enterprise from the family spaces and cut off the light from the windows that surely lit the family room behind it. The open door provided some light, but with only one lamp on either side of the wide but shallow space, it was somewhat dark. She could hear a woman—probably the tailor's wife—conversing with children in a language she did not recognize, on the other side of the curtain. A long counter separated customers and the merely curious from the tailor's crowded work area.

As her eyes adjusted to the din, Isabela could see tools of the man's trade arranged on shelves and tables: buttons, thread, needles, scissors, tape measures, fabric. Her eyes were drawn to an exquisitely designed and decorated gown. Hung high on a hook, it was if the gown could speak.

"My master may spend his time repairing sleeves and lowering hems, but look what he is capable of."

On the left wall hung an unusually large, heavy crucifix. The crucifix too had a voice.

"Witness the devotion of this modest family."

On the right a statue of the Madonna reached out her arms toward the customers. The gesture and the Madonna's expression were ambiguous. Was she saying, "Blessed are all ye my children who enter here," or "Oh ye of generous hearts, save my son, save me, save yourselves?"

And books! More books than all the ones Diego had taken from her home. A solid Bible that looked too heavy for any one person to lift lay open on a tall lectern built to showcase it. A few other books lay open on small tables, on benches. Still more were arranged neatly on floor-to-ceiling shelves. Isabela was frustrated by the tantalizing titles—most too far away and too obscure for her to decipher. She had a brief image of herself, belly and all, climbing over the counter to reach them. She could spend months, perhaps years, exploring the languages, stories, and ideas in those volumes.

The tailor wove a thick needle through the fabric he was sewing, much as he might place a marker in a book so he could return easily to the correct passage of his interrupted reading. He stood to greet his clients. A thin man who wore spectacles, he had a slight roundness to his shoulders that forced him to bend his head up and back to speak.

Pronouncing each word with a pause in between he asked, "Ladies, how can I be of service?"

His voice was exceptionally deep. His intonation, with the question ending on a high note, was unlike that of most inhabitants of the region.

Cook, whose eyes and ears missed no detail, wondered, 'Do the tailor's peculiar speech habits reflect unease with the Spanish language? A speech defect? Or is he simply dazzled by the beauty of the young woman who has just entered his shop?'

Indeed, Isabela, who had arrived in Santos Gemelos as a travel-weary, food-deprived skeleton, was a transformed, full-figured expectant mother.

"I'm wondering if you could let out the waist of these skirts and dresses for me, Sir," Isabela said, showing him the garments. "An inch or two."

The tailor, whose customary gaze was downward, could not help but glance at the belly of the well-spoken young woman who gazed at him from alluring, large dark-brown eyes. He was not surprised to see the beginnings of the bulge which explained her request.

Having witnessed both the skittish nature of the little girl she longed to see again and knowing that Briana was probably just on the other side of the curtain, Isabela said in as casual and sweet a voice as she could muster,

"Mr. Valverde, I understand you have a young daughter—a gifted child with a singing voice so pleasing as to open up the very Heavens above. She performed at my wedding in the square several months ago."

The tailor's expression became hard and skeptical.

"You are mistaken. That could not have been my child. She is not permitted to go wandering on her own. Your garments will be ready in a few days."

The tailor turned toward his workbench. He sat, found the spot where he had left the needle, and began stitching.

"The little girl was about six, I believe," Isabela said, trying not to sound as if she were pleading.

"She was dressed in gray. I couldn't understand all the words to her song, but it seemed to be about a bird taking flight. I was quite moved and grateful for her performance."

Isabela's voice faltered as she recalled the child's lilting tone—the few bright moments the child provided her in an otherwise dismal, disheartening day.

"I brought her some gifts. I would like to give them to her directly, if I may."

The tailor sighed and called in the direction of the curtain.

"Reza, bring the girl here." Then as an afterthought, he called, "A lady is here to see her."

When mother and child appeared five minutes later from behind the curtain, Isabela understood that "A lady is here to see her" may have been code for "Make the child as presentable as possible." Over the ankle-length gray skirt she wore in the plaza, the little girl wore a crisp sky-blue apron. The fabric of the bonnet that held her black curls matched the apron. When Briana caught sight of Isabela on the other side of the counter, she pulled her mouth up into a thrilled smile and gave a startled little cry.

"Briana," her father said in a tone that caused the child to hang her head and pout. "Briana, Doña Isabela tells me you sang for her. In the plaza. Is that so?"

In a barely audible voice, Briana answered, "Yes, Papa."

"You know you are not allowed to leave our house unless you are accompanied by your mother, me, or your brother. Why did you run off? You must have understood it was wrong. You were gone for such a short time that none of us even registered your absence."

Isabela began to regret that she had mentioned the incident. She had simply wanted to thank and reward the little girl—and yes, meet her, perhaps even hear her sing again. Now she had to endure watching the child suffer a scolding.

Briana looked at the floor. Her small lips quivered. She made an effort to compose herself, but could not. Finally between little sobs that shook her narrow shoulders she said,

"I wanted to see the princess, Papa. The princess in the castle. On the hill. I wanted to see her dress, Papa. Her wedding dress. I thought it might be as beautiful as the one you made for Mama."

Briana had been wringing her hands in front of her. When she spoke of her mama's wedding dress, she swung around and pointed at the gown Isabela had noticed when she first entered the shop. Now Isabela saw that the gown hanging from several pegs high on a wall was the most elegant and elaborate gown she had ever beheld. It seemed to be designed with four distinct sections. At the top a delicate light red/beige lace in a V shape tucked into a narrow band of a different broader lace, then into a gold ribbon. Red satin covered the bodice and small waist and came to a point below the waist, echoing the V shape of the top layer of lace. From there layer upon layer of perhaps five different sumptuous scarlet fabrics fell in graceful folds.

To highlight its beauty and allure, the skirt had been spread out to its full width and tacked to the wall. In contrast to the tight-fitting bodice, the bulging sleeves were made of various golden layers each draping over the next, ending in a row of wide tucks at the wrist. The mounds of fabric dominated the back wall of the shop.

After her tearful explanation, Briana startled them all. She ran the length of the counter and darted under an opening Isabela had not noticed. She ran to Isabela, threw her arms around her and held onto Isabela's bulging belly. Isabela bent down so that she could look directly into Briana's eyes.

In the sweet, understanding voice she used with the orphans, Isabela said "Your father is right. Of course, you shouldn't run away alone. Not for any reason. I did so enjoy your song, though, Briana."

Holding Briana's hand, Isabela turned to the parents.

"May I give the child a small thank-you gift?" she asked.

The parents looked at each other, torn between the need to discipline their child and their deference to Doña Isabela. Their mutual glance apparently convinced them to acknowledge and accept Isabela's appreciative gesture.

"Yes, you may," the tailor said with some reticence.

Reaching toward the basket held by Cook who silently watched the scene from the doorway, Isabela said,

"This is Cook. She makes the most delicious almond cakes. This one is for you."

Reaching again into the basket, Isabela retrieved the coin and placed both offerings in the child's hands.

Isabela sensed that, having fulfilled most of her reasons for going to the tailor's today, she should take her leave and let the family return to its routines. She could not pull herself away, though, not from this delightful child who was about Nelleke's age, also spunky like Nelleke, but more contrite. The thought of trudging back up the bluff without fulfilling the most important reason for being there made Isabela sad. The time of her confinement was arriving quickly. She might not have another opportunity like this one.

Even while fearing that she might be disrupting further, Isabela found she could not stop herself from asking quietly, hopefully in a tone that gave the parents permission to refuse,

"Might I hear the song again? It cheered me so that day. Its echoes continue to give me comfort."

Isabela could not imagine being in a marriage where mutual decisions were made without a word, just by a look exchanged between husband and wife. She suppressed a stab of jealousy. The father spoke, but it was obvious that he sought the opinion of his wife before doing so. After one of their glances and a slight lifting of the mother's chin which apparently indicated acquiescence, the father looked down on his child from his side of the countertop.

"Do you wish to sing the song for Doña Isabela, Briana?"

"Oh, yes, Papa. Oh, yes, I truly do. Please, Papa. May I?"

"What song did you sing for the bride, Briana?"

Briana motioned for her father to bend toward her over the counter. She whispered in his ear.

"Can you sing the song entirely in Spanish, Briana? No foreign words?"

Briana hesitated. Did she understand her father's warning? Did she know the difference between Spanish language and what her father called "foreign words"? She thought another moment and then, not taking a chance that he might prohibit her performance, she stepped away from Isabela, pulled herself straight, cupped one of her small hands in the other, held them in front of her waist and launched into the song.

The pureness of the child's voice was even more evident within the small space than it had been in the open plaza. Isabela would not have been surprised to see Briana sprout wings and ascend into the Heavens along with the disappearing bird who was the subject of her song. The performance was briefer than Isabela remembered though, or perhaps she just did not want the song to end. Its melancholy tune in a minor key was haunting. Isabela dismissed a sudden longing for her harpsichord.

If she had more ready access to the instrument, she might be able to replicate the melody. Yet like the elusive bird, she wasn't sure she would ever be able to capture the feeling of the piece. She suspected that Briana never sang it the same way twice.

After the last lilting notes rose and thinned, Isabela knelt and put her arms around Briana.

"You have given me great joy today with your performance, dear child."

Reza spoke for the first time.

"I do hope you enjoyed Briana's singing today. She composes so many songs that she sometimes forgets previous ones."

"Shall I make a drawing of the bird for you, Princess?" Briana asked.

"I should like that very much, Briana. You may call me Doña Isabela. You can give it to me when I return to pick up the work I left with your father."

Cook and Isabela bid the tailor and his wife goodbye. Isabela wondered if in all those books there was an answer to the question that came to mind when she kissed Briana on both of her still damp cheeks.

'Why is it that human tears taste like the sea?'

Chapter Eleven
Village Friends

rudging up the bluff, Isabela spoke excitedly to Cook.

"What an interesting family, Cook, don't you think so? 'Sing in Spanish with no foreign words,' the father instructed. Foreign words, Cook. What could that mean? Do they know other languages? I could sing for them in French, Dutch, and English if they like. I could teach Briana and she could teach me. And she writes her own songs? She illustrates the songs? And all those books, Cook. I hope they will let me visit again—and not JUST for my tailoring needs. But they're a little guarded, wouldn't you say? They remain isolated somewhat? That long counter with the wall beneath it seems to say, 'Bring us your business, but stay in your place.'"

When Isabela arrived back at the de Vega home—and that was the way she thought of it. THEIR home. It was not HERS. She did not have a home any more—she found her in-laws in their usual places by the fire. Doña Juana was wearing a new shawl. Unlike the black one with uneven fringe that continually slipped off her shoulders, this was a tightly woven deep brown with large yellow flowers. Captain Vicente smoked away contentedly on a shiny new white long-stemmed pipe. The room smelled of fresh tobacco. What's more, a third chair had again been placed in front of the fire.

"Diego was here," Doña Juana explained. "He sails tomorrow early. He has a new shipment of textiles he believes he can sell for a tidy sum. He looks forward to meeting his son upon his return. He met our request to provide a chair here by the fire for you. Perhaps it will help prevent your wandering."

At first the three of them assumed that the knock on the door indicated that Diego had returned, but Diego never knocked. Doña Isabela went to the door.

"Cornelius, how nice to see you. Do come in. Do you know Doña Juana and Captain Vicente?"

After acknowledging the couple in Spanish and bowing slightly, Cornelius addressed Isabela in Dutch.

"I'm leaving with Diego tomorrow. You asked me to take responsibility for a letter you've written?"

"Thank you SO much for remembering, Cornelius. You told me you could never return home. What can you do, then, to safeguard my letter and see that it reaches its destination?"

"There's no foolproof manner of delivery, but I'll tell you how it works, Isabela. We leave fighting to the soldiers. Trading is too lucrative for both Spain and Holland to let hostilities always interfere. When we see that a ship flying a foreign flag is not a military ship, and they determine that we too are no threat to them, we pull alongside each other. To communicate, we shout through cones made of iron. We exchange news and sometimes toss packages and letters too. Other times, we meet strangers in taverns onshore. We inquire about each other's homelands and destinations. We entrust each other with deliveries. Sailors from all countries long to communicate with their loved ones, to assure them that they are still alive. I've even written letters myself for a sailor or two who was illiterate. My own letter to my Amsterdam family will be with yours. I will do whatever I can to see that your letter reaches the City Orphanage, Isabela. It could take many months, though."

Isabela ran to her room to get the letter she had written, addressed, and sealed weeks ago, hoping for this very moment. She kissed the letter and placed it in Cornelius' hands.

After Cornelius took his leave, she explained to her suspicious in-laws that the letter was destined for Nelleke who was like a sister to her, that she wanted the little girl to know she was alive and well and expecting a child.

To appease the couple further and to provide some comfort for her own increasingly heavy body, Isabela brought three cushions from her room. Her in-laws seemed grateful for the gesture. Doña Juana and Captain Vicente nodded off, unaware that they were sitting on a near fortune. Isabela helped them to their room and retired to her own where she soothed her loneliness with thoughts about her next visit to the tailor's.

Isabela could not venture down the bluff to the village alone. It was not until Friday of the following week that Cook was free to accompany her. By then Isabela had imagined many scenarios that might deepen her relationship with the Valverde family. What could she bring into their lives that they might find useful, entertaining, interesting? In order to get to know them, to spend time with Briana, to borrow one of those many books, she must be able to give something in return. Her life felt so paltry and her existence so simple and uninteresting in comparison, but she would think of something.

Increasingly, Cook's days were filled with providing herbs, counsel and encouragement to villagers and farmers. Not only did they come from Santos Gemelos. Some walked half a day or more to reach her. A few came in boats from places she had never heard of. Finally, Cook had a free hour before serving the evening meal.

As they approached the tailor's, Isabela became more and more excited. She had several plans for engaging them. She also needed those enlarged skirts and dresses. When they arrived, the door to the dwelling was shut. A worn sign read, *"We are sorry we are not available to serve you. Friday nights in our home are dedicated to educating our children. Please do not disturb their lessons. Thank you. The Valverde family."*

* * *

"Stop taking chances with my grandson," Doña Juana would say every time Isabela left the house for anything—even to visit Cook. She couldn't sneak out like a wayward adolescent. Her in-laws were always in their chairs by the fire. It would be Monday, then, at the earliest before Isabela could visit the tailor's family and then only if Cook were free to accompany her.

'But how about Mass on Sunday?' Isabela thought. With the oversized crucifix and the pleading Madonna plus the open Bible on its lectern, the tailor's family certainly appeared devout. Perhaps she might see them at the church? Isabela herself rarely went to Mass. Ironically, it was while living in Calvinist Amsterdam that she attended Mass every Sunday. Calvinists had taken over Catholic churches and destroyed all the images and alters. Catholics were not permitted to worship openly, but hidden worship was tolerated.

Sunday morning was Isabela's only opportunity to be away from the orphanage. She was devoted to her group of twenty little girls, but while other big sisters marched them off to the Nieuwe Kerk, Isabela stuffed her mantilla up her sleeve and headed in the other direction. When she reached her destination, she gave the coded knock. After greeting Isabela, the mistress of the house led her up three flights of stairs of what from the outside appeared to be an ordinary canal house. At the very top of it, however, was a secret worship place where she knelt with fellow Catholics and allowed herself to be lulled by the priest's familiar Latin cadences and blessings.

Finding someone to accompany her into Santos Gemelos was difficult. Once a month or so Friar Fernando climbed the bluff to check in on her elderly in-laws and pray with them. Sunday was Cook's most demanding day. Not only did she try to add something special to Sunday's meal preparation, she was meeting the needs of what she had begun calling "my flock." She used the phrase in jest, but the truth was that people wanted to be in the presence of the woman who exuded the calm assurance one might expect from someone who had visited Heaven.

The locals continued to call her "Cook," but those who came from afar referred to her as "Healer." She never used that term to describe herself, but she didn't correct those who did.

"WHAT they believe helps them heal as much as any herb or salve I might give them," Cook told Isabela. "If they believe I have a healing touch, they will heal that much faster."

Even Friar Fernando always stopped by to see Cook after praying with the de Vega's. Whatever Cook gave him soothed his aching hips and knees.

Tía Lucia remained content with her convent life and steadfastly refused to go any farther than the garden. Nonetheless, after her usual light breakfast, Isabela set out on the path toward her old home, telling Doña Juana that she was visiting her aunt. That was true, but it was not her only purpose. She knew that one of the younger nuns was bored and unhappy, that she would welcome the opportunity to escape for a morning to the village. The challenge for Isabela would be to convince the head sister to allow such an outing.

When Isabela slipped in quietly, she saw the nuns kneeling in the chapel. With lips moving in prayer, eyes closed, heads bowed and hands clasped, most remained motionless. The young nun, however, raised her head to gaze worshipfully at the bleeding, agonized Christ figure above her.

Isabela's visits cheered Sister Mari. When she caught sight of her, she smiled and lifted her hand to wave, but stopped herself and tucked her hands back together in prayer pose. Tía Lucia did not participate in morning prayers. Isabela entered her aunt's cell, found her dressed, sitting on her bed and reading the Bible. The previous night Isabela had felt life stir within her for the first time. She took Tía Lucia's hand and placed it on her belly.

"This child belongs to you too," she said.

Tía Lucia let out a little cry when she felt a small motion.

"He's sending a silent message," Lucia whispered. "He's saying to us, 'Hello. Get ready. Here I come.'"

When the nuns had gathered around the table for bread, Isabela motioned to Sister Agathe, the severe French nun who governed the others. After listening to Isabela's request, predictably, Sister Agathe said,

"No. We need Sister Mari here. And who knows what temptations she might encounter in the village."

Isabela remained calm while she explained that she was asking a favor for herself, that it was important to her to pray in the church of her childhood, to pray to Mary for a safe birth and healthy baby, that she could not go alone. She sympathized with Sister Agathe's concerns. She promised that Sister Mari would never leave her side. They would attend Mass and return immediately. She needed assistance to make what for her was a sort of pilgrimage. By granting permission for Sister Mari to accompany her, Sister Agathe would have done her part to ensure that Isabela's baby came into the world blessed and healthy.

Sister Agathe sighed and relented. Mari's restlessness was affecting some of the other young nuns who had begun to complain and bicker. Perhaps this brief outing would satisfy her for a time and help her focus on her convent duties. At least Sister Agathe hoped so.

When Sister Mari and Isabela entered the church, every bench was filled. Mass had not yet begun. The congregation was laughing softly. Friar Fernando must have said something amusing as part of his welcoming remarks. He was a beloved figure. Small farmers walked up to an hour to receive his blessing. Some member of each family had to stay home to attend to animals or prepare a meal, but nearly every village family was represented. People on the back bench closest to the church door crowded together to make room for the latecomers. When Mari brushed shoulders with the youth to her left, any thoughts she had of sitting attentively through a second service evaporated.

Isabela strained to look over the churchgoers. Yes, the Valverde Family was there—in the front row, in fact. They must have arrived early. Mother, father, Briana, and the son whom she had not yet met were the first to rise and take communion. Mari and Isabela were among the last. Isabela thought she might exchange a smile with Briana, but Briana sat between her parents with bowed head and closed eyes.

Emerging into a noon sun and pulled home by their many duties, most of the congregants scattered quickly. A few lingered to have a word with the friar on the church steps. Neither Mari nor Isabela was anxious to trek back up the cliff. Finally, the four members of the Valverde family exited. The tailor became involved in some kind of deep discussion with the friar. Briana caught site of Isabela, dropped her mother's hand and came running over. When Isabela introduced Briana to Sister Mari, she led the two young women back to where her mother waited. "Can Sister Mari and the princess come to our house for the Sunday midday meal, today, Mama? Please, Mama?"

Señor Valverde joined the group just in time to hear his wife say, "Not today, Briana. Perhaps another time."

Briana still held Isabela's hand, but her expression changed from hopeful pleading to acute disappointment. Isabela tried to think of something that might comfort the little girl.

"Briana, I have an idea. I'm returning to your father's shop soon to pick up my skirts. You offered to make a drawing of the bird in your song. If your mother agrees, would you do that for me when I visit?"

Briana brightened. The possibility of sharing an activity together—even a brief one—cheered them both.

"Indeed," the tailor said after greeting Isabela and Sister Mari, "your items are ready for you. We look forward to your visit to our humble shop. Did you meet my son, Bernardo?"

Isabela found herself looking at a boy of about twelve. With his long wiry frame and face, the prominent cheek bones and tightly curled black hair that hung down to his shoulders, he looked like a young version of his father, but without the stoop and the squint. Bernardo bowed slightly to acknowledge the introduction.

Isabela knew it was time to let this family return home, but she did not want to let them go. Even fearing that she was being rude and unforgivingly bold, she could not stop herself from saying,

"Would it be impertinent of me to ask if I might borrow a book? Something to keep me company during my confinement?"

The tailor's response reassured and comforted her.

"I know just the one. It will be waiting for you," he said.

Isabela would have preferred to follow them home and receive the mystery book that very day. Instead, for two days she imagined what book it might be. For a young expectant mother, might the tailor choose something light and playful? Some silly poetry? A book about flowers? Or would he be tempted to challenge her? Loan her a text so dense that her inability to decipher its meaning would frustrate her? Or was he just being kind when he said that among the many volumes on his shelf, he already had chosen the one for her? Perhaps he would not take her request seriously? He would forget all about it and grab something quickly at the last minute?

Two days later, Cook accompanied Isabela to the tailor's. With some hesitation, Isabela packed the paint set she had salvaged from her home. She had been saving this gift from her father to give to her own children. She had looked forward to telling them about their grandfather and how his gifts were so appropriately chosen for her age and interests, how watching her open and exclaim over the gifts gave him much joy, how the gift giving was a ritual celebration each time he returned home safely. But it would be years before her children would be able to enjoy the paints and Briana was just the age now that Isabela was when she received them.

When Isabela and Cook arrived, Friar Fernando was behind the counter. Isabela felt utterly foolish at the stab of jealousy she experienced. 'The friar has been invited into the shop, whereas I am kept at a distance separated from the family by this half wall and long counter.'

"Wonderful to see you looking so bright and fit, young lady," the friar said in his warm, fatherly, jolly way.

Then, as if he needed to offer an explanation for his presence, he explained,

"This fine tailor is preparing a new robe for me—the finest wool, he tells me."

The community was accustomed to seeing their friar trudge around the area administering to his flock wearing a dusty loose garment that was stained with fish oil and smelled of stale beer. One day a week, he "dressed up" by covering that robe with a full-length white vestment embroidered with a gold cross that began at his saggy chin and ended at his sandaled feet.

"How lovely," Isabela said. "What is the occasion? A wedding? A christening?"

"Oh, those occasions occur nearly every week," the friar responded.

With the next utterance, his voiced tightened. He continued in a tone Isabela had not heard from him before—stiff, serious, possibly even with a touch of fear.

"Madrid has sent word that high church officials will honor us soon with a visit."

Isabela and Cook chatted with the friar while the tailor measured his shoulders, the length from his neck to his ankles, his arms, and finally his considerable girth.

"Your robe will be ready next week, friar," the tailor said. "Don't let your new look change you now. We're all fond of you just as you are."

Isabela puzzled over how the friar—and other customers—exited the tailor's workspace. Surely they did not pass through the curtained-off part of the room in the back? The friar walked down to the far end of the counter to the area where, on her previous visit, Briana had ducked under a small opening. The tailor followed behind, raised a section of the counter for the cleric and set it down once the friar was on the other side. A hidden horizontal door—that was the answer.

Would Isabela ever be invited into the workspace? It would not be appropriate for the tailor to measure her in the way she had just seen him do with the friar. If a woman orders a new gown, Reza must do the measuring. When she brought her skirts to the tailor and met him for the first time, he glanced at her mid-section. Many people did that—out of curiosity, she wondered each time, as if they might see through her flesh to the infant inside? She suspected that for some people too— men and women both—seeing a woman's protruding belly conjured thoughts of the act that created the child. Now it occurred to her that the tailor with one quick experienced look could probably estimate the size of her waist and predict how much extra fabric to add in order for her to be comfortable for the remaining months—no measuring necessary. Still, whether from a knowing grandmother passing her in the street, to a mocking adolescent boy, to the tailor himself who was simply conducting business, the glances seemed simultaneously intimate and invasive. Even though the tailor had never touched her and probably never would, she blushed remembering his brief contemplation of her belly.

With Cook off to the market to purchase fresh fruit—and probably to pick up some of the latest gossip, Isabela was alone with the tailor. To demonstrate his work, he placed one of Isabela's skirts on the counter. He had constructed a front panel, cut a section of the waist and added ribbons. The skirt could be tied snugly or loosely. She could adjust it as needed. The accommodating skirts would accompany her on her journey toward motherhood. By just imagining stepping into one of them and fussing with the ribbons until she got just the right fit, she seemed to breathe more easily.

After paying the tailor, Isabela showed him the paints she had brought for Briana. She could see that he was apologetic, that he understood the growing bond between his daughter and the young woman before him.

"I'll see that she gets these. She'll put them to work immediately, I'm sure. She'll be crestfallen not to have received your gift in person. She's off on an errand with her mother."

When Cook returned at that moment and took charge of the carton of skirts, she noted that it was surprisingly heavy. As Isabela climbed the bluff, leaning at times on Cook, she became sadder with each carefully placed step. Her wish to watch Briana use the paints, her plan to use Briana's interest in drawing to share an activity with her—none of it had worked out. There was no mention of loaning books, either. Although she was excited about having a child of her own, she was also anxious about Doña Juana's often expressed possessiveness toward the child. Were it not for Cook, she would feel entirely isolated and abandoned.

Chapter Twelve
Confinement and Correspondence

nce in her room alone, Isabela opened the carton to change into one of the skirts. When she examined the contents, she saw a skirt that did not belong to her. Had there been a mix-up? As she lifted the skirt out of the package, she realized it had been used for wrapping something bulky. Carefully pulling back the folds, she found the treasure the skirt had been hiding—three books.

Isabela noted with surprise and pleasure that the author of the smaller volume was a woman and a saint. She would eventually reread, savor, and ponder every word the author penned, but for this first exploration, she opened the first page and read the introduction:

"One of Spain's greatest mystics, Santa Teresa de Jesús (1515-1582) created perhaps the finest poetry and prose found in Spanish Renaissance literature. Her published writings include her Autobiography, *The Life of Teresa of Jesús*, her seminal work, *El Castillo Interior*, as well as *Christian Mysticism*, *Christian Meditation*, and *Camino de Perfección*. Her unaffected, but brilliant style reflects her religious intensity and describes how her soul—and therefore any human soul—reaches divine essence through prayer."

Holding the the other two volumes on her lap was like holding small, compact human twins. Due to both their weight and the voluminous number of pages, the books had heft. They seemed alive. She stared at the hard covers which contained no illustrations. The words were etched so deeply and in such ornate type, she had to bring her lamp closer to decipher them. The titles appeared to be *El Ingenioso Hidalgo Don*

Quixote de la Mancha. Authored by Miguel de Cervantes, the first—Part I—was apparently first published in 1605—thirty-seven years ago—in either Portugal or Madrid. The second volume followed in 1615. Although the expression was not used much by the time Isabela came of age, she remembered from other literature her aunts read to her that an *hidalgo* was a nobleman. By extension an *hidalgo* might also be a man of noble and generous spirit.

How did she know that definition anyway she wondered? Where did it come from? As she continued to stare at the title, memories came back to her. This same book was part of her father's library—now dispersed. It was Tía Anacleta who became particularly fond of the hidalgo's journey and his quest. Although she never read from the book directly to Isabela, she shared stories from it, simplifying them probably so that Isabela could grasp them. Sancho Panza on his donkey. Windmills in the distance mistaken for giants. Isabela had laughed at the images Tía Anacleta described, but Tía Anacleta seemed moved by them.

With her thumb Isabela ruffled through the pages until she reached the final one—page #1090. Tomorrow she would begin to immerse herself in this demanding tome the way her aunt had a decade ago. Life was circling back on her.

Impatient yet too exhausted to begin reading, she opened the cover. A folded note on white linen paper lay there patiently waiting to be discovered.

Dear Doña Isabela.

Per your request for reading material during your confinement, I have enclosed two possibilities. I am not certain of your literary tastes. Therefore, I have enclosed two very different books for you to choose from . . . or perhaps you'll like them both? Should these not meet your need, however, I will send my son, Bernardo, with additional choices for you. Doña Reza and I wish you a safe and joyful birth. We look forward to seeing you again and to meeting your child.

Sincerely,
Your Tailor

Isabela sat for a long time clutching the two loaned books along with what was apparently a gift—a brand new skirt—a practical gray, but oh, so clean and unworn and fitted with the required panel and ribbons.

By the time she had read the note for the third time, tears spilled down her cheeks. It had been so long since anyone had been that kind to her. It occurred to her that the definition of hidalgo—a noble and generous man—described the very person who had chosen and loaned her the pair of Don Quixote books. Did the humble tailor see himself in this hidalgo? She hoped her reading would reveal more similarities. For now it was the writers and characters of the books who would keep her company. But she was sure she would visit the family again when her child was old enough. "We look forward to seeing you . . ."

For the next two months, Isabela barely left the house. The path to her former home was too treacherous for visiting Tía Lucia, and even the much shorter path to Cook's cottage could be slippery. Doña Juana's warnings frightened her.

"If you fall, you'll have a baby with two heads. He'll never walk. You'll be carrying him in your arms for the rest of your life."

All day long she sat near a window, knitting and sewing—baby blankets, bonnets, wraps. In the early evening she sat with Doña Juana and Captain Vicente. She encouraged her father-in-law to share exploits about his shipping days. If he remembered anything interesting, he didn't share it. Twice, though, he did tell the exact same story about her father's bravery; how in his youth, until Isabela's mother begged him to stop, his ship was enlisted to transport medical crews. In the heat of battle, his small, versatile, easily maneuvered ship appeared quickly alongside a battleship that had raised its red "Wounded" flag. Through the fog of gun smoke, the crew scrambled aboard with bandages, remedies, and whisky.

"There were always some sailors they could revive and save," Captain de Vega said. "If necessary they were prepared to amputate. As for the dead soldiers, well, they stripped them of their swords, guns, and ammunition, wrapped them in the remaining torn pieces of their own uniforms, crossed themselves, and tossed the bodies overboard."

Isabela tried reading to her in-laws from Santa Teresa's poetry, but they nodded off. She trained her ear to listen for Cook entering the warming kitchen through the back door, so she could have a chat with someone/anyone other than the de Vegas, but Cook always had people waiting for services and did not linger long.

Once while Doña Juana sat snoring in her chair, the old woman woke with a start and fell forward. Isabela kicked her leg out to stop Doña Juana from hitting the hard floor. Even though she was frail, helping her up to a standing position was a strain. The incident was a warning that the three of them could no longer cope without assistance. The de Vegas would never agree to hire a helper because they had no money to pay or feed anyone. Isabela did have the funds, of course. The challenge was to pay someone without their questioning the source of the money. She hated to lie.

Once she led the de Vega couple to their room and helped them undress, she was free to devote her evenings to Don Quixote's exploits. After a week of reading on her own though, she felt she had such a need to discuss the many questions the text incited that she wrote a note to Señor Valverde. Cook regularly visited the market only two streets away from the tailor's shop and would happily deliver the message, she was sure. Yet the note sat in her desk for a week. 'There is nothing I desire more than to hear the tailor's views on this book,' she thought. 'So why do I not send the note? Because I fear the gesture would be regarded as impertinent? Because I will appear as lonely as I really am? Because my questions may sound naïve and ignorant?'

As she read further, the pressure to learn more and understand better became intense. She felt ridiculous. 'An 18-year-old woman about to give birth to her first child on this isolated bluff in 1642, obsessed with the story of a batty old man who thinks he's a knight wandering around the countryside in 1605?'

When she could tolerate her questions no longer, she wrote a second note. Before she allowed herself to reread the notes which she felt were simply a reflection of her own naïve and tangled musings, she sealed both with the sealing wax and personal stamp she had salvaged. The curly "I" and "C" of the stamp only reinforced her feelings of ridiculous girlishness.

The very next day, Cook delivered a reply:

Dear Doña Isabela,

Doña Reza and I are thinking of you and hoping that you are strong and healthy as the birth of your child approaches.

I am most pleased that you find the skirts useful and comfortable and that you are enjoying the two books I sent you. Your comments on the Miguel de Cervantes novel raise some interesting and thoughtful points, many of which have been discussed among serious literary critics in the decades since the book was released. Many scholars continue to address these issues, yet the ideas expressed are open to interpretation. That means that there are no definitive answers, only opinions. Your reactions are as valid as any other reader's. I encourage you to approach the story with the same open and imaginative mind you display in your notes to me.

My opinion is also only one among thousands, but I am happy to direct my comments to two of the questions you pose:

First of all to understand Cervantes, one must recognize the single major influence on his thought: the renaissance philosopher and theologian, Erasmus of Rotterdam (1466-1536) who died only nine years before Cervantes was born. Although Erasmus was an ordained priest, he never served the priesthood. Instead, he lived as an independent scholar who treasured the freedom to develop his intellect and devote himself to literary expression. At the end of his life, he was an active correspondent with approximately 500 other scholars. In some ways Cervantes continues Erasmus's thought or perhaps expresses it in a different form—the novel. Both are critical of the Catholic Church's excesses. Both are writing in the shadow of the Church and Crown decision in 1492 to give Spanish Jews three choices: 1) leave the country in thirty days, but leave your gold and silver behind; 2) convert immediately and publicly to Catholicism; 3) prepare to die.

I interpret Cervantes' writings as a continuation of attacks on the Catholic Church, the Spanish Inquisition and the ruling Catholic Spanish nobility. In his other writings, Cervantes points to his own Jewish ancestry and to the Jews' plight in Spain and abroad following the expulsions and mass conversions.

So as to your statement that you thought that Spain is a Catholic country with no Jewish residents, the situation may be true on the surface, but because so many Spaniards chose to convert rather than flee or die, their offspring continue to rile the Church. Outspoken writers, Erasmus and Cervantes among them, must live as Catholics while expressing their view that the Church has strayed from its original mission and now, in cooperation with royalty, seeks only power and wealth.

As for your question about the implications of Don Quixote's mistaking harmless windmills for threatening giants that must be slain, I believe Cervantes uses those scenes to draw attention in a satirical way to the rationale and actions of Spain's rulers and policies.

As for Santa Teresa of Avilés' writings, do share with me your thoughts.

Very truly yours,
Tailor Valverde

* * *

Making sense of the jumble of reactions she felt upon reading the tailor's letter kept Isabela awake much of the night. First, profound gratitude. Perhaps she didn't have 500 correspondents like Erasmus, nor would she ever, but she had one significant correspondent. And the mystery of the man. He himself was a serious scholar. Why was he not teaching in a major university instead of ruining his eyesight stitching hems? Amazement too that he expressed admiration for the thoughts she had shared. And what about Erasmus? A DUTCH scholar born in Rotterdam in the country where she herself had lived and loved? During their few exchanges, Isabela had never told the tailor about her experience abroad, but perhaps he, like most villagers, knew it. Was the connection some kind of coincidence or a sign of some sort?

Isabela was an avowed Catholic. Even surrounded by Holland's Calvinists, she never wavered or questioned her upbringing. Erasmus remained a loyal Catholic too while also criticizing the Church. It had never occurred to her to think of the Church as anything but benevolent. Was the tailor explaining the writers' opinions or were they also his own? Such a devout family who sat in the front row of the church at Mass, who displayed the Madonna in their shop. The tailor himself worked beneath a large crucifix. Could one display such devotion while simultaneously criticizing? If one were to begin to question the Church, where would one begin? How would one choose what is good and what is . . . well perhaps if one were to believe Erasmus and Cervantes?

As she lay in the dark thinking and rethinking, it occurred to her that she had not felt movement in her belly for many hours—perhaps not since she had thrust out her foot to stop Doña Juana from falling forward. Could that spontaneous gesture have harmed her baby? Dozing she dreamed that the tailor kneeled in front of her as she stood in his shop—on the OTHER side of that barrier where she had never been. He peeled back the panel he had sewn into her skirt to reveal a hidden door—like the horizontal one on his counter. He pulled a lever that opened the door and peeked into her belly. He closed the door, carefully reset the cloth panel, stood and said to her in his serious, scholarly way, "Your baby is unharmed. Soon you will hold in your arms a beautiful, healthy boy."

The dream woke Isabela, but the comfort it gave her was brief. She knew the baby must be curled up and crowded. She felt around until she touched what she thought might be a foot and tapped it. The foot, if that's what it was, remained inert. She explored her belly further and began tapping it all over, frantic. When she thought she felt mild movement, she didn't stop. She wanted her boy to jump and turn and ask, "Mama, what are you doing? Now I can't sleep." She got her wish. Her overly active infant kept her awake until morning.

At dawn when she finally raised herself and her heaving belly out of bed, her feet rattled a paper on the floor beside her desk. She had been so keen to read the tailor's words that she must not have noticed something else he sent.

As she unfolded the page it was as if the birds drawn there were lifting off and soaring right there in her room. In a straight diagonal line like an arrow that cut across the page from bottom left to top right were five separate drawings of a bright yellow-and-red bird as it took off from the ground and ended up in the clouds. The drawing was whimsical and joyful. Isabela wanted more. She longed to sit and watch Briana create and to ask her all the questions this drawing evoked.

"Where is the bird going? What does he see up there? Will he come back down? Is this the first time you've used paint? You are so talented, my sweet child."

For now she would write a thank-you note and send it with Cook along with the message answering a question in the tailor's recent message:

"Yes, I am enjoying Santa Teresa's mystical writings. They provide me an antidote to and a contrast with Cervantes' apparent accusations. I have to confess I'm confused. I don't know enough to be able to take sides and form my own opinion."

* * *

Isabela was forced to put aside the stimulating, esoteric and often puzzling readings and dedicate her time to more earthly concerns. As her day approached, Cook checked in with her every time she brought a meal. One afternoon she found Isabela pacing her room, moaning softly, and clutching her belly as if to keep it from dropping onto the floor. Within the hour a midwife joined the other two women attending Isabela.

Without consulting Doña Juana, Isabela had arranged with Sister Agathe to allow Sister Mari to live at the de Vega house for an indeterminate amount of time. Because Mari was helping cook in the cottage, joining Isabela as she prepared for the baby, or sleeping in her little nook in the warming kitchen, the couple did not complain about what Isabela feared they might see as an intrusion. They even accepted Mari's assistance in the evening when she brought them tea, accompanied them to their room, and helped them into bed.

One June morning Cook posted a notice on her cottage door apologizing that she could not meet with any visitors that day. Everyone who read the notice understood what it meant. Word of the impending birth spread quickly in the village. Isabela had assigned Cook the task of keeping Doña Juana away during the birth. Not only was she sure to criticize and complain, Isabela feared her presence might actually curse her child.

Chapter Thirteen
Pedro

ushing Pedro out into the world was much less laborious than Isabela expected. Perhaps, she thought, in spite of Doña Juana's warnings, those walks up and down the bluff actually strengthened the very muscles she needed.

Isabela had assumed that every new mother knows automatically what to do with her babe. She was surprised by the panic she felt when the midwife placed Pedro in her arms. She had never seen a newborn, much less held one. What had she been thinking? But Pedro himself taught her.

A small face with red splotches and blinking eyes tried to make sense of what had just happened to him. A mass of dark hair like hers and like Diego's covered a head slightly dented on one side.

"You poor darling. This was difficult for you too, wasn't it?"

When she held him tight enough to kiss his forehead and nose, he caught her scent. His tiny mouth began twitching. Isabela thought of the piglets she once watched being born. Several batches of kittens too. They all knew exactly what to do. The baby became impatient. Where was the thumb he had sucked on for months in the womb? Swaddled, he could not raise his fist to his face. Isabela lowered her night dress. Did her mother feed her right after she was born? She never thought to ask. She always assumed she had. Perhaps Tía Luisa would know. When her Pedrito let out a frustrated wail, a sudden jab of missing her mother grabbed her.

When the baby, still hoping for its thumb, did not recognize the nipple immediately, she squeezed it against his thirsty lips. When drops of yellowish liquid landed, the baby latched on. He sucked twice. Rested. Sucked twice more. Rested. Raised his eyes to hers. When he began sucking in earnest, confident now, reassured, Isabela experienced the sweetest sensation of her life. A pressure in both breasts, a soft pumping of liquid forward into the mouth of her son. A tightening of her womb, as if it too had understanding of this situation. The sucking was proof the baby was expelled. The womb could begin to return to its normal size and shape.

When she comforted, dressed, read to, or held a little orphan girl, Isabela was focused on the task. But she was also aware of the sensual effect of the child's soft skin on hers. What she was experiencing now was far more powerful. Salty tears ran down her cheeks, chin, and neck and landed on the baby's face.

What followed was an intrusion so brusque, unanticipated, and harsh, it left Isabela shaken and furious. Her mother-in-law burst in for a look at her first grandchild. What she saw horrified her—her tearful daughter-in-law with open night dress, sweaty, sticky, suckling a hungry newborn. The baby's slurping sounds sickened her.

"The wet nurse is here, Isabela," she said. "Women of our class do not feed our own infants."

Isabela had learned to tune out Doña Juana's nearly constant disapproving tone. As her belly grew, she became less and less compliant, no longer anxious to please or ready to obey.

"Send the woman away, Doña Juana. I will nourish my own child."

* * *

When Pedro turned two, Isabela felt reasonably comfortable leaving him with Mari for a few hours. Mari stopped wearing her nun's habit as soon as she arrived at the de Vega home. There was never any talk of her returning to the convent. She was devoted to Pedro. Isabela was grateful for Mari's help, but Mari was illiterate. Conversations were limited. She longed for the Valverde family. Yet in spite of both Briana's and the tailor's attentiveness and encouragement by letter during the past two years, she felt shy approaching them.

After descending the cliff, to build up her courage, she first walked through the village to the plaza. Perhaps a dozen women were gathered at the public well. Even though many of them had a private well, they came here most days to converse and share gossip. She could hear snatches of their conversations as she approached: "Consuela lost all her front teeth. She's frightful looking." "That goose lays more eggs in a day than I can sell in a week." "My husband would never allow that." "Do it anyway." "I don't dare."

When they caught sight of her, though, all chatter ceased. She found it disconcerting that they all knew her and she knew none of them. She had seen them greet each other with a shout of recognition, with a pat on the arm or an elbow punch. The women greeted HER by holding the sides of their skirts and bending one knee quickly. Their curtsying seemed awkward and set her apart. 'A curtsy takes the place of words,' she thought. 'It might mean Hello. Yes. I agree. I understand. I will do as you say. Good-bye.' In any case, the curtsy demonstrated a subservience that Isabela did not welcome. It reinforced her loneliness.

She smiled and nodded at the women and went directly to the tailor's. Although she and Mari could easily have removed the pregnancy panels themselves, she was using them as an excuse to visit the shop. Her waistline had returned to its normal size. Briana saw her first.

"La princesa!" she shouted as she darted under the opening and rushed to greet Isabela.

She looked as if she would throw her arms around Isabela, but stopped herself, apparently seized by the shyness Isabela had witnessed before. Isabela bent down and held out her arms to the child whose head now nearly came up to Isabela's chest.

Briana led Isabela to the horizontal door and lifted it open, inviting her to pass to the other side. The tailor saw Isabela's hesitation. He stood up from his work table and gestured for her to accept Briana's invitation. When he moved away from his work space, he removed his spectacles. Isabela noted that the rims were made of leather and that the bow-shaped piece of steel that held the rims together was tightly covered with a piece of black silk. The tailor placed the spectacles in a wooden case with round holes dug out that fit and protected the spectacles perfectly. Isabela did not refer to the correspondence she and the tailor had maintained for the past two years. She was on her second reading of Don Quixote. The tailor knew exactly on what page, in fact. Their written discussions of the book had sustained her. When she found herself looking directly into his dark, unfathomable eyes, however, Isabela was quite shaken. She felt her face redden. She took a deep breath to compose herself.

Chapter fourteen
Coping

"**P**lease," the tailor said, reinforcing Briana's invitation. "We have looked forward to your return. How is your little boy?"

Reza was sewing on a button. She did not stand, but she did nod and say, "Good morning." Isabela observed that Reza seemed pale.

Briana held out two closed fists.

"Which one?" she asked.

Isabela played along. She tapped the right fist. Briana showed her open, empty hand. Briana teasingly shook the still-closed fist. If there was anything inside, it made no noise. Briana slowly opened her fist to reveal an exquisitely carved horse. Proud and commanding with its head raised, chest thrust forward and mane trailing down its back, the carving ended on a small flat stand halfway down the horse's neck. Briana placed the carving in Isabela's hand. Pure and smooth in its whiteness, it was also weighty. As Isabela caressed the handsome horse, Briana led her to a table on the opposite side of the tailor's work area.

When Briana explained, "It's supposed to be a Knight," her brother, Bernardo, came rushing from the other side of the curtain.

"Don't touch that board, Briana. Leave it alone. Father and I are in the middle of a game and I'm ahead. You've picked up the white Knight? Where was it? Put it back."

"I know exactly where it was," Briana said with certainty. "It was on G1. You hadn't moved it yet. You better be careful. The black Knight will swallow it up. Show THAT piece to Isabela, why don't you?"

Reluctantly, and taking time to note its placement on the checkered board, Bernardo carefully lifted up the black horse/Knight and held it up for Isabela's viewing.

"Onyx," he said. "The white pieces are made of ivory. Do you play chess?"

"I must confess I'm not familiar with the game," Isabela said, "Do you think I could learn?"

"Father says it's a game of strategy. You have to analyze all the possible moves. It requires daring too, Father says."

"Correct," the tailor called from his side of the shop where he had returned to bend over his work. "Hopefully, it also teaches a young man patience."

Bernardo blushed and pointed out the other pieces. Kings and Queens represented by carved crowns. Bishops in the form of a cap with a cross. Rooks and Pawns.

"You have to study the board and determine both your openings and endgames. Ultimately what you want to do is maneuver the King of your opponent into a position where it cannot escape. When you're sure you've got him you say . . ."

"Stop," Briana said. "Let me tell."

"Okay, you go ahead and tell it then."

"You say 'checkmate.'"

"Good, Briana," the tailor said with understated praise.

The tailor left his work again and went to his bookshelves. He motioned for Isabela to approach. She saw an entire shelf dedicated to the game, with titles in Italian, Portuguese, French. The tailor plucked a book from the shelf and handed it to her—*Repetición de Amores y Arte de Ajedrez* (*Repetition of Love and the Art of Playing Chess*).

"Written by a Spanish churchman," the tailor informed her.

"Luis Ramirez de Lucena. See what you make of it. Bernardo, what do you say? Do you want to match wits with Isabela in a game some day?"

As she took leave of the family, the tailor surprised her by accompanying her to the street. In a low voice he said,

"Isabela, I'm not sure you're aware that a new priest has arrived in town. Just yesterday Friar Fernando was sent away. They did not even give him time to say good-bye to the many families he has served for dozens of years. The church is watching who attends Mass, who comes to confession . . . and who does not. It would be wise for you—and Cook too—to demonstrate your devotion."

As Isabela took leave of the Valverde family, she marveled, 'No matter how brief a visit with them might be, I come away with so much to ponder and learn.'

She clutched the book tight—another treasure to explore in the privacy of her room. The tailor's advice about attending Mass made her tense, though. She trusted his judgment. She knew that Cook's busiest day was Sunday when villagers and farmers felt they could justify a few hours off to seek Cook's help with whatever ailed them. Cook would not turn them away in order to attend Mass. In order to attend Mass herself, Isabela would have to leave Pedro with Mari and descend the bluff alone. Attending Mass unattended with the staring villagers was disconcerting. It would be awhile before she met the new priest.

Then, of course, there was the loss of Friar Fernando. Just knowing he was making his rounds, mixing with his people, sharing joy or offering condolences—she had always felt safe. Now with his sudden departure without a good-bye, not knowing where he was and not having yet met the new priest, she felt unmoored.

When she arrived at the de Vegas's she found two surprises. In the past two years, Diego had stopped by briefly to see his son only three times. What she saw when she walked through the front door made her gasp. Diego was throwing Pedro up into the air above his head and catching him. The baby had no sense of the danger, of course, and was enjoying himself thoroughly. Every time Diego set him on his feet, Pedro grabbed his father's legs and begged for more. Diego began throwing him higher and higher. Isabela intervened.

"Diego," she said without greeting him, "I'm afraid Pedro will get sick from being tossed around like that. He has a delicate stomach."

"A delicate stomach, eh?" Diego said. And then tossing him up again, he added, "I've seen no hint of a delicate stomach. What I've got here is a strong healthy boy."

The next time Diego set Pedro on the ground, Isabela took the child's hand and led him to their shared room. Pedro was not happy. As she dragged him away, he wailed and called, "Papa. Papa."

Diego called after her, but did not insist. He was probably tired of the game already.

"You'll make a coward out of him, Isabela. He'll grow to resent you if you keep him from enjoying himself."

Diego left abruptly as he always did . . . to go where and to do what she did not know.

After she was successful in distracting and calming Pedro, she noticed two mailings on her desk—both from Amsterdam. She tore open the one from Nelleke and scanned it to see if there was any mention of Pieter. Yes, he was pacing the floor while his sister, Anneliese, translated Isabela's letter from English to Dutch. So he knew now of her marriage, that she was going to have a child. Nelleke, with the help of her new mother, wrote a long letter. The little girl Isabela loved for her chatter, energy, and verve came leaping off the page through her words. How wonderful that she had a new family now and one that responded to her need to question and learn! That Nelleke and Isabela would probably never see each other again seemed cruel.

The second letter was from the Housemother of the City Orphanage, Mrs. Heijn. In her brisk, business-like manner, Mrs. Heijn inquired about what to do with the few items Isabela left behind "after her disappearance." Mrs. Heijn seemed to imply that Isabela ran off and abandoned her duties, but hopefully by now she knew the truth. Isabela wrote a quick note agreeing to Mrs. Heijn's suggestion that she give her final wages—a mere pittance—to the orphanage Regent and now father of Nelleke, Mr. Broekhof, so that he could invest the money on her behalf.

Making a decision about the second item Mrs. Heijn inquired about was more difficult. As for the dress—the one that Mrs. Comfrij had made for her in order for Isabela to attend Mrs. Comfrij's daughter's wedding—she instructed Mrs. Heijn to give it to Nelleke. She and Nelleke attended the wedding together in identical dresses Mrs. Comfrij sent. For that one night those party dresses replaced their usual red-and-black orphanage uniforms. It would be years before Nelleke was big enough to wear the larger dress, but it might be fun for her to receive it as a gift.

Pedro enjoyed the ritual of kneeling with his mother to pray before she tucked him in each night. The rhythm of the childish prayer calmed him. While Isabela spoke the words carefully and distinctly so he could eventually memorize them, Pedro mumbled along with her. She stopped before the final word of each line so that Pedro could triumphantly call out all the rhyming words he knew perfectly.

Matthew, Mark, Luke and . . . JOHN!
The bed be blest that I lie . . . ON!
Four corners to my . . . BED!
Four angels round my . . . HEAD!
One to watch, and one to . . . PRAY!
And two to bear my soul AWAY!
Together they chorused *AMEN!*

Once he fell asleep, Isabela said her own prayer. No matter how much she asked of Mary—"Please help me to be the best mother I can be. Please keep my child healthy. Please protect my boy that he may grow up to be a good and strong man," she always arrived at the end of her prayer with strong feelings of gratitude. "For the friendship of the tailor's family. For the new book I can't wait to devour. For the fascinating game of chess I plan to learn. For Nelleke's recent letter which I will reread a dozen times. I thank you oh, Mother of our Lord. Amen."

To this litany of thank-you's, she felt like adding "and thank you, Mary too, that my husband rarely visits and does not pester me about my wifely duty." She might think those words and feel them profoundly, but saying them out loud in a prayer would seem somehow shameful. "Amen," she repeated.

She was sitting at her desk responding to the letters when she heard the Captain and Diego engaged in one of their arguments. So he had returned. The two fought nearly every time Diego was in the house. She assumed their conflicts centered on the business, money, or Diego's waywardness. She didn't think the disagreements had anything to do with her. She had always ignored their raised voices. They were shouting now. When she thought she heard the Captain say her name, though, she stepped to the door of her room and opened it a tiny bit.

"We need more grandchildren to carry on our name. Do you understand what I'm saying? I am talking about legitimate children— not those bastards you sire with that whore of yours."

She heard a chair scrape and fall, her mother-in-law's cry, "Diego, NO!" and then again the enraged voice of her father-in-law.

"You would strike your own father? You are not worthy to carry my name. I am putting my hope and faith in my grandsons. THEY will restore honor on our family."

Isabela gasped, trying to understand the repercussions of this conversation. That Diego had another family now made sense. He must be with them when he's not sailing. She felt relief actually. Or did he have children with several women? Some of those children playing in the dirt in the town center—where they his? And those women by the well who gathered to gossip—were some of them his mistresses? Did everyone in the village know all the sordid details? Everyone except her?

She had no time to ponder further. Diego burst into her room and motioned for her to lie down on her bed. Since their wedding night, he had left her alone and she was not prepared in any way for this moment. The vinegar, ointment, and orange essence Cook had given her were hidden away. She registered his impatience and dared not delay. She also sensed that she would bear the brunt of the anger he felt toward his father.

"Not in here near the child," she hissed, trying not to cry.

She gathered her wits and brushed past him. He followed close behind to the small room beside hers where he rarely spent the night. For the next two weeks husband and wife met five times in the ugly, bare room. As long as Diego's ship was visible from her window, while anticipating but dreading his visits, she followed Cook's instructions. After each encounter she returned immediately to her room and washed herself in the fragrant water waiting in the porcelain green-and-blue pitcher she had salvaged. The calm, reassuring intimacy of the pastoral scene mocked her situation. Surrounded by sheep grazing on a gentle slope, a beautiful young woman sits by a rock close to her beloved. He has one arm around her shoulders. With the opposite hand he brings her delicate fingers to his lips, all the while gazing at her adoringly. They will remain in that idyllic position for as long as the pitcher remains whole.

Usually Diego rose immediately after their encounters and left the house, slamming the front door behind him. Once, though, he fell asleep. With all his weight on her, she could barely breathe. His beard, rough and stiff from salty sea winds, felt like needles piercing her throat through the lace at her neck. Her nightdress was still raised. She could not move her arms, but one leg was free. She controlled her impulse to gather all her strength and kick him off. But what if he landed on the floor, hit his head, was injured? She might end up caring the rest of her life for an invalid she hated. Or he might be so furious that he would harm her.

If she remained still and endured the discomfort and humiliation? What if Pedro should awaken and come looking for her? The lamp still burned next to the bed. It was the thought that her little boy might see her in this position that gave her the courage to rouse her snoring husband. The moment he raised his head slightly, she shoved him, squeezed out from under him, leapt up and ran back to her own bed. She felt her femininity mocked. Her womanliness tainted. Her soul robbed of strength.

The encounter left her trembling and unable to sleep soundly. When she dozed she saw Kings and Queens on miniature horses, some black, some white. They paraded, faced off, jousted. The conflicts became more threatening. They ran at each other—even the Queens, threatening with weapons. The scene turned into an all-out war. "Strategy," one of the horses kept yelling. "Endgame," one of the Queens shouted out. Then all the pieces, black and white, joined forces. They surrounded the white King. For a moment it looked as if they would capture him. Instead the crowd pushed him off a high cliff and watched as he plunged shrieking onto the sands below.

* * *

Isabela's second child was born the evening of 3 March 1647. As she had written in her first letter to Nelleke after arriving back in her village, she named the little girl Nelita. Captain de Vega lived long enough to hold the infant and delight in her sweetness and beauty. For Isabela the Captain's death was bittersweet. Except for Tía Lucia whose memory was nearly gone, the Captain was her last link to her father. Yet it was he who was responsible for Diego's forcing himself on her. As long as Captain Vicente was alive, Diego used Santos Gemelos as a base for his business dealings, but with her unpredictable, uncaring husband now the head of her family, her future felt tenuous.

Her most fervent wish was that he would simply disappear. In order not to arouse his suspicion, she had spent only a tiny fraction of the cushion money. She could survive here alone. As Doña Juana became frailer, she also became more belligerent and critical. But she had no real power in their home any more. Isabela had Mari to help with the children and household chores, Cook to prepare meals and look after the family's occasional ailments, the tailor's family for the rich friendship she craved.

By the time Nelita was born, she had read and studied the chess instruction book from the first page to the last. Because Bernardo and his father and, increasingly, Briana too, were always in the middle of a game, she did not have the opportunity to play herself, but she watched and tried to figure out what her next play would be if she were the one sitting at the board. About half the time, whoever's turn it was performed exactly the move she had decided on. She doubted she could ever win a game were she given the chance, but concentrating and imagining all the possibilities was a rewarding diversion.

Chapter Fifteen
Sad Encounter

ne day when Isabela was feeling restless, she invented an errand, left Pedro and Nelita in Mari's care, and descended to the village. She avoided the plaza with its gossiping women where she did not feel comfortable and headed to the outskirts of town to an area she had never explored. The modest wooden structures became farther apart and isolated from one another. She feared she might get lost, but also felt some exhilaration at discovering this area she didn't know existed.

One cottage caught her attention because of the profusion of flowers leading up the long path toward it. A strange sound emanating from the cottage made her stop and listen. Concerned, she moved toward the cottage. At first she thought it was an injured animal or a hog being butchered. Once, for a holiday celebration, Cook was too busy to go to the village to purchase pork. One of her many grateful visitors had given her a small pig. When she killed it, the animal's cries reached the main house—a long, angry, defiant scream, a furious protest that its life was ending, but also outrage at the brutal, slow manner of its end—hung upside down, its belly sliced, its blood drained, the drips caught in a barrel at its dangling feet.

But this was not the sound of butchering. It was the sound of miserable, disbelieving loss. Human loss. It was uncontrolled mourning. Thinking that perhaps she could offer solace, Isabela approached the modest cottage and knocked softly. The wailing continued. She heard hammering coming from behind the cottage, but her concern was focused on inside the door—someone in extreme distress.

After Isabela rapped on the door a number of times, a girl of perhaps seven opened the door a crack and peeked out. Startled, the girl curtsied and opened the door wider so that Isabela could enter. Anticipating that her eyes would need to adjust to darkness, dampness, and cramped surroundings, Isabela automatically squinted as she took a step into the room. Instead she found a surprising amount of light, whitewashed walls, lit lanterns, burning candles. This family was not as poor as the front of their dwelling would indicate. It had a narrow front typical of the region, but it was deep. There might be a second room.

On one side of the large room a fire glowed. On the other side a woman sat facing a window and the trees beyond. Isabela approached the weeping woman. When the woman glanced at Isabela, for a moment she appeared frozen with shock. Then, with trembling lips, she began to sob again. Tears fell down her cheeks, rolled over her chin, dripped onto a bosom soaked with breast milk and landed on an infant—gray and unmoving. Without a word, Isabela put her arms around the woman. The little girl who had opened the door did the same. The little group of four remained that way for some time. Two mothers, a little girl who Isabela observed was clean and tidy and whose large dark frightened eyes moved from the dead baby to her mother to Isabela and back again.

The hammering stopped. A girl of perhaps twelve and a boy of about fourteen entered from the back with a small box and gently placed it beside the weeping woman. With his hammer, the boy gave the box a quiet final whack which made the mother jump. The mother turned, hung her head and kissed the infant's cold forehead. She allowed her oldest daughter to take the bundle from her and place it in the blanket-lined box.

The oldest daughter answered another knock on the door and stood aside for the town's new priest. Young, stern, and brusque, he nodded to the family and motioned for them to follow him outside. Isabela accompanied the family to an area beside the cottage where a small rectangular hole, freshly dug, awaited the tiny casket. As the son lowered the box, all bowed their heads and joined hands. The priest gave a clipped benediction.

After the son finished shoveling and patting dirt on the burial site, the oldest daughter invited the priest to join them for the midday meal. It was the first time any member of the family had spoken. The girl's gracious manner and voice and her ability to take charge under such trying circumstances impressed Isabela. The priest nodded dismissively to indicate that he did not accept the invitation. Before his departure, he turned to the mother, who had stopped weeping but stood staring at the pile of fresh dirt at her feet.

"Doña Leonor," he said, "you are a loving and devoted mother. We do not always understand why God takes from us what is most precious. But I must warn you. You are aware that the Church does not look kindly on bastard children. I cannot guarantee that my benediction assures your son a place in Heaven. I encourage you to avoid bringing more children into this world only to suffer in the next."

Before he took his leave, he turned his attention to Isabela. Although he had never met her, he, like everyone else in the town including this family, knew her on sight. Addressing her with a stern look, he said,

"Señora Calderón, I have yet to see you at Sunday Mass. Neither have I heard you confess."

Shaken by his scolding tone, especially under these sad circumstances, Isabela said nothing more than a contrite,

"Yes, Father."

With her arms now empty, Leonor composed herself somewhat and turned toward her three living children. She seemed to fully grasp for the first time that Isabela was there. With the same gracious manner as her daughter and even with a small smile, she said,

"Thank you for coming to comfort us during our sorrow. I so wanted this boy to grow into a man who would take care of us. Within a few years my oldest son may leave to sail with his father. So many young men never return, you know."

Taking Isabela's hands in hers, Leonor added,

"We would be most pleased if you joined us for the midday meal, Doña Isabela."

Isabela had just met this family and did not want to impose on them, yet she was very pleased to be invited. During the years of her friendship with the Valverde family, discussing shared readings, learning chess, and exchanging gifts, and although she had helped with sewing projects from time to time, they had never once asked her to share a meal with them. When Leonor placed her arm through Isabela's and led her to the back of the cottage, Isabela had a chance to observe the grieving mother up close.

'She's probably at least ten years older than I am and she must have been quite beautiful at one time,' she thought. Isabela found herself slowing down to match Leonor's steps. 'She has a dream-like quality. A genteel reserve; sweet, but cautious.'

Although Isabela was concentrating on Leonor, she did take note of the many flowers. Like those she had noticed approaching the house, these too were arranged in neat rows. They bordered paths to a well-ordered orchard and a vegetable garden. They lined this very path that led to the back door of the cottage. The blooms were so profuse and bright, Isabela bent to sniff them. What struck her most, however, was the back wall of the cottage—whitewashed like the front room and painted with giant sunflowers that nearly touched the roof.

When Leonor noticed Isabela admiring the unusual outdoor wall, she said,

"Whitewashing one's home is said to prevent the spread of disease, you know."

As they stepped into the large kitchen, Leonor washed her hands and put on a fresh apron. Tucking the ends of a clean shawl into her waist, she proudly made the formal introductions. Even in their plain frocks, aprons, and bonnets, the girls carried themselves with the grace of their mother. Each smiled and curtsied before returning to her duties.

Twelve-year-old Catalina arranged five wooden plates on the long table, then five goblets, two pitchers and, of course, a vase of flowers. In the table's center, arranged around a large wooden bowl with floating blossoms, four small wooden bowls held dates, olives, pistachios, and sliced apples. To the soup brewing in the pot above the fire, seven-year-old Marianna added the mushrooms and parsley she had been chopping.

Leonor's son placed an armful of logs next to the fireplace. When Leonor introduced him, Angel smiled, nodded, and said,

"Doña Isabela, thank you for coming today."

The young man disappeared into the front room and returned with an extra chair. When he placed the chair at the table, he smiled and nodded again to indicate that this was her place. She had never before felt so comfortable and welcomed in anyone else's home.

Marianna passed the bread to Isabela who tore off a piece and passed the loaf to Leonor. No one spoke until each person had a large chunk. After Angel said the blessing, the girls rose in unison. Marianna carried each bowl to the soup pot. Catalina filled the bowl and Marianna carried the bowl back. First she served Isabela, then Angel, then Leonor. She placed a bowl at her sister's place and then her own. The formality of the meal, the way each child quietly went about her/his duties, the lack of bickering, seemed amazing to Isabela. Were they always like this, she wondered, or were they on their best behavior because of her presence?

When everyone was served, the children waited until Isabela had taken the first sip and commented how delicious she found the soup. Angel stood to fill the goblets with warm spicy mulled wine. For the first time she noticed that he leaned ever so slightly to his left side.

When he sat directly across from her, she glanced at him, trying not to stare. Leonor's son had the strength of a peasant and the skills of a craftsman. Isabela could see that this youth was the man of the house, the one who chopped wood, did repairs, carried heavy buckets of water, and probably also consoled an often despondent mother.

During the years of her close friendship with this family, Isabela would learn that when he was young, Angel was desperate for his father's attention and approval. As he matured he found little in that father to admire or emulate. He saw him as a disruptive presence to be endured, a usurper, an irritant, but, fortunately, a temporary one. It was his mother and sisters who had more influence over Angel's nature. Unusual for a young man his age, Angel had the intuitive sensibilities of a woman.

So that first day, like his mother and like Isabela herself, he felt the nervousness among them. He saw the cautious smiles, the small attempts at friendship followed by awkward withdrawal. Isabela sometimes accompanied Cook on healing missions and was known among the villagers for her acts of kindness. Bringing flowers to a sick person. Comforting the bereaved. Distributing Cook's delicacies to the poorest among them. In that sense, it was natural that she arrived to comfort his mother when she did.

Yet he knew what his family was thinking. 'Does Doña Isabela know who we are? Could she possibly be the only person in this village who has never known we existed? Why is she here really?'

Isabela too had many questions about this family—their relative wealth compared to most villagers, the painted sunflowers, the absent father, their origins, and now this resemblance to the de Vega men, but she let Leonor take the lead.

"Tell us about YOUR children, Doña Isabela. You have two, don't you? I hope you'll bring them to meet us."

The two women chatted companionably while Leonor's children listened, cleared the soup bowls, refilled the wine glasses, placed another log on the fire, and brought wooden plates with small knives for cutting fruit. Neither woman referred to her husband and Isabela saw no sign that a man lived there. Leonor apologized for the wooden plates.

"I preferred the pewter ones I once had, but they are gone now."

The children looked away.

When Isabela stood to take her leave, Leonor rose and accompanied her. As they passed through the front room, Isabela glanced toward the window where she had first seen Leonor weeping. The chair where Leonor held her infant was covered with a large cloth, but a section of the chair's cover was visible from the back. The fabric resembled the matching chair and divan Diego had removed from her home and supposedly sold in Madrid—the red damask set her father had ordered from France.

Marianna came running up to Isabela and curtsied her good-bye.

"Will you visit again soon . . . please, Doña Isabela?"

She reminded Isabela of the little girl orphans she so adored and missed.

"Of course, Marianna, if your mother wishes."

Before Leonor opened the front door and took a few steps with Isabela down the path to the main road, Isabela took another moment to look around the room.

"You have some lovely things," she said as her eyes landed briefly on a familiar-looking cushion.

"I wish I could return the favor and invite your family to dine at the de Vega home, but my mother-in-law is elderly. She finds it difficult to adjust to visitors."

Leonor closed her eyes as if to shut out unpleasant memories or thoughts.

"I am familiar with her character," Leonor said.

"You and I can visit here any time. Please bring your children soon. We have much to talk about."

How could Isabela refuse such a generous offer? She felt an immediate kinship with this woman.

"It would be a great pleasure to introduce you to my children," she said.

Isabela noticed tears in Leonor's eyes as she turned to walk back to her cottage. Isabela had been a distraction. Now Leonor had to face the fact that she would never again hold the baby son whom she had named Rafael.

* * *

Angel caught up with Isabela just as she turned from the lane and entered the main path.

"May I accompany you for a short while, Doña Isabela?" he asked.

"Of course," she answered.

When they had taken several steps in silence, Isabela initiated the conversation by repeating the names of the family members.

"Leonor. Catalina. Marianna."

'She may know the names of others in the village,' Angel thought, 'but she apparently just learned ours.'

"And you, Angel," she said smiling in her affectionate, appreciative, but cautiously curious way. "A memorable name."

Angel liked the way she said those words. "A memorable name." She did not say "Where did you get a name like that?" Or "Why did your parents choose that name?" She pronounced the words more like an invitation. It was if she were saying, "I'd like to know how that name was chosen, but you may decide whether to share that information with me or not."

"Yes," he explained. "Fourteen years ago just before I was born, my father gave my mother a small painting of an angel. My mother loves color and form. She notices the way the sun makes different patterns as it moves through the sky. It was her idea to whitewash the interior walls. Light lifts her spirits. She loved that painting. That's why she chose my name. By custom, she should give me a Biblical name, of course, or the name of a saint. She knew, though, that my birth might alienate her from the church, that I might not be baptized. She gave me a name she loved instead."

Isabela was startled when Angel said, "Later my father sold that painting."

"I'm so sorry," she said. The family had resources. She wondered what kind of man would do such a thing. She told Angel about a favorite painting given her by her father, the one that went down with her father's ship, about how later she met the man who painted it. Rembrandt. She realized then that it had been a self portrait.

"She is brave your mother." Isabela said with a genuineness that Angel could see was real. "What is the family name may I ask?"

'She really does not know.' he thought.

"My mother's family name is Zindicado." Angel hesitated. "My sisters and I use our father's family name."

Isabela could see he was struggling. Was there something he was ashamed of? Embarrassed by? Or was there some other reason he was hesitant to give his last name.

"de Vega," Angel said quickly.

As if to divert her from that reality, he laughed lightly and said, "When I was a child they called me Angie."

Isabela nodded. She would puzzle this out later. Diego had no brothers. How were her children related to this family then? For now she had to return home.

Isabela took a few steps and then turned around. Angel was standing where she left him.

"Please come back, Doña Isabela," he called. "Visit us often."

Isabela nodded her consent and waved good-bye.

His smile and thoughtfulness had already captured her heart and prevented her from noticing other similarities. Yes, like her father-in-law, husband, and son, this young man's left shoulder was slightly lower than the right. The two Captain de Vegas never smiled like this young man did. Yet she was looking at the same high forehead, those deep-set eyes, the distinctive black eyebrows with subtle red tints.

During the long walk back through the village and up the cliff, Isabela thought about Leonor. Could she herself ever be as independent and strong as her new friend? Yet her thoughts kept returning to that cushion. Yes, she was sure it came from her home. Memories of the cushion became clearer. It was her first attempt at crochet. Tía Anacleta taught her. She was probably six. Tía let her choose the design and pick out the colors—red and blue for the blooms, green for the stem and leaves. Until then they did not trust her with the sharp needles. She felt so grown up when she first picked them up.

She tried very hard, but balancing the large needles and weaving them in and out of the stiff fabric was difficult. In a fit of frustration, she even threw the whole project—needles, thread, fabric—onto the floor. Tía Anacleta was patient. "Leave it alone for a day and return to it when you feel like it." Weeks later Isabela showed her mother her completed handiwork, not quite aware that what was supposed to be a symmetrical

116

arrangement with two identical flowers on each side growing from a single stem in the center had come out lopsided. All four flowers were crushed together on the left. She had finished only half of some of the leaves and they seemed to float on their own, unconnected to the plant.

Her aunts might easily have thrown out the cushion and suggested she start over, but they praised her effort. As her needlework improved, the pillow became a family joke and a favorite. "Pass me that cockeyed cushion," one of them would say and everyone would laugh. So some of her family's belongings had found their way to Leonor's home? Perhaps there was too much for Diego to transport and he sold some items in the village after all?

Chapter Sixteen
Growing Friendships

or the next two years, Isabela led what she regarded as a perfect life for herself and her children—dividing their days between visits with Cook, the Valverde family, and Leonor's brood. By the time she returned to Leonor's home the week after she met her, she was convinced that this gracious woman was the "whore" she heard her father-in-law refer to. Yet if Diego was the father of all of Leonor's children, he apparently was as little involved in their lives as he was in hers.

The five children were delighted with each other's company. They played, argued and sometimes competed for attention like siblings. Leonor had a cupboard full of toys: dolls, wooden horses, tin horns, drums. The older ones pulled the younger ones in a wagon up and down the garden paths. Isabela brought the contents of her childhood dollhouse—the one she had found on its side the day Diego emptied her home of nearly all its contents. The girls spent hours arranging and re-arranging the miniature chairs, tables, beds, pots, platters, griddles, dishes, cups, and goblets.

After the spring rains when the soil began to dry, the women spread cloths throughout the garden and gave each girl a weeding tool and a basket. The child who pulled the most weeds, got a cinnamon stick, but they all got a sugared anise seed for every weed in the basket. They also learned to count into the hundreds. Together the mothers invented other activities that combined learning with practicality and reward. With their children they rolled letters from dough and made them into spiced cookies. Whoever arranged the most correctly spelled doughy words got to eat the most cookies once they were baked.

Under his careful supervision and with Isabela's permission, Angel taught Pedro to chop wood. Pedro had his own small hatchet and woodpile. Pedro nagged Angel to engage in the mock swordfights the two boys sometimes staged, but Angel took his role as the oldest male seriously. He put Pedro to work mending a fence, plugging a hole in the roof, and scaling fish—an oily task the females disliked. Pedro chopped off fish heads with gusto. His favorite activity was hunting with the older boy, not because they brought home game for an evening meal, but because Pedro got to load and fire Angel's musket. Initially it was so heavy, Angel held the weapon while Pedro fired it. It was a happy day for Pedro when he grew strong enough to acquire and fire his own musket.

Although she kept a few chickens behind a fence, Leonor did not like farm animals—neither their noise nor their filth. She could never kill one, anyway, so what was the use, she reasoned. Isabela held the ladder for Leonor as she picked oranges, grapefruits, pomegranates, and olives. Leonor taught Isabela how to cut back the trees so that they had space to absorb sunshine and produce more fruit. Occasionally one of the women would shop in the village market with her own child plus the child of the other. Villagers both marveled at and mocked their friendship, but gradually came to think of them as two sisters raising cousins together.

It was during the quiet moments when the two women sat mending or knitting that Isabela gradually learned how Leonor came to live on the outskirts of Santos Gemelos.

"I was born in the city of Málaga. My mother died when I was quite young. I don't remember her. My father made a good living as a skilled craftsman. He made time pieces. It was intricate work for which he apprenticed many years, but personal time pieces to keep in a pocket or on a chain were becoming popular. In his prime, my father's shop employed three men—each skilled in making one part of the complicated device. Only my father knew how to combine the pieces into an attractive and functioning whole.

"When my father lay dying, he arranged for me to marry one of his frequent customers, a man his own age—an older, wealthy man who he thought was a widower and who would provide for me. My father died before the marriage could take place. I learned that the man's wife was very much alive, that he had grown children. He had convinced my father that he would be my husband and I his only heir. Instead, he installed me here in this isolated place as his concubine. I was fifteen years old. He did partially honor the second half of the bargain he made with my father though. He visited for weeks at a time and provided for all my material needs. He hired a housemaid for me and a gardener. After he noticed my interest in art, he even sent an artist who taught me how to paint. They all became my friends and my tutors. Their skills became mine. My father had left me all his worldly goods. Fortunately, my master, who had misled my father about marrying me, WAS honorable about money. He taught me how to manage a household. When he died ten years later, I was frightened and sad. I had no children, but I did have resources. I could continue to live well. I knew how to survive.

"One night when I was feeling especially lonely, my housemaid suggested we go into town to celebrate the feast day of St. Stephen. I reveled in the music and the crowds. I gorged on all the delicious food. I danced and I danced. I also drank a lot of wine. A young man followed me back to my cottage. That night was the beginning of a long, but uncertain relationship which produced my three children. The young man was eight years my junior—an only son who hated his strict, critical parents. They forced him to accompany his Captain father on long trips and to learn every aspect of sailing, which made him ill. He found intolerable the desolate and dangerous sailing life they forced upon him and the way they controlled him, not only deciding his profession, but betrothing him to an infant when he was a mere child."

Leonor stopped and looked at Isabela apologetically. "I'm sorry," she said. Isabela shook her head no and urged Leonor to continue.

"On those long trips at sea during the short stops on land, my man sought company in the taverns. He discovered a talent for cards. He became a gambler. He remains a gambler. After one of his visits I noticed that a set of knives I inherited from my father was missing. We fought after that. Later all my pewter disappeared. I asked him not to return. A few months later, I relented. When his father injured himself, he was forced to take over the business. He comes and goes, but he's never stolen from me again. He remains the careless, irresponsible youth I met years ago, but he is the father of my children and I allow him to stay when he wishes. He rarely gives us money, although sometimes he lavishes us with gifts. Other times he asks for the gifts back. His erratic behavior is hard on my children, but we've learned to tolerate it. We know not to depend on him. We are self sufficient. In addition to the wealth I inherited from my father and master, I add to our income in various ways. My children help me sell fruits and vegetables . . . and occasionally my paintings at the market."

* * *

Meanwhile, Isabela continued her correspondence with the tailor. It was difficult for her to decipher his real attitude toward her and she hated that his opinion of her mattered so much. When referring to a letter of hers, he wrote, "If Erasmus had lived long enough to read Cervantes, he would have made the same observation."

'He must be exaggerating ridiculously,' she thought, 'or has he taken pity on me? Is he just being kind?'

Gradually she came to accept that he too enjoyed their exchanges, that his praise was genuine. She loved him for believing in her intelligence. Although Isabela longed to continue their written communication with spoken words, she resisted the temptation because she did not want to exclude Reza, especially since she had concerns about Reza's health. Once she tried to engage Reza in one of their debates, but Reza was not interested in participating.

One day when she stopped by to pick up some new trousers for Pedro, Reza and Briana were out on an errand. The tailor said to Bernardo, "Let Doña Isabela take Briana's place at the chess table." Isabela studied the board. It took all her concentration. She shut out all other thoughts. When she read the chess instruction book in her room, she sometimes acted out moves using thimbles. Now she picked up a Rook for the first time. As she held it by its slender neck, it felt so solid and sure. It seemed to guide her. After two more moves, she found herself asking more than announcing, "Checkmate?"

At that moment, Briana came bursting into the shop. When she heard Isabela's questioning tone for a word that is usually spoken with quiet pride and decisiveness, she ducked under the counter to hug Isabela and study the board herself. On his side of the board, Bernardo maintained a noncommittal silence. He was still hoping to salvage the game for himself. In her uncertainty, Isabela had placed the Rook in the winning spot, but had not let it go. She was still clutching it. When she looked toward Briana for guidance, Briana lifted Isabela's hand off the board. They grinned at one another and together yelped their triumph: "Checkmate!"

"Unfair," Bernardo said. "Two against one. I'll get you next time."

Isabela was always trying to think of some way she might be useful to this self-sufficient family. During one visit, she inquired about the dress Reza was making.

"Actually, I'm just making part of it," Reza explained. This is a wedding dress for one of Santos Gemelos' poorest families. They remade an old dress, but asked me to cover it with a fresh new apron and collar. That's all they could afford."

"You've given the apron and collar a special cut, haven't you, Reza? The rounded scallops match. They draw attention away from the shabbiness of the rest of the dress. Do you think the bride might like some color on the new pieces? I learned to embroider when I was working as a Big Sister in the Amsterdam City Orphanage."

When Isabela noticed Reza's hesitancy, she offered,

"If you provide me with a piece of cloth and some thread, I will demonstrate what I'm thinking."

Isabela twirled red thread into small raised tulips and secured them to the cloth with two dainty stitches down their center. Next she made the connected step-like stitches that outlined leaves on either side of the flowers. Reza studied Isabela's designs carefully. In this family, only Briana acted spontaneously. Before accepting Isabela's offer, Reza showed the model to the tailor. He too studied it, placed it alongside the plain collar, and finally approved. Isabela realized that part of their concern was that if she made mistakes, the entire collar which covered the bride's shoulders would have to be redone. Still she felt irritated that they did not leap to take advantage of her offer.

After that, Isabela had an excuse to visit more often.

"Any embroidery work needed?" she would ask playfully.

She was given her own table, needles, and thread. Reza and the tailor worked mostly in silence, but Briana was learning the skill too from her teacher/princess. Nelita was not yet old enough to use needles. Sharing this activity with Briana took Isabela's mind back to her own childhood and also to Amsterdam.

Like everyone in the village, the tailor family knew Isabela had lived in Amsterdam. Only Briana asked her about that experience.

"Doña Isabela, you grew up in the princess house, the castle up there on the bluff. Isn't that right?

"Well, it's really just a house, sweet Briana, but yes, that's where I lived until I was fifteen."

"And then you went far away? On your father's ship?"

"Yes. I ended up spending a year and a half in a big city called Amsterdam. I knew a little girl who was about your age. Her name was Nelleke."

"What was Nelleke like?"

She was a little smaller than you. She had big eyes that were almost black, her hair was yellow and her head was covered with tight little curls. She was a most curious child. She asked questions constantly. 'What number comes after 99? How many stars are in the sky? What's the highest number ever?'

"She didn't like to sit still. She loved to run. Running was considered unladylike, though, and besides, she was just one child among hundreds living in the orphanage. There were a lot of rules."

"Poor Nelleke. I would like to meet her some day. Do you think I ever will?"

"Maybe. Amsterdam is a long way away, Briana."

"Briana, every time you show me a new drawing I can see how much you've advanced. Do you realize that? Look here. A few months ago you drew butterflies with their wings outspread. NOW you're drawing THREE levels of wings with different designs on each plus the slender body between, and the head with antennae. You've painted the whole butterfly in such vibrant colors. Did I ever tell you about the time I met one of the most famous Dutch artists?"

"You don't mean Rembrandt, do you, Doña Isabela?" the tailor called from his workbench without lifting his eyes or turning.

Isabela never stopped being amazed at how well informed the tailor was. How did he know so much about the world when he sat here in this hovel sewing day after day?

"The very same," she answered. "I was with my favorite little orphan—the one I just told you about."

"Nelleke," Briana said. "She was my age when you first knew her and she's ever so lively and curious."

"Yes, exactly, Briana. Well, I just got a letter from her and you'll never guess what."

"What then?"

"Rembrandt asked her to pose for him. She's now in the largest painting he's ever made. The painting is so big, it would cover the whole front of your house and there she is, she wrote, right in the middle all

123

lit up, dressed in a gold dress. Of all things, though, hanging from the waist of the beautiful dress, Rembrandt painted a chicken!"

They all chuckled. Isabela experienced a particular delight that something she had said amused this solemn family.

"A chicken? Dead? Alive? Upside down? Squawking?" asked Briana.

"Yes, a chicken. Dead. Upside down. Definitely NOT squawking."

They all laughed again.

"I want to see Nelleke in that painting some day," Briana sighed. And I STILL want to meet her."

Chapter Seventeen
Mounting Frustration

$\mathfrak{A}$s their correspondence became more frequent and intense, Isabela found herself hoping with each visit that the tailor would accompany her outside when she bid the family good-bye. She experienced acute disappointment when he remained at his work table.

After a long exchange about the mystical writings of Santa Teresa de Avilés, he told her that Santa Teresa was descended from Conversos.

"In other words," Isabela wrote back, "her ancestors were Jews? Given her devotion to God, that seems unlikely."

"Jews are devoted to God," he explained. "They also believe in the coming of the Messiah. They just don't think Jesus was the anticipated Messiah. They believe the Messiah will appear at some future time."

He began including a philosophical question in each of his letters:

"If God is all powerful and all knowing, why does he allow evil to exist?"

"If God created the world in seven days what existed before the creations? Was there another world before the one we know?"

"Can something everlasting be made from nothing?"

"In order for something to be created, must something that already existed be destroyed?"

"If God is love, how could he not welcome a child—even an unbaptized child—into His Heavenly home?"

Isabela became obsessed with his questions. She tried to record her thoughts but, when she read them back, she hated what she had written. She did not want to appear ignorant and stupid in his eyes. She pondered the questions so much she sometimes could not sleep. She could no longer concentrate on the most simple task. When Nelita yanked on her skirt and yelled, "Mama, Mama," she realized the child had been calling her for minutes, but she had been lost in her thoughts.

It was as if he were supplying her with exercises—assignments to challenge her—yet after she thought about his question for days, wrote a response, tore up the page, pondered some more, wrote and sent him something totally different, he never reacted. He just sent another question.

By the time she responded, 'had he forgotten he even posed the question in the first place?' she wondered. When she visited they never spoke of their correspondence. The questions hung above them like silent taunts. As her children grew older, she sometimes brought them with her.

The tailor sat on one side of the shop beneath the commanding crucifix. Isabela sat on the other side studying the chess board, her children playing marbles at her feet.

Outwardly, she was a calm focused young woman adding roses to a gown. Inwardly, she was filled with barely contained longing—to stop writing, writing, writing, and CONVERSE—to have a conversation, many conversations, to sit with the tailor, remove his glasses, look into his eyes, see beyond his eyes into his mind. "What do YOU think?" she wanted to scream at him. "Tell me. Share with me YOUR thoughts."

She began to hope and live for the rare occasions when he rose from his work table and accompanied her out into the street. It was a sign he had something special to share with her. Even in the dusty street with people and animals passing, with Briana hugging her good-bye, with her children pulling her toward the market because she's promised them a cinnamon stick, in that moment she felt cocooned with him. There were just the two of them rapidly exchanging unexpressed thoughts, yet saying out loud only,

"Good-bye." "Come back soon."

* * *

One evening as her children slept and she sat at her usual place reading or writing, she became restless. She rummaged among her letters and half re-read them. She reached into the back of drawers where she rapidly shoved material years ago as Diego emptied her home.

She opened a folder and found herself staring at a document written a month after she was born in 1625. A stamped official seal clung to the document beneath the signatures of the two men who decided her fate. Their careful handwriting agreeing to the betrothal of their daughter and son filled her with anger.

As she read the specific terms of the betrothal, she began to understand not only how this document had shaped her life, but how it affected the three members of the de Vega family. Her father gave Captain Vicente a sizeable sum to celebrate their agreement. The remaining part of the dowry was to be paid out in yearly amounts until the day of their marriage. She now realized that since Captain Vicente's accident when he had to stop working, her future in-laws were depending almost entirely on her father's annual dowry payments.

Given what Leonor told her about Diego's gambling, even THAT money probably did not last long in the de Vega household. She also realized that because of her father's death, the payments stopped years ago. Doña Juana and Captain Vicente had no income at all beyond what Diego chose to give them. He was willing to risk incarceration and quite possibly his life to travel to Amsterdam and marry her for one reason. It was his intention all along to sell her home and every moveable object in it. She now knew that he may well have gambled it all away rather than sold it. Could he have treated his own home with such callousness? Might the de Vegas home have once been full of the unique intriguing objects she had expected to find here?

That night she wondered for the hundredth time what might have happened if her father had not entered into the marriage agreement with Captain Vicente. If her aunts had not shared her letters and her father's business records with the de Vegas, where would she be now? Married to Pieter? Living in his three-level canal house on the Heerengracht? Running her own household? Raising their children? And Pieter? Would he not have become so "restless" as Anneliese describes? Would he have completed his apprenticeship with Rembrandt? Would he have become a famous painter in his own right?

Although she felt like ripping it into bits, Isabela reburied the document deep in her desk drawer. She picked up her quill pen, dipped it in black ink, and composed the first written question she had ever sent the tailor.

She reread her question. They had never written of personal matters, never alluded to human love in any form. The next morning she read it once more, sealed it, and sent it with Mari. How would he react? Would he respond as thoughtfully as she had tried to respond to all his questions? Would he regard the topic as too uninteresting to dedicate time to? Too childish? Too nonacademic? Inappropriate?

The tailor's response arrived two days later. To her surprise and delight, he took her question seriously. He wrote a treatise in fact!

You pose a challenging question: 'Do you believe it's possible to betray someone you love deeply?'

First I would define what appear to be two contrasting verbs. Though 'love' comes in many forms, it conjures up positive words like 'affection, devotion, beloved, attraction.' 'Betray,' on the other hand, is associated with 'cheat, give away, denounce, and deceive.' At first glance they seem like opposites, but human behavior is so complex that I must answer your question in the affirmative.

Although Judas betrayed Jesus, whom Judas supposedly loved, by identifying him to the Romans in exchange for a few gold coins, there are other examples of a more caring nature. I believe one might be justified to deceive the person one loves in order to instruct, protect, or even save the life of one's loved one. As a parent, one is sometimes forced to make decisions that a child experiences as unloving, yet which are designed to improve the child's life in some way. I'm sure you and I can come up with other examples.

Isabela wrote to thank him and immediately sent another question: "Do you think it is possible to live fully in one place when your mind seems to live elsewhere?"

The tailor wrote back that he believed many people live several lives at once over a lifetime—*the one where they are physically present; the often peculiar ones they experience in their dreams while sleeping; and the ones they construct and dwell on when their hands are busy, but their hearts and minds are full of imaginings. Without that part of our mind— our imagination, our dreams—would we have Michelangelo's David? Would we have the wheel? Or would we still be sitting in the dark trying to ward off lions and bears from the opening to our caves?*

She desperately wanted to follow up with more questions. 'What is in YOUR heart and mind, Señor Valverde? What do YOU imagine as an alternative life?'

Fearing that her questions might push their correspondence into such a personal realm that he would retreat altogether, that she might even drive him away, that he might end their communication, she never sent him those questions. Whenever she saw him, the questions seemed to beat in her head, begging to be spoken out loud. Yet she dared not utter them.

If she had no excuse to visit the shop, she forced herself down the bluff alone to Sunday Mass where she knew she would see at least the back of his head, sitting with his family directly in front of the new young priest. This option was frustrating, though, because a visit never followed. It was also unpleasant. This priest approached his congregation not as people who deserve God's love, but as sinners who should live in fear of God's punishment: "You and I," the priest often repeated in a threatening tone, "are aware that we live among sinners, zealots, false Christians."

"Look around you," the priest demanded. "Which of your neighbors demonstrates the characteristics of a witch? Where might reside those with tainted blood—those Conversos who practice their poisonous ways in secret? It is your duty as a pure Christian to report such suspicious behavior to the church. God bless you."

Isabela was not the only parishioner who avoided the priest and his accusations. Some mornings there were more people lined up outside Cook's cottage than there were on the hard church pews. The Valverde family remained among the priest's most consistent followers.

One Sunday, to her delight and astonishment, the Valverde family sat not in their usual front row, but in the back of the church. They must have arrived late just as she had. She greeted them and joined them for the service. Afterwards, after one of those quick, silent visual exchanges she sometimes noticed between Reza and the tailor, Reza led Bernardo and a protesting Briana toward their home.

The tailor stayed behind, took Isabela's arm, and led her a few paces away from the church beyond the plaza. He stood so close to her that she was sure he could hear her heart pounding, that he would notice the effort she was making to hold her knees steady. The encounter was quick, however. He took her hand and folded in her palm a tiny package. "Do not open this until you are alone," he said in a hushed tone. "The note will explain." He left abruptly, leaving her standing there bewildered.

* * *

Isabela spent the rest of that day playing with her children. A trip down the mossy stairs to the beach. Blowing bubbles through a pipe out to sea. Watching the bubbles burst in the surf. Digging holes in the sand. They removed their shoes, held hands and walked through the water parallel to the shore, kicking the water ahead of them. The package in her apron pocket was so light, she could not even feel it, but her curiosity was barely containable.

Finally, Pedro and Nelita were bathed, dressed, and sleeping. Because Sundays were a particularly demanding day for Cook, Isabela had asked Mari to reheat some of the week's previous meals, thus freeing Cook to give attention to the crowds seeking her healing balms.

As dusk settled in, Isabela slipped over to Cook's cottage for some warm honey water for Doña Juana. Lingerers moped about hoping for a moment with Cook even at the late hour. Isabela entered the cottage. 'How can a woman look utterly exhausted and yet still have more to give?' she asked herself. As Cook always did before sending one of her "visitors" on their way, she held the hand of a young, tearful woman in hers.

"You don't need me to heal," she was saying. "You can heal yourself. You can be your own miracle worker."

Cook urged the woman toward the door.

To those outside, she said, "I apologize. I realize that some of you have come a fair distance and that you have been waiting for some time. I am a cook. That is how I earn my living. I must give my attention to my duties. Please come back tomorrow if you can. But I want to share something with you. Each of you can be your own healer. God has given us a healing resource that is free, that is everywhere, that surrounds us. That healing resource is . . . AIR."

As Cook pulled herself up straight and breathed deeply, the air seemed visible passing through her belly, her lower lungs, and her upper lungs. With an audible sigh, she exhaled. She demonstrated again.

"Air. Allow it to circulate throughout your body. Allow it to linger over troubled areas. Exhale all the stale air. Breathe in again. Do this several times a day. Imagine the pain, the sorrow, whatever ails you disappearing, carried away with each exhale."

Although impatient to claim the warm milk, return to her room, and explore the tailor's package, Isabela joined the gathering. She followed Cook's instructions.

"Inhale slowly. Fill your belly. Your lungs. Your chest. Exhale."

"Inhale once more. Feel the fresh, clean air enter your veins. Allow the air to caress your heart. Hold the air in your heart. Exhale all distress."

* * *

After delivering Doña Juana's evening drink and helping her into bed, at last Isabela had a few hours to herself. Instead of going to her desk as she usually did to read or write, she reached into the pocket of her apron. The package the tailor had given her in such a hurried and mysterious manner was flat and barely covered her palm. Sensing there was something precious inside, she slowly removed the twine and folded back the layers of thin brown paper.

There was something else, something tiny wrapped in a strip of cloth. Before examining it, she read the tailor's hurriedly scribbled note,

Doña Isabela. Do not protest or return this gift. Doña Reza and I agree that you should carry this with you wherever you go. One never knows in this life when it will become necessary to start over. Sew this into your petticoat. Destroy this letter. In fact, you would be wise to destroy all my letters. May God bless you, Isabela.

She unwrapped the tiny package to reveal a stone. 'No, it must be a jewel,' she thought. Studying it under the lamp, she saw that it was only about the size of the tip of Nelita's smallest finger. Roughly hexagonal in shape, smooth and clear, it refracted the light, sending her twinkling messages whose meaning she could not decipher. She grabbed one of the books the tailor had loaned her, the kind of book she hadn't even known existed—a dictionary it was called. She searched through the "D's" until she found the word "diamond."

"The stone's name is derived from the Greek word *adamas*," she read, "which translates to 'unconquerable.' This symbolic meaning lends itself well to the diamond's historic commemoration of eternal love."

"Unconquerable!" Is that what she would feel with the diamond—and she was sure now that's what this stone was—hidden on her person? But what about the association with "eternal love?" "There are many kinds of love" the tailor had written in a previous exchange. If this jewel had anything to do with love, it was not of the romantic sort. Much as she had to admit to herself that she sometimes craved a declaration of love from him, she knew he had already made such a pledge. Besides, he made it very clear that the gift was from both him and his wife.

Isabela read, reread, and memorized the tailor's note. "One never knows in this life when it will become necessary to start over." Start over? Begin a new life? She had thought that she would live out her days in this house, in this village. After Doña Juana dies, she would be the mistress. She has thought often of the changes she'll make, how she'll whitewash the inside to brighten it like Leonor's. She'll ask a carpenter to build a new sturdy table, comfortable chairs. She's never counted the cushion money, but maybe there's enough to purchase another harpsichord. These were dreams. She had not yet fully solved the puzzle of how to explain such purchases to Diego, of how to prevent his taking them away.

When she arrived here from Amsterdam, she had virtually no family left. But since then she had built a life for herself here. She had her children. Leonor was like a sister, her children nearly as dear to Isabela as her own. She had Cook. She had the Valverde family. Why would she ever leave here? Where would she go?

Once she was sure she would always remember every word of the note, she followed the tailor's instructions. She secured the diamond into the hem of her petticoat. She threw the note into the fire and watched it burn. "You would be wise to destroy ALL my letters," the note said.

'That I cannot do,' she thought. 'Every word the tailor has written is precious to me.'

Chapter Eighteen
Domesticity Interrupted

Each morning Isabela's children looked forward to their morning rituals. The days began when Cook awakened them with a light knock on the door of the bedroom they shared with their mother. Some mornings they pretended to still be sleeping.

As Cook moved quietly through the room and placed the tray with cheese, oranges, and warm bread on the table by the window, Nelita and Pedro slipped out of bed, tiptoed behind her and grabbed her around the waist from behind. Cook, pretending to be surprised, turned around and asked,

"Well where did you come from, you little rabbits?"

Other times the children hid under their quilt. Cook snuck up to their bed, reached under the quilt and tickled them until the room filled with their delighted giggles. Usually, though, as soon as they heard her footsteps in the hall, the children leaped out of their beds and ran to open the door and greet Cook. Whatever playful scene they acted out always involved lots of kisses and embraces. Cook had known these children since the moment they were born. They were like the grandchildren she would never have.

Isabela sat up in bed enjoying the sight. Cook might point out a chipmunk just beyond the window or a spider crawling up the wall.

"Where did it go?" Nelita might ask.

"It ran away from YOU, Nelita. YOU scared it," Pedro would tease.

"I did NOT scare it, Pedro."

"You know what I think?" Cook would say to stop the bickering. "I think it has a secret hiding place. Its very own crevice. It's up there right now eating its breakfast. And YOU, my darling children, are going to eat YOURS. Sit here."

When they were very small, Cook held the children on her lap and fed them. Once they were old enough to feed themselves, she sat with them, told them a story, asked about their studies. When Isabela wanted some morning time alone with Cook, she summoned Mari to take the children to the warming kitchen for their breakfast. Although the children complained, Isabela was firm.

During her two pregnancies, Cook brought her remedies for nausea, bloating, and swollen ankles. For years now early mornings were the only time she could be alone with Cook and she shared everything with her—meeting Leonor, visiting with the Valverde family, letters from Nelleke, the fears about her unsettling marriage. Since Cook had told Isabela about Gérard, she shared little of her own thoughts. Isabela knew only that Cook filled her days with gardening, food preservation, and, of course, the nearly constant demands of her "visitors."

The morning after Isabela saw Cook dismiss some late visitors and show them how to take healing breaths, Cook went through the usual playful times with the children, but seemed to hold them unusually tight, even to the point where they squirmed to be released. Cook sent the children off to join Mari and closed the door behind them.

Isabela was still sitting up in bed when Cook came to sit next to her. She reached into her blouse and slipped over her head the chain that held the unique and exquisite double cross Gérard had given her. She pressed the cross to her lips and said,

"I'm giving this to you, Isabela. I want you to wear it now. It has protected me all these years. Just as Gérard gave it to me, I want to give it to someone I care for. You have many more years to live. I would ask that you carry on the tradition. When you no longer feel you need the protection the cross provides, give it to someone who may need it more than you do."

Before Isabela could protest, Cook slipped the chain over Isabela's head, turned, walked away, and closed the door behind her. Isabela pulled a skirt over her nightdress and ran after her. She caught up with Cook just as she was going out the back door of the house to return to her cottage.

"Cook, Cook, wait," she called. "Please. The cross belongs to YOU. I don't need it. I don't need protection. I am fine."

Cook did not turn around. She kept walking away. Isabela ran and caught up with her just as they both arrived at Cook's cottage door.

When Isabela noticed there were no people waiting to see Cook, she felt a sense of panic. Something had changed. Something was wrong. She approached Cook, took hold of Cook's shoulders and turned her around so they were facing each other. Cook's face was streaked with tears. Cook—the strongest, most assured, wise, and loving woman Isabela had ever known—fell into Isabela's arms.

Her sobs seemed eternal. Isabela stood holding Cook tight, saying nothing, but feeling bewildered and afraid. What had happened? What could she do to console this woman who for decades had comforted so many others?

Finally Cook raised her head. Isabela noticed the wrinkles around Cook's reddened eyes. She had always thought of Cook as vibrant and youthful. Now it occurred to her that Cook might not be much younger than Doña Juana. Cook took Isabela's hands and held them in her own still smooth, white, unblemished hands. That same warm touch that had comforted Isabela so many times calmed her even now. Isabela could not imagine the source of Cook's distress, but as she stood there hand in hand with Cook, high on the bluff with a gentle wind rustling their tight white caps, a rabbit hopped by, a bird landed on a limb above. She felt the new sensation of the weight of the double cross on her chest and she felt certain they would both be all right.

As Cook turned to enter her cottage, she indicated that Isabela was not to follow. Her parting words were,

"When they question you, just tell them the truth."

Chapter Nineteen
Interrogation

That very night they came for her. Isabela learned later that they always came at night. Mari was sitting on a rock behind her warming kitchen in the dark with a suitor. In the distance, they noticed four torches moving up the path from the village. Occasionally they disappeared, only to come into view again—closer, larger, burning brighter, more threatening.

Frightened, the young woman slid down behind the rock in the arms of her friend, Miguel. Every minute or so, Miguel peeped up from their hiding place and described the scene. The torches were held by four soldiers who followed behind the village priest. They kicked in Cook's door. Only moments later they dragged Cook out, surrounded her and pushed her ahead of them. One of them held a bulging satchel. Miguel watched the torches disappear back down the path. If any words were spoken, they couldn't hear them from where they sat.

The couple waited uncertainly in the dark, unsure what to do. Mari urged Miguel to follow at a safe distance behind the soldiers and learn what he could. An hour later he returned to report that the soldiers had taken Cook to the town prison. Mari decided not to wake Doña Juana or Doña Isabela.

The next morning the knock on Isabela's door was different than usual. Louder, more insistent. Cook did not sweep into the room in a playing mood with a breakfast tray of fresh-smelling bread and smooth butter. Fearing the knock might be Diego's, Isabela got out of bed, wrapped herself in her bed quilt and with the children peeking out behind her, opened the door to find Mari with a few slices of day-old bread. Mari broke down in tears and told Isabela everything Miguel had seen. The children began to whimper. They clung to Isabela.

Isabela dressed herself and the children and walked with Mari to Cook's cottage. In addition to their fears about Cook's disappearance, they were all hungry and Doña Juana needed to begin her day with a substantial breakfast to ward off her various ailments.

The door to the cottage swung back and forth, creaking on its hinges. The combination of a warm fireplace and Cook's smiling greeting always made this one-room cottage seem so welcoming. Now the fire had burned down. The embers were cold. The first thing Isabela noted was that Cook's many, varied pairs of gloves no longer hung on the line in their usual place. An open bottle of the lanolin she so prized sat on a shelf above her mussed bed. Whole shelves of herbs were empty. Some of the vials lay broken on the stone floor, their dried contents spilling out, their curative powers destroyed.

Finding no bread, Mari and Isabela picked some fruit and cut cheese for their breakfast. Isabela asked Mari to walk into town to the market to buy something for their mid-day and evening meals, but Mari politely refused.

"After what I saw last night, Doña Isabela, I'm too frightened to go into the village alone."

If Isabela had to accompany Mari, they would need to take Pedro and Nelita with them. Doña Juana could barely take care of herself let alone two lively grandchildren. The outing would require most of the day, would exhaust them all, and they could carry enough for only a few days, but Isabela felt she had no choice. They had to eat. They could not subsist on only carrots, beets, and parsley from the garden. They must supplement the vegetables with meat and eggs.

As they neared the back of the main house, they saw a young man approaching the front door. When they reached the large room, they discovered a note slipped under the door.

Addressed to both Señora Isabela Calderón and Señora Juana de Vega, the brief note read: "You are instructed to report at once to the prison of Santos Gemelos." It was signed by the local police warden. Doña Juana was far too weak to undertake such a jaunt. Isabela would have to go to the prison herself while Mari shopped with the children in tow.

Finally, loaded with baskets, taking turns carrying Nelita who would simply sit down in the path and not move when she was bored or tired, the foursome arrived at the town plaza. Shaken and frightened, Isabela left Mari with the children and reported to the prison.

"Follow me," the guard said after she gave her name and showed him the note.

The guard led Isabela to a bare room with one candle and one chair. For the next two hours a representative of the Church grilled her with questions and took notes while two soldiers stood by sneering. A green cross reached across the chest of the interrogator and down the length of his white robe, from just under his chin to the hem of the garment. A pointed hood made him seem far taller than he actually was. Towering over the seated Isabela, the cowardly man hid his face with a full face mask. Only his threatening eyes were visible.

"How long have you known Señora Zalamea?"

"I first met her on the eve of my marriage when she, . . ."

"Just answer the question. How long have you known Señora Zalamea?"

Isabela had to think. How long had it been since that evening when Cook, in her caring way, came to warn her about what was about to happen?

"About six years I would say."

"Describe the nature of your relationship."

"Señora Zalamea is the family cook. She brings us our breakfast, our . . ."

"Answer only the question you are asked. We've been told she claims to have visited Heaven and returned. What do you know about that?"

"Cook is an entertaining storyteller. When she talks of having visited Heaven once in the company of a Compostela pilgrim, I believe she is speaking metaphorically."

The interrogator stopped. Isabela felt throughout her body and soul the stare coming through the eyeholes of the intimidating mask.

"Make an effort to speak clearly and precisely," he finally ordered, as he continued to write in his notebook.

"It is well known in the community that she also claims to be a healer. Have you witnessed such so-called healings?"

"I have never heard her refer to herself as a healer."

"Many seem to feel she has special powers—powers that do not fall within the range of most humans. What do you have to say about that?"

"I believe her power—as you call it—is entirely human—of the most human sort in fact. Her strength comes from a heightened sense of love and caring."

"Strength, you say. Define what you mean by that word."

"I mean strength in the sense of giving and listening to many distressed people—sometimes a dozen in one day."

"Yes, we are aware of how many people she has duped. How much does she charge for such . . . SERVICES," the inquisitor snarled.

"Nothing. She charges nothing. She simply gives her time and attention."

"Is a basket of oranges NOTHING? Is a small pig NOTHING? Perhaps she does not CHARGE, but she does BARTER. She is paid. If you continue to give misleading and dishonest answers, I must warn you that as a close associate of the accused, you too may become suspect."

Isabela sighed. She felt herself weaken with the fear of a cornered animal. She tried to hold herself rigid so that her trembling was not visible.

"May I have some water, please?" she asked, suddenly aware that her mouth was so dry she felt she might choke.

"You can drink plenty once the questioning is over, Señora Calderón. Are you aware that women are not permitted to practice medicine, that practicing medicine without professional training, without a license from the medical board is against the law?"

"Yes, I understand that more or less."

"You understand it more or less, do you? What does that mean? Do you understand or do you not?"

"Yes, I understand."

"You understand what?"

Isabela could not remember what she last said. She did not remember the last question. She only knew she was getting desperate to return to her children, to Mari, to trudge up the bluff. For the first time the de Vega house felt to her like home, like a haven.

"You understand WHAT?" repeated the interrogator.

'I understand that you are a despicable person,' Isabela wanted to say, 'that it is YOU and not my dear COOK who deserves to be sitting in a cell somewhere nearby.'

Instead she answered with a meekness that disgusted her, "I understand that practicing medicine without a license is illegal."

"Your cook dispensed medicine, though, did she not?"

139

"She never referred to it as medicine. She used common herbs or a plant found in the field."

"Precisely. What she was doing was practicing WITCHCRAFT, Doña Isabela. You deny that fact at your peril. And . . . the next time you are called for questioning, bring Juana de Vega with you as the note instructed. You are dismissed."

Isabela saw that it would be useless to point out that Doña Juana could barely put one foot in front of the other and would collapse on the bluff long before she reached the village. Without much hope, though, she did ask,

"May I visit Cook?"

"So that she can perform some witch spell on you right from her cell? Certainly not."

The interrogator left the tiny room. Isabela stood and walked out, one guard in front of her, one behind. She walked slowly through the small prison, straining to hear any sound of Cook. She was sure Cook was close enough to hear if Isabela called out to her, but the interrogator's threats had so frightened her, she remained silent. Once free of the horrible cold stone walls, she made her way to the plaza, trying not to run which would draw attention. She wanted only to hold her children close.

On a normal day, if she did not find Mari and her children immediately, she would wander among the stalls until she located them, enjoy the smells, stop to admire the crafts, make a purchase and converse with the seller, smile when a parrot authoritatively squawked some common phrase. Now, not seeing Mari, she felt panicked. She felt like overturning every stall and screaming, "Where are my children? Have you seen them? Have you taken them?"

After moving up and down the narrow spaces between the stalls and becoming overwhelmed by the noise and shouts, even by the guitar and violin music that she usually enjoyed, she spotted them—in the grass just beyond the plaza. Nelita contentedly gobbled an anise cookie. Pedro dipped a small pipe into a bowl of liquid and blew bubbles. Miguel had joined them and offered to help carry the baskets of provisions. Isabela noted with relief that Mari had stocked up. The baskets were full. Neither of them wanted to return here soon.

When they arrived at the top of the bluff, Isabela experienced a moment of confusion. When Cook's cottage came into view, she realized she was thinking, 'I haven't seen Cook since yesterday evening. I'll stop by and share with her all that's happened since.'

She imagined Cook shaking her head sympathetically at the absurdity of it all. She would reassure Isabela with an embrace, followed by a hot cup of one of her delicious brews. Isabela could see Cook—the way she took pleasure stirring a generous dab of honey into the tea, squeezing in a few drops of lemon.

There was no smoke coming out of the chimney. The door still swung in the breeze. Miguel offered to secure it to keep wild animals from taking shelter inside.

A torn letter from Nelleke did little to cheer Isabela. When she read the date—Fall 1644—she realized with dismay that the letter had been written three years earlier. How many hands had it passed through? How many ships had it sailed on before landing at her doorstep? It felt to her as if she and Nelleke lived on different stars, hundreds of thousands of miles apart, as if their lives no longer had anything to do with each other. She didn't know how to respond. Nelleke must be twelve by now. What about her own life could she share with a happy, secure and sheltered Amsterdam child?

Fall 1644
Dearest Isabela,

I am now nine which means you are nineteen years old. As you can see from this handwriting, I write my own letters now. I don't need Mama's help any more. I just realized another parallel in our lives—parallel—that's like when two boats go side by side in the same direction through a canal. I'm keeping a notebook of three-, four-, and five-syllable words. Parallel— I'm taking a moment to write that word in the three-syllable section. It's the discovery of FIVE-syllable words that I find the most enjoyable, though. I sometimes note too when I first learned the word—from a person who spoke it or from reading it. Here's one: "Exoskeleton." What is an "exoskeleton?" Do you know? My brother, Daniel, taught me that word.

How about if I ask you at the beginning of each of my letters a question about insects or spiders or butterflies and answer the question at the end? Here's your first question:
"How high can a flea jump?"
Now for that parallel. I believe that my little sister, Katje, and your boy, Pedro, were born about the same time. That means I can imagine you

and your little son playing just as Katje and I do. I have three brothers, but Katje is my first and only sister. She is so funny trying to walk. She doesn't seem to care how many times she falls down. She pulls herself up and tries to take a step. Mama and Papa bought Katje a wooden walker which helps. Sometimes I try to entertain her like you did with us in the orphanage— with a funny story or song. You were so good at just making up something right on the spot. I wish I had that talent. But I can make her laugh just making faces. She loves it when I tickle her toes. Do you tickle Pedro's toes?

Papa imported a parrot—a beautiful, exotic one with a green head and blue feathers. Excuse me while I write "exotic" in my three-syllable notebook. At first it just squawked. Now it imitates Katje's cries and I can't tell the difference. I run to help her and it's really the parrot.

Papa had a silver ring made for Katje—not a ring for her tiny finger, but a large one she can hold in her fist. It has a piece of coral attached that she can chew on. Except she drools a lot and I find that somewhat sickening. When Mama will let me, I run around the house with a little windmill. It twirls and makes a swishing sound which Katje loves. I hide behind a wall or doorway or chair and pop out with the windmill. Katje squeals and claps her small hands together. I wish you and Pedro lived with us so we could all play together.

For Saint Nicolas Day, I placed some taai taai in Katje's little fists. Taai taai is the baby name for koek—a long, thin, sweet bread. I don't think we had any in the orphanage. We break off pieces for her. It's her favorite food because it's both tough and chewy, but also flavored with honey. She's always begging for more taai taai.

I must send this letter now and hope it gets to you. Please tell me about your little boy, Pedro. Does he look like you? Does he have your thick, dark curls? Remember how we discovered the night I arrived in the orphanage how we both had under our bonnets those tight curls? But yours were almost black and mine were yellow. Our skin, too, was similar. Not the pale white of most of the orphans, but a light beige.

Answer: A flea can jump 100 times its own height. I measured it. Watch out for fleas!

Your devoted "little sister," Nelleke

Chapter Twenty
Explanations

For the next two months, Isabela heard nothing from Cook. Mari went once or twice a week to the market—for information as much as for supplies. She reported that many people had been questioned—some two or three times. No one had seen Cook. Mari herself was too frightened to deliver the notes and food that Isabela sent to the prison. She would not go anywhere near it. Miguel offered to make the delivery, but Mari would not hand over to him the notes and packages. She felt they were all at risk.

With Cook gone, it was more difficult for Isabela to leave the children and the household chores in order to descend to the village and visit with her closest friends. In her next communication to the tailor she wrote:

I'm not sure if you know how close I felt to Cook. I am bereft with missing her and worrying about her fate. They questioned me at the prison. I told the truth, of course, but the inquisitor twisted my words. They seem determined to condemn her for one thing or another—all of it totally unjustified. Why is this happening, I keep asking myself? Can you explain it to me?

The tailor wrote back. "*Yes I will explain, but first you must promise me that you have destroyed my letters to you and that you will destroy this note and any future communication just as I, with sadness, destroy yours.*"

"I don't understand," she wrote, *"but I will do as you say."*

"First of all, I am upset that you were questioned. I know you are brave, but I can only imagine how frightening that must have been for you. I hope you are recovering. Of course your friend is innocent of wrongdoing, the tailor continued. Her caring is legendary. That is part of the problem. Her very strengths and her powers as perceived among the people are a challenge to the combined authority of the Church and the Crown. Did you not tell me that on any given Sunday there are more villagers waiting to meet with Cook than there are attending Mass? That people are travelling further and further distances for a moment of her time?

The Church and the King operate in unison to keep all power in their hands. They encourage neighbors to spy on one another and report what they perceive as suspicious behavior. Anyone with a grudge could misinterpret or deliberately frame someone they dislike. This, of course, is the very opposite of Christ's message of acceptance and forgiveness.

What we have here is a young and ambitious priest. Perhaps you are aware of the expression, 'auto-da-fé?' The English translation is 'burning at the stake.' Most are carried out with great spectacle in one of Spain's major cities. The King and Queen attend. The Grand Inquisitor himself leads the parade. Thousands cheer. Santos Gemelos is an insignificant village. Our priest wants a larger role on the national stage. Since he arrived, he has been searching for some justification, for some reason to accuse a local person of heresy. In so doing, he hopes to convince the authorities at the highest levels that he is worthy of a more important, more visible post, that he can quickly identify so-called 'heretics' and destroy them. Thus Santos Gemelos will possibly, dear Isabela, I am sorry to tell you, have its own spectacle.

Although this is not true in Cook's case, such violence is also often about wealth. The main victims of these killings are New Christians— Conversos with Jewish ancestors whose property is confiscated after their deaths. Their gold and silver enter the coffers of the Church and the Crown, both of which require enormous amounts of wealth to maintain.

Isabela, please take care of yourself."

While desperately wanting to savor and cling to the handwriting she cherished and to the folded notes the tailor had touched, Isabela, nonetheless, carried out his instructions. Although she hated to lose forever any words the tailor had penned, she watched as the neat, thoughtfully arranged sentences became consumed by flames. She listened to the paper crinkle as it turned black and disappeared.

* * *

Miguel and Mari were married in a simple ceremony in the church, presided over by the village priest. Isabela could not face the man— priest turned traitor. She was appalled at the hatred she felt toward him. She refused to cower and obey him by attending Mass. She would not step inside the church. But she did give a reception for Miguel and Mari—the first gathering she had ever organized in the de Vega house. Doña Juana had not left her bed for weeks and was nearly deaf. Fortunately, there had been no second message demanding that she report for questioning. As long as her meals were served and she was cleaned, the celebration would not trouble Doña Juana.

Mari was still alienated from the parents who had sent her to the convent after she gave birth to the child of a married neighbor five years ago when she was fifteen. The child's father was raising the little boy. Mari was pleased, though, that her older brother did attend. Miguel's family, although at first skeptical of Mari as a suitable wife, had accepted her. His large family—mother, father, three sisters, two brothers, aunts, uncles, cousins—filled the large room with their feasting, music, and dancing.

After their wedding and with still no word from or about Cook, Mari and Miguel sought permission to move into Cook's cottage. They had already been tending the garden and were using the yard there to raise the chickens given them as wedding gifts. At the sight of smoke rising once again from the cottage chimney, Isabela put her arms tightly around herself and rocked back and forth.

* * *

The next day, a letter from Nelleke.

Winter 1648
Dearest Sister, Isabela,

I am fifteen so you are twenty-five.
Insect question: What insect feeds on hazelnuts and how does it reach through the shell to the meat inside?

I do so love your letters. Your tailor sounds like a very interesting man. He seems so learned. It makes me wonder why he is a tailor and not a writer/scholar or a professor at a university. In any case, your friendship reminds me of my relationship with my cousin. Willem is nineteen now, but we have adored each other since we were very small when we used to play hide-n-seek in his big house.

His mother, my Aunt Elsbeth, has always been very rejecting of me for reasons I do not understand. She never invites me to their home. Willem and I meet in secret, but that makes our meetings all the more delicious, really. We talk and talk. He was a foundling, you may know. He still has the half playing card that was pinned to his blanket the day my father found him on the front steps of the family print shop. Willem showed me the card. It must have been formidable and frightening when it was whole. Half the card was scary enough.

It was cut at a jagged angle like a puzzle piece. You really should see it some day. The partial head of a demon-like snake with a forked tongue, thick black lashes rising above one large human eye, which stared straight at me in a most threatening manner. My father made and sold cards like that in the taverns. He had quite an imagination apparently . . . and skill too.

Actually the card he showed me is a replica. Years ago during an altercation I don't understand, Aunt Elsbeth lost the original. Willem then drew and cut the card as he and his mother remembered it.

Willem wonders about his origins. He suspects that his real mother has the other half of the card, but he doesn't know how to go about finding her. Anyway, he's starting at the University soon in Leiden. I will miss him terribly. He has a calm and rather quiet demeanor. He never seems to tire of my constant talking and wondering and questioning.

Did I tell you I'm writing a story for children? It's about a little girl whose younger sister has just died. She becomes attached to a caterpillar who somehow found its way into her room. She hides it from her mother and the maid so that they don't throw it out. It's her secret. She names it Wooly and watches it nibble the fresh leaves and grass she gathers for it every day. She talks to it. She's convinced Wooly recognizes her voice. Whether he's anticipating more food or he just likes her company, she likes the way he twists his head toward her when she bends down to peek at him in his hiding place. She borrows a container from the kitchen, but her cook hasn't noticed yet that it's missing.

When Wooly wiggles out of his caterpillar skin and turns into a butterfly, the little girl feels loss all over again. She realizes that she cannot confine the butterfly to her room, that it needs to get out into the fresh air and explore the world. Tears fall from her eyes when she watches the butterfly take off from her window sill without a backward glance or a word of thank you for her care. Yet she feels exhilaration (Excuse me. I'm stopping to write 'exhilaration' in my five-syllable notebook).

She feels exhilaration, though, when she sees how free it is. It rests for a moment on a branch nearby. She hopes it will come to visit. She decides that her sister turned into a butterfly too. She didn't really die. Her sister is enjoying her explorations in the trees, skimming along the canal waters. Perhaps her sister and this butterfly will become friends, she thinks.

Willem does not make fun of my stories like my brothers might. He loves this story and helps me sometimes. He'll suggest a better word here and there or revise a sentence. It's a poignant story he says. I love it when Willem uses words I don't know. When I ask him to define them, he does so in such a vivid way with examples. I know I'll never forget the words. Here's what he said about poignant. I can hear his voice saying it as I write. I can see the serious expression on his face.

"Poignant means touching, affecting."

"Synonyms?" I ask him. (I no longer write down three-syllable words. That notebook is full and three-syllable words are too common.)

"Intense," he suggests. "And maybe sincere, heartfelt. Yes," he says shaking his head with satisfaction. "Heartfelt is a good synonym. What's interesting about poignant is this—it can be positive or negative, but it always describes an emotion. Poignant regret, for example, but a poignant scene as when a mother holds her newborn for the first time."

Doesn't Willem sound just so intelligent, Isabela? He reminds me of your tailor friend. Aren't we both lucky to have such people to converse with and learn from?

Answer: A hazelnut weevil. It's like a living drill. Using its long, slender snout with tiny jaws at the tip, it chews holes in the hazelnuts. I've now watched the process three times.

All my love, your not-so-little-anymore sister, Nelleke

Chapter Twenty-One
Punishment

Attention residents of Santos Gemelos—

**A major event will take place
in the Santos Gemelos Plaza
at 12:00 noon the 10ᵗʰ day of June
in the year of our Lord, 1649
immediately following a special Mass.**

**All villagers—men, women, and children—
are required to attend.**

Posted at the prison, the town hall, and the church, the notice was circled by the words "Tribunal of the Holy Office of the Inquisition of Spain," written in elaborate script and stamped with an elaborate crown atop the outline of a human face whose features consisted of a cross, a sword, and a palm leaf—the seal of the Inquisition.

Flyers appeared in every market stall and every home. While coping with losing Cook's steady, reassuring presence and care, Isabela had been living with the fear of what was happening to her in that prison. Every night when she prayed to Jesus and Mary, she clutched the double cross, hating herself for keeping it when it was Cook who needed the protection. Yet, at the same time, she tried to prepare herself for Cook's death. How could Cook survive there away from everyone who loved her? In a place where even a request for water might be denied?

Mari brought the flyer to Isabela with the most horrible news possible. Cook had been judged a heretic and was to be burned at the stake. As the tailor had predicted, the event was planned as a spectacle, a celebration of the church's triumph over evil forces and proof that the Crown will not tolerate deviant behavior.

The flyer made it clear that "men, women, and children are required to attend," but Isabela would never subject her children to observing their beloved Cook meet such a violent end. She herself would go out of deference for Cook, and in the hope that Cook would see her in the crowd—that she might hear Isabela's voice crying out to her.

By the time Isabela arrived, a crowd had already gathered. In the center of the plaza next to the well someone had erected a thick, wooden pole with a raised platform and a neatly stacked pile of logs. Hoping not to be noticed, Isabela slipped through the men, women, and children chattering and calling to one another in what Isabela considered a far too exuberant and expectant mood. Lute and guitar music competed with each other from opposite sides of the square.

When the church doors were thrown open, a surge of "ahhh's" and shouts of "Here she comes!" followed. A man who wore the same cassock as Isabela's interrogator led the procession—the dreaded green cross dominating its front panel. This time he did not wear a mask, although his face below the coned hat appeared like one—severe, haughty, self-righteous, in charge.

Lesser ecclesiastical figures followed. Behind them marched the village priest, proud chin raised, looking straight ahead.

Next, apparently representing King Philip IV, came a dozen nobles dressed in full finery. Isabela had never seen any of these people. They must have been invited by the Church as witnesses, or were they so idle they would simply show up for their own amusement? She studied one particularly pompous noble who walked in front of the others. Below the man's small pointed nose and slit-like lips was a beard so neat, it must have been trimmed daily by his personal barber.

The clothes looked as if they had never been worn. He wore a black-felt full cap with a tight brim just below his hairline. A matching dark tunic whose full upper sleeves had slits that allowed the expensive silk shirt beneath it to show through. The white embroidered shirt's wrist cuffs and matching stiff collar contrasted with the bright red of the shirt itself. The man's red patterned pants ballooned out at the hips and tapered into his high, buckled black boots. A gold ringed belt around his waist held his sheath and sword.

As the procession reached the waiting people, the humble villagers curtsied or bowed.

"Duke," they mumbled. "Marquis." "Baron." "Most illustrious lady."

Perched on their parents' shoulders, awed children's voices echoed their parents.

"Duchess." "Count." "Most excellent Lord."

Behind the nobles marched the municipal and town authorities. The noon sun gleamed off the silver helmets of the three dozen soldiers who followed. The last two soldiers held torches and completed the procession. Between them, secured to a wooden ladder by her neck, wrists, waist, and ankles, was an old woman who barely resembled the most famous villager so many had revered and admired.

Having been distracted by the pomp and pageantry, the crowd suddenly fell silent. They pushed closer to catch a glimpse of the condemned woman. Cook with her blouse ripped and drooping over one bare shoulder. Cook with a cone-shaped hat. Fastidious Cook now filthy, with matted hair, barefoot, still in the skirts—now threadbare— that she was wearing the day she was taken. Her once youthful satiny hands were rough skinned, the veins visible from where Isabela stood. The music stopped. The procession moved slowly twice around the small plaza.

When Isabela was close enough to observe Cook, it seemed to her that Cook's serene, calm expression with the faint smile was a deliberate attempt to reassure those who, like Isabela, would be feeling tremendous distress.

"Do not worry," her expression seemed to say. "I will be all right. You will prosper without me. You can heal yourselves. You can heal each other."

"Cook! I love you, Cook!" a woman shouted.

More joined in. Isabela recognized next to her the man whose scalp Cook treated in his youth. His wife beside him, he was holding an infant.

"Thank you, Cook," he yelled. "See how healthy I am now. See how content. Thank you, Cook."

Soon the crowd began chanting in unison. "Cook! Cook! Cook!"

As the procession completed its second turn of the plaza and opened up a path to the waiting pole, the most daring in the crowd began to shout,

"Healer! Healer! Healer!"

One old man, who knew Cook when she was a girl, yelled the name everyone had forgotten,

"Aurelia! Beautiful Aurelia! You are loved, Aurelia!"

Isabela did not shout. She did not believe that Cook would ever distinguish her voice from all the others. In the hope that Cook would see her, though, she had rummaged among the belongings that Cook had left behind and that Mari had placed in a special container. Most of the gloves were missing, but now reaching as high as she could, Isabela shook the single white glove she had found. Although Cook could not move her head tied tightly to the ladder, her eyes seemed to pick up the motion of the familiar object she herself had sewn. Isabela thought Cook saw and knew that only Isabela would be waving that glove.

The soldiers attached the ladder to the wooden pole in such a way that Cook's feet rested on the woodpile. An official climbed up to the raised platform and read a proclamation.

"Aurelia Teresa Zalamea has been tried, found guilty, and confessed . . ." The crowd murmured an objection.

"Not guilty," someone shouted. "She would not confess."

"She is innocent!" yelled others.

"Found guilty and CONFESSED," continued the official, "to the following crimes: blasphemy, practicing medicine as a woman, practicing medicine without permission, false claims, heresy, and witchcraft. For her transgressions Aurelia Teresa Zalamea has been condemned to die by fire."

Before climbing off the raised platform, one soldier removed his thick leather gloves. When he placed his hands around Cook's neck, she closed her eyes and smiled—the smile Isabela had seen many times, a smile of quiet recognition, of welcoming joy. 'She believes that Gérard has come to take her to Heaven again,' thought Isabela. 'This time she will not just SENSE God's presence, she will SEE God. She will sit with Him in Heaven, with Gérard, with Mary, and with Jesus. She will live forever, my beloved Cook.'

The soldier's thumbs pressed on Cook's throat. Her head slumped to one side. There were no prayers for her soul, yet Isabela felt Cook's spirit set free. Her body was not free, however, and neither Isabela nor any other observer was prepared for what followed, even though they had been told to expect it. The inquisitor nodded to the two soldiers holding torches. They lit the pile of wood at Cook's feet.

Isabela had remained strong for Cook's sake but, as the flames licked at Cook's feet and began mounting up her body, Isabela could no longer tolerate the loss, the injustice, the horror. The soldiers threw into the flames Cook's gloves and the contents of her vials. Villagers watched as the herbs that had soothed and cured their ills turned to ashes.

Several adolescent boys who did not know Cook, who had never sought her healing and advice, began yelling,

"Witch! Witch! Burn witch!"

Isabela pushed through the mob of people who remained transfixed as the flames consumed Cook's body. She did not look back. She sought comfort. When she had run past the two streets behind the church, she found that the youths had arrived there first. Threatening with planks, hatchets, and hammers, they shouted at the closed door,

"Come out you traitors. You cowards. You with tainted blood. We know what you are. Liars. False Christians. Judaizers. Show yourselves."

They began pounding on the door and trying to kick it in. They smashed the shutters on the windows. More people arrived. Some tried to stop them, but the youths resisted and encouraged each other.

"Get them. Drag them out here. Let THEM be tried."

Isabela could not make sense of the words. She thought only of the four people she loved hovering in their home. She saw that the youths were drunk on the violence they had just witnessed, that they wanted more. Finding the door tightly secured, they hacked at the front of the cottage. The walls gave way. The youths scrambled inside still shouting. One had a torch. The blows had knocked the heavy crucifix off the wall. It lay fallen face down across the tailor's table. The blow had cracked the table into two pieces. The outstretched hand on the Mary statue had been knocked off and lay split in two halves. Books were strewn about.

"Hey, look at these," one of the youths yelled out. Several of them moved toward the chess board. They tossed the Rooks and Kings and Queens back and forth to one another. They stuffed their pockets.

When the youths began tearing down the curtain that separated the tailor's work area from his private space, a female voice screamed,

"No. No. Leave them alone. They are innocent. Do not hurt them."

The voice stopped when Isabela fell to the ground, unconscious.

* * *

Strong arms lifted her up. On and on the arms carried her, supporting her head, holding her close. She woke in a bright room with a warm fire and white-washed walls, a cold cloth on her forehead, stretched out on Leonor's bed with Leonor sitting next to her, holding her hand.

"Are you awake, dear Isabela? How do you feel? Angel told me what a terrible fright you've had. I'm so sorry you had to endure that, Isabela. He's gone back to the town and will return to us when he has something to report."

Chapter Twenty-Two
Alarm

efore Angel walked into the house several hours later, Isabela felt sufficiently recovered to sit up and sip the soup Catalina had prepared. Yet when she saw Angel's expression, her stomach tightened so she feared she would lose the soup all over Leonor's bed.

"The news is mixed and not entirely clear at this point," Angel began in his gentle way.

"Cook's remains have been taken away. No one knows what they will do with them. They only know that she will not be given a proper burial. As for the tailor's family, after battering down the walls of their home, the youth stomped inside and leaped across the counter. One of the boys yelled out, 'Aha! Look here.' On the back of the fallen crucifix in neat black paint were the words, 'Jesus himself was a Jew.'

Among the splintered bits of the Madonna's hand someone picked up a small scroll. It must have been inside her pointing finger all that time. By then, the priest had heard of the looting. When he arrived and learned about the scroll, he asked to see it and placed it in the pocket of his Cassock.

"Evidence," he said.

"Evidence of what?" Isabela asked, trying to delay hearing what happened next.

Angel shook his head and continued.

"They tore down the heavy curtain to reveal a room like that in any village home. Fire burning in the fireplace, beds, tables, chairs, kitchen utensils, oil lamps. I'm not sure what the priest expected to find, but he seemed disappointed."

"But the tailor?" Isabela cried. "The family?"

"They were not in that room. They were not in the garden. Their shoes, their clothes, all their personal items were still in the wardrobe. The priest was not satisfied. The youths were bored now, but he kept encouraging them to scour every inch of the room. I don't know what he hoped to find.

"I knew you would want to know everything that happened, Isabela. I didn't say anything, but I followed along as if I were one of those horrid youths. I saw a second scroll tucked into the hand of the Madonna statue. It was small and lay on the floor mixed in with the bits of ceramic from her smallest finger. I heard one the boys unroll it and yell.

"'Hey, look at this scribble! What is this thing?'

"He ripped the little scroll in half, threw it on the floor and kept going. I picked it up. Here it is. I saved it for you. The boys kept looking through the family's belongings. They did not notice me. Neither did the priest. They were distracted by a large pewter candelabra left behind."

Isabela glanced at the two halves of the tiny scroll and put it in her apron pocket.

"But one of the youths cried out, 'Hey, come over here. Look at this.'

"He had moved the wardrobe to look behind it. In the shadow cast by the large piece of furniture, one could barely make out an opening in the wall. The excited boys shoved the wardrobe over on its side. Yes, there was a space large enough for someone to pass through. The youth ducked in, but came right back out.

"'It's dark in there,' he said, apparently afraid to venture very far.

"The priest was excited. He lit a lamp and gave it to the youth who took a few more steps into the space.

"'I think it's a tunnel,' the boy yelled back, his voice echoing.

"The priest encouraged the other youths to enter the space first and then followed them.

"The crowd that witnessed Cook's ordeal was dispersing. Some had returned to their homes on this same street. Others were passing by. Soon both the Valverde house and the mysterious dark space were filled with villagers. Many began rummaging and pocketing whatever they saw. The tailor's tools, furniture, food, candles. Women reached into the wardrobe lying on its side, its doors swinging open. They took bonnets, skirts, blouses, bedding."

Isabela was appalled, but these stories were not what she wanted to hear.

"Did they find the family?" she asked dreading the answer.

"They followed the tunnel for a long way. It became very narrow in places, but it ended in a cave that faced a small secluded area of the harbor. People probably expected to see the tailor's family huddled against a cliff. They spread out along the beach, but no one could find them anywhere. It's not at all certain that they even escaped through that tunnel. As everyone knows they close their business on Friday nights. No one had seen them for at least twenty-four hours. They could be anywhere."

Isabela slumped down onto the bed. She tried to crowd from her mind the day's images—of Cook's body, of the tailor's family frightened and fleeing, of everything they owned destroyed or stolen. Then she remembered something she rarely thought about—the secret jewel which at this very moment was hidden in the petticoat she was wearing. Of course, this was not their only diamond. 'Wherever they go, if they arrive safely, they can rebuild their lives.' This thought comforted Isabela, but the trauma of losing so many dear friends in one day was overwhelming.

"It's nighttime now, Isabela, and you've experienced so many shocks today," Leonor said to her. "Mari and Miguel are with Pedro and Nelita, are they not? I don't think, even with Angel's help, that you should try to climb the bluff tonight. If you're feeling better in the morning, Angel will accompany you home. Do you feel well enough to sit with us at the table for the evening meal?"

Isabela had never spent a night away from her children, not even when the nuns notified her one evening that Tía Lucia was dying. Now she hesitated. She knew that Mari and Miguel would worry, but might not be surprised knowing that the day was such a desperate one for Isabela. Perhaps they would assume she was with a group of mourners or finding comfort with friends—just as she was. The thought of climbing up the bluff in the dark . . . no, she thought, I cannot, I haven't the strength. I will leave at dawn. She was probably not the only one feeling exhausted by the day's events. She did not want to ask anyone, and certainly not Angel, to venture up the bluff and back tonight to deliver a note.

Twice she screamed in her sleep and woke the entire family. Another time she sat upright, trembling, sobbing, trying to push away the nightmares. Each time Leonor placed her arm around her and soothed her back to sleep.

As Leonor had predicted, by the next morning, in spite of the fitful sleep, Isabela woke up feeling somewhat stronger and anxious to return home.

"After you've eaten," Leonor said, as she prepared bread, cheese, and cider for breakfast and tucked oranges and apples into a small basket along with a flask of water.

"Keep drinking and eating as you climb up. Take care of yourself, Isabela."

Weren't those the last words the tailor wrote? She began to cry softly again. Part of her wanted to stay here with Leonor and be cared for. But the caring had always been mutual. Before she embraced the girls and Leonor and thanked them, she asked Leonor about the bandage on her hand.

"Did you hurt yourself?" she asked with concern.

"No," Leonor said, "there was no injury. It's a sore. It comes and goes. I have some on my back. In a few other places too. They don't hurt."

"I'll search for Cook's special plant. It cures every skin condition."

"No, Isabela," Leonor said with alarm. "You must not. Stay away from all of Cook's cures. Destroy them. Did she not suffer confinement and death because of those cures? If the sores continue, I will seek the advice of a doctor. Now go. We will see each other soon again, my dearest."

* * *

When Isabela and Angel arrived at the de Vega home, she spontaneously invited him inside. He was such a strong, dependable young man, a contrast to the brash, destructive youths he described the day before, and she was so fond of him she didn't want to let him go. She also felt that her household might be more likely to forgive her quickly for the night she'd spent away if she brought Angel inside to visit with them. The children looked up to Angel and regarded him as an older brother.

Angel hesitated, knowing that his mother was despised by the de Vegas, that they had not once reached out to him or his sisters. This was the closest he had ever been to his grandparents' house.

Seeing his reluctance, Isabela reassured him,

"You know that Captain Vicente died some time ago. Doña Juana is frail and remains in her bed all day. She's forgotten all our names. It's doubtful you'll even cross paths with her but, if you do, she'll just assume you're another member of her family—which, in fact, you are. You know, Angel, that Pedro and Nelita would delight in your surprise appearance. Stay a little while."

Isabela held open the door and encouraged Angel to enter first. Indeed, the children were surprised, so much so that they stopped their play and stared for a moment. Then they ran to Angel. Pedro thumped him on the back and on the arm. Nelita reached up to be held. They seemed far happier to see Angel than their mother. Apparently, they had hardly missed her. Isabela always enjoyed watching the siblings enjoy each other, but she did want to be acknowledged. Just as she reached out her arms to them and said, "How about me?" she noticed a man's muddy boots propped on one of her cushions by the fire.

When, without turning around to face the group by the front door, the man spoke, everyone was suddenly silent.

"Oh, you've decided to return home, have you, Isabela?" the voice growled.

"I arrive after a challenging voyage to find my mother has just died, my cook has been condemned as a heretic and a witch, and my property is in the hands of a young peasant I've never met. As if all of that were not bad enough," he continued, pausing to take a puff on his pipe and a sip of his beer, "the mother of my children seems to have abandoned them. Is this the way you behave while I am gone? While I'm away earning a living for us all? Isabela, WHERE HAVE YOU BEEN?"

As he spit out the final word of this tirade, Diego stood and spun around to face her. Anyone else looking at what Diego saw might think the group of four framed in the doorway was posing for a family portrait, albeit a tense, unsmiling one. Pedro clung to Isabela's skirts. Isabela's hand rested on Angel's arm. Nelita circled her arms tight around the neck of Angel who held her close.

Father and son, only seventeen years apart and looking like the good and evil sides of a coin, stared at each other. What Diego experienced when he saw them all huddling together was betrayal, a loss of power.

Angel spoke up.

"Hello, Papa," he said calmly. "Isabela had quite a fright yesterday and collapsed. Mama and I urged her to spend the night with us recovering."

"A fright? Collapsed? Because she lost a cook?"

Then addressing Isabela, he said, "Haven't you already hired another one?"

To ward off more of Diego's insensitive attacks and to avoid an accusation of neglect, she said,

"I am sorry about Doña Juana, Diego. Did you and the children have a chance to say good-bye to her? Even though she no longer recognized us, every night we sat with her for a time. I fed her the evening meal while the children read to her or sang softly. She didn't know who we were anymore, but it seemed to help her sleep."

Diego showed no emotion. He said simply, gesturing with his stubby chin, "We will bury her now—over there with all the children she lost."

Diego returned to his chair by the fire, propped up his feet on the cushion and filled his pipe. Angel turned toward the door with Nelita still clinging to him. Pedro and Isabela accompanied Angel outside and a little way along the path until it began its sharp decline.

"Will you be all right?" Angel asked Isabela. "I've never seen him speak that harshly."

"Don't worry. I'll be fine. He has never struck me, if that's what you're thinking. Take good care, Angel. I am so grateful to you for rescuing me from that horrible scene and to you and your mother for caring for me. I really don't know what I would have done without you."

Mother and children stood and watched Angel descend. When he approached a bend, he turned to wave. They waved back. Angel disappeared. They turned back to the house.

* * *

Isabela washed Doña Juana's body and selected a fresh blouse and skirt for her burial. Mari helped dress her. Miguel carried her body to the grave he had dug for her. The family followed. Isabela and her children each said a prayer. Diego stood staring. He said nothing. When the hole was covered, he turned and headed down the bluff.

* * *

When Isabela entered her room that evening, she found that someone had left two packages for her. After the children were asleep, she opened the lighter one. When Isabela saw what was inside, she let out a groan of protest. 'No, no,' she thought. 'This is not mine. I should not own it. I should not possess it. I could never wear it. Why? Why did they leave it behind? It's too bulky I suppose. They left with so little. But why entrust ME with something so precious?'

She removed the torn pages of the scroll from her apron pocket and looked at them for the first time. In a thin neat handwriting she saw words in a script and language she did not know, had never seen, had never heard. She rolled the two fragile pieces together and tied them with a slim ribbon. She reached down through the folds of Reza's wedding dress until she felt its hidden pocket. She tucked the scroll into the pocket and closed the lid on the box.

Next she opened the heavy box. Books. She looked at the titles and their authors and concluded that only one person she knew would have owned these books. *General History of Spain*—Juan de Mariana. *Songs of the Soul*—San Juan de la Cruz. *Castle of Love*—Diego de San Pedro. She sat at her desk to look through *Anonymous Poems* whose titles intrigued her. "The Kiss." "Glove of Black in White Hand Bare." "The Siesta."

She stretched out on her bed still holding the book of poems, and began to cry softly. She knew that reading any page in any one of these volumes would fill her with questions and thoughts, but now there was no one to discuss with, no one to write. Knowing that every time she held one of these books in her hands, every time she read a line, she would be consumed with frustration and feelings of longing and loss, she was tempted to place the books under her bed and ignore them. Then she noticed in the center of the book a small piece of barely visible brown paper. A bookmark? A message? Printed on the page was a long poem entitled "Love and Death." She skipped to the final stanza and read:

What a world, so topsy-turvy!
What a change in people's lives!
Cupid giving life destroys,
Death destroying life revives.

She turned the paper over. In the tailor's handwriting were the words, "Wherever you go, go with all your heart. Confucius, 551-479 BC."

Chapter Twenty-Three
Losing Leonor

Mari and Isabela scrubbed every inch of Doña Juana's room, opened the windows and replaced the feather mattress. That room became Diego's room. Pedro, who had become too big to sleep with his sister, took over the small room next to Isabela's. Diego had his side of the house. Isabela and her children the other. They met in the large central room on those rare occasions when Diego took meals with them. Finally, she washed and mended the four heavily used, smoky cushions whose secret treasure she had not touched. From the six original cushions she stuffed with coins years earlier, she had emptied only two. As usual, as long as Diego was in Santos Gemelos, Leonor and Isabela did not visit or contact one another.

Isabela was now the mistress of her own home, yet she did not move to fulfill her dreams of a whitewashed interior, comfortable furniture, a harpsichord in the corner. Like the housewives she had seen in Amsterdam, with Mari's help, every day she scrubbed the walls, floors, and furniture. They rearranged the shelves in the warming kitchen, threw out chipped plates and broken goblets. Next they turned their attention to the cottage which Isabela had not entered since Cook's death.

The cottage was Mari and Miguel's home now and Mari was expecting their first child. Miguel had asked permission to add a second room. The steady sweetness of the young couple cheered Isabela somewhat. She wanted only to go through Cook's things which Mari had set aside.

161

Isabela gave to Mari Cook's bonnets, blouses, and skirts. She kept for herself the shawl knitted by the mother of the young man whose scalp Cook had healed, believing that's what Cook would have given her if she hadn't been taken away so abruptly. Knowing little of their healing power, finding them merely decorative, Mari had watered and cared for several of Cook's plants, moving them around so that each day they caught some sun.

Isabela recognized the plant with the long, slender leaves whose sap had soothed Gérard's wounds and set Cook on the path of becoming a life-long healer. She found dozens of vials of dried herbs marked, "Stomach" "Kidneys" "Birth pains" "Toothache." With Leonor's warning words in her mind—"Destroy them all"—she kept only the plant and one vial Cook had marked with the word "Seasickness." Why that particular one, she couldn't say since she herself planned to live out her life in Santos Gemelos.

Perhaps she chose to save that vial because, of all the ailments on the labels, it was the sickness of her two voyages that was most debilitating. Perhaps, although she suppressed the thought, she was preparing for the time when Diego took Pedro on his first voyage. Perhaps it was the possibility that the tailor's message, "Wherever you go . . . . ," was prophetic. Although she did sometimes think about taking her children and leaving, she had no idea how to escape or where to go. Diego certainly wouldn't miss HER, but he might search for his son. If Diego could find her in an enemy land far from Spain in a protected orphanage, he could find them anywhere.

* * *

After Diego had been in Santos Gemelos for two months, he arrived home one morning. Every day, Isabela looked out her window at the harbor and beyond. Diego's ship was anchored in the same place. With no explanation, he announced abruptly,

"Prepare to sail, Isabela. I've had enough of this dead town. I know where there's fortune to be found. That's where we're going. It will be an adventure."

Isabela spent several long sleepless nights going over in her mind every bit of information she could drag out of her taciturn husband. He became irritated so quickly with her questions that she asked only one or two at a time. Eventually, she understood his intensions. Where did he intend to take them? "To the New World." Where specifically in the New World? "A place called San Agustín." How far away is it? "It's across the sea. About five weeks journey at least." Why there?

On that subject, Diego was more effusive. "Gold and silver. The Crown is mining in South America and shipping the precious metals back to Spain. The ships pass by San Agustín in order to catch the Gulf Stream back home. Some of these ships are attacked by pirates, but the attacks are quick. The pirates rarely find all they're looking for. Other ships are downed by storms. Some get stuck in shallow water. The sailors drown and the ships sink. There are dozens of lost ships loaded with treasure and I aim to locate them. Bars of silver. Silver and gold coins. Gold time pieces. Jewelry. Necklaces. Earrings. Bracelets. Crosses. Swords with gold inlay. Pewter and silver goblets. Plates, tableware, forks, spoons. Just imagine."

"The ships are at the bottom of the sea. How are you going to get the treasure?"

On this point, Diego was less clear, but he replied in his usual sure, cocky manner,

"They're developing new methods all the time. What's needed are men brave and determined enough to locate and raise the booty."

* * *

Isabela pondered her choices. 'Concentrate. Strategize. Dare. Analyze,' she told herself. Isn't that what she learned from chess?

1) She could refuse to accompany Diego. She could suggest that he make an exploratory trip. If New Spain and his plans appeared promising, he could return for them or send for them.

Problem for her: He was determined to take nine-year-old Pedro with him. Isabela was not ready to turn over her only son to his irresponsible father, but she could not prevent his leaving either.

Diego's likely reaction: "Fine. Stay here if you want, but I'm taking Pedro with me."

2) She and Nelita could accompany Diego and Pedro to the New World. Once Pedro was settled and an adult, she could return to Santos Gemelos, to her home here. Although she had lost some of her most beloved friends, she still had Leonor and her family. With Diego off exploring, she could remake the house into the lovely home she sometimes imagined.

One problem among many: this scenario would take years. By then perhaps Nelita would have become attached to life in New Spain. She might not want to return to Santos Gemelos with her mother. Isabela would be stuck there.

Diego's likely reaction: "Fine. Come with me—all of you—and we'll see what happens. I told you it's an adventure, didn't I?"

* * *

When Isabela tried to discuss some of her possible scenarios with Diego, he dismissed them impatiently.

"This is forever. We're not coming back here. No one is coming back to Santos Gemelos. In one month we'll no longer have a home here anyway. How do think I'm financing this voyage? I sold the property. There was no one wealthy enough to buy it outright, so I sold it in sections."

Isabela was momentarily shocked. Then she berated herself for her naïveté. Of course, this is exactly what Diego would do. He had done it before hadn't he? Sold off HER family's property without discussion, without warning?

Her concern turned to Leonor. Even after Angel accompanied her up the bluff after her collapse, when he had defended her and addressed Diego as "Papa," they never discussed Diego's other family. When she asked, Diego's response dealt a double blow to her heart.

"Angel is coming on this trip. Leonor has always known he would sail with me and learn the business just as you've always known Pedro would do the same. You women try to hold on to your sons forever. Are you suggesting that Leonor and her daughters come with us too? I thought you knew. I THOUGHT the two of you were such good friends. Leonor is ill. She has the *mal francés*. She could never travel.

"And by the way, don't even think of visiting Leonor. The disease is highly contagious. And if all that isn't enough reason, she doesn't want to see you anyway."

Isabela was crushed and alarmed at Diego's casual revelations, but not surprised by his sarcasm—"I THOUGHT the two of you were such good friends." Not only was Leonor dying from a horrible disease, but she was losing her son—possibly forever. Isabela remembered the first time she met Leonor, weeping over the body of her dead infant. She knew then that Angel would leave some day and she so wanted that second son to live, grow up and take care of his mother and sisters—at least for a time.

Before writing her friend, she looked up *mal francés* in the dictionary the tailor had given her. Remembering the sore Isabela had seen and the others which Leonor had mentioned, she read with increasing horror:

Spread through sex or through contact with an open sore. Recommended treatment for a skin ulcer: cover it with a spider's web and a band of violet fabric. Late stages of the disease may involve deafness, heart problems, dementia, and mental illness. Large ulcers may deform the face and other areas of the skin.

Immediately she sent via Miguel a note of concern.

Dearest Leonor,

Diego has told me that you are ill, but he has forbidden me to visit you. Please write to tell me how you and your girls are faring. I so miss our visits and so do the children. Please share with me what the doctor has told you. Are there effective treatments for the disease? I owe you so much, Leonor. I can't stand the thought that you might be suffering and in pain.

If it were my choice, I would live out my life in Santos Gemelos with you as my closest friend—like sisters. I hope you understand that as a mother, I cannot allow Diego to take Pedro away. He is too young to defend himself. For his sake, I must be vigilant on this voyage and in the New World.

I cannot express to you how distressed it makes me to think of you losing Angel even for a short time. He is such a devoted son that I'm sure he will return here, even though Diego is determined that both his sons be trained as ship Captains.

I give you every assurance that I will watch over Angel as if he were my own.

I send all my love to you and Catalina and Marianna

After sending off the note, Isabela spent much of the night remembering all the wonderful times her family and Leonor's spent together. As the two women became closer, Isabela hoped for more shared confidences. One time a door on their private lives seemed to open a bit. They spoke about the men in their lives. Leonor said only,

"My father, my master/caretaker/husband and the father of my children. Those are the only men I've known well."

She shared no real details or opinions about these men, though, and pulled the conversation in another direction.

"Unless you count someone who I'm convinced will be the most wonderful of all—the man my son is becoming."

Then with her gift for soliciting others and waiting quietly for the other person to share her thoughts, she said,

"And you, my dear, Isabela? Did you meet anyone memorable on your travels?"

'Anyone memorable?' Isabela felt an irrepressible urge to share every detail about Pieter—his eyes, his teasing twinkle, how they met, what it was like to pose for him, to sit still with his eyes taking in every detail and transferring it to canvas. She wished that she and Leonor could giggle and whisper like the other Big Sisters at the orphanage. But how well does she know Leonor really? About Leonor's longings and dreams? Does she desire Diego or put up with him from time to time because he is her children's father? Might she love someone else?

Besides, something held Isabela back. Diego captured her and brought her back here because her aunts shared their concerns about a possible growing attachment with the painter. How much of that had he told to Leonor?

In order to have something to share, Isabela told Leonor the story of Jules's picking her up with his left arm and placing a hard rain-soaked, salty kiss on her mouth before he dove into the sea to escape the sinking ship.

"That is incredibly dramatic, Isabela. I'm sure you're the only woman in this village who has been kissed by a French sailor, much less one who is moments from his death."

"Yes, and he was injured too. Cornelius had already scooped me up and was beginning to lower me into a secret rowboat that my father had made in case I needed to escape. During one of the many flashes of lightening, I saw Jules plunge head first into the waves. Blood ran down his arm from his shoulder and dripped off his dangling right arm."

"Any kisses from anyone else?" Leonor pressed gently as she kneaded bread and waited with an air of feigned lack of interest. "Anyone who kissed and lived to tell the tale?"

Isabela did mention Pieter then, but she dwelt on the comedy of the posing sessions.

"Yes, there was another kiss—a quick one, without all the chaos of the first. A student of Rembrandt needed a painting to submit to the artist guild. He asked the Housemother if she could suggest a suitable subject. He also offered to donate the finished painting to the orphanage. For some reason, the Housemother suggested me.

"He was a handsome young man who drew a lot of attention. The cleaning maids and other Big Sisters kept finding excuses to pass by the hall and peek in. I tell you that floor was never scrubbed so often as when Pieter was painting me—and it had nothing to do with flecks of paint falling on the floor. He spread a wide canvas to catch those. The women fell on their hands and knees and cleaned around the canvas. Even the little girls were curious. Sometimes I could hear three or four of them hiding just beyond the open door urging each other forward."

Leonor sprinkled cinnamon on the bread dough, rolled it up and cut it like pinwheels. "So . . . . a kiss?" she asked, "amid all that spying and confusion?"

"A simple peck on the cheek once," Isabela lied. "Probably an apology for the stiff neck I got from sitting so still for so long."

They never spoke of men again, but Isabela wondered after that why, in her calm way, Leonor was so insistent. Her interest seemed to go beyond mere curiosity. Could she have been spying for Diego for some reason?

Once Isabela had seen a gypsy troupe perform in Amsterdam's Dam Square. In one of the acts, a younger woman saunters up flirtatiously to the betrothed of her older sister. Shocking the impromptu Calvinist audience, the man sends her off with a loud slap to her behind. While the younger seethes and hisses, the older sister reclaims her man by slipping her arm possessively through his and sticking her tongue out at the younger woman. In spite of themselves, the spectators laughed uproariously.

Before chasing each other into their make-shift tent, the three actors ended the performance with a wink and a little dance to a tune whose words were something like,

"May the Lord damn the mister who threatens my devotion to my sister."

They drew out that last syllable on a high note before finishing with,

"May the Lord send straight to Hell the sister who threatens to steal my man!"

Isabela had always felt somewhat intimidated by and immature around Leonor who was twelve years older, but it occurred to her now to look at their situation from Leonor's point of view. 'I'm the younger and the legitimate wife. Leonor always knew about Diego's early betrothal. Did she hope that Isabela would never return to Santos Gemelos, that she herself would eventually marry the father of her children? Would she really want that? Her life seemed so well ordered and peaceful.'

Isabela was also the mother of Diego's only legitimate son. It would be Pedro and not Angel who would inherit Diego's possessions if he hadn't gambled them all away. Could Leonor be jealous of Isabela then?

Chapter Twenty-four
Another Unwanted Trip

I sabela turned her attention to making the voyage as livable as possible. She and Mari made lists of all possible foods that might last on a long journey. At the beginning of the trip they could eat fresh fruits and vegetables. Before having to resort to dried meats, they would take with them and slaughter a few live chickens and lambs. Mari dried apricots, apples, pomegranates, and figs. She soaked in brine and placed into glass jars every ripe olive from every olive tree in the garden. They wrapped cheese and stuffed bags with dried peas and beans.

Knowing that after a week of travelling they would be eating dried crumbs, they baked and wrapped dozens of loaves of bread. To the longer-lasting but thin, brittle hardtack, they added some oil to give it a tiny bit of flavor.

Eventually they would be left with smoked meats and dried fish, although there would be a constant battle to keep even those foods from turning putrid or being consumed by vermin and determined rodents. They filled barrels with water and marked them "for drinking" or "for washing."

Diego concentrated on supplies of a different nature. Every day for a month he and his two sons rowed out to the docked ship. What seemed most important to Diego were the large quantities of rum he hauled onboard.

With the assistance of crew members, Diego taught his sons to either repair, make, or purchase everything needed for a long voyage. Since this was Diego's first voyage across the Atlantic, he needed accurate sextants and telescopes, new navigational books and maps. He gave the boys their first lesson in how to navigate and how to calculate the ship's location. He hired a carpenter who reviewed the tools on hand and supplemented them as needed. Saws, hammers, nails, adzes to cut and shape wood.

They loaded the ship with sails, cordage, rigging and rope, with sand, paint, and brushes to keep the heavily used deck in shape.

Like the other crew members, Angel and Pedro packed their personal items, their clothes, and whittling knives—even sewing kits since maintaining their own clothing would become their responsibility. Two of the eleven crew members packed musical instruments.

Angel absorbed every bit of information Diego presented and asked frequent questions. Pedro did not seem particularly focused on much of the instruction, but became quite excited when the focus turned to weapons. Even though theirs was a merchant ship not a military one, it was equipped with one cannon on each side, plus gunpowder, balls, and equipment to maintain the cannons.

In case of a threat from pirates, the cannons afforded a first line of defense. If unwelcome parties made it on board, the crew would use axes, boarding pikes, cutlasses, and daggers to repel them.

Isabela knew from her two previous voyages that the men were nervous with females on board, but she was determined to improve on the makeshift space Diego had assigned her some ten years earlier. She and Mari made a curtain of double thickness that reached from the ceiling to the floor of the area below deck.

One day she convinced Diego to allow her to visit the ship. For herself and her daughter, she claimed an area that was double the amount of private space Diego had set aside for her on their previous trip. She took one of the new hammocks which she and Nelita would share and asked the carpenter to build shelves around the space. Reluctant to "take orders" from a woman, he eventually agreed and found that he actually enjoyed designing them a small area they could call their own.

He surrounded the hammocks with shelves which he bolted into the floor. He seemed quite pleased with himself when he pointed out to Isabela that he had nailed in place a barrier on each shelf to keep the items from falling as the ship rocked.

Isabela dreaded having to hear every belch, grunt, snore, and swear word from the crew just on the other side of the barriers, but at least they were *visually* separated from the crew. The renovated ship also had a hole on deck which the men would use for urinating and defecating. That meant that she and Nelita would not be subjected to their splashes and stench below deck.

Finally, Isabela faced the hardest work of all—making decisions about what to take with her and what to leave behind. No furniture, which meant giving up her beloved desk. Only a few changes of clothes meant she would arrive in a new town looking like a scullery maid.

"Only essentials," Diego told her, but what did that mean? Essential for her body, her mind, her soul? She placed the tailor's books in her only trunk, a doll and toys for Nelita. The treasured boxes that contained her letters were too bulky. The letters themselves did not take up much space, but two other precious items would.

For days she agonized over whether to pack Reza's wedding dress. On the one hand it seemed so foolish and utterly impractical. Would she take it apart and use the fabric for something else? No, she would never destroy the garment. She only knew she did not want to part with it. Even though it did not really belong to her, Reza and the tailor had placed the exquisite unique gown in her care. She felt responsible for it. It was a work of art. Most of all, it connected her to two people she admired and cared for and prayed for every night. Even if they themselves had perished, the dress worn on their wedding day would live on.

She removed everything she had packed, folded the dress and placed it on the bottom of the trunk. The books weighed it down so that it didn't require as much space as she had feared. Now for the cushions—the four that still held hidden coins. While she was pondering the challenge of how to pack those, Diego walked into her room.

"I hope you're ready," he said. "The ship is and you better be too."

Spotting the pillows which he had enjoyed sitting on, but disdained as decorative, feminine fluff, he said, "You're not going to be so ridiculous as to take up space with THOSE, are you? Leave them with Mari."

After he left the room, she again removed everything from the trunk except the wedding dress, placed the cushions in next, then books, letters, clothes, and toiletries. On top she placed the toys, small books, chalks, and notebooks to amuse Nelita during the long days at sea. The totality of her belongings had shrunk to the contents of that trunk. She shut the trunk and sat on it for a moment, then called to Diego to tell him it was ready.

Isabela held her breath when Diego re-opened the trunk and ruffled through the contents. He examined and raised an eyebrow at the vinegar and salve she hoped never to need again plus the three bottles of white cream—the lanolin she had saved from Cook's cottage. Apparently satisfied with her choices, he did not rummage down as far as the pillows and the dress. After he closed the lid and dragged the trunk away, Isabela reached down, lifted her skirt slightly and felt for the hidden jewel. The diamond was always just where she sewed it months ago—tiny and hidden, but so utterly reassuring.

During the pressured weeks of preparation, Isabela continued to write Leonor. She never received a response. Angel was so busy preparing the ship and learning everything he could about how to sail it that she had not seen him either. The night before they left, she wrote a final message to Leonor saying again how much the friendship meant to her and expressing the hope that they would someday see each other again. She also penned two quick notes—one to Anneliese and one to Nelleke—telling them she was sailing to San Agustín in New Spain. Perhaps there would be an opportunity during the voyage to send the letters to Amsterdam.

Two days after packing the trunk, Isabela woke for the last time in the room that had been her sanctuary for almost ten years. She and Nelita washed their hands and splashed their faces using the fresh water in the blue-and-green porcelain pitcher and bowl. She held the objects up to the dawn light and allowed herself a favorite memory—her father slowly, teasingly unwrapping the beautifully painted pastoral scenes, the squeals of delight from her aunts and from Isabela herself, her mother's gentle caressing of the smooth sides of the bowl, the way her mother lifted the sizeable pitcher and hugged it to herself, the smile her parents exchanged. The lovely objects that greeted her every day would be acquired by new owners. The memory of them would never leave her.

PART II
New Spain

Chapter Twenty-five
Departure

"See our ship's bow, Mama? How it slopes? Down in the middle and up on the sides? 'Graceful,' Angel calls it, 'the way a Gypsy dancer turns and looks over her shoulder. It entices you,' Angel says. 'It's like an invitation. To exactly what, you're not sure. There's a certain mystery in that shape.'"

"You like words, Mama, and you'll like this one. Caravel. Ca-ra-vellll. Angel says the sound carries you away just as a ship takes you somewhere. Caravel. That's the type of ship, not its name. Papa didn't want to call it *Nuestra Señora de la Concepción* any more. 'That was the old name. The name your great-grandfather gave this ship,' Papa said. He wanted something short. Something simple. 'Why not call it *El Oviedo* then?' That was Angel's idea—the name of our capital. You know, Mama. The capital of our province, *Asturias*."

Pedro chattered away in the rowboat, his admiring and excited eyes fixed on El Oviedo becoming larger as they approached it.

"You know what Angel says about the Caravel-type ship, Mama? 'If it was good enough for Columbus, it's good enough for us. The Niña and the Pinta made it across and so will we.' Oh, we'll see much bigger ships. But El Oviedo is FAST. 'And easily maneuvered,' Papa says. SAFE too, Mama. So don't you worry. As merchant ships go, it's tiny really. More like a passenger ship. But we do have some cargo. Papa has stored a few Spanish textiles on board. He thought they might come in handy for bartering or selling when we arrive in New Spain."

It had often been challenging to hold the attention of her nine-year-old son. Isabela had struggled to get him to sit long enough to learn his numbers and letters. She had not been able to excite him about languages or art, or music either. He preferred to practice his mock sword fighting and set up pretend battles with his wooden soldiers—in the sand, on a table, on the floor. She was always tripping over them.

She thought he was focusing on the weapons on board. Now after a month of working with Angel, Diego, and the crew, he had learned . . . what? Not only scores of nautical terms, not just how to prepare for a voyage, determine location and distance, how to steer. During these short minutes in the rowboat, he had shared historical facts and displayed knowledge of geography. New words rolled off his tongue: "Easily maneuvered. Handy for bartering. Caravel. Graceful. Enticing."

With Nelita holding onto her skirts, Isabela climbed up the plank from the rowboat to the deck of El Oviedo. In her arms, Isabela held Cook's healing plant and the vial of herbs marked "Seasickness." She hoped not to need the plant's healing properties, but she expected to drink lots of tea made from those dried herbs.

Pedro's excited chatter continued as he led his mother and sister on a tour. Isabela was relieved to see the many improvements Diego had made since she last sailed on this ship ten years ago. With its shiny, freshly-painted dark-brown deck and the light-colored coils of new rope, she hardly recognized it. Pedro continued his recitation.

"Look up, Mama. Brand new. Aren't they handsome? Made of silk. They're VERY strong too. Papa says they can even resist a hurricane."

Isabela gazed at the three white square sails with the red emblem of the Spanish crown swaying gently as if warming up, waiting in the wings before given a chance to show what they were really capable of.

"I have a title, Mama. Did you know that? I'm the Cabin Boy. I have duties. Come in here, Mama," Pedro said motioning her toward the space at the very front of the ship.

"THIS is a compass. It has 32 points on it. THESE are sandglasses. Don't touch them, Nelita. You may think they're toys, but they're OFFICIAL. And I know how to use them. We keep time with them. And here's where we keep the log-line and half-minute glass. We need those to check our speed. It's my duty to record that information on the traverse board—over here. Now if you'll excuse me, Ladies, I need to get to work."

"Ladies?" Isabela had to smile at hearing her son use that form of address with his mother and sister. He really was enjoying the male environment and he was taking his new responsibilities so seriously.

Nelita tugged on Isabela's skirts. During Pedro's excited introduction to the vessel, she had followed along, but her lips were quivering. Isabela understood why. The noise and activity must be overwhelming for her. The men shouted and jostled one another as they moved around bulky and heavy objects. Nelita was so small.

And where was Angel? Everywhere it seemed. From across the deck, he greeted them with a smile and a tip of his cap, but he was immediately called over by the carpenter to do a last-minute check of supplies. Then by the cook to do the same. Next by the boatswain to do a final inventory of cordage, tackling, sails spikes, needles, twine, sailcloth, and rigging. He compared everything he saw with the lists in the notebook he carried.

Isabela searched for a spot to place the valued plant. Angel noticed and pointed to a tucked-away area where, for now at least, it would be safe and catch the sun. She placed the vials of herbs in her apron pocket. She sat on a bench where she was least likely to be in the way, pulled Nelita up on her lap, and tried to distract her by pointing out the names of the crew members she knew and giving her own explanation of what they seemed to be doing. No matter how much ship lingo she learned, she'd never catch up with her son.

But the Captain? Where was he? Shouldn't he be observing? Supervising? Advising? Isabela was so accustomed to NOT seeing Diego that she now realized she had not set eyes on him once since they climbed onto the ship.

"There he is! There's our leader!" one of the sailors said with a sarcastic guffaw. Everyone went to the back of the ship and watched as a rowboat with two men approached. Both were rowing, but one stopped to rest frequently. The lazy rower turned and looked up at all the faces peering down on him.

"Well what the hell are you looking at?" he snarled. "Get back to work. We're pulling anchor. We're sailing for The New World."

When Diego climbed aboard, Isabela saw that the smart, new Captain's jacket with the gold tassels and buttons did lend him an air of authority. Yet the jacket, matching trousers and commanding leather belt could not hide his otherwise unkempt appearance—the straggly hair and beard, the red eyes, the smelly boots. And didn't a handsome new felt hat come with this ensemble? Yes, Isabela remembered that Pedro had showed it to her.

"It's like what our Spanish soldiers wear, Mama. It has a broad brim, see? But the brim is tacked up on the sides and front. When it rains, the water runs off onto the shoulders away from the face. The Captain can always see clearly. Isn't that clever? Papa said he would buy me one someday. One for Angel too."

Although the ship was anchored in a relatively calm area, Diego teetered across the deck. With no greetings, inspections or fanfare, he yelled, "Pull anchor. Set sail." Angel and Pedro were waiting. Whether Diego remembered or not, they did. He had promised them that they would be allowed the privilege of pulling the cables that secured the vessel in place. The ship had been in this same spot for many months and dislodging the anchor was hard work, but the brothers refused aid. "Anchors away!" the boys yelled as they felt the anchor loosen. Eventually up it came, giving a loud clang as it hit the deck. The boys hauled it to the side of the ship and tied it securely.

"To the New World!" yelled Captain de Vega. "To New Spain!" yelled every man on board. The steersman turned the ship eastward. The sails whipped and sighed. Isabela had been grappling with whether to turn and take a final look at the beach, at the twin houses where she had lived for nearly all her twenty-seven years. When she decided she should not miss this chance, she placed Nelita on her feet and turned around.

She could make out a few people—probably family of the crew—gathered on the beach waving handkerchiefs. In front of the people stood the village priest. He must have said a blessing for the crew. She was grateful she hadn't heard his words. She regarded anything he said as insincere and false. It occurred to her that in his voice, a so-called blessing might even be a curse. She drew Nelita close to her and reached for the double cross in her bosom. Clutching it tightly, she said her own private prayer of hope.

A mist had lifted off the sand and was rising up the bluff obliterating her view entirely. When she turned forward again to take her place with Nelita on the bench, she noticed Angel paused, staring at the bluffs. 'He so resembles his father at that age,' she thought. But thank goodness, their characters are totally different.'

Diego was fourteen on one of the two occasions she had seen him before he turned up beside her bed in the Amsterdam orphanage a decade later. He was leaving on his first voyage with HIS father. His mother was teary. It was the only time Isabela ever saw her cry. But the young Diego was completely stoic and unsmiling, unwilling to betray any emotion, be it fear or excitement.

When Isabela and Angel exchanged a glance, she saw tears in the young man's eyes. 'He's not yet sixteen,' she thought, 'and it's unlikely he'll ever see his mother alive again.'

The mother/son bond had been so strong. What must the young man be feeling? The same mixture of sadness and anticipation she was experiencing probably, but also regret? Guilt? Angel was called away. After a brief discussion with the cook, he whipped two chickens around by the neck and began plucking their feathers. Once he had turned over the chickens to the cook, he strode over to make an adjustment on one of the sails. As Angel turned the mechanism and then climbed the mast to check on the new position, he began whistling. Up above them all, working away, concentrating on catching the strongest wind, he produced a fierce, strong, confident sound that not only entertained her, her children and the crew, but buoyed their spirits. The crew stopped their work for a brief moment and added their whistles to his.

From the far side of the deck Isabela noticed Diego staring at her as if startled. Had he forgotten they were coming on this trip? He shook his head—whether from confusion, irritation, or regret she could not tell. Then he descended below deck where later in the afternoon she found him face down in a hammock still wearing the new jacket and the muddy boots.

Chapter Twenty-Six
Monsters

To Isabela's surprise and delight, just one week into the voyage, they encountered a friendly French ship whose captain agreed to make every effort to see that Isabela's letters were passed on and delivered to Amsterdam.

Her days with Nelita fell into a pattern. Natural light did not reach below deck. They were awakened by the crew's stomping and shouting above, washed using as little water as possible, ate the remains of the previous night's evening meal, and climbed the ladder to the deck. On calm days they spent the morning reading, playing, sewing, helping the ship's cook prepare the midday meal. In the afternoon they descended for a nap, then showed up again for the evening meal, some conversation and music before bedtime.

In fact, contrary to her fearful expectations, the first two weeks of the voyage went amazingly smoothly. Feeling responsible for the Señora, the little girl, and the young men on this voyage, the cook reasoned that perhaps fresh fruit might help them avoid the lethargy, bone pain, and loosened teeth he had suffered as a young sailor. Eventually he lost every tooth in his head. For this trip he packed a barrel of limes, lemons, oranges, and grapefruit. The chickens, ducks, and lambs made hearty stews. The hard cheeses retained their flavor.

Although it became apparent early that the ship was understaffed for this cross-ocean voyage, the crew, not to be outdone by the Captain's two hard-working, enthusiastic sons, did double duty when necessary.

* * *

As the fourth week began, the rations began to dwindle. The water supply had a layer of scum on top. The hardtack was infused with bugs. They ate it anyway. Nerves were on edge. The Captain spent late evenings playing cards and drinking. He slept much of the day below deck. The lack of leadership began to wear on the men. They argued. Wordlessly but forcefully, Angel broke up two fistfights. He did not blame or call for punishment. He was aware of his youth and inexperience, yet the men respected him and included him in every major decision. He never descended below deck, choosing instead to grab a coil of rope for a pillow and curl up on the bare floor to snooze for a few hours.

Every day the men had been fishing casually—almost as a form of amusement. Now a serious effort to catch fish became imperative. The men took turns throwing out nets. The cook fried up or boiled whatever squirmy, protesting sea creatures turned up. Although some days the crew stuffed themselves, other days there was very little to share among them. Angel made sure that Isabela and Nelita always received at least a few bites.

One morning Isabela and Nelita came upon a scene that terrified Isabela. A disheveled Diego was leaning over the stern. In his hands were two bare feet—the smallest male feet onboard. Isabela dropped Nelita's hand and ran to the scene. With nothing but his father's unsteady hands to support him, Pedro was upside down, trying to entice fish to the water's surface with pieces of hardtack. "Almost got that one, Papa," Pedro yelled up. Her husband, who at age thirty-two should have been in his prime, was actually the weakest man onboard. Like all the men except for perhaps Angel, neither Pedro nor Diego knew how to swim.

When a wave grabbed Pedro's useless spear, it disappeared instantly in the rolling waves. Diego made an attempt to pull the boy up, but his arms shook from the effort. All of this had transpired in a second before Diego was even aware that Isabela was near him. For fear of startling him, she suppressed a scream. She stepped away and yelled for Angel who, along with two other sailors, ran to haul a protesting Pedro up the side of the ship. When they set him upright, he said,

"Hey, I almost got a couple of 'em. We could have had a feast."

'He is as unrealistic and carelessly risk-taking as his father,' Isabela thought, her heart still pounding wildly. She wanted nothing more than to pull her child to her and hold him, but she knew that such a gesture in front of the crew would humiliate him.

That night after Isabela and Nelita shared a meal of hardtack and rotten tangerine, they were awakened by stomping and shouting above their heads. In the dark, it was impossible to know the hour. Midnight? Early morning? Diego raised the hatch and yelled down to them, "Isabela. Nelita. Come up here. You've got to see this."

Diego left the hatch open, but very little light reached below deck. Isabela climbed the ladder and peeked out. She heard Angel's voice yell to her "Watch out. Go back down until we've killed this thing." Isabela kept her feet firmly on the ladder, but she did not close the hatch. For days the men had been fishing nearly around the clock and setting the nets lower and lower with little result. What she saw in the lamplight mesmerized her. Even with Nelita tugging on her skirts from the rungs below her, she could not move.

This sea creature's two long thin tentacles and eight arms reached in all directions, from one end of the deck to the other. Isabela had a moment of imagining how gracefully it must move through the water, but here, confused, out of its element and under attack, it writhed and slammed its arms in every direction. Accustomed to only one enemy— the whale—its huge eyes looked up at six two-legged humans towering over it making loud noises unheard in its natural habitat.

The men used hatchets and swords to cut away at the powerful arms. "Is this thing ever gonna die?" one asked. When the sailor gave the giant a hard kick, he found he could not pull his foot away. "This damn thing has teeth under its arms," he cried, as he tried to shake off the boot and free his foot.

After another ten minutes of valiant resistance, the creature seemed to succumb. It lay unmoving. Its severed and chopped-up limbs were strewn all over the deck. The men stopped and watched. The dismembered head with those large eyes stared up at them. They did not yet trust that it was no longer a threat. When the one-boot sailor reached down to claim what was his, the suction and teeth held fast. The arm seemed to jump. It became a tug of war. Afraid of losing a hand, the sailor let go and gave up—at least for the moment.

* * *

The cook wasted no time boiling up the creature's remains. The starving crew feasted the entire day. Once their bellies were stuffed, they began to wonder at what they had conquered. Did the creature have a name? Was it male? Female? Both? Neither? Were others like it out there?

'This can't be the first ship to have encountered such a creature,' Isabela thought. 'The tailor would know exactly what it was—its name, its habits, what it ate, how it reproduced.' She felt certain that, unlike everyone else on board this ship, the tailor would share the respect and sadness she felt seeing such a magnificent being destroyed bit by bit. Suddenly, she wanted desperately to ask him, "Can such brutality be justified, do you think, is it in fact necessary if humans have no other ready food source? What makes us better than this animal who seemed intelligent, who knew—I'm convinced—what was happening to it?"

This is what the rest of her life would be like then? She would always have questions she felt only the tailor could answer for her?

That night she dreamed she was back in that narrow shop with the Valverde family. Briana drew the creature as Isabela described it to her. Bernardo was teaching Pedro how to play chess and Pedro was actually concentrating. Isabela shared with the tailor the questions she had earlier in the day. He was bent over his work. His back was to her. She waited. She repeated the questions. He did not turn. He did not answer. She was hurt. She felt foolish and rejected. Villagers began yelling out in the street.

"There they are. Get them."

A mob struck the walls of the tailor's home and shop. The small cottage shook. The Crucifix fell—barely missing the tailor's head. The family did not move. They kept doing what they were doing. The tailor's glasses remained on his nose. His fingers continued to move the needle in and out of fabric. The cottage continued to shake. From its display space, Reza's wedding dress fell in a crumpled lump on the floor. The shouts became more threatening. Isabela remained with the family until her terror woke her.

* * *

The movement and shouting were real.
'Not again,' she thought. 'Another creature?'

She shook off the dream and listened. The trampling was heavier than she'd heard the previous night. The shouts were more frantic. Was this creature even larger? The men sounded more panicked than amazed this time. She realized she was hearing not only Spanish from the protesting crew, but another language. English. It was English. She was sure.

"Give us everything you've got," a voice boomed. "Goods or death."

Frightened to her core, Isabela heard someone yanking on the hatch. She had double bolted it as she did every night, but the hatch was shaking and she feared that whoever was just above her might succeed in dislodging it.

Then Angel's calm voice reached her. The sound of his sword placed on the deck. He spoke no English, but she could imagine him gesturing so that they would understand.

"We are a small passenger ship," he said. "We have no goods. We can give you something to eat. Yesterday we caught a huge fish. With eight arms."

She heard the cook scurry to bring the remaining fish—slices he had hoped would feed the crew for three days, would now be gobbled by these pirates. If it meant saving a single life, of course it was worth it. They needed every man on board to run this ship.

There was silence for perhaps two minutes. She imagined the foreigners grabbing the fish with their fingers and shoving it down their throats. She heard empty wooden bowls ricocheting off the deck.

"We'll search every inch of this ship. If you're holding out on us, you'll know the consequences."

She heard them banging, turning over barrels, smashing crockery. Again they pounded on the hatch. "Who's down there? Open up!"

Isabela trembled behind her curtain, holding Nelita tight against her.

Apparently looking out over the exhausted scant crew members, the pirates relented. Isabela heard the booming command, "Retreat." She heard the intruders scramble down to their ship. It did not occur to her that there was only one thing on the ship that might be of value to these pirates—a human being, an impressionable young person. Someone who might adjust to their way of life, whose small size would be useful for sneaking on and off ships in the night. Someone they had already seen fighting bravely in spite of being just a boy.

Isabela waited for perhaps twenty minutes after she heard the pirates leap back onto their ship. Angel did not call to reassure her that all was well. No one did. She sensed movement on the other side of the room below deck. A cat? A rat? She lit a lamp and saw Diego sitting up in his hammock, wide awake. He had heard everything, yet he had made no effort to join his crew's battle.

Disgusted, she rapped on the hatch. When no one responded, she undid the double bolt and looked out. The crew saw her, but they kept their eyes cast down. No one greeted her. Something was wrong. Where were her boys? In a total panic, she climbed up and looked around. A slender body lay on the deck with one injured arm held up by the carpenter. Blood soaked a bandage wrapped around the wrist. Angel.

Isabela ran to him. He was conscious, but in pain.

"I think we can save the hand," the carpenter said. "He's young. He'll heal."

No one else spoke. They were fond of Angel, of course, but why were they all so downcast? Why did they avoid looking her in the eye?

Suddenly she knew. She looked around and did not see what she wanted desperately to see. She fell to her knees and grabbed Angel's good hand.

"Tell me," she pleaded. "Tell me it isn't true. Tell me my boy is safe."

"I tried to keep them from taking him, Isabela," Angel said weakly as he too began to cry softly. "We all did. They beat us back. They tried to cut off my sword arm. They put a hand over his mouth, picked him up and threw him in the boat before any of us could stop them. We were outnumbered. They were experienced fighters. We're lucky they didn't kill us all. I'm so sorry, Isabela."

Isabela clutched Angel's hand in hers and wept.

Over and over, as she held her aching stomach, as her entire body rippled and trembled with grief and disbelief, she kept repeating, "My boy. My boy. Oh, my little boy."

When she heard from behind her, "Mama! Mama!" she thought for a moment it was all a bad dream or a joke or a staged rehearsal of some kind. Pedro was there all along, wasn't he? He had just been helping the cook and was out of sight?

"Mama! Mama! Papa wouldn't let me come up on deck," Nelita said as she fell into her mother's arms.

'So, this is my family now,' Isabela thought. 'Nelita, Angel, and I. It was a miracle that no one was killed.'

Diego climbed up on deck, approached and peered down on the three of them lying, sitting in a clump, in shock, not speaking, clinging to one another.

"Son?" he asked Angel?

Angel assumed he was asking about Pedro.

"Gone, Captain. I did everything in my power to stop them. They were so quick. Pedro was on their ship and sailing away almost before I realized it. They took him, but left other pirates on El Oviedo to keep fighting us—to block us."

Diego shook his head.

"But YOU, Son, are YOU seriously injured?"

Angel told him exactly what the carpenter had told Isabela.

Diego looked out over the deck where crew members were assisting others. Mending a sprained ankle. Cleaning blood off a face wound and inspecting it. Making a sling for a broken arm.

Diego made no offer to assist. He made no apologies. He spoke no comforting words. No words of thanks either for the crew's bravery, for their efforts to save his son.

Before she realized it, Isabela's anger and despair overcame her. She peeled Nelita off her, stood up and ran straight toward her husband. With a red, distorted face and the ferociousness of ten years of pent-up rage, she struck him repeatedly on the chest. Diego stood looking down at her as the blows fell. He did not try to stop her.

She took a step away from him and screamed at him through her sobs, "Coward! You are a coward, Diego! Look at you! This is your ship. This is your crew. Pedro is your son. You heard what I heard. Yet you did nothing. You hid below. You let them carry away my boy, Diego."

She began pummeling him again, first with one fist then the other in rapid succession, then with both fists together.

Although he barely felt the blows, Diego was now embarrassed by Isabela's uncontrolled outbursts and the ugly accusations heard by his entire crew. He took her fists in his hands and held them so that she could not move. When she began howling, she remembered Leonor's desperate cries of mourning the day they met.

"I hate you, Diego. I wish they had taken you instead."

Diego dropped her hands, walked to the other side of the deck, turned his back, and looked out at the sea.

* * *

186

Isabela tried to gather her wits and concentrate. She had one boy left and she was determined not to lose him too. She was relieved to see that the sword had not punctured Angel's wrist, but there was a deep, straight cut across the fleshy part of Angel's right hand just below the thumb. She tried to think. 'What would Cook do?'

For the next week she boiled and cooled water twice a day and gently cleansed Angel's wound. After each cleansing, which at first caused Angel to wince and gasp, she broke off a stalk of Cook's healing plant and spread its thick green substance before bandaging the wound again.

She had never shown the double cross to anyone, but now kneeling over her patient, she pulled it over her head. Dangling it above his eyes she said,

"Angel, this is a very special cross—a double one, do you see? When you're better, I'll tell you the whole story of its origins and how I came to possess it. It provides powerful protection to anyone who wears it. I want you to wear it. I want you to have it from now on."

When she tried to lift Angel's head and place the chain on his chest, he shook his head vigorously.

"Absolutely not, Isabela. It is yours. YOU need the protection. YOU keep it. I will be fine."

With Angel incapacitated for a few days and Pedro gone, they were more shorthanded than ever. The crew went about its duties. Diego rallied and worked harder than he had since the voyage began. When on the third day Angel sat up and began whistling, everyone cheered. The crew helped him to his feet. The boatswain figured they were just one week away from their destination.

On the fourth day after Pedro was taken, Isabela and Nelita returned to their routine. That Diego was not in his hammock did not surprise her. He had been sleeping above like the others. After she emerged and took her place on the bench, she still didn't see him. She assumed he was in the steering cabin with the boatswain. All the men, even Angel working with one hand, were at their stations.

After an hour or two, one of the crew said, "Can somebody wake up that useless Captain of ours? We need more help here."

Isabela was puzzled because she knew he was not below deck.

"He isn't in his hammock," she called out.

"Who has seen the bastard this morning then?"

"Not me. Where the Hell is he? Three days of work and he goes into hiding again?"

Angel kept coiling a rope as best he could. He said nothing.

They searched both the entire deck and below deck. They searched the Cook's galley. They searched the steering cabin. They even searched behind Isabela's privacy curtain. Captain Diego Carlos Blandón de Vega was no longer present on El Oviedo.

Chapter Twenty-Seven
Arrival

Crunchy walnuts. Succulent grapes. Tasty beans. Nourishing millet and corn. Clams the size of her fist.

For a week now, Angel had been rowing across the bay to San Agustín with one of the Captain's textiles which he bartered for food. He sold half of the remaining textiles to pay the crew who scattered through the town on a search for food, drink, card playing, women, and work. Every day at noon and again in the evening, Angel rowed back to the ship with food and news for Isabela who wished to remain in place until Angel found suitable lodging for her and Nelita.

Isabela understood that in order to settle her reduced little family of three, be it temporary or permanent, she would have to dip into her cushion money. Nelita was too young to be sworn to secrecy. At any time in any company, she might blurt out, "Did you know my mama is rich? She keeps money in her cushions. So many coins! I saw them!"

Isabela had to tuck Nelita into one of the hammocks, wait to be certain she was asleep for her nap and then, working right beside her as silently as she could, lift the lid to her trunk and remove every layer of clothing and goods until she reached a cushion. After cutting the threads that covered the opening, she grabbed a fistful of coins, placed them in a small purse, tucked the purse low in her apron pocket, stitched the cushion back up, rearranged it on top of Reza's dress, put everything back in place, and closed the lid.

She was never sure just how much to remove from the cushions, partly because she had no idea what costs they might incur in San

189

Agustín and partly because she had shoved the coins in the cushions in such haste so many years ago she had no idea of their total worth. Once, just as she put down the lid, she turned to find her sleepy-eyed daughter looking at her curiously. Isabela was able to distract the child quickly and Nelita never asked what she was doing.

"Well, look at my girl, all awake now!" Isabela said trying to distract Nelita from anything she may have witnessed. "Let's go up on deck and see if Angel is on his way with our midday meal."

She assumed that both she and Angel would need to find work to survive. Although they had not discussed it, Angel indicated that he assumed the same. He was looking not just for lodging, but for opportunities for both of them to earn a living. He was terribly apologetic.

Isabela was feeling little enthusiasm for moving into the town. Angel and the cook had given the ship a good scrubbing and it had become a home for her and Nelita. Freed from the constant jostling and dangers of sailing, she felt anchored here in the bay. She felt no pressure to explore or adapt to a new life. Besides, Angel's descriptions of the town offered nothing enticing. She allowed herself to be lulled by the off—shore breezes—warm and gentle.

She wrote brief notes to Anneliese and to Nelleke telling them she and Nelita were safe, but that her husband and son had disappeared during the voyage. She considered herself a widow now, she wrote, and was frightened for her boy. She was trying to adjust to the idea that she would never see him again.

It had been so long since Nelita had a playmate. She had become quite independent and imaginative. Sometimes she pretended the ship was a castle. Other days, the ship was just a ship with herself serving as both Captain and crew. She might be a teacher one day, a great artist another. She arranged her dolls and books and toys and drawing materials according to that day's fantasy, weaving long conversations with her dolls and her mother as she acted out elaborate scenes.

Isabela overheard her explain to her favorite doll, "Papa has gone away again. My brother now too. Don't you worry, *Muñequita*. Papa always comes back. Pedro will be with him. Oh, the tales he'll tell. Would you like a bit of honey on your bread? A slice of orange?"

Occasionally, Isabela allowed herself to be drawn into Nelita's play. Under Nelita's direction, she became a queen giving orders to her subjects or a pilot guiding the ship into harbor or a one-person audience for a theater production, and even, reluctantly, a pirate, stomping and yelling threats. Mostly she spent her days with one of the tailor's books in her lap, reading occasionally, but gazing at an island off to her left thick with various shades of green and what appeared to be families of exotic birds.

How could Isabela explain to her five-year-old that her father and brother would never return, that they would never see them again, when she herself had not yet accepted that truth? When she was struggling with her own denial and guilt? There was nothing of Diego that she missed really. She missed only what she never had, only what might have been were Diego a totally different kind of husband and father.

But her son, her child, her boy. She had no energy for throwing herself into a new village without him. She became obsessed trying to recall every detail of his life. She relived his birth, the first time she put him to the breast, his first steps. She relived the anger that seized her when she came upon Diego throwing him carelessly up in the air and later holding him by his feet over the side of the boat. She recalled Pedro's rejection of her attempt at lessons and his recent enthusiastic learning as he helped prepare for the voyage. Clearly, he was destined for a life at sea, but as a pirate? She could not think of him in such a role.

'What would he be like as a man,' she wondered. Although his nature was the opposite of Isabela's—impetuous, rambunctious, always in motion—he resembled her in appearance. He was small for his age, had long dark lashes and a delicate mouth with the corners always turned up with a slight smile. Would he eventually look more like his father and brother? He would probably never be as tall, but would he develop their broad shoulders with the left slightly lower than the right? Would those hints of red show up in his hair and eyebrows? She did not believe he would ever have been as careless and uncaring as Diego, but it was also difficult to imagine that he would become a thoughtful, sensitive young man like Angel.

Questions haunted her. 'Will he ever know the love of a woman, have children? Do pirates even have families? How will he adapt to such a life? He always loved his mock sword fights, but could he steal, plunder, and kill? How long would he survive such violence?'

Nelita worked her mother's weeping into her scenes.

"Oh dear lovely queen, is the servant late with your breakfast today?" Or "I'm so sorry you did not enjoy today's performance. I shall rewrite the script."

* * *

After two weeks Isabela forced herself to turn in the direction of the town, to see what it looked like from this distance, to listen more carefully to Angel's descriptions. She remembered his saying it had been carved out of a wilderness of swamp and beach surrounded by dense forest filled with abundant wild game. But what was the tiny town like?

"Imagine Santos Gemelos many years ago, when it was first being settled," Angel said. "The houses are primitive and usually have only one room. Made of wood slats connected by mud. A few with tiled roofs, but most with roofs made of overlapping fronds. There don't seem to be fireplaces or chimneys. Women cook over open fires behind their cottages. A lot of the activity is outside, actually. The wells are simple and not very deep. They dig a hole for burying refuse. It's difficult to keep chickens and pigs because they attract wolves, wild boars, even bears sometimes. Most women know how to shoot a firearm. And speaking of women, there aren't many.

"This is a man's town, a military outpost, really. I've heard it referred to as a 'garrison town.' Someone called it a 'frontier town.' Apparently, few colonists come here willingly. When the King was told there's no gold in La Florida—that's what they call the larger area around San Agustín—La Florida—he wanted to abandon it. When he learned that the French and the English have permanent settlements in the New World, though, the king listened to his advisors and continued to fund this little place.

"The soldiers' pay is often late, I've learned. Their lives are difficult. They're on duty in the fort twenty-four hours, then off twenty-four hours. Most are young, illiterate peasants who have nothing in Spain to return to. They act pretty bored. Listless. They drink and play cards. They clean and re-clean their muskets.

"From what I gather so far, the town's purpose is to protect the area for those ships coming from South America on their return to Spain. Since there's no silver or gold in this area, those ships are the ones Captain Diego talked about, laden with gold that comes from south of this hemisphere. The gold is destined for the Church and the Crown, of course, and the captain was right that some of the vessels never make it. Many sunken ships lie out there, but no one knows how to reach the buried treasure they carry. The land itself must be worth something. Spaniards have battled the French for it. They've killed off many of the native people for it. The town also serves as a center for Christianizing the natives.

"Now they are what I find most fascinating here, Isabela. The natives. I can't even begin to describe them. Their dress, their knowledge . . . their legends, their tawny skin. Some of them are strikingly beautiful too. You must come see for yourself . . . and soon, because—and this makes me quite sad—they're disappearing. Thousands of years here compared to our mere one hundred years, but we've rounded them up and forced them to move into missions. Uprooted from their land and traditions, they are dying often from our diseases. It's all about converting them to the Church. They really must become like us if they want to survive. Yet that's probably too simple. I don't understand it all yet, but Big Owl—you'll meet him—has told me that the residents of the town would not survive without native labor and large corn supplies. In many ways we depend on each other.

"And there are Africans here too. Their skin is so dark it has a blue-black sheen. I try not to stare at them. Some were brought here as slaves. Others live free, having run away from other parts of the New World.

"The town used to be just helter-skelter. A hut here. A fence there. A trail or two. In the late 1500s they laid out a plan. Now you see three parallel streets and three cross streets. The fronts of the cottages open right onto the street itself, and each has a sizable space behind it to garden. As you know from the food I've brought, they've planted fruit trees and they've learned so much about new food from the natives.

"The only nice structures in the town are the governor's house—quite elaborate, really—the church at the corner of the central plaza, and, of course, the mission that houses the Franciscans."

Just hearing the word "Franciscans" made Isabela shudder. They were the fanatics who killed Cook and many others.

Noticing her alarm, Angel said, "They're not all bad, Isabela. Conversion is their main task, but they also care for people. They set up a hospital. Best to get used to seeing them when they're in town. Seventy of them, apparently. By now they've moved all the natives out of their villages, into some thirty-eight separate missions.

"But, Isabela, I think I've found a situation for you. When do you think you might be ready to move off the ship?"

Chapter Twenty-Eight
A Roof of Sorts

I sabela was touched by Angel's pursuit of a "situation" he felt was appropriate, but he was terribly apologetic that it was beneath her. This was the best he had found for now, he said.

"A widow. Doña Maria Luisa. She was married to a Spanish soldier who died from smallpox two years ago. Very nice woman. About forty, I'd say. She takes in laundry, mostly from soldiers. But she needs someone to mend the uniforms. A woman who used to help married an officer and moved into one of the somewhat better cottages.

"It's primitive, Isabela, I admit, but it's a start. You and Nelita would have your own place, but you would share the garden and well with Doña Maria Luisa. Did I mention she's a native? She loves to talk and has so many stories to tell."

The very thought of moving into a one-room cottage made with vertical planks held together with mud, palms for a roof, no fireplace, a loquacious woman as her close neighbor—it all exhausted Isabela. She understood that mourning was wearing her down. She was living in an unreal world where Pedro was still with her, where he would always be with her. People recover, don't they? But how?

She missed the tailor more than ever. She sensed he had known loss. He would be able to help her. When she thought of the Valverde family, the chess board leaped into her mind. Once again she tried to apply the lessons the game had taught her. Define options. Analyze pros and cons. Take occasional risk.

But her mind was so muddled she couldn't get beyond the first step. All right, then. Define options: stay on this ship forever OR go on land and explore this town. Were those her only choices? Neither enticing? The first probably unrealistic? People would refer to her as "that hermit lady" who lives "out there." It wouldn't be fair to Angel either. Nor to Nelita. She should be helping both of them.

What about the option of returning to Spain? The Dutch Republic, even? Pieter's sister, Anneliese, had invited her several times to live with her family in Amsterdam. What held her back? A lack of independence, perhaps, of not having her own home? Or the thought of Pieter arriving from one of his many trips abroad with a bride on his arm?

Facing another long and dangerous voyage discouraged her further. At least in San Agustín she apparently had the possibility of a home of sorts, and work. Yet still, she could not force herself into town even to explore a little.

One day Angel, who continued to bring delicious food every day and slept on the ship, mentioned a chapel he had discovered.

"Small. Very sweet. Tucked in among palm trees near the water. At first I thought it might be a sort of shrine to lost sailors. But no. When I approached I saw the chapel's name. *Nuestra Señora de la Leche y Buen Parto,* Our Lady of Milk and Happy Delivery.

"I went inside, where I saw one pregnant woman kneeling and praying on one side of the chapel and another woman weeping on the other side near the back. In that town dominated by men, someone has constructed a place where women can find solace. A statue of Mary nursing her baby looks down from a pedestal. Really, Isabela, looking at her, I felt like I was being bathed in her love as I sat there. She has the most consoling, understanding look. I've gone there twice now, although I'm careful not to disturb the women. Every day someone places fresh flowers at Mary's feet. Flowers surround the entrance to the chapel too. May I show it to you?"

Isabela found the image of Leonor's young man seated in a chapel for women quite natural, and also touching. Raised in a female-centered household, he had, since she first met him, demonstrated some of the sensibilities she associated with her own sex. Did he know intuitively that his description of the loving Mary might be the one incentive to draw her to the town? Or had he contemplated how to entice her off the ship? In any case, she felt deep gratitude that even though she had lost her own son, she had inherited Angel. As long as she was able, she vowed again that, as she had promised Leonor, she would care for him too.

That afternoon Isabela and Nelita made their first foray into the town. Angel helped them out of the rowboat, past the fort where a line-up of pelicans seemed to serve as a welcoming committee. Side by side the three of them passed through the gateway of the palisade, made of vertical tree trunks lined up tight against one another.

'What are those logs with sharp points on top of each log supposed to keep out?' Isabela wondered.

As if reading her mind, Angel said, "You'll be living in a fortified garrison, Isabela. Colonists in. Enemies and wild animals out."

Angel led them up and down the town's three streets, around the plaza, by the church.

"One hundred twenty markets, shops, and houses are crowded inside the palisade," he said.

Along the way they passed scores of soldiers in groups of three or four, women returning from the fish market, children playing with sticks. Wandering pigs, goats, and a cow or two gave the entire town a farm-like atmosphere and odor. Although made of wood like all the houses, the Governor's house was imposing. At one corner of the plaza, with its own fence, two floors, and large garden, it dominated the corner opposite the church.

Isabela saw a primitive sign pointing to a hospital. When she passed the fort's watchtower she could almost hear Pedro's feet scrambling excitedly up to the top and his voice yelling down, "Mama, Nelita. You've got to come up here. I can see everything. I even see El Oviedo from here."

Isabela found it unnerving that every man, woman, and child they passed stopped what they were doing to stare at the newcomers. During the two weeks Isabela remained isolated on the ship, rumors and gossip had apparently developed.

"There's a woman living out there?" "Yes, her son brings her food every day." "What's she hiding from?" "Got something against us?" She wondered if all those days spent in the harbor where she felt free of curious eyes, she'd actually been under scrutiny. The look-out tower, manned day and night and positioned to be able to look out over the inlet, islands, and harbor provided the perfect spot for observing her activities.

The sudden appearance of Isabela and Nelita put to rest the suggestion of one resident—"She must be too ugly to show her face among us."

Now, as she passed by and made a weak attempt to smile at the few women she saw, she heard behind her, "Why she's beautiful!" "Her little girl too." "Lost a boy to pirates, I hear." "Poor thing." "Lovely with that olive skin, those large dark eyes." "Yes, but she's delicate. You can see the sadness in those eyes."

She smelled both the leatherworks and the brewery before she passed them and heard the sharp rhythmic blows of the blacksmith. For a brief moment, it felt like she was back in Santos Gemelos.

Suddenly, Nelita let out a squeal and hid her face in her mother's skirts. "Mama," she cried in a muffled voice, "that man is naked." Nelita had just gotten her first glimpse of a native. Isabela was startled too and did not know how to react. He was coming right toward them and she was so riveted by the sight of him, she couldn't look away. He was surely the tallest man she had ever seen—perhaps four inches taller than either Diego or Angel. And the most stately. He carried himself like a king. He might be about twenty-five years old she thought, but it was hard to tell with two broad horizontal red lines painted just below the prominent cheekbones under large dark brown eyes. His hair was pulled back tight and twisted into a neat bun secured with a painted stick. A long piece of gleaming metal dangled from one ear. A blue-and-white feather from the other. Around his neck he wore a necklace made of beige-and-white shells interspersed with stones and what may have been fish bones. He carried a thick spear covered with rope.

No, he was not naked as Nelita feared, but he was nearly so. His body was shiny and the color of dark copper. Powerful chest muscles were visible on either side of a pouch secured to his shoulders leaving his arms free. An evenly cut patch of dangling leather covered his privates, but came only to the top of his thighs leaving his solid legs entirely visible. Isabela felt unnerved and struggled to maintain her composure. With Nelita's face still buried in her skirts and Nelita's arms tight around her thighs, Isabela clutched the double cross in her bosom and scuttled awkwardly by the dignified man.

Years later when she learned that the Spanish colonial government had murdered this princely man, she remembered the words that came to mind when she first saw him—"magnificent, simply magnificent."

Angel greeted the native by name in the same natural tone he had used to greet several of the soldiers. "Big Owl," Angel said as the two men acknowledged each other with a nod.

"Angel, how are you?" Big Owl responded in an authoritative, resonant voice in perfect Spanish.

"White men call his tribe 'Timucuan,'" Angel whispered after Big Owl had passed by. "Spaniards estimate their numbers once reached at least 200,000, but now there are only about 13,000. Most are wearing clothes like ours now, but Big Owl's clan tries to maintain some of the old ways."

"Are you ready to meet Doña Maria Luisa?" Angel asked.

But he had already stopped in front of one of the cottages.

"She's expecting you."

The first thing Isabela noticed about Doña Maria Luisa as she stepped into the street to greet them was that she too was exceptionally tall—especially for a woman. Imposing and erect, she was only slightly shorter than Big Owl. The beauty of her youth was still evident in the tawny hue of her skin, the high cheekbones of her elongated face, and her almond-shaped eyes that did not hesitate to look carefully over her visitors from head to toe. Apparently the pair passed whatever judgments Maria Luisa made about them.

"Hello, Señora Calderón. Señorita Nelita. My name is Maria Luisa de Aguilar," the woman said in precise, but slightly accented Spanish. "Angel"—and here she stopped to glance toward Angel before returning her intense gaze on her visitors—"Angel tells me you seek lodging. Paid work too possibly? I myself earn my bread as a laundress. Widowed all these many years. Making my own way in this town. My husband—a brave soldier if ever there was one—was killed defending that very fort." She stopped and pointed forcefully with a long, wrinkled finger toward the bay. "The Buccaneers, you know. They are merciless.

"The lowly soldiers now. They do their own washing. It's those few officers who earn a little more. They pay me to keep their uniforms clean. At least when the King sees fit to send them their wages. Life is hard here for us women, but we make do.

"Now, Angel here has made it clear to me that you are a lady. I can see that for myself."

Doña Maria Luisa again let her eyes pass quickly over Isabela's simple but well-made blouse, skirt, apron, and bonnet.

"Washing for you would, I suppose, be . . . out of the question. Unsuitable, let us say. But I understand you're a recent widow yourself, Señora. My condolences."

Without taking a breath, the laundress continued.

"Here is my thinking. The officers and sometimes the Governor's wife herself need attention to their clothing. More care than I can give. Replace a torn sleeve here and there. Repair a dropped hem. Sew on a button or two. It's routine work you understand. Not particularly demanding. I could pay you by the piece. Now I suppose you'd like to see the vacant dwelling."

Maria Luisa took a step toward the garden and looked back over her shoulder to be sure her guests were following behind her. She led them through her one-room house that contained little more than a narrow bed, a small table, one chair, and several large baskets overflowing with dirty garments.

When they stepped out of the dark cottage into the large garden, it was obvious to Isabela that this was where Doña Maria Luisa spent most of her time. Half a dozen chickens surrounded her and clucked demandingly.

"You've had your grain for the day," she said to them. "Hush now."

With one wave of her commanding arms she scattered the chickens across the courtyard. A nanny goat tied to a post also greeted her with a loud baaaa, which Maria Luisa ignored. Men's underwear, trousers, shirts, vests, and jackets were strung up on lines that stretched across the courtyard from one cottage to the other. Three or four wooden vats were lined up.

Smoke rose from smoldering charcoal beneath a grill set in an iron frame. "The *brasero* we'll share for cooking," Maria Luisa explained. Stretched out on the rack was a dead animal unfamiliar to Isabela. Greenish gray with a long snout and a tail that dangled over the rack, it looked like a large, scaly lizard.

"A baby alligator. You should see the full-grown ones. And if you ever do . . . run! They may seem to be moving slowly, but they can lunge in the blink of an eye. They'll catch a muskrat in those jaws and moments later it's gone . . . right into the belly of the beast. They're tasty, though. My nephew, my brother's son, just brought that alligator for me as a gift. Within an hour, it will be smoked enough to last several days. I'll give you a taste if you like."

Indeed the available dwelling was "vacant" as Maria Luisa had described it. "Barren" was the word that came to Isabela's mind. Other than several ant hills, a spider web, and a few dried fronds that lay scattered on the floor, this single room contained nothing. It seemed to Isabela like a shed to shelter a horse, not a home for people, not for her and her daughter. Suddenly she was exhausted.

"Thank you, Maria Luisa. I will consider your kind offer."

Turning to Angel, she said, "I would like to visit Our Lady of La Leche before returning to the ship."

Chapter Twenty-Nine
Comfort and Resolve

ur Lady of La Leche was nothing like the church in Santos Gemelos, nor as carefully constructed as the church in the corner of the plaza in San Agustín. As Angel led Isabela and Nelita through the woods on a curved path of crushed stones, she caught her first glimpse of it. A lowly chapel. Humble. Made of planks darkened by the rains. No steeple. Six small arched openings on each side. Yet someone had thought it important to provide a space dedicated to women's cares, desires, and fears. The Franciscans perhaps? Was Angel right that she should not pre-judge all of them? Or did a soldier build it? A man whose wife cried all day long lamenting that month after hopeful month, God did not give her a child.

They stepped inside the musty building where one woman kneeled as she prayed to the statue of Mary set high in a nave. Before the woman stood and brushed by them, they heard the end of her earnest prayer.

"Intercede with Him now, my loving Mother, that, in accordance with His will, I may become the mother of other children of our Heavenly Father. This I ask, O Lady of La Leche, in the Name of your Divine Son, My Lord and Redeemer. Amen."

Keeping her face partially covered with her shawl, the woman did not acknowledge them, but stopped to light a candle before leaving the chapel. Isabela took Angel and Nelita by the hand. She did not want to pray alone and Pedro was not just her son. He was their brother too. She led them down the narrow center aisle, past a few crude benches.

As they approached the statue, Isabela thought of the Mary statue that was such a strong presence in the tailor's shop. That Mary must have been an older one than this one. The tailor's Mary had either known the pain of losing a child or sensed that such a loss was in her future. Even with Angel and Nelita on either side of her, Isabela missed the tailor desperately. If he knew of her loss, he would look at her with his wise eyes. He would console her with words of wisdom. Perhaps he would quote Aristotle on the meaning of death. He might share his own experience with personal loss. There was so much she did not know about him . . . and where was he now? Were he and Reza and their children even alive?

The little group of three gazed upward at Mary who calmly looked down on the chubby babe nursing at her breast. When they knelt, Isabela began haltingly, to pray out loud.

"Lovely Lady of La Leche," she murmured, "most loving mother of the child Jesus, and our mother, the mother of us all, please listen to my humble prayer. Your motherly heart knows my every wish, my every need. You too lost a son. To you only, His innocent Virgin Mother, has your Divine Son given to understand the sentiments which fill my soul. Yours was the sacred privilege of being the Mother of the Savior.

"My child was also taken from me. Cruelly. Suddenly. I beseech you to intercede on behalf of my child, Pedro de Vega. Bless my child. Be with him wherever he is. Watch over him. Keep him safe that we may one day be reunited. Comfort us, his mother, his only brother, his only sister as we face a future without him. This I ask, O Lady of La Leche . . ."

Isabela reached to her left and her right to take Nelita's and Angel's hands in hers. They added their voices to her familiar closing words.

After they had remained in that position for a full minute, Nelita spoke up,

"And my papa too, Mother Mary. Bless him too."

When Angel began a prayer, Isabela felt a stab of guilt. So absorbed had she been in her own grief, she had not given a thought to Angel's. Awkwardly, slowly, and simply, Angel said,

"Blessed Mother. I have lost MY mother—a lovely, dedicated mother like yourself."

His words shook Isabela. Was he referring to Leonor's illness and his voyage away from her or did he have information he had not shared with her?

Angel continued.

"Having learned of her death only recently, I am full of guilt. I abandoned her in her moment of greatest need."

A sob escaped from the young man. Isabela held his hand tighter.

"Please forgive me. If ever there was a woman who deserved to join you and your son in Heaven, it was my mother, Leonor Validado. Yet there are those who would see her burn in Hell along with her lost child. I beseech you, Mary, Blessed Mother, to intercede on her behalf, to secure her a place in Heaven, in Heaven with you for eternity."

Angel could not say more.

"Amen," Isabela murmured for him.

How selfish she had been focused on her own suffering, oblivious to all this young man had been feeling, to all he had endured including a serious painful injury trying to save her son. She squeezed his hand, dropped it gently and placed an arm around his shoulders as he hung his head and attempted to stifle a sob.

After each of them lit a candle and stepped outside the chapel, Isabela asked gently,

"You've received news from Santos Gemelos?"

"Yes," Angel, said, regaining some composure, "just yesterday. I didn't want to tell you yet. I didn't want to upset you. You probably saw the ship that arrived. A letter. From my sister, Catalina. My mother died soon after we sailed. Catalina beseeched me, she begged me to return."

Again, guilt pulled at Isabela. Were Angel to return to Spain, she felt she might not be able to cope with life in this sodden, desolate outpost. Yet she could not face another journey either. And other questions nagged at her. What would she do there? Where would she live? COULD she live in a country that threatened and killed innocent, good people? Yet she had no right to detain Angel.

* * *

One week later, Isabela and Nelita moved off the ship to the cottage that, except in size, barely resembled the abandoned hut Maria Luisa had offered her. Angel had replaced the old roof fronds with fresh ones and interwoven them tightly the way Big Owl showed him. Several heavy rains that week proved that for now, the new roof would keep the droplets out.

From the ship, Angel had brought cooking utensils and water storage barrels. Until they could locate beds—and afford to purchase them—Isabela and Nelita would continue to sleep in hammocks. At least they each had their own now. The floor was swept and the dirt packed down firmly. Isabela had a work table, shelves, hooks, lamps, two chairs and, best of all, her trunk. If she wanted anything else, something would have to be removed. They could barely turn around in this new home and it would soon also become her place of business.

Angel promised to construct a barrier in the garden—around a space he had negotiated with Maria Luisa—a space for Isabela to grow her own vegetables if she wished, although she had never gardened on her own. She could plant an orange tree for shade. Nelita could play outdoors where Isabela could see her at all times.

Her walk through town convinced Isabela that even if she were to sell her petticoat diamond—and who here would have enough money to buy it was a big question—there was probably no other affordable property superior to this one. Constructing something new might be possible, but first she must adjust to current circumstances. She and Nelita had a home of sorts. Angel spent his days in the town, but slept on the ship.

Maria Luisa approached her immediately. After a brief greeting— "Well, it's not the governor's palace, but welcome anyway"—she left a pile of clothes for Isabela.

Isabela sat down and immediately set about reducing the pile of mending. 'How bizarre,' she thought, as she sat with needle and thread reattaching a sleeve to a shirt, 'I've become a tailor. Señor Valverde was a serious man, but he would probably find the situation momentarily amusing.'

That very night, she decided to write him. It was unlikely she would ever see him again, but she could sort of pretend they were still corresponding like they used to. Finding that the awe and intimidation she had always felt in his presence was as strong as if he were right in front of her, she dipped pen in ink and wrote:

11 November 1651
Dear Señor Valverde,

I wonder how you would react if you could see me at this moment. Would you be alarmed? Sad for me? Amused?

Here I sit in a space smaller than your Santos Gemelos work area. Yet this space serves as my entire home—mine and Nelita's.

But I realize you do not even know where I am. I am in a part of New Spain. After selling off our property, my foolish husband set sail with his family for San Agustín in search of sunken gold. Then in the middle of the voyage he disappeared off that very ship. Mysteriously. Just gone. I consider myself a widow now. But the hardest thing to tell you is that I also lost my son on that trip. My boy, Pedro, was taken by pirates.

I thank my blessings that Nelita and I are safe and that, although we are only twelve years apart in age, Leonor's son, Angel, has become like my own son.

I think of you and your family often. Once when my children were little, I was playing with them on the beach. Pedro went off to explore. Before I could call him back, he yelled for me and insisted I come find him. He was hiding in a rowboat—abandoned apparently and tucked into a barely visible opening under the cliff. My fervent prayer is that you somehow escaped in that rowboat—to where I cannot imagine. To a waiting ship? To another part of New Spain? To Europe? To the Far East?

I will probably never know, but I will never forget you either. Right now for the first time in months, I am going to read—from one of your books, of course. I could not read on the journey because of the constant jostling. Since Pedro's abduction, I have not been able to concentrate enough on the words on the page.

I am opening your copy of Don Quixote to any random page—page 384—and I read: "We firmly believe that she is forced upon this journey; and gather from her dress, that she is a nun, or which is more probable, going to take the veil and finding herself very little inclined to that way of life, is melancholy at the prospect."

It occurs to me that with your insight, you would see some connection between this passage and my current circumstances. Is there meaning in the fact that out of a book filled with thousands of words, my eyes fall tonight on this particular passage?

I forgot to tell you how I am making a living, how my reading just now is a respite, a much-needed pause from my work—sewing and mending. I hope wherever you are that you have found work more worthy of your intelligence and knowledge, something more stimulating than the labor of needle passing through thread, although I have to say I do find the final result satisfying.

I pray for you, Reza, Bernardo, and little Briana daily. That you are safe. That you are alive. That wherever you are, Briana is free to sing from her heart whenever and wherever she wishes in any language that comes to her.

Your friend,
Isabela Calderón

Chapter Thirty
Offer

After a month, Isabela settled into a routine. She and Nelita awoke shortly after dawn and lowered the hammocks which at night stretched the entire length of the small shelter. They tucked the hammocks into a corner so that the space was opened up, ready for meal preparation and for Isabela's growing body of work. The arrangement with Maria Luisa meant that Isabela was a servant of sorts. Isabela performed the tasks that Maria Luisa assigned. Maria Luisa collected payments and paid Isabela half of whatever she earned. That half also helped pay for the rental of the shed which provided Isabela and Nelita their only protection from the burning sun and torrential rains.

Customers were supposed to deal directly with Maria Luisa but, because the heat was often stifling, Isabela left her street-side door open in search of fresh air. Although there was no sign, more and more customers were coming directly to Isabela's door. Isabela suspected that the curiosity that had followed her all her life contributed to the growth in the sudden need for her sewing services.

She overheard two customers talking as they left her shop.

"I see what you mean. It's not just her beauty, is it? It's what I'd refer to as her aura."

"Good breeding one might say. A grace. The way she approaches each customer so politely."

"Not like the rough pioneering women we're used to around here, is she?"

At first she directed customers to Maria Luisa who would then pass the garments to Isabela. But this was awkward, especially since she easily fell into conversation with her customers and they did not want to take the time to go around to the front of Maria Luisa's place, knowing that the work would be completed by Isabela herself anyway. Isabela began taking payment directly and then gave half to Maria Luisa. Although this was the reverse of what Maria Luisa had planned and at first Maria Luisa resented the loss of control, she did trust Isabela and she appreciated the increase in income that Isabela was generating.

For the midday meal and often the smaller evening one too, Maria Luisa and Isabela cooked together over the coals on the raised iron *bracero* in the garden, where they also shared a privy and a covered hole in the ground for refuse. Several times a week Angel joined them and occasionally Big Owl too. Big Owl, it turned out, was the very nephew who had given Maria Luisa the alligator. He never arrived empty handed. Deer already skinned, chopped and ready to roast on the open fire. Snake. Fish. Clams. Lobster. Goose. Duck. And corn. Always corn. And always lots of talk. Big Owl was the son of Maria Luisa's brother and that brother was an Indian chief. The gift of dramatic storytelling seemed to be a family trait and they especially enjoyed telling the newcomers about their ancestry.

"About two hundred houses to a village, wouldn't you say, Auntie?"

"Yes, that's right. Covered with mud. That kept the dwellings cool in summer. Warm in winter. We knew how to keep ourselves comfortable. That's why our grandfathers wore their hair tied up on top of their heads too, you know—with bands of river reeds. It kept their necks cool."

"Was that the real reason? I always thought they favored that style as a way to dare other tribes to try and scalp them. You dress like a white person now, Auntie, but what about your grandmother. Wasn't she a chief?"

"Yes, your great grandmother. After she stared down a wolf one night when she was two, they named her "No Fear." Women became *caciques* when there were no sons. The inheritance was through the mother's line. The women owned the family hut. I never knew No Fear, but my mother showed me some of No Fear's clothing she had saved. A skirt made of moss. Necklaces of shell and pearl. Bracelets of fish teeth. A band she wore around her hips made of silver-colored balls. Even brass ornaments around her ankles. My mother let me wear them sometimes.

As a little girl, I was enchanted by the tinkling sound they made. It was like wearing bells."

"The chief has always been the only one who was permitted to be tattooed, right?"

"At least in our tribe that is true. Describe for our newcomers the tattoo your father wears, Big Owl. Did you know, Isabela, that Big Owl is the first son of the current chief? He will one day be chief himself."

"I've grown up looking at that tattoo and knowing that I too will have one when I become a *cacique*. My father let me trace the patterns when I was small—with my finger or a stick. The tattoo was made with sharp thorns. It's hard to describe, but I'll try. It runs from his right thigh down to his ankle. It's an interlocking set of complicated designs with sharp angles and an occasional circle or eye. The mix of red, black, yellow, and blue is stunning."

Nelita had fallen asleep in Angel's arms. Isabela ventured a question.

"How did you get your name, Big Owl?"

"Ever since I was small, I had trouble sleeping at night. I wore my mother out because I would wander out of the house through the village. She was afraid to fall asleep. The village was surrounded by a high palisade, but still there were a lot of ways a small child might hurt himself. I noticed that of all the birds in the woods, the owls were the ones, who, like me, prowled at night. I often saw them with their big open eyes and those amazing necks that can turn all the way around. They're really magnificent.

"I learned to imitate their cries exactly. It's a complicated language." Big Owl broke into a series of calls, trills, barks, and hoots that woke up Nelita and left the others amazed.

"They're very generous I noticed—at least with their own brothers and sisters. They share food. The largest owl of all trusted me and began landing on my shoulder. We'd walk around in the dark like that. I named him '*Silencio*' because he would land on my shoulder with no warning. His wings made no sound when he flew. When my mother spotted me with that owl, she named me 'Big Owl.' That big daddy owl and I were friends for years until an enormous hawk carried him away."

* * *

Since settling into the cottage, Isabela had returned to the pattern set early in her adult life. She devoted an hour or two each evening to her reading and writing. Nearly every night she wrote a note to the tailor.

Dear Señor Valverde,

I've just found the most charming poem in one of the books you left behind for me. "Cassandra's Song of Celibacy." Are you familiar with it? It's written by a Renaissance poet, Gil Vicente, who wrote plays as well as poetry in both Spanish and Portuguese. Although I'm no maid, the words mirror my feelings. I cannot imagine marrying again. This young woman resists the efforts of everyone around her. The last stanza reads:

The man has not been born, I ween,
Who as my husband shall be seen;
And since what frequent tricks have been
Undoubtedly, I know,
In vain they say, Go, Marry! Go!'
For I'll no husband! Not! No!

Even as Isabela wrote the words—both hers and the resistant maid's—she realized that perhaps she was not being fully honest. Was there any man she could ever be happy with really? Did he exist? Or was she too defiled by Diego to be worthy of such a man? Although it seemed somewhat shameful given his devotion to his family, and foolish too, she found herself imagining what it would be like to be the wife of her "correspondent." What might she write him if he were her husband and they were separated for a time? She dipped her feather quill into ink and allowed her thoughts to wander. After all, no one but she would ever see these words.

"*Dear . . . .*" But she got only that far before her pen stopped. She did not know the tailor's first name. His children called him "Papa," of course. Reza was a woman of few words and she never used his first name. Everyone else, including Isabela herself, referred to him as Señor Valverde or simply "the tailor." All right, in her imaginary world, she would simply use an affectionate term. She began again.

My love,

I pray that you will return to me safely and soon.

What is it about you that I miss so? Your eyes mostly, I think. Wise, like Big Owl's night-time companion. And the mind behind those eyes. With more thoughts, knowledge, and opinions than you could share with me in a lifetime. Sometimes I wish I could leap into your mind and devour it all at once. Of course, then I would miss the thrill of discovering daily the breadth of your interests, the constant surprise when you spout from memory, for example, a passage from a theater production that perfectly addresses the very issue we've been discussing. Or when you pick up a piece of Briana's charcoal and draw a diagram that serves to analyze, dissect, and clarify a complex issue.

Yes, that is what I miss, but it's not all that I miss.

Isabela stopped. What she wanted to write was highly inappropriate . . . but who would ever know?

I miss the way your eyes adjust in the evenings. Yes, I don't know if you realize. When you remove your eyeglasses, there are a few moments when your eyes look somewhat startled. Then they relax. You seem to be seeing your surroundings in a different way. You seem to see ME in a different way. I have a confession to make. The sight of your eyepiece on the bedside table excites me. It's a signal. I'll soon have you all to myself. No more tedious sewing and mending. No giving your attention to customers or to children's chatter, questions and needs. Just me. Beside you. In your arms. You always seem reluctant to blow out the candle. I've never asked you why. I like to think it's because seeing me stretched out, under the quilt, waiting for you—that image pleases you. I must ask you when you return. In those moments, what exactly do you see? I'm certain you'll use some poetic language that will make me feel beautiful.

Oh, there's something else I want to tell you, my darling. I've hung up the wedding dress you entrusted to me. It made no sense to keep it in my trunk. Angel helped me tack it up so that it spreads out nearly covering an entire wall of my little cottage—the way you displayed it in your shop— like a work of art. Its delicate beauty and the memories it conjures up simultaneously cheer me and fill me with longing. Tomorrow I'll ask Angel to build a shelf above the gown to protect it from falling debris. Every evening I brush it free of threatening insects. I must say, it does attract a lot of attention. Women, men, and children stop by to admire it.

    Your loving Isabela

* * *

    Midmorning, Isabela stood up from her work table, stretched, and walked the four steps to her front door. She was afraid that by bending over her mending for hours every day, she would develop the tailor's rounded back. Every time she forced herself into an upright position, she thought of those shoulders and how she longed to massage away the stiffness he must have felt. Did Reza do that for him? Was she still doing it?

    In the distance she spotted Angel running toward her waving something over his head.

    "Isabela," he said breathlessly when he reached her, "a letter for you. From Amsterdam."

Chapter Thirty-One
Choices

Winter 1651
Dearest Isabela,

I am 17 so you are 27.

Here is my insect question: Which insect is large enough to kill vertebrates? A vertebrate is an animal with a backbone, by the way. So you reason that it must be a powerful insect.

I worried so about you taking another long voyage on a ship. I was relieved when your quick note arrived telling me you were safe. Anneliese and I often share your letters. Your note to her contained the same tragic news. Our hearts are filled with sorrow for you, Isabela. We both long to embrace you and hold you. Losing both a husband and a son and then arriving in a new town in a new land. That must be so difficult.

We are grateful to Angel for looking after you and to Nelita who I'm sure brings joy and amusement into your life. As you say, your family now consists of the three of you. You are not alone. It makes me want to get on a ship myself, find you, and bring you back to my country forever. But Mama would never let me and I have no money of my own. Please write again and tell us how you are doing there. You know you are always welcome to come live with us in Amsterdam. Please consider that option.

At least our two countries are no longer at war. 80 years! I cannot fathom such destructiveness and foolishness. So many deaths.

Willem has designed insect trays for my collection. They even have a glass tray that slides over the display to keep the insects from deteriorating.

He also gave me a lovely silver-tipped quill and high-quality ink, so I can clearly identify each insect. He studies at Leiden now, but returns often. Mama watches me carefully now that I am fully grown and does not like for me to go out of the house without her or Anna, our old housekeeper. She knows I have a wandering nature—probably because I'm really half Gypsy and lived going place to place until I was four.

I did sort of "escape," though, one day last week. I just went to the milliner to have a new hat made—at least that was my excuse. A man followed me home. For the third night, he's sitting outside my window under the Linden tree playing a lute. I just peeked out. He's still there. The past two nights I've fallen asleep to the music and singing. In the morning he's gone. I'm afraid Mama and Papa are searching for suitable suitors for me. They're whispering more than usual and urging me to pay more attention to the way I dress. I haven't told them about the performer. Their room is on the back of the house, so they don't hear him. I think they would find his presence alarming.

Pieter is off again on one of his long trips. We don't know exactly where this time. Perhaps he doesn't either. Why are men allowed to wander and women must remain so confined?

I want to get this note off to you quickly, so I'll just answer the question and say good-bye. Answer: A diving beetle. It goes underwater. It can even catch a salamander.

Your adoring sister, Nelleke

When Angel said those words "Isabela. A Letter. From Amsterdam," Isabela was foolish enough to think for a moment that the tailor had found his way to that city, had learned where she was, that the letter was from him. 'I am being ridiculous,' she thought, ashamed that when she saw the letter was from Nelleke, she felt a twinge of disappointment. The energy and enthusiasm in Nelleke's letters were beginning to make her feel old and stodgy. Plus, was she jealous of Nelleke in another way? Nelleke certainly was getting lots of attention from that cousin of hers. And from other men too . . . like the stranger who serenaded her. 'Whereas I,' she thought, 'must resort to secretly writing letters to a man who may not be living and who, if he is alive, is a committed husband wed to someone else.'

Angel waited until Isabela had finished Nelleke's letter before settling down for a chat and a drink of coconut milk.

"Isabela, there's something I want to discuss with you. About the ship. About El Oviedo. I searched through some papers and found the ownership documents with the official seal. The ship belonged to Diego, of course, and naturally he had named Pedro as his heir. Where does that leave us? You and me? I suppose since . . ." Angel hesitated, not wanting to upset Isabela, but she knew what he was going to say and said it for him.

"Since Pedro's whereabouts are unknown and, in fact, we're unlikely to ever find out where he is . . . It's all right, Angel. I made a promise to your mother that I would look after you. Actually it's you who have cared for me in so many ways. What are your thoughts? About the ship? It's just sitting out there."

Angel shared his idea hesitantly and quietly, trying in his thoughtful way not to upset Isabela. She had stated the situation correctly. It was doubtful that Pedro would ever claim the ship.

"As you know, I've found paid work here on several vessels—doing repairs, helping with purchases, even suggesting new design elements. Apparently there are plans afoot to replace the current fort. This would be the ninth fort the Spanish have built and they want this one to last. Like this one, the other forts kept rotting. Until a reliable source of stone is found near here, we're stuck with structures made of wood.

I've seen the plans. It will be square-shaped with four square bastions. They'll need a lot of skilled manpower. I can make a living this way, but I don't want to do carpentry work all my life. Although Diego did update the ship before we sailed here, it is still old and it has just completed a long journey. Were we to sail it again, we would have to make further investments. I've decided that I want to stay in New Spain. I have the impression you do not want to return to the old country either."

"That's the way I'm feeling now, yes."

"One option is to sell the ship, of course. But I have another idea. This entire area—and I'm referring to the whole region they're calling La Florida plus other Spanish holdings like Cuba. More and more people will come here I believe. Big Owl tells me there is a vast network of rivers north, west, and south of here. He's willing to introduce me to all the waterways and estuaries, to a vast number of small and large islands.

"If we don't do something to save it, El Oviedo may be eaten up by sea worms. The shipwright and blacksmith suggest covering the bottom of the boat with iron to discourage those pests. What's more, Isabela, unlike a heavy galleon, our caravel can sail in water that's only four feet deep. I'm thinking we should set up a business to navigate both the rivers and the islands as well as the shore. Commerce is only going to grow. We could remodel El Oviedo to serve as a passenger ship too.

"The question of who owns El Oviedo remains, though. I believe you, as Diego's wife, are the rightful heir, that is if women are allowed to own property here. In any case, if I did the remodeling, we could go into business together, you and I, and split the profits. Of course, you may prefer to just sell the ship outright and take the money. I understand that."

The idea of a source of income beyond the meager amount her sewing brought in was certainly appealing. So far Isabela had dipped into her cushion money only once since she arrived. If she ever needed to depend on her hidden currency, it might disappear quickly. Then where would she be? The town residents mostly bartered to meet their needs, but what did she have that might be useful to someone else?

"May I take a few days to think about your idea, Angel? Before you leave, I wanted your help with something."

Before Isabela could explain what she needed, they both moved toward the open door to see what was causing some commotion in the street. The streets were narrow. They alternated between a layer of mud and a cover of dust, depending on the weather and the temperature. Everyone just trudged through. Yet here was someone arriving on horseback. No. Two horses. A woman and a young girl. Both well dressed even at this early hour in layers of lacy tulle. Jewels around their necks, ribbons fluttering from their broad-brimmed felt hats. Each horse was led by a man. A third man held a parasol over the woman's head. Apparently the women did not wish to dirty their dainty shoes or darken their ivory skin. Only one household in San Agustín might house such women . . . and they had just arrived at her door.

"Oh, look, Elizabeth," the woman said from the doorway before she had even greeted Isabela or Angel. "There's the gown. It's true what they've been saying. It is delectable."

The elegant woman clapped her hands together several times as if applauding a performance and stepped inside Isabela's cabin. She made a move to touch the dress, but stopped herself.

"I'm sorry," she said looking at Isabela and Angel after quickly surveying the humble cottage. "I should introduce myself. I am Estefania Mendoza D'Avila, wife of Nicolás Ponce de León, Governor of La Florida. May I introduce my daughter, Elizabeth."

Isabela curtsied slightly and said, "Welcome to my humble shop, Señora Mendoza. Señorita Elizabeth. My name is Isabela Calderón. This is my son, Angel de Vega. And my daughter, Nelita. We have recently arrived from Santos Gemelos, Spain."

"Yes, so I've heard, Señora Calderón. I am so sorry for the losses you endured on the voyage. Although I miss my family and Madrid terribly, I do dread the return trip."

"I see you want to explore the gown, Señora. Please do come closer. It's not easy to see it with so little light."

"Oh, but its reputation precedes it. I see that no one who has spoken of it has exaggerated in the least. The layers. The way the sleeves bellow and then narrow. The bodice and skirt contrast and connect with each other at the same time. And these colors? Tell me, what is this fabric? Did YOU make this splendid garment yourself, Señora Calderón?"

"I believe the fabric is mostly silk, although the skirt appears to be a blend of silk and light wool. I can take no credit for the dress, Señora Mendoza. The tailor in my native town made it as a wedding dress for his bride."

"A talented man, your tailor, I must say. My daughter will marry soon. I would like to commission this tailor to design dresses for her, my younger daughter, Fania, and for myself."

"I'm afraid I don't know the tailor's whereabouts, Señora."

As she explained, Isabela felt her throat tighten. She became anxious that her voice might reveal the personal loss she felt. The Governor's wife was focused on the gown and did not seem to notice. Isabela continued.

"He was forced to flee our village. I only pray that he and his family are safe."

"Oh, how truly unfortunate! A talented dressmaker and they drive him away! The times we live in! My husband has imported some intriguing fabric from China, Señora Calderón. I should like to show it to you. Can you come for tea the day after tomorrow?"

"I would be most pleased to accept your invitation, Señora."

"Oh and I see you have several books. Perhaps you've noticed how rare it is to find books in this town. Is that French I see? Do you read French?"

"Yes and I speak it some."

"And other languages as well?"

"Some English. Some Dutch."

"Oh my, I can see we have much to discuss. You'll visit us then in the Governor's house? Thursday afternoon this week?"

"I shall look forward to it, Señora."

Isabela had two days to ready suitable outfits for herself and Nelita.

* * *

The following Thursday a servant greeted them and led them to a parlor set with fine china, matching teapot, and a serving dish covered with grapes, pomegranates, and orange slices.

When the Governor's wife and daughter entered the room where Isabela and Nelita were waiting, they beheld a mother and daughter whose shiny, clean and brushed locks, simple but fresh blouses, and polished boots charmed them immediately.

"Do tell me about yourself, Señora Calderón. And may I call you Doña Isabela? I find that many of the formalities I was raised to honor back in Madrid seem, well, silly, here in this frontier outpost. Please call me Estefania. I can't tell you how delighted I am to have met you. I could see at once that you are a woman of good breeding, an educated woman. I am weary of trying to make conversation with the officers my husband insists I invite to share our meals. Their topics range from musket firings to complaints about Spain's neglect, to . . . well too little that is of interest to me. Do you take honey in your tea?

"Sometimes I wonder how I ever ended up here. I must admit I was fascinated when I first met Nicolás. Oh the stories he told! Born in Colombia. Growing up in Peru and Venezuela. Of course, there is some prestige attached to being the wife of a Governor, but I never could have imagined the isolation . . . and well, the constant fear of attack. You know, it might be pirates like that beastly Englishman, Sir Francis Drake, who burned the town to the ground in the past century. It might be the French. Were it not for the hurricane of 1565 that destroyed all five of their ships, this territory would belong to THEM. Then there are the natives, of course. Yes, we've subdued them. Made believers out of them. But the truce feels uneasy to me. They seem so foreign. How do we really know what they're thinking and planning? But do tell me what brought YOU here, Isabela."

In many ways it was delightful for Isabela to be able to tell bits of her life story to this woman, who although certainly interested, was so starved for company and talk that she interrupted continuously. She doubted that Doña Estefania would be a real confidante like Leonor, but sitting in the pleasant surroundings with a woman of her station was a welcome change.

"Now let me show you what my husband found for me," Estefania finally said as she reached for a bolt of cloth on the top shelf of a delicately carved, oak wardrobe.

"Of course, Spain too produces excellent textiles, but have you ever seen anything like this?"

As Isabela ran her fingers across the delicate silk cloth, Estefania continued,

"Look at this deep blue. The red. And the designs. The bridges. The elaborate fans. The delicacy of the women. All on a piece of cloth. How do they do it?"

Hostess and guest began to imagine a design suitable for the wife of a high official and mother of the bride.

"Could you sew such a dress yourself, Isabela?"

Isabela had remodeled dresses, but she had never made one from the beginning, yet how could she refuse the Governor's wife?

"My aunts did all the dressmaking in our family, Doña Estefania, but I will attempt it."

The Governor's wife then shocked Isabela with an additional proposal.

"Making a gown for me, others for my daughters . . . that will leave you little time for your business, Doña Isabela. I would like to see you freed of that tedious work you've been doing. As well as free of all household responsibilities, I might add. Why not move in with me, into the Governor's house? You and your daughter? Your son is creating a life for himself in the region. He would be welcome to visit any time. Let me take you on a tour of the grounds. You'll love the oversized well. Our servants use a large amount of water to make wine. The Governor entertains frequently. Do you ride? We have our own stable, of course, and two gardens—the flower garden and the kitchen garden outside the servants' quarters. We imported the gravel for the veranda. There's no suitable material for that purpose around here."

By the time Isabela and Nelita said good-bye to their new friends, Isabela had taken Doña Estefania's measurements and cut out paper patterns for the gown's bodice, sleeves, skirt, and ruffles. Although they held each pattern against the cloth, neither woman yet had the courage to cut into the elaborate fabric.

During the afternoon's long visit, Elizabeth and her younger sister, Fania, entertained Nelita. On the patio they jumped rope. In the kitchen they tasted cook's almond delicacies sprinkled with chopped dates. The sisters stood Nelita in front of a long mirror to show her how lovely she looked draped in their shawls, adorned with their necklaces and bracelets. All three laughed when their jeweled rings fell off Nelita's small fingers and landed on the carpet.

Using the Tarot set her father imported from Italy, Elizabeth delighted the child by telling stories about each elaborate card. When she overheard her mother's invitation to move to the Governor's house, Elizabeth told Nelita,

"The Tarot cards tell your future, you know. Close your eyes and I'll describe what this card predicts for you. Ready? I'm looking at a painting of a tree dripping with ripe, juicy golden pears. I see you pluck a pear from the tree and bite into it. Juice runs down your chin. Wait. Don't open your eyes yet. Suddenly, you find yourself in a room larger than the whole house you live in now. The room is on the second floor with two windows. Breezes ruffle the pale-yellow curtains. You're wearing a ruffled pink-and-purple dress with rows of lace from waist to hem. You dance until you fall into the bed you share with your doll. No more hammock."

Chapter Thirty-Two
Suspicion and Confession

Isabela and Angel stood in front of the notary while he examined both the ship's documents and their own identity papers.

"Ship name: 'El Oviedo,'" read the notary.

"Year constructed: 1597. Home port: Santos Gemelos, Spain. Permission to drop anchor: San Agustín, 3 August 1651. Owner: Diego Carlos Blandón de Vega. Disappeared 18 July 1651. Neither seen nor heard from since that date. Presumed deceased. Heir: Pedro de Vega. Kidnapped on 14 July 1651. Neither seen nor heard from since that date.

"Let's begin with the events of July 14," the notary continued.

Isabela described what she knew.

"After an arduous voyage from our home port, a few weeks before reaching San Agustín, my nine-year-old son was captured by pirates."

"Did you witness the kidnapping, Señora Calderón?"

"No. I heard it, though. From below deck huddled with my young daughter."

"What did you hear?"

"Stomping. Fighting. Shouting. Then silence. I was terrified. When I again heard movement above me, I climbed up onto the deck to find my son gone and Angel, here, seriously wounded. He had fought to save his brother."

"And your husband?"

"I'm sure, Sir, that you know how dark it can be below deck. Only after the sounds of struggle above, did I realize that my husband was below deck too. He had made no move to join the fight above our heads.

221

It was four days later when my husband disappeared. The night sentry saw nothing out of the ordinary. No approaching ships or boats. But he did hear what sounded like a splash. My husband has not been heard from since. I suspect that he was despondent over his inability to save our son."

"You're suggesting that he may have deliberately thrown himself from the ship?"

"I believe that's a possibility. He may also have been ill."

"Ill? What was the supposed illness?"

"*Mal francés*, I'm afraid. Again I have no proof other than his symptoms of lethargy and weakness."

Angel looked at Isabela with surprise.

"The point is, Sir, that both my husband and his heir were lost to me in the middle of the vast sea. I have spent months trying to reconcile the fact that I will never see either of them again. Meanwhile, my husband's first-born son, Angel de Vega, has proven to be a very capable and knowledgeable sailor. He has also been a great comfort to me in dozens of ways. I wish to grant him half ownership of El Oviedo that he might secure his future and make a decent living from it."

"I must ponder what you have told me. The disappearance of both the owner and his proper heir within two days time shortly before the ship reached its destination—that sounds suspect to me. I would like to interview other members of the crew. I will also consult with the magistrate. I will notify you when I've reached a decision. I will begin my interviews with the sailor who was on sentry duty that night. What is his name? Is he still in port here?"

"There were always a minimum of two sentries, Sir." Angel answered. "I was one of them that night. We had a small crew. The other sentry that night was the ship's cook. Please feel free to interview me now if you wish."

"Yes, I do so wish, young man. Let's begin this discussion once again." The notary dipped his pen in ink.

"Your full name, please."

"Angel Carlos Validado de Vega."

"Father's name."

"Diego Carlos Blandón de Vega."

"Father's date of birth."

Angel looked at Isabela for that information.

"4 January 1617," she said.

"Mother's name."

"Leonor Validado."

"Mother's date of birth."

"6 March 1611."

"Your profession."

"Sailor and carpenter, Sir."

"Relationship to Isabela Calderón."

"Doña Isabela is the legitimate wife of my father. Since the death of my mother, Leonor, Doña Isabela has been like a mother to me."

"Answer the questions as posed, Señor de Vega."

"Yes, Sir."

"Señora Calderón, I'd like to ask you to step outside. I wish to interview the young man alone."

"Please remember, Sir, that Angel was wounded in his efforts to save my son."

"Save your son? Save himself? Or save the ship for himself? That is what I must determine, Señora. What exactly happened on that ship to cause both the owner and his legitimate heir to disappear? That is what I need to know. The door is to your left."

* * *

Isabela stood in the street outside the notary's office fuming with outrage. How dare that man accuse her dear Angel of plotting, of stealing, of . . . murder? 'Isn't this still another example of the paranoia the Church and Crown continuously display?' she asked herself. 'Attacking the innocent. Setting neighbors, friends, and even family members against each other?'

The longer she stood there, the more shaken she became. She worried that the notary might call the constable to arrest Angel right there, this very night. What's more, although she wanted fiercely to believe in Angel's innocence, she feared the notary might actually have cause to do so.

Finally the door opened. Angel, looking grim, took her arm and gently led her away.

"The notary wants to continue his investigation. For now I'm free. Let's try to talk in the chapel," he said. "I have a confession to make."

Silently they made their way through the streets toward the harbor and across the grassy knoll that led to Our Lady of La Leche. The heavy door creaked as they opened it. No women kneeled in prayer. As they entered, the light from several candles swayed and bowed before returning to a restful, watchful state in their metal holders. Angel lit several more candles and guided Isabela to one of the benches. They sat side by side for several minutes before he explained.

"I can barely remember a time when I did not despise my father."

At first Isabela felt shocked hearing that strong, ugly word, especially when applied to a parent, but she had to admit that "despise" might well describe her feelings for Diego as well.

"I've struggled all my life to understand why my mother loved him, how she could forgive him again and again. Although in many ways she was an intelligent and capable woman, she remained a frightened, abandoned girl whose father arranged for her a hasty, poor match to an older man. A man who already had a wife. That man did take care of her, however. He gave her anything she wanted . . . except a child.

"My father was the opposite of that first "husband" if you will. Youthful, handsome, reckless, and enormously uncaring. Once I was born, perhaps she felt it was her destiny to be no one's legal wife. She always knew that Diego intended to honor the two Captains' agreement and marry you some day. But to grow up watching my mother pamper him, always available to him during his sporadic visits. From the time I was a small boy, I rejected him. I tried to be the responsible man of the house."

"I know, Angel. Beginning with my first visit with your mother, I saw how much you did daily, hourly to care for her and your sisters, how tenderly you comforted them all when your baby brother died."

"Thank you, Isabela. But imagine what it was like for me. This gruff, demanding man shows up two or three times a year. He becomes the center of my mother's world for a few days. I felt utterly unappreciated by both my parents at those times. I tried to hide my growing resentment from my mother, but she must have been aware of it. At least I hope so. My God, he even stole from her.

"I did not want to leave my mother, knowing that she would die alone. I was furious that Diego sold our home and all our belongings. That he broke up the family was an added cruelty. He sent my sisters to live with an elderly aunt in Málaga—the city where my mother was born, but where my sisters may feel totally lost. Did you know that?"

Isabela shook her head in sympathy and disbelief.

"And they must have been miserable too far away to comfort or care for their mother."

"Before she was forced to move in with the nuns, my mother spent days moving candles and lanterns around the house. She would sit and study the shadows they cast as if she were memorizing the shapes. Then she would move them again and stare at the new flickering patterns. The nuns took care of her, but she died surrounded by strangers, not by those she loved.

"At first I refused to obey my father's command to accompany him here to the colony. Eventually I felt I had no choice. Not after my father said, 'You have no future here, Angel. Don't you realize that? No home. No money. No family other than me. The Church has not been kind to you. You were born a bastard. You are not valued here. You are not respected.' He made me feel like I was an outcast. I came close to striking him then, Isabela, but I was also ashamed at the fear I felt. I believed my father might be capable of killing me, his first-born son, and no one would pay attention.

"So I bid my mother a painful good-bye. We both knew we would never see each other again on this earth. My hatred toward my father grew more intense on the voyage. All I could think about was the callous way he treated her always and then discarded her when her beauty and youth faded. The way he broke up our family, sold our home and property, sent my sisters away. WE should have inherited our property. Somehow before we knew it, he had manipulated a sale.

"I resolved to learn everything I could about running the ship. My father was eager to teach me and marveled at how quickly I learned. 'It's in your blood,' he told me. 'Your grandfather. Your father. Now you. You will be a great seaman.' I remembered when I was very little, how I craved attention and praise from him. Those words came too late. I did not trust a single word he said.

"I learned how to read the charts, man the sails, interpret the wind. But I could see that working with a crew was, not surprisingly, my father's weakness. He needed a committed team, but with his harsh way of barking out orders, his threats to lower their wages if they did not perform, his dismissive attitude toward every one of them, they did not respect him. He didn't even make any attempt to remember their names. They were objects to him. More people to manipulate.

"At first, since they knew I was his son, they expected the same from me. But I strove to become their comrade. I listened to their stories. I learned more from them than I did from all my father's instructions. When I realized that I knew enough to run the ship by myself and I believed the crew would follow me or at least work with me side by side, even though I was young, I began to think about how to get rid of him.

"In my fifteenth year my intolerance for his presence in our home turned to rage. I understood that he was the cause of my mother's illness. By then you and your children felt like part of my family, Isabela. When I became aware that he was just as insensitive, blaming and harsh with you, his legal wife . . . and now that I know that his irresponsibility and recklessness killed her . . ." Angel stopped to collect himself. He closed his eyes, took a deep breath and continued.

"Although I felt tremendous guilt leaving her in that delicate state, I took advantage of the chance to break away, to get out of Santos Gemelos. It held no future for me. My father was right about that. I needed to learn a trade. Preparing for the voyage with Pedro, knowing that you and Nelita would be on the ship with me, gave me the courage to throw myself into learning all I could.

"When the privateers took Pedro away, when the crew and I fought with all our strength—and oh the courage they all displayed—for the ship, for the cargo, for you and Nelita, for themselves—while my damnable father—Mother Mary forgive me—I could not take it anymore. I thought I might leap overboard to drown my feelings of disgust for his despicable, cowardly behavior."

Isabela grabbed Angel's arm and held onto it as if to hold him back from such an act.

"I was embarrassed to be his son. By then he was sleeping nearly all night and all day. It had never occurred to me that he might have the same illness he gave my mother. Not until you suggested that possibility tonight to the notary. I don't know why. I guess I was too focused on my own feelings of hate. In any case, illness was no excuse for his total neglect of life aboard that ship and his indifference to his families for years.

"When he made no attempt to join us, showed no remorse when Diego was taken, I prayed for relief from my hatred. That night when the ship's cook and I were assigned sentry duty, the cook fell asleep. The sailor guiding the ship had his back to the deck. I was standing on deck looking out over the sea when I heard the hull's trap door open and shut.

"It seemed that Diego did not see me. As if he were in a trance, he walked directly to the opposite side of the ship from where I was standing. He leaned over the side. I thought perhaps he was sick at his stomach. I experienced an almost irresistible temptation to stride across that deck, strangle him and push him into the brink. In order to control myself, I turned away. I turned my back on him. I heard a splash.

"I ran over and held a lamp over the spot where I had just seen him. When I looked down, I saw only black waves hitting the sides of El Oviedo. It was as if my father never existed. I confess I felt a great sense of relief, Isabela. But I had been seconds away from committing the grave sin of patricide. Forgive me." Angel covered his face with his hands.

"I am so very sorry that you had to suffer so much, Angel. I love you. You know that, don't you? We're only twelve years apart in age, you and I, yet I've loved you like a son. Often, though, especially since we began the voyage, I've felt that our roles were reversed. That must have been how Leonor felt sometimes too—that YOU were the parent.

"I do so hope that by sharing these feelings with me, you feel unburdened, that you can forgive yourself. Please do not dwell further on these matters. You have so much to give the world. A wonderful life ahead of you. Really, Angel."

"I've thought of confessing to a priest or a friar, but I can't bring myself to do it. I simply don't trust them to understand. Even THINKING of killing a parent must be a sin. God will punish me, I know that. But the worst part of going to Hell is that I know for certain my father will be there too."

Chapter Thirty-Three
Modeling and Remembering

Isabela never discussed Diego's fate with Angel again, but she did take steps to protect him from the notary's suspicions. By the time they met with the notary that first time, hoping merely to legally transfer ownership of El Oviedo, Isabela and Nelita had been living in the home of the Governor for two months.

The Governor was based in La Florida's capital, San Agustín, but he was responsible for the entire La Florida region and was often away. When he was home, the atmosphere changed considerably. The ladies tucked away their sewing, their books, their art projects and their games. They quieted their chatter and laughter. They became more sedate and feigned a seriousness and dignity that were not apparent during those long periods when they had the house to themselves. They also attended to the guests the Governor invited nearly every night.

The Governor adored his wife and daughters. On his first visit home in weeks, he was delighted to find that his household had expanded to include two more lovely Spanish females. The few memories Nelita had of her father were fading. Isabela was grateful that her daughter had more positive male models like Angel and now Governor Ponce de Leon who took the time to admire Nelita's art projects and to play checkers with her.

One of the Governor's favorite pastimes was to challenge his dinner guests to a game of chess. Isabela had shared with him her admiration of his ivory pieces which, like the fabric she was working with, were imported from China. Although she longed to join in, she did not immediately reveal that she knew how to play the game. The most frequent visitor was Lieutenant Benedít Catalán, who like the Governor before him had risen to the position of Accountant of the Royal Treasury. He also held the position of Supervisor of the Royal San Agustín Prison.

Estefania noticed Lieutenant Catalán's awkward attempts to engage Isabela in conversation both during meals and afterwards on the veranda.

"He's definitely interested, Isabela, and you could certainly do well by marrying him. I know he's older and has a son nearly your age, but his second wife died recently in childbirth along with her baby. He comes from a wealthy Spanish trading family and he has two important positions in the colony. Why won't you encourage him—at least a little?"

Isabela had no interest in relating to such a possible suitor or any suitor. She smiled and answered his questions, but otherwise made few comments.

"Señora Calderón, I'm told you once lived in what we in the military still refer to as 'enemy territory.'"

"If you are referring to Amsterdam, Lieutenant, yes, I did live there."

"My goodness, how horrible that must have been for you, a young Catholic woman, living among those heathens."

"Actually, I found them quite welcoming and generous. Now if you'll excuse me, I must put my daughter to bed."

To the Lieutenant, she remained mysterious and that, combined with her beauty, made her even more alluring. She preferred to banter with the Governor, though. As her aloofness toward the Lieutenant continued, his regard of her became more daring, even leering, especially when he'd had several glasses of the Governor's brandy. To avoid him completely when he, like her, was a guest of the Governor, would have been impossibly rude, but her continued distanced responses to his overtures did not seem to discourage him in the least.

One evening as the Lieutenant and the Governor were bent over the chess board, Isabela slipped over to study the game herself for a moment. She quickly surmised a way for the Governor to beat his opponent. She moved to a position behind the Lieutenant and managed to communicate to the Governor by mouthing and motioning that by moving his Rook two spaces, he could capture the Lieutenant's Knight.

Completely taken by surprise both by Isabela's knowledge of the game and her boldness, the Governor studied the board for another moment and made the winning move. Isabela soon became his favorite chess partner, thus freeing her from the Lieutenant's overtures. The Lieutenant no longer attempted to talk to her, but his stares became so direct and lustful that whenever she was near him Isabela habitually reached for the cross on her bosom and held it tight in her fist.

The evenings he visited the Governor, fearful that she might encounter him alone, she avoided the arbor and flower garden even though the air there offered some relief from the relentless heat. She also needed to ask a favor of the Governor and did not dare complain to him about how uncomfortable the Lieutenant made her feel. He had not actually DONE anything offensive. It was his manner and his inappropriate facial expressions that upset her.

One evening soon after Angel and Isabela's threatening encounter with the notary, Isabela sat across from the Governor who was studying the chessboard carefully. Determined to outshine her at the game at least once, he was taking his time before making a move. She casually mentioned Angel's business plans. Always open to such ventures that might bring taxes and trade to his colony, the Governor stopped playing and listened. Isabela saw a way to take advantage of the Governor's position, but she allowed him a move which actually hurt her own chance to win.

"I think it's a marvelous plan, Governor. You've met Angel. Although he's my husband's son by a previous marriage, he has been like a son to me. He is just the kind of man who will help this colony thrive: intelligent, hard-working, skilled, determined. You may have noticed that he also has a sensitive side—much like you, I would say."

The Governor was listening carefully and enjoyed the compliment, but he took time to smile triumphantly when he captured her Knight.

"We've encountered a small problem, though, in transferring the legal ownership of El Oviedo into Angel's name," Isabela continued. "I'm wondering if you would have a word with the notary to resolve that small impediment and allow Angel to prepare the ship for passage on La Florida's riverways."

Governor Ponce de Leon did not hesitate to reassure the pretty and clever woman across the chess table even though he was alert enough himself to know that she had let him win. "Consider the matter closed, Doña Isabela," he said. "Your energetic young man will soon be trading throughout New Spain."

Isabela felt tremendous relief. She gave the Governor a big smile of gratitude and a quick pat on the arm. Her sense of satisfaction was short-lived, however. Although Angel would get his wish, she could not know that soon she would be involved in a situation that would pit the lustful Lieutenant against their mutual friend, the Governor.

* * *

"I know you're spending a lot of time preparing for Señorita Elizabeth's wedding, Isabela, but do you think you could squeeze out some time for another project? It has to do with modernizing my ship."

"Updating El Oviedo, Angel? I can't imagine how I could be of use. There are some excellent shipwrights in San Agustín."

"Indeed there are, but there is also an excellent sculptor who specializes in figureheads. I have this hope. Wherever I go, you will accompany me. In fact whoever approaches El Oviedo straight on will first see YOU. Or at least a bust of you. Your face. They say the figurehead is the soul of the ship, Isabela. I mean it as a tribute to you, but I also feel that a replica of you would comfort and protect me and the passengers. I've spoken to the carver. He first draws a portrait. Then he carves the wooden figure using that portrait. You wouldn't need to be available during the entire carving process."

For the second time in her life, Isabela found herself sitting perfectly still while an artist attempted to capture her features on paper. This artist was primarily a sailor and older than her father. With some difficulty, he repeatedly rose from his stool and approached her with squinty eyes. She felt like a tree or house or some other unmoving object. He looked at her hairline, penciled in a few marks on the board he held, returned to his stool, scribbled some more, and rose again to peer at her and compare his scribbles with her actual features. 'Are his eyes strong enough to see the widow's peak that I, my mother and aunts all have?' she wondered.' The process continued with her forehead, her nose, her chin, and finally with her eyes—one at a time.

She amused herself by trying to remember every detail of the first time she posed—ten years ago in the entrance hall of The Amsterdam City Orphanage. Curious maids, cooks, and other Big Sisters wandered in, trying to look purposeful. Orphans, including Nelleke, passed through on their way to and from the school room or dining hall. The Housemother poked her head in every so often to be sure she and the young artist were behaving themselves. This time it was the Governor's family that gathered round. They were quiet and respectful of both artist and sitter.

But the major difference was how she related to the artist. Pieter had convinced the Housemother to free Isabela from her duties for an hour each day for two weeks. Only when he offered to donate the finished painting to the orphanage did Mrs. Heijn agree. The portrait would do double duty. It would serve as an example of Pieter's best work. As his submission to the artist guild, it would be the most important step in the multi-year process to become an official member of the artist guild that licensed all artists and oversaw the sale of all art. Pieter's master and teacher, Rembrandt, was supervising his work.

Secondly, the orphanage would have on permanent display a painting of a beautiful young woman in the traditional orphanage half red/half black uniform with a crisp white top ending in a "V" at her cinched waist. A bonnet held in place by silver pins below her ears, the thick black curls spilling out. Sedate. Holding the Bible open in her lap. The woman's dignified and contented expression would speak well of the staff and the quality of the care. It would reflect positively on the Housemother herself.

In addition to these two "formal" goals, though, posing for Pieter gave the pair an opportunity to spend time with one another, albeit in a rather public venue. Isabela and Pieter who had met only once before the sketching began, developed a secret way of communicating. A very slight role of the eyes when the Housemother repeatedly gave them the countdown—"Thirty more minutes." "Ten more minutes." "FIVE more minutes." "Isabela has duties, you know." An amused small smile when one of the orphans stopped to stare at them—well, at Pieter mostly.

Isabela's companion Big Sisters could not suppress a giggle or resist dawdling, so titillated were they by the scene. Pieter was continually amusing Isabela with a twist of his lips, a scrunch of his nose, by raising his eyebrows, or sucking his cheeks—all in a mocked reaction to some curious person who had just passed out of view.

Isabela could not help laughing and sometimes had trouble re-assuming the pose. While she tried to gather her wits and become the serious model again, Pieter tapped his feet feigning impatience and irritation, even though it was he who was the cause of the disruption.

The easel was set up facing the wall. Only Pieter could see it. He did not want anyone gathering around and commenting. Isabela never did see it. The maid found a way around this obstacle. She determined that the stone floor near Pieter required a great deal of extra scrubbing when he was working. When the maid had finally taken her bucket and scrub brush and moved to another room, he put down his paintbrushes, got on his knees and imitated the maid's movements, eliciting more giggles from his amused model.

The cat came to investigate what he was doing. When she decided Pieter wasn't very interesting, the cat stretched and placed herself right up against him. Not to be outdone, Pieter, still on his knees, stretched his back in perfect imitation of the cat. For fear she would cause still more of a stir, Isabela suppressed an urge to laugh aloud but she took advantage of the break to stand and stretch herself. Their child-like playfulness was short-lived—snatched during moments when the bustling orphanage was still. They both knew that if the Housemother ever caught them at it, she would end the sessions.

It was the intensity of his eyes on her that Isabela remembered most—when he was working hardest, struggling to translate what he saw onto the canvas. At those times, in spite of Pieter's occasional antics, she felt the seriousness of her role. She wanted the project to be successful for him.

Then there were the times when the children were in the schoolroom with the other Big Sisters, the maid had duties elsewhere, and the Housemother was meeting with the Bookkeeper. During those few moments, they could actually attempt a conversation. Pieter explained his life plan. Two more years of study with Rembrandt. Approval by the guild. A life dedicated to art. A wife. A family.

As she continued to sit for the peering, squinting carver, she allowed her memories to linger over the only evening she spent with Pieter—at the celebration of Saskia's wedding. Pieter arranged with the mother of the bride, Mrs. Comfrij, to seat him next to Isabela. The joyfulness of the occasion mirrored their own happiness at finally being together for an entire evening. They talked. They drank. They feasted. They danced. They laughed out loud. Pieter comforted her when she broke down in tears telling him about the shipwreck that killed her father. And oh those embraces under the linden tree when Pieter walked her back to the orphanage—when Pieter covered with slow tender kisses the eyes, nose, cheeks, and mouth he had been studying and translating to canvas for weeks.

Isabela was on duty six and a half days every week. They saw each other once more after Saskia's wedding—the afternoon of the following

Sunday. It was then that Pieter guided her hand to draw the canal—the lesson he gave her on perspective. The next morning before dawn, Diego came for her. Now Pieter existed only in her imagination and in the night-time dreams that occasionally took her on those brief, intense Heavenly visits.

"That will be all, Miss. I think I have what I need. Thank you."

Isabela barely heard the carver dismiss her. She was still immersed in her thoughts about Pieter. How sad she was for him that none of his life plans came true. He never finished the painting. He never became a member of the guild. Last she heard he had never married. He just travelled. 'What is it he seeks?' she wondered. 'What will become of him?'

Chapter Thirty-four
Invasion Warning

Estefania's dress was complete and Isabela dedicated her days to finishing the younger sister's ensemble. Fresh cotton undergarments and petticoats. A parasol covered with cloth to match her new dress. The second dress—this one for daughter Fania—was easier now that Isabela had practice in designing and making the first one.

She never got over the surprise of using straight pins made of real gold. But what she wondered is the bride herself, Elizabeth, going to wear? Wasn't HER dress the most important of all? Yet Estefania had never mentioned it. All at once, Isabela realized. Estefania was hoping that Isabela would offer Elizabeth the tailor's bridal gown.

My love,

I've never thanked you for leaving Reza's exquisite wedding dress in my care. I supposed it was because you preferred to travel lightly. I am not alone in admiring its unique beauty. It has caught the eye of the Governor's wife who I'm sure would like to see her daughter married in your very gown. In addition to loving the gown myself and feeling responsible for it, every time I glance at it I am reminded of your absence, of how much I miss you, of my fear—overwhelming at times—that I may never see you again. I am trying to put myself in your place, to enter your thoughts. You would certainly have a strong opinion, but, I wonder, what would it be?

The gown is yours. What might you say to me? I will try to conjure up your voice: 'Keep the gown intact. Display it if you wish, Isabela, but Reza will be the only woman to actually wear it.' OR 'Of course, loan the gown to your new friend. It was meant to be worn on the most joyous of occasions.'

It's enough, my darling, for me to try to understand my own mind and now I must puzzle over yours as well. The last thing I ever wish to do is disappoint you in any way.

Your devoted Isabela

* * *

Estefania had planned the wedding for mid-March. "Before the wretched, clinging heat sets in," she said. One morning in early February as Isabela was cutting out a new petticoat for the dress she had made for Fania, Estefania called Isabela into her bedroom.

"Look at this. It was my mother's wedding dress. I had always hoped that one of my girls would wear it. What do think? How would this look on Elizabeth do you think?"

Was this an obvious ploy to encourage Isabela to offer Reza's dress or was Estefania blind to the condition of her mother's dress?

"My mother was the second daughter in the family to wear it. Then it was passed to the third sister and several cousins. That was before the family became wealthy. We shared whatever we could with one another in those days. By the time I was married to the Governor, my father could afford more lavish garments, but with such limited space on our sailing vessel, I left MY gown in Madrid for my nieces."

Sitting on her bed next to the faded garment, Estefania caressed the dress and looked at it forlornly. Without saying anything more, she raised her eyes pleadingly to Isabela.

"It may have been lovely once, Doña Estefania, and I'm sure your mother looked beautiful in this dress. I fear that now it is worn beyond repair," Isabela said.

She was being generous. The dress, made of cheap imported cotton may have been passable for the first bride, but it was now a faded and stained jumble of wrinkles. No lace or altered sleeves could salvage it.

"Do you think Elizabeth would wish to borrow my tailor's dress?" she asked tentatively.

Estefania leaped up from the bed and embraced Isabela. She tapped her palms together five times the way she had the first time she set eyes on the gown.

"Why what a truly generous offer, Isabela. Let's ask Elizabeth what she thinks."

Before they could reach Elizabeth who was doing embroidery with Nelita in the downstairs parlor, a frighteningly loud boom shook the house and aroused the entire town. They heard soldiers running up and down the streets shouting,

"Enemy ship sighted. Enemy ship sighted. All soldiers report to duty. All civilians take cover. Enemy ship sighted."

They could hear screaming and running. At first the women were paralyzed. When they heard the military scurrying through town, muskets drawn, and then heard a second boom, they ran and huddled with the servants in the kitchen.

"Cannon. They're shooting cannon. Who is this supposed enemy? The French wouldn't dare return after what we did to them. The natives don't use cannon. Is it the English? Buccaneers?" Doña Estefania whispered. "What a time for the Governor to be gone—visiting the chief of one of the missions—half a day away by canoe."

Angel and Big Owl rushed into the kitchen to check on the safety of the women. El Oviedo was now docked close to the town. The two men were the first to see the small ship—little more than a boat—with a foreign flag.

"Did you recognize the flag?" Isabela asked.

"I believe it's a Dutch flag," he said. "I wanted to be sure you were all right. Don't go out. I'll try to get more information."

Isabela grabbed hold of Angel.

"Stay here. We'll learn soon enough what this is all about."

But Angel broke away from her. As Big Owl, ever polite, exited behind Angel, he stopped, turned around, gave the women a small nod, and said in a warning tone that was both gentle and commanding.

"Ladies?"

They understood. They nodded in unison. They would not budge.

* * *

"We've confiscated their weapons, Lieutenant, Sir. As you'll see when you inspect the contents of their boat, the weapons appear to be mainly for hunting and fishing purposes. Three muskets. Four spears. Six knives of different sizes. Hardly the weapons of war."

"I'll be the judge of that. Show me everything you found. I want a list of every object on board. Plus the names, occupations, nationality of every man. Men only, correct? No women or children?"

"That is correct, Lieutenant Catalán. No women. No children. There's a problem compiling that list, however. There were only four men total. Naturally I interviewed the Captain first—or attempted to. Neither he nor any of the men speak Spanish, Sir. We did not get very far in our investigation."

"Well what language do they speak?"

"Dutch I would guess since they are sailing under a Dutch flag."

"Dutch? I know a woman who may be able to help. I'll send for her. Meanwhile, bring the Captain to the interrogation room."

"Yes, Sir. Right away, Sir."

Lieutenant Benedít Catalán's position as Accountant of the Royal Treasury of La Florida took up most of his time. The only occasions when he was called upon to fulfill his second position—Supervisor of the Royal San Agustín Prison—were when a non-Spanish ship was either sited or sought permission to dock. Otherwise, he left the day-to-day running of the prison in the hands of his deputy.

The Lieutenant was pleased that he could use his powerful position to order Isabela to appear. To date, his only contact with her had been within the Governor's compound. The Governor was his superior and he could do little there to alter a situation that both displeased and tantalized him.

By the time the soldier sent to fetch her arrived at the Governor's house, people had begun to stir and poke their heads out of their homes. Except for the two cannon warning shots, there had been no other sounds, only reports that four men had been taken prisoner and were being questioned. When Isabela walked toward the prison with the armed soldier behind her, the gossip began.

"Now they're going to question her too?"

"She lived in that country, you know."

"She must be a false Catholic. One of them heretics."

"Could she be a spy maybe?"

When the soldier led her to the interrogation room, Isabela thought of Cook and all she had endured—accusations, isolation, probably torture, a violent public death. She could not imagine what the authorities wanted with her. The soldier pointed to a crude bench.

"Sit here while I call the Lieutenant."

She was beginning to feel the walls closing in on her in the windowless, airless space when Lieutenant Catalán opened the door, walked in, and closed the door behind him. His sneer made her feel like a captive butterfly that he intended to tear apart, wing by wing. She panicked and clutched the bench with both fists.

"Good morning, Doña Isabela."

"Good morning, Lieutenant."

She waited for an explanation. 'What did Cook advise? Deep breaths.' She attempted to calm herself without being obvious, but with his standing over her, with his beady eyes on her, she felt totally exposed.

"You once told me you lived in Amsterdam for a time."

"That is correct."

"Would you please tell me how a young lady of your station—a good Catholic woman, I'm sure—ended up in the capital of our enemy, in a city that viciously threw out from our churches our nuns and priests and all the symbols of our religion? Never allowed them to return? Did not allow them to worship openly?"

Isabela decided not to defend the actions of the Dutch. She had already told him that they had treated her well. She did not wish to defend herself either by explaining that she had continued to attend Mass every Sunday in that city, in a makeshift attic chapel in the home of a Dutch Catholic couple. In fact, although the chapel was hidden and it was true that Catholics could no longer use their churches, the Dutch DID allow Catholics to worship in their homes with a priest leading the Mass. Unlike her homeland where Crown and Church ruled together with an iron hand and encouraged citizens to spy on one another, she had found The Dutch Republic to be a mostly tolerant society.

"I was taken to the city when a storm destroyed the ship I was on—a ship destined for Spain, I might add. My father's ship."

"What happened to your father?"

It took all of Isabela's strength to keep her voice even when she said the words,

"My father went down with the ship."

"How did you escape the same fate?"

Isabela knew this questioning had something to do with the ship that had appeared in San Agustín's harbor, but she could not see where the questioning was leading. Perhaps the Lieutenant had no scheme in mind either. He was just using the incident as an excuse to frighten and detain her.

"One of the sailors—a Dutchman—saved me. He took me to Amsterdam."

"What did you do there during your time in that country?"

"His family cared for me while I recovered. I found work in The Amsterdam City Orphanage."

The Lieutenant took a step toward her. For a moment she feared he might grab her or strike her. She would not cower. She looked him directly in the eye. She took another deep breath.

"Yet you came to San Agustín directly from Spain, did you not?"

'Here in this suffocating space, alone with him, I dare not rebuff him,' Isabela thought. 'Here I cannot escape. This despicable man is holding me captive. He can demand answers to all the questions he has attempted to ask me in the Governor's house.'

"My betrothed came for me."

"What a brave man your betrothed must have been finding his way through enemy territory to save you."

When Isabela said nothing, the Lieutenant did not comment. He knew she was recently widowed. Perhaps he interpreted her silence as sadness caused by her loss.

A soldier knocked and opened the door. "The Captain of the Dutch ship, Sir. You wanted to interview him first?"

"Yes, bring him to me.

"Doña Isabela, it seems that our prisoners speak no Spanish. I assume you learned some Dutch while you lived in Amsterdam? How long were you there before your future husband rescued you?"

"Eighteen months. Yes, I speak a little Dutch."

In fact she had become quite fluent during that year and a half. She loved the language even though her accent, grammar errors, and strange constructions sometimes induced giggles among the staff and even the orphans. Pieter told her he found her accent endearing. During the ten years since she left there, she had received many letters from Nelleke plus some from Pieter's sister, Anneliese, and two from the orphanage Housemother. She read these letters aloud to herself repeatedly, regularly. She sang songs in Dutch to her children. The language was somewhere in her mind, somewhat buried, but possibly accessible—just how accessible she was about to find out.

* * *

The guard gave a shove to a man who could barely control his disdain for the situation in which he found himself. Although dusty, disheveled, and disgusted, the man shook off the guard and strode into the room in the authoritative manner befitting the Captain of a ship, albeit a small one. He tipped his hat to the Lieutenant in charge, nodded at Isabela, and spoke forcefully in his native language. To the Lieutenant, the sounds coming out of the man's mouth sounded like gargle and spit.

"Good afternoon, Mr. Authority. Whoever you are. How do you do? Captain Middelcamp here at your service. I must thank you for that warm welcome announcing our arrival, not once but twice. I'm certain the entire town knew of our presence before we ourselves were yet certain we had arrived at our destination. Oh, and did I mention the accommodations? Splendid. That dirt floor. No pillow. No cover. Best sleep I've had in years. May I ask, Sir, why we are being detained? I see by your uniform that you are a military officer. Surely then, you are aware that Spain and The Dutch Republic signed a truce nearly three years ago? Eighty years was enough, don't you think? We are no longer at war. Thank you for getting out of our country and leaving us alone, by the way."

Although he was making no threats and he smiled from time to time, the guttural nature and unbroken barrage of the Captain's words, none of which the Lieutenant understood, combined with the Captain's confident manner, alarmed the Lieutenant. He took a step backwards. Really he was tired of this whole business.

'Maybe I should turn over the questioning to my number two man, my deputy,' he thought. When he glanced at Isabela he changed his mind. 'An opportunity to impress her. A unique situation. I will show her I am the man in charge here.'

Yet he was dependent on Isabela for a translation. The Captain had been jabbering in Dutch nonstop since he entered the room and she had not yet said a word. In an attempt to stop the stream of nonsense sounds, Lieutenant Catalán raised his hand, nearly pressing his palm against the Captain's chest. He turned to Isabela.

"All right, young lady. You're the expert here. What is this loquacious idiot babbling on about?"

Isabela stood up from the bench, curtsied, and addressed the "intruder" in Dutch as if she were the hostess of the ugly, damp hovel where the three people were gathered.

"Captain, what a pleasure to meet you. I'm only sorry it has to be under such ungracious circumstances. May I apologize on behalf of my countrymen. My name is Isabela Calderón. This gentleman is the Supervisor of the Royal San Agustín prison. I once had the pleasure of living in your country. Now the Lieutenant has asked me to translate for him."

Feeling more secure now that the jovial, loquacious, and apparently fearless Captain had joined them, she asked sweetly in Spanish.

"Lieutenant Catalán, what is it you wish to ask the Captain?"

"I wish to know his business here. That's what I want to know. Tell him that. Using few words."

"The Lieutenant is responsible for the safety of the population, Captain. As you might imagine, the town has endured many threats in the one hundred years since its founding. He merely wishes to know the purpose of your visit. Obviously you did not come directly from The Netherlands."

"I asked you to translate a simple question, Doña Isabela, not to translate a whole book."

"We came from New Netherland, from New Amsterdam to be specific. I immigrated there with the wife and family four years ago and set up this passenger service. I move people and goods up the North River and back. So apparently, this guy wants to know why San Agustín? I'll tell you why. One of my countrymen arrived in New Amsterdam, took one look and decided he'd rather come here instead. Offered me a nice pile of money to bring him directly to San Agustín with the understanding I'd make no stops in between. Pretty impatient, that one. Awfully nice fellow, though. Three weeks later . . . here we are. In jail."

"He runs a passenger ship out of New Amsterdam, Lieutenant. He's brought a paying customer here."

"I think you're gathering a lot more information than you're sharing, Señora. Nothing you've told me is particularly helpful. Who is this passenger the Captain refers to and what does he want?"

"The Lieutenant wishes to know what business your passenger has in San Agustín, Captain."

"Well, why doesn't he ask my passenger himself, then?"

"The Captain suggests you ask the passenger directly, Lieutenant."

The Lieutenant called for the soldier guard. "Set this guy free and the crew too. Hold the passenger until I have time to interrogate him."

Chapter Thirty-five
The Passenger

he passenger's artist eye quickly took in the alert stillness of the woman seated on the wooden bench ahead of him and to his right. A woman in her late 20s, still youthful. A woman who had been married for nearly a decade. Married—all that time to someone else. That thought always surprised him with its power to seize him with envy. Now, as he learned only weeks ago, a widow. The mother of two children—one lost, a boy, Pedro, named with his own name in mind, perhaps? Did she wish the boy had been his then? Did the husband know that? Did the husband know anything about him?

A daughter, Nelita, still alive, and surely named after the orphan, Nelleke, who brought this woman into his life on a rare sunny morning in Amsterdam—a perfect day to follow his mentor and master painter out of the studio, into the light. A perfect day to capture the effect of that light in the pastoral scene spreading out beyond the city wall. A scene that took her breath away. That same wall where he first spotted her as she climbed up in pursuit of Nelleke after refusing the assistance of his proffered hand.

He had imagined meeting this woman in a hundred places in a dozen different ways, but never like this, never in an ugly, windowless, prison that smelled of blood, sweat, and rotten fish. A woman little changed from the girl he knew briefly and whose sudden disappearance had haunted him without ceasing, embedding itself in his waking hours, in his dreams, in his wanderings and in his art. The same grace and delicacy. The same light-olive skin. The perfectly symmetrical arched eyebrows above the soft, intelligent brown eyes. The nearly black curls, perhaps somewhat looser now but visible on either side of the tight gray bonnet. Oh, and he had forgotten about the way her hairline peaked in the very center of her forehead. Had he gotten that right in the portrait? It had been so long since he looked at that canvas.

But what is that? Just to the left side of the peak a thin line of silver. How he longed to trace that silver trail with his finger to where it disappeared under the bonnet, to remove the bonnet and continue to trace the enticing narrow silvery path. Did it disappear into the black or did it follow through across the top of her head and down her back all the way to the tips of her tresses? Would he be able to capture the magnetism of that silver in a portrait?

Portrait. With hands clasped in her lap, knees together under her skirts and feet lined up touching each other in the thin leather boots, her profile unmoving, she could be posing for a portraitist at this very moment. She looked to her left. To greet him? To take stock of the next prisoner? Just before she recognized him, he caught in her features a wariness, a guardedness that was not there in her youth. Where before there was mystery and reserve with an occasional shy openness, now there was mystery mixed with distrust. But, of course. After what she had endured. The losses. A father. A husband. A son. Possibly more losses and disappointments that he knew nothing about.

The moment passed quickly. Her whole face and body reacted to the shock, the puzzlement followed by the surety. Her lips parted. Her eyes widened and moistened. She raised her hands and clasped them against her chest as if attempting to calm her throbbing heart.

Fortunately, the Lieutenant was sizing up the prisoner himself and did not notice Isabela's reaction. He posed a question. He looked to Isabela to translate. He posed the question a second time. A third time. His tone was impatient. What was she waiting for? Suddenly Isabela and Pieter realized why they were in this bare windowless room.

"NAME. WHAT is your NAME?" the officer asked in Spanish.

"Name," Isabela said in Dutch. "What is your name, Sir?"

She struggled to keep the corners of her mouth from rising. She kept her chin steady. It was so tempting to slip into the playful expressions they developed long ago—a secret way to communicate with one another without words. But they mustn't. She could see he was as overcome as she was. She must get hold of herself. She must convey to him the danger they might be facing.

"Pieter," he answered. "My name is Pieter Hals."

"Pieter," Isabela said, unwilling to move her gaze away from the man she remembered so fondly. Finally, she turned to the Lieutenant and said in Spanish, "My name is Pieter Hals."

"Profession?" the Lieutenant barked.

"Artist," Isabela answered without hesitation.

"Are you making up your answers, Doña Isabela. You have not even asked the prisoner what his profession is."

"Profession?" Isabela asked Pieter in Dutch.

"Artist," he answered.

"Artist," she said again to the Lieutenant.

"Where is he coming from?"

"From where you coming?"

Pieter could not keep from smiling. He always found her twisted use of his native language so amusing.

"New Amsterdam," he answered.

"New Amsterdam."

"What prompted this trip to our town?"

"Why you come here?"

"Because I received a letter from my sister—a letter in which she informed me that the woman I love is living in this town," Pieter answered making no attempt to hide his delight in locating that woman so quickly.

Isabela remained stiff and professional.

"The passenger is an artist. He has documented the great cities of Europe. Now he is doing the same for The New World."

"What does he intend to do with these drawings?"

"Do not say you know me. I told him you document the New World. He wants to know what will you do with the drawings?"

"I will share them with my countrymen. Interest in the New World is growing in Europe."

Isabela translated Pieter's answer into Spanish.

"How long do you intend to stay in San Agustín?"

"For as long as it takes to convince the beautiful woman before me to become my wife."

Isabela struggled to keep her face expressionless. "Until he is satisfied that he has captured the nature of our humble town, Lieutenant."

The Lieutenant could see no reason, no way to justify detaining the artist.

"Tell him he is free to go. Like all non-Spanish citizens, however, he is required to check in once a week with the Mayor's office. Tell him to complete his business as quickly as possible and go back where he came from."

Isabela translated.

"How about tomorrow? We can get married in New Amsterdam and set sail for Europe."

"The prisoner—Mr. Hals—says to tell you that he would like to make you a gift of one of his drawings before he leaves. He plans to explore every aspect of the town. You will have your choice of many excellent sketches, Lieutenant." Isabela said.

The Lieutenant shrugged and left.

Isabela stood and walked out of the horrible suffocating space. Pieter followed.

"Any idea where a serious suitor can get a wash and a shave before he sets about courting?" Pieter asked her.

"Limited choices, Pieter. I'll introduce you to the laundress, Maria Luisa, first. She knows plenty about making a man presentable—and that is what you must be, Sir, if you wish to visit me at the Governor's house where I am living. You can use the washtub in her garden. She may volunteer to scrub you herself and you may want to accept. She's a good-looking woman. She'll also wash everything you have on from that dusty cap to your worn stockings.

"Ask her for directions to the only boarding house in town. I warn you, it's not what I would call luxurious. By the way, when the Governor is out of town we have few visitors for the evening meal. I feel quite certain that the all-female household will be delighted to have you as their guest tonight."

The man who knocked on the door of the Governor's house several hours later had become more recognizable as the artist Isabela remembered. He had recovered his confiscated belongings from the prison and was dressed in the expensive clothing befitting the son of a wealthy Amsterdam merchant. Yet his style—far less formal than his father would have preferred—reflected his own profession and his easy way of interacting with the world.

A reddish-brown, high-quality felt cap set back on his head. 'How old would Pieter be now?' Isabela wondered when she noticed his thinning hair. 'About 32 maybe?' Loose white shirt. At least the sleeves were buttoned at his wrists this evening. Most of the time he kept them rolled up to his elbows she remembered, so they wouldn't end up covered in charcoal or paint. A light-wool, tan open vest over matching trousers that ended below the knees. Dark-brown stockings. Shined black boots that reached mid-calf.

Isabela showed him into the parlor and introduced him to the ladies of the house, all of whom wore their best jewelry in anticipation of meeting the gentleman from Amsterdam, the friend of Isabela. They were all hoping to be chosen as a model.

"Doña Estefania Mendoza d'Avila, wife of the Royal Governor of La Florida. Doña Elizabeth Ponce de Leon, older daughter. Fania Ponce de Leon, younger daughter."

Pieter lifted his cap, bowed, and smiled, as each was introduced.

When Isabela moved to stand behind the smallest child and placed her hands on the child's shoulders, when she said "Nelita de Vega, my daughter," Pieter's poise and composure left him. His fingers actually twitched, so anxious was he to set charcoal to paper and draw the child—a perfect replica of her mother. Sweet and shy, yet aware of the sensation she was creating, Nelita peeked out from behind her mother's skirts.

The women, who had been rather giddy when he arrived, fell silent when they noticed the dampness in Pieter's eyes. He bent down on one knee in front of Nelita and very slowly reached out his palm to her. She regarded him cautiously for a few seconds, looked up at her mother who nodded her approval, and placed her hand in his. Pieter raised the child's hand to his lips and kissed it lightly.

"Do you think your mother would give me permission to draw your lovely face, Nelita?" he asked.

"He thinks you're pretty," Isabela explained to her. "He wants to draw you. Would you like that?"

"Yes," Nelita, nodded, her hand still resting in Pieter's.

The maidservant entered with a tray of crystal wine glasses and a carafe of wine.

"Made from pomegranates grown in our own arbor," Doña Estefania said. She served the guest first and then the others. Nelita had her own small wineglass and was given a watered-down version. Pieter raised his goblet,

"I wish to toast to friendship," he said. "To peace between our countries. To the joy of meeting new friends wherever one travels."

Raising his wine higher, he turned to Isabela.

"And rediscovering old friends."

After the sumptuous meal and lively chatter, Nelita gave good-night kisses to everyone, including Pieter, and went upstairs for a bedtime story from Elizabeth. The remaining two members of the family discreetly withdrew to their private rooms as well, leaving Isabela alone with Pieter on the veranda.

As exhausted as she was from the emotion of seeing him again and from the challenge of translating the entire day, she was reluctant to say good-night. Finding herself suddenly alone with Pieter was never awkward—not during their few contacts ten years ago and not now. Since Pieter was adept at the give-and-take of conversation and could probably have sat with her until dawn, it would have to be she who ended the evening.

"What a meal! Do you eat like that every night?"

"Only when the Governor is home. Otherwise we eat rather simply. Doña Estefania told the cook that we had a special, foreign visitor, a distinguished artist I believe she said."

"Bit of an exaggeration, I'm afraid. I simply draw the life around me wherever I happen to be. What was that succulent meat dish? Some kind of fowl? In all my travels I've never tasted anything like it."

"Quail. Cook roasts it in a clay oven with fresh herbs and garlic, and smothers it with lemons—all grown on the property. The squash and beans—the Spaniards learned to grow those from the natives. Wait until you see THEM. Oh, you've already met one. Maria Luisa. You must have been able to imagine how beautiful she once was."

"She's still beautiful. All of her."

"All of her?"

"Sure. She said I was so filthy that I needed a personal scrubbing. In order to do the job right, she felt she had to get right in the tub with me. A generous and thorough woman."

Isabela slapped Pieter on the arm. "She did not. But just in case, that's the last time I send you to Maria Luisa for any service of any kind. Speaking of decorum . . ."

"Oh, I didn't realize that was the topic. I thought that was just the way you do things here in this little frontier town."

"This is a garrison, a military outpost. Governed, controlled, financed by the Spanish Crown and Church, I might add. The Franciscans are watching. If you don't behave, they'll drag you into Mass and force you to confess your sins."

"My Calvinist soul is doing just fine without that kind of supervision, thank you. Speaking of our religious differences, I developed a deep hatred of myself after you left."

"You? Full of self-hatred? What was it? Nothing to do with me, I hope."

"Everything to do with you.

"We hadn't known each other long, but I thought I wanted to spend the rest of my life with you. First I would have to speak with my father. I knew your Catholicism would be unacceptable to him. He lost two brothers during the eighty-years war. I'm sure the fighting was vicious on both sides, but my father knew only the brutality of your countrymen. He was virulently anti-Catholic. The thought of a Catholic daughter-in-law and Catholic grandchildren would have been abhorrent to him."

Isabela and Pieter were sitting next to each other on a curved wooden bench imported from Italy and painted a shiny white. An elaborately painted life-size sculpted parrot kept watch between them. Fortunately, it was made of porcelain and would not be repeating any of their words. A torch sent out flickers of light that lit up their faces and the immediate area of the garden. The delicate fragrance of lilacs and roses reached them from all sides. Pieter took a deep breath and hung his head for a long moment.

"I dreaded talking to my father, Isabela. I kept putting it off, practicing what I would say, coming up with ways to counteract what I knew would be his immediate refusal. He would have dismissed my interest in you as passing youthful folly. He would not have given me his blessing and approval. I believed that once he met you, he would understand why I was so smitten, but to even get to the point of introducing you, I had to move him to an initial level of partial acceptance.

"I thought I had time. I kept telling your Mrs. Heijn I needed more sessions to finish your portrait, but she was running out of patience. Switching to the voice of the Housemother—speaking in the severe tone Isabela remembered so clearly, Pieter said, 'The regents want to see your work, young man. They're always thinking of new ways to raise money for the orphanage. If they find it of sufficiently good quality, they're considering organizing a celebration of the portrait's completion, possibly an auction. Finish up the project.'

"I was nervous about being able to see you often enough once I completed the portrait. I was sure that eventually I could think of a way to convince my father, that until then you and I could continue seeing each other during those few precious Sunday hours when you were freed from your duties with the orphans.

"I knew you were betrothed, but you never spoke of your future husband. He was far away in a country The Dutch Republic was still fighting. He didn't seem real to me. He didn't seem like a threat. Your father arranged the betrothal, but he was no longer alive to honor it. I thought your betrothal posed no obstacle. I couldn't have been more wrong. Suddenly without warning or good-bye, you were gone. I never spoke of you to my father. I've spent ten years wondering if I had been more courageous, more forceful, if I hadn't kept trying to come up with the perfect convincing words, if I had dared to talk to him, perhaps I could have prevented your leaving.

"Your disappearance caused a great deal of upset and worry, you know. The children were terribly frightened. The police came. They interviewed everyone. When the guard was found bound and gagged, when your fellow Big Sisters discovered that you'd left behind your slippers and your uniform, they concluded that wherever you were you must still be wearing your nightdress. We believed you were taken, possibly against your will. I was desperate to know that you were all right. I felt helpless and utterly useless.

"Then months later Nelleke came running into our house with her new mother, your letter flapping in her little hand. Mrs. Broekhof was deeply apologetic about interrupting our noon meal, but once Anneliese learned the letter was from you, father could not keep her at the table. You began the letter in Dutch but switched to English which I guess was more comfortable for you. Waiting to hear each sentence of your letter, Isabela, waiting for my sister to read your English and then translate it out loud for us into Dutch, it was agony. I was relieved that you were alive, that you were back in your home village, but the thought of you married and expecting a child was, I admit it, devastating."

'If he knew how much I suffered in my marriage, if I were ever to tell him of Diego's rough and thoughtless treatment, of his neglect, Pieter would only blame himself further,' Isabela thought. 'Best not to tell him now. Perhaps never tell him.'

During Pieter's confession, Isabela reached across the parrot and placed her hand on his. She did not know how to comfort him. 'How sad that now so many years after my religion caused him so much grief, I no longer feel such strong ties to it,' she thought. 'Best not to tell him that either. Now it is I who must not delay the initiation of a delicate conversation. I must tell him soon that I can never marry again, that I will never again be anyone's wife—even his.'

15 January 1652
My love,

I'm not sure I ever mentioned Pieter Hals to you. He was the young artist who painted my portrait as a gift for The Amsterdam Orphanage. After Diego came for me, Pieter never finished the painting. I'm not sure what became of it. He wouldn't show it to me while he was working on it and now I'll never know what he saw in the young girl I was then.

Pieter is so unlike you, my darling. Not a scholar or a thinker, he does not analyze or philosophize much. He lacks your wisdom. He does have a wonderful eye, though. Tonight after dinner he delighted Doña Estefania and her daughters by sketching in two minutes one woman after another while all three posed at the same time. I remember that Rembrandt had that ability. Just after we met Rembrandt for the first time, he studied Nelleke's face for a very short while, told her to turn her back, and sketched away. One minute later she appeared fully formed on his slate. I remember Nelleke's delighted squeal when she called out, "It's me!" She was right. The sketch was uniquely Nelleke.

Pieter has that same gift. The women had to guess which one of them appeared in each of Pieter's sketches. They're mother and daughters, sisters. He caught both their similarities and their differences and, oh, were they charmed. They could easily recognize themselves and each other. With an exaggerated bow he presented each of them with their own "minute portrait" as he called them. They're impatient to show their father. Tomorrow Pieter will show me a selection of the hundreds—perhaps thousands—of sketches he's made on his travels, including some from New Amsterdam from where he sailed to get here. Most are in storage, but he keeps a few with him.

Like you, he does have deep feelings though, especially, if I can trust his word, for me. He declares that he wants to marry me. In fact he said so almost the first moment of our encounter—in the town prison. Yes in the prison—a dreadful place. It's not worth the waste of ink and paper to tell you about it. A long and strange story I will share if we ever meet again.

For reasons I have never discussed with anyone, even with you in these letters which you'll never read, I will never marry again. Oh, never, never, never—three "never's" in one sentence. I'll find something I can speak of more positively.

I do hope you and Reza don't mind. I have decided to loan your wedding gown to Elizabeth. She leapt up and down with delight when I told her. How sad that I will never wear it on such an occasion.

I've had little time for reading lately and I miss it. Doña Estefania has borrowed my French books. I'm sure she hides them from the Governor. Everyone in this town despises the French . . . and the English . . . and the Dutch, all Protestants, and probably the Jews too. I keep my silence. I must if I am to live among them.

Yours forever,

Chapter Thirty-Six
The Roman Life

"**S**o this is what your life has been like the past ten years, Pieter? I've been concerned, worried for you. Every time I receive a letter from your sister telling me that once again after a short "visit" home, you were off to another country. After one month, I now understand that what others see as itinerant and ungrounded, really suits you.

"In one month your presence has added quite a bit of excitement and merriment to our isolated little outpost. I know you're not a man of routine and sometimes during the day I try to imagine where you might be at that moment. In the plaza with curious off-duty soldiers gathered round? Children too." Isabela lapsed into the voice of a demanding child. "'Me next, Mister. Do me next. See how still I can be, Mister?'

"Or you're down on the docks drawing the exhausted crew as they exit from the most recently arrived ship? Anneliese wrote me that your favorite subjects are women, though. There aren't many of us here. By now you must have sketched Maria Luisa a dozen times plus the few female tavern owners in town plus women on their way to and from Mass, nursing a baby, chasing a runaway toddler, coaxing a rebellious young son down from a palm tree?

"It's so generous of you to give away most of your drawings, Pieter. Your subjects will treasure your depictions of them for the rest of their lives and pass them on to their grandchildren. I can hear them telling the story years later.

"There was this artist. Brown felt cap set on the back of his head. Dutch, I believe. Didn't speak Spanish all that well, but oh my he got us talking anyway. My sisters and I followed him everywhere. Mama tried to stop us, but we kept on. He kept putting us off. 'Hey, stay away from me, you three. You think you're the prettiest girls in San Agustín is that it? You think I've got time to sit here and draw YOU?' Meanwhile he learned our names and our ages. 'Let's see if I can figure out who's the oldest.' Then he'd point to our youngest sister. 'YOU,' he'd say. 'I can see you're the boss.' Of course we'd all giggle. Then one day he spun around and pretended to glare at us. We knew that mean face wasn't real. He'd fooled and entertained us plenty with his face-making. 'I give up,' he said. 'Sit down on that bench there.' Then he arranged us. Me, the oldest, sitting. My middle sister standing behind me. The youngest on my lap. Here it is. Here's that drawing. Weren't we adorable back then?"

"Isabela, that's quite a story. What stories are YOU going to tell YOUR grandchildren, do you think?"

Pieter always had a way of deflecting conversation from himself to her and often in ways that made her think about her nebulous future. He had not once referred again to marriage. After an entire month of talking about everything but that particular subject, she thought it would be presumptuous and inappropriate to bring up the topic only to tell him why she could never be his wife. Besides she was enjoying their daily meetings far too much. She didn't want to risk driving him away. He'd leave soon enough.

"I simply speak Italian with what I think is a Spanish accent," Pieter said after Isabela complimented him on his growing knowledge of her language.

"You're just being your typical modest self," Isabela answered. "Let's trade," she suggested. Let's speak in Spanish half the time and Dutch half the time. And let's correct each other."

"Fine idea. Although why you feel the need to become more fluent in Dutch, I can't imagine," Pieter said taking a long moment to look at her. His stare was part tease, part serious question. She blushed, then closed her eyes and looked away. She couldn't answer. She didn't know.

"I love your language, Pieter," she finally responded. "It reminds me of the eighteen months I spent in the orphanage. I grew up with no siblings. Suddenly I had twenty little sisters as well as four sisters my age or older—the "Big Sisters" who like me took care of the little ones.

It was a lot of work, but I loved it. I met Nelleke. Did you know that we still correspond?"

"Nelleke Broekhof. My neighbor. The child responsible for my meeting you. I am indebted to her for life."

"Or are you indebted to your dog . . . Runt? Was that his name?"

"Good memory, Isabela. I don't get the connection, though."

"Oh, maybe you didn't realize why Nelleke was so determined to climb up on the city wall that day? Runt had invited her to play. I guess he had to ask his master for permission first."

"An obedient little fellow, that Runt. Of course I granted him permission. It meant I might be able to provide some distraction for Nelleke while I engaged her lovely caretaker in some conversation. You were pretty standoffish, though."

"SHY is the word. My life at that time consisted of six and a half days a week focused on my little charges. I was not accustomed to being out in society."

"Yes, I remember, but we found a way around that, didn't we?"

"YOU did, yes, you clever man. Pieter, where is that portrait? You wouldn't show it to me while you were working on it."

"I've now drawn almost every woman in this town from the lowliest to the wife of the Governor. I'm not going to make a drawing of YOU here. I have a full-blown portrait of YOU already. It requires only five more sittings to finish. It's been waiting for you to reappear. It's turned against the wall in the third-floor studio of my home on the Heerengracht in Amsterdam. You know what you have to do if you want to see that portrait."

Isabela refused to be drawn into such talk.

"Of all the countries you've visited, which was your favorite, Pieter?"

"Italy," Pieter answered without hesitation. His usual chatty cheerfulness had left him for a moment.

"What was so special about Italy?"

"Well, I made every attempt to involve myself in the lively artist community there and I ended up staying for five years. And I met Michael Sweerts. He was from Brussels. He spoke Flemish, which you probably know is almost the same as Dutch. Yet he didn't spend much time with the Dutch painters, at least until I came along. Even though he was a deeply devout Catholic, we became friends. I was fascinated by his unique style. Intimidated really. The melancholy dignity of his figures. The way he infused his portraits with a mysterious silvery tone.

I found it exquisite. I tried to imitate it, but I couldn't. He refused to tell me how he achieved it. It seemed to evoke both an earthy richness and a humble Heavenly quality at the same time. I felt pretty inferior. I followed him around for awhile.

"Sweerts was still in Rome when I left. He talked about returning to Brussels and setting up a drawing school. That's something I've always thought of doing too. But I'd still have to become a member of the artist guild—a possibility that is looking less and less likely. Michael and I have lost touch now. He was always a bit wayward. Inconsistent too. Off to Mass on a regular basis, but could drink with the best of them. A different prostitute every night."

"A different woman every night? You were so young then, Pieter, weren't you? Twenty-one when you arrived in Rome? Twenty-six or so when you left? I can't imagine YOU behaving like that. Or is there a side to you I don't know at all? Anneliese mentioned in one of your letters that you had written something about a woman. Was there someone special in your life? What happened?"

As soon as she asked the question, Isabela felt it was a mistake. Best to keep their friendship light. It was too intimate an inquiry. Too probing. It might be upsetting for him. She had no right. She started to put her arm on his hand and stop him from answering, but it was too late.

"Lucy." he said a little too dreamily, Isabela felt. "I called her Lucietta."

'Oh, he had a pet name for this woman,' Isabela thought.

"She was from Venice."

'Venice? That romantic city that rises from the sea?' Isabela imagined a dark, voluptuous, seductive beauty with green seaweed wound through her thick black hair flowing below her waist. Her stomach tightened. She was having trouble breathing.

"She was older than I was. Not quite thirty. She was the sister of a painter and had been the wife of another."

'Older. Experienced. Well, I hope this Lucy enjoyed herself seducing my friend.'

"She found it quite amusing that her mother had named her for a saint—Santa Lucia who was an early Christian martyr."

"'If my mother only knew,' Lucietta would say with her raucous laugh. Married at fifteen. Widowed at twenty, she just wanted to have a good time. She found a community among the painters. Everyone wanted her to pose for them."

'And you? Did you ask her to pose for you?' Isabela thought, but did not ask out loud. It was the next logical question, but she had heard too much already. She refused to ask him more.

"Pieter, Elizabeth's wedding is in one week. You've met Estafania's sister, Margareta, who came all the way from Madrid for the wedding and plans to stay for two months. Margareta wants me to add a layer of lace to the dress she brought with her. As if it's not already fancy enough. I better get some rest."

"Oh, I don't think I've told you. You know that I've been doing a lot of drawings of Angel's boat. Of Angel and the men working on the renovations. The carver did a marvelous job, by the way. He really caught your likeness—from a piece of wood. That amazes me really. And even though his eyes are no longer strong." 'I'll have to give this up soon,' he told me sadly. "He's a Converso. Maybe you know that."

"You mean . . . ?"

"Yes, he told me the whole story. One hundred and sixty years ago, his entire family—mother, father, grandparents, sisters, brothers, aunts, uncles, cousins were well established and educated, living in a bustling community in the center of Madrid. Some of the men were tax collectors. They worked for the Crown and were well paid. The King and Queen were often short of money. It took/still takes an inordinate amount to maintain their lavish style of life. They borrowed money from the carver's family.

"Without warning, the Crown sent a proclamation throughout Spain. 'All Jews are ordered to leave the country. Within thirty days you must leave your businesses, your homes, your gold and your silver. You have two other choices. You may remain in the country if you formally, immediately, convincingly, and permanently convert to the religion of our blessed Lord—if you become Catholic. If you refuse to leave or convert, you will be killed.'

"The carver's great-grandfather was ill and unable to travel. The family made a quick decision to convert. Some of them. Others left. Siblings were divided. But the Church has never been convinced that the conversions were genuine. To avoid suspicion and return to their own religion, they left after the great-grandfather died. They moved to South America. The Church continued to threaten them. The carver lost two wives. The only child of his to grow up died recently. The carver couldn't stay any more after that. He came here recently looking for work.

"'Ironically, I'll probably die here,'" he said. "'Here where more and more natives are being converted every day. I can't escape those Franciscans.'

"Anyway, all this is to tell you that Angel and Big Owl are taking El Oviedo on a practice run—up the big river north. The carver's going. They've invited me to come along too. We'll be gone at least a week."

3rd March 1651
My love,

Did I tell you that Angel hired a carver to make a likeness of me to serve as a figurehead for El Oviedo? Pieter says he did quite an excellent job. That it does indeed resemble me. But Pieter's story (he's learned so much about everyone in such a short time) about the carver got me thinking. I'm worried that you and Reza are Conversos too. Perhaps that's the reason you left Santos Gemelos so abruptly. But to where? The carver's family fled to South America where they could speak Spanish, I suppose. But the Church still threatened them.

I have so many questions I want to ask you. I'll close with this quote. Do you recognize the source? Pieter will be gone for at least a week. Perhaps I'll have more time to return to the daily reading of the books you left for me.

> *Sad on the daisied turf Salicio lay;*
> *And with a voice in concord to the sound*
> *Of all the many winds, and waters round,*
> *As o'er the mossy stones they swiftly stole,*
> *Poured forth in melancholy song his soul*
> *Of sorrow with a fall*
> *So sweet, and aye so mildly musical,*
> *None could have thought that she whose seeming guile*
> *Had caused his anguish, absent was the while,*
> *But that in very deed the unhappy youth*
> *Did face to face, upbraid her questioned truth.*

Do you recognize it? It's from a poem by Garcilaso de la Vega. As you probably know, the poor man died on the battlefield when he was thirty-three. Just think how much more beautiful poetry he might have written had he lived.

Good night, my darling.

Chapter Thirty-Seven
In Pieter's Absence

⌒

The El Oviedo trial run stretched into ten days, then two weeks. By now it had been nearly a month. At first Isabela felt independent and confident. 'I can get along just fine without Pieter's daily companionship,' she thought. 'My days are filled with lessons for Nelita, chatting with Estefania and her daughters, reading, errands, planning meals with the cook. All that and the seemingly never-ending need to change a button or clasp here, lower or raise a hem, lengthen a sleeve. The gowns are so consuming.'

The most tedious task had been adapting Reza's dress for Elizabeth who was apparently thicker around the waist than Reza had been when she was a bride. Isabela had not predicted that she would have to alter what she regarded as the most perfect gown ever made. It was painful to rip out the waist, to separate that magnificent top from the skirt. Of course she had no matching fabric either. She added some fabric on the sides where it was least likely to be noticed. Yet the whole process seemed destructive. She felt disloyal to the tailor as if she had fouled a work of art.

Elizabeth's wedding was certainly small and modest by Madrid standards as her aunt let her know, but appropriate Isabela felt for the daughter of a Governor in a simple church in a garrison town. She was proud of the role she played in making it a success. After the ceremony, the couple paraded around the plaza while the town's soldiers and craftsmen plus a few families and their children threw flowers and shouted their best wishes. By then many residents had seen the gown that previously hung in Isabela's sewing cottage. Seeing it on an actual bride created more excitement.

"You'll be next, Isabela," Estefania whispered.

Isabela shook her head.

"Absolutely not," she protested.

The celebration at the Governor's house was private and lavish. Cook had worked all week and hired extra help. Estefania brought out her best silver platters, serving forks and spoons. The military officers made toasts. The Governor blessed the couple and announced that he had appointed his new son-in-law to the position of Accountant of the Royal Treasury. Isabela was relieved that the Governor, after learning of his hostile treatment of Isabela's friend, had dismissed the Lieutenant from that position and sent him to an isolated post in Peru.

Not until the tables were moved to the side of the veranda to make room for dancing did Isabela admit to herself that she missed Pieter. The whole scene would be so much more lively and amusing if he were there to share it. She could imagine him sitting on their favorite bench next to the porcelain parrot, charcoal in hand, board and paper in his lap, eyes alternately raised and lowered as he captured the scene.

As she watched the others dance, she realized that something in her life had shifted. She had been invited to live at the Governor's house in order to help prepare for this event. Where did that leave her now? Might Estefania expect her to return to Maria Luisa's cottage? Although they certainly had grown close over the past months, she might regard Isabela as little more than an educated servant.

Besides she could tell that Estefania was impressed by her sister's tales of the Madrid life. It would not take much urging for her to say to the Governor, "Almost four years here, my dear, and you've done a marvelous job of governing this wild place. Can we talk about moving back to Spain now? I think two military officers in the family are enough don't you? My sister has a number of possible matches in mind for our Fania—back in our own country."

Yes, the family would leave—perhaps soon. Would they invite her to accompany them? Would she want to? Where would Nelita be better off? What kind of life would they both have if she remained here? Yet nothing Estefania's sister described appealed to Isabela. Parties, fashion, gossip, constant vying for position, for the attention and favor of the Court. She did not want to return to a country controlled by a powerful Crown/Church partnership. She knew The Dutch Republic was different. She would ask Pieter how it operated. Who actually governed? She felt so naïve. All the poetry reading in the world did not seem to help her make decisions about her own life. After the Governor twirled her around once, she could see that others were about to approach her. She excused herself and took a protesting Nelita up to bed.

With the music and the merriment just below right outside her window, she lay brooding. 'Pieter will soon leave here,' she thought. 'He will return to Amsterdam for a short time before taking off again—perhaps for the Orient next time or Paris. New sites. New experiences. New people to charm and to capture on paper. That is his life. His memories of San Agustín will blend into memories of Italy, Brussels, France.'

* * *

"Governor, you have a visitor. A native. A high-ranking one I would guess. With an entourage and four horses. Shall I show him in?" Isabela had been playing chess with the Governor before the evening meal was served when she went to answer a knock on the door. Although she had by now seen a number of natives, this one startled her in the same way Big Owl did when she passed him that first day as she walked through the town.

The dignity and bearing of the man. The tail of a raccoon fell down his back. And the ear pieces! Were those pearls in one ear? And in the other ear tiny carvings etched in what? Copper? His lips were outlined with blue paint. When Isabela returned to the door to invite the man into the parlor she caught sight of the brightly colored tattoo that began on his right thigh, continued down his leg, and ended in a circle around his ankle. 'An interlocking set of complicated designs with sharp angles and an occasional circle or eye.' Wasn't that the way Big Owl described it? 'With a mix of red, black, yellow, and blue?' This must be Big Owl's father.

'Besides their skin color, the way they wear their hair in a knot, their clothing, there is something else that makes them seem so different from European men,' Isabela thought. 'What is it exactly?' She tried to act calm and natural. She certainly would not stare. Then it occurred to her. She had never seen a native with a beard. Not only that but they had not a single hair on their chests, arms, or legs either. Their bodies were smooth canvases—perfect for all that decoration.

'What does one serve a Timucuan chief at teatime?' Isabela asked herself. Estefania had taken her girls and Nelita to the market to purchase some vegetables for the evening meal. "A little outing," she called it. Isabela went to the kitchen to ask the advice of the cook.

"Oh THEY'RE the ones who taught US how to live off this land, but I'll prepare a platter of something. Just give me a minute. Meanwhile, would you mind, Isabela, taking drinks to the Chief's men out in the street? They've walked some distance. The Governor always treats the tribes with respect. He needs their cooperation I heard him say. I'd ask the maidservant to do it, but she's so scared at the sight of them, she's probably hiding somewhere."

When Isabela arrived with a tray of fruits and sweets, she found the two men deep in conversation, sharing a smoke. Every chair in the room was piled with gifts—bows and arrows, dried herbs, animal hides, moccasins in all sizes, ornaments that appeared to be made from some kind of bone. Shells, bowls, hickory nuts. Two large pumpkins sat side by side on Estefania's damask settee like twin invited guests. Isabela overheard the Chief say that the large quantities of blackberries were for the ladies. After the Chief's men had unloaded barrels of corn and accepted gifts of blankets, live turkeys, and oranges from the Governor, the natives' visit was over.

Isabela returned to the chess table. "You seem quite at ease with the Chief, Governor. Does he visit often?"

"Several times a year. It's important for our little colony to maintain good relations with these people. Your move, Isabela. I know your strategy of trying to distract me from the game with provocative questions."

The Governor studied the board and moved one of his pawns one square forward.

"We're so dependent on Spain for supplies. These natives have everything they need right here. There have been times when we Spaniards might have starved without their friendship.

"Yet we've endured a lot of tension since we landed here. Violence too. The Chief is struggling to maintain order, he told me. The Franciscans have broken up their clans and moved them into missions with strangers from other villages. Although most have embraced our Lord as their Savior, they're struggling with so much change. The Chief told me how in the past his people would go to war if one village takes the best clay along a river, if one person steals corn from another village's field. By 'war' he means killing only a few people, just to show you're strong. They didn't try to kill everyone or take their land. Compare that to the vicious way we wage war. The fact is we are still trying to understand each other. We need each other yet we never completely trust one another."

That night at the Governor's table the family and guests feasted on more gifts from the Chief—five varieties of fish, acorn bread, and bowls of blueberries mixed with cream from the Governor's milk cows. Elizabeth and her new husband, Luis, exuberant with his new position, engaged the Governor in talk about restlessness among the natives.

Isabela could not help noticing that Luis took time to turn often to the bride at his side. 'Whatever he whispers certainly makes her smile,' she thought. She felt the same tug of familiar jealousy—those times in Santos Gemelos when she noticed the tailor and Reza arrive quickly at a mutual decision just by looking at each other without exchanging a word.

* * *

One week later Nelita came running into the house.

"Mama, Angel's back."

She had been strolling down by the docks with Fania. I saw YOU first, Mama. Well, not you, but that statue sure looks like you. On the front of Angel's boat. Then I saw Angel at the same time he saw me. He waved and smiled. His passengers are disembarking. Many of them. And it looks like he's got a lot of goods to unload too. He looked happy, Mama."

Isabela pulled up her skirts and ran several yards before she stopped herself, took a deep breath, and slowed down to a dignified pace. 'I am no longer a little girl running to meet my Captain father,' she said to herself. But to see Pieter again after an entire month. To hear his stories. To see his drawings. To feel his eyes on her. Those playful, twinkly adorable eyes. As she approached the pier, she strained to catch sight of the cap set back on his head. He would no doubt be helping women and children step off the boat. When he saw her approach, Angel jumped on land and came to meet her.

"It looks like your first run was a success, Angel," she said trying not to strain to see behind him.

"I'm pleased, Isabela. I think you and I may have a good business here."

He started to give her a few details. "Big Owl is amazing. He led me to inlets, islands, hidden communities, and prominent villages. Everyone was eager for news—once they got over their reluctance of talking to strangers. Pieter was so adept at putting them at ease. At getting them to trust us. All he had to do was smile and draw them. They forgot their fear."

When Angel saw Isabela standing on tiptoe looking toward the boat, he realized what she was looking for. Something more important to her than a possible business success. More important than the stories he wanted to tell her.

"Pieter said he had never experienced anything like what we saw. He's lived in beautiful cities—he said Rome, Genoa, Brussels, Amsterdam— but the wilderness was new to him. He kept looking ahead and couldn't wait to see what lay beyond each curve in the river or stream. After a month we had only begun to explore really. They say the big river empties into the ocean, but there's so much land north of that. Pieter made arrangements with another owner of a small passenger ship. He wanted to keep going. 'Just a little farther,' he said. 'Before turning back.' Angel reached in his pocket and handed Isabela a crumpled piece of paper.

Embarrassed that Angel should see her tears of disappointment, and impatient to read Pieter's words, Isabela nonetheless unfolded the note that very moment.

To my friend, Isabela,

Angel will tell you what a time we've had. I look forward to showing you my new drawings. *I gave most of them away, but I saved a few.*

Pieter

Nothing about missing her. Nothing about when he intended to return. She said good-bye to Angel. She did not want to return to the Governor's house and face Estefania's questioning expression. If she were back in Santos Gemelos she would have walked along the bluff or descended the stairs to walk along the beach to comfort herself. In this small, enclosed, dirty town only one spot offered her the solitude and comfort she needed.

To get there from the docks she had to pass dozens of people—the blacksmith standing in his doorway taking a break from the heat of his hut; workers loading, unloading and delivering cargo; soldiers guarding the watchtower; women going to and from the market. They all knew her by name. They all greeted her. Some attempted to engage her.

"Doña Isabela, beastly hot today, eh?"

"Señora, how is that sweet daughter of yours?"

"What a wedding that was—for the Governor's daughter. We've heard you made that gown yourself. Is that true?"

She tried to smile, but kept going. She did not answer back.

The more people nodded or spoke to her, the more isolated she felt. Her acute disappointment was beginning to feel like something worse. 'What is it?' Isabela asked herself. 'I feel as if I have a beast in my heart and belly pounding on my insides. This feels almost as bad as . . . as the grief I endured after Pedro was kidnapped.' Grief. Naming the feeling only made it increase. 'No, not grief. It's anger that is gripping me. It's fury.'

She slid through the door and entered the still coolness of the Chapel of Our Lady of La Leche. She moved to the front of the chapel and knelt, trying to quiet her self-pity so as not to disturb the other two women on the benches behind her, eyes lowered, clutching their rosaries.

Reaching for the double cross Cook had given her, she prayed, "Oh, Mary, Mother of our Lord, Mother of us all, forgive my hateful heart. Soothe this rage that has taken over my soul. Show me the way to forgive my husband. Return to me the feelings of love and respect for my father whom I once so adored. Give me the courage to speak the truth with my friend, Pieter, and to send him on his way. I beseech you, oh blessed Mother, show me how to move forward. I remain your loving servant. Amen."

* * *

That night, Isabela determined that she would count the hidden coins. She gathered three cushions placed around the room she shared with Nelita—from the chair by the window, from her bed. The fourth cushion supported Nelita's sleeping head. When Isabela attempted to gently remove that cushion—the last one Tía Lucia ever decorated—

Nelita sighed and clutched the cushion with both hands. Isabela folded up Nelita's castoff petticoat, raised Nelita's head, pried the little girl's fingers away from the pillow and slowly pulled it out from under her. She lifted her daughter's head and replaced the cushion with the petticoat, kissed Nelita gently and waited. The child continued sleeping.

She ripped out the stitches she had so hurriedly sewed the last night she spent in her childhood home, removed the stuffing, and shook out the coins all along her bed quilt so that they would make as little noise as possible. She saw that the coins could be divided into four categories. Fifteen minutes later she had four piles: thirty-two *reales de plata*—Spanish silver coins; one-hundred-three *maravedíes* which were worth some fraction of a *real*; five *escudos de oro*—gold coins worth, she thought, sixteen times a *real*; and miscellaneous coins her father had apparently collected from countries he visited or monies he used for trade—including the coin she believed with an engraving of Emperor Julius Caesar. 'Could this really date back to Roman times?' she wondered. She removed the Roman coin and put it in its own category.

She was most familiar with the *maravedí*, the smallest in size and least-valued coin and also the most common coin in San Agustín. Although just recently she had heard the Governor and his son-in-law speak of the possibility of initiating the minting of coins in La Florida, almost everyone bartered. She had seen the Governor place five or six *maravedíes* directly into the native Chief's hand as they bid each other good-bye.

She stared at her stash and tried to make sense of it. She began with the most valuable—five gold coins worth perhaps sixteen times a *real* and many, many times more than a *maravedí*. She realized with a shock that even without the diamond she was probably the wealthiest woman in the town. Estefania and her daughters lived well, but they were dependent on their husbands. These coins destined for Diego's control after her father's death were now Isabela's own. But what were they worth to her and what could she do with them? She would have traded all these coins before her for a kind and loving husband—the husband she would now never have.

She placed all the *maravedís* in a wooden box, covered the box with a cloth, and slid it under her bed. She spent the next several hours restuffing the cushions, carefully distributing the remaining coins in the cloth so they would not clink against each other. She sewed up the openings—slowly so that the new stitches matched the original ones.

Nelita was puzzled when she awakened the next morning to find her head on her petticoat. Isabela explained casually that she had borrowed the pillow to support her back which had been a little achy. She returned to Nelita her favorite cushion.

Chapter Thirty-Eight
Return of the Wandering Suitor

"Isabela!" Fania called as she ran down the corridor toward Isabela's room. "Isabela! I thought you would want to know. I saw Angel. He told me that your friend is in San Agustín. But he's ill, Isabela. He's at the boarding house."

Just before Fania spoke, Isabela had been absorbed in two passages from a book of medieval writings the tailor had given her. Composed by Alfonso X, King of Castile in the 13ᵗʰ century, the first was a charming description of Isabela's native land entitled *Of the Good Things of Spain*.

More than all other lands of the earth, Spain has an over-flowing abundance of every good thing. Spain is like God's paradise. Spain is fruitful in crops, delicious with fruits, abounding in fish, rich in milk.

The second passage was darker. Entitled *The Jewess of Toledo*, it recounted the story of King Alfonso VIII's fascination with a Jewess named Fermosa.

He remained in seclusion with the Jewess for almost seven years during which time he did not think of himself, nor his kingdom. The good men of the kingdom held a meeting to determine how they might put an end to that wicked and unseemly situation and they decided that they should kill the Jewess and thus they would regain their master whom they considered lost.

When she heard Fania say, "Your friend is in San Agustín," Isabela's first thoughts were, 'Oh glorious day, the tailor has found his way here. But he's ill?'

She threw the book aside. Before she reached the bottom of the stairs, she realized her error.

'How absurd I am,' she thought. 'It's Pieter who has arrived and is ill, not the tailor.'

Isabela knocked at the door of the boarding house. When no one answered, she reached to open it just as a male boarder was exiting. The boarder directed her to Pieter's room. When Isabela entered she thought, 'How horrified Pieter's father would be that a Catholic priest should deliver the last rites to his son.'

She saw Pieter's forehead and nose covered with a white cloth, a Franciscan leaning over him, the rest of Pieter's body, immobile, stretched out under a blanket. She imagined a crucifix dangling in Pieter's face and over his chest, his ears forced to listen to chants in Latin which would be meaningless to him. If he could still hear. If he were still alive.

The friar spoke to Pieter quietly, knelt, said a prayer, and rose to leave. He seemed surprised to see Isabela hovering inside the door.

"Are you this man's wife?" he asked.

"I am a friend," she replied.

When Pieter heard her voice, he tried to remove the cloth and turn his head toward her, but he could not free his arms from under the blanket.

"I'll return soon with the ointment," the friar said.

In spite of her suspicions, Isabela noted that the friar's tone was kind, that he was attempting to be reassuring. She realized with some relief that he was a medical friar—someone who probably worked at the hospital. Yet she feared she may have arrived too late to say good-bye to her beloved friend, that the ointment the friar spoke of was part of a death ritual, a way to prepare the body.

The friar left. Isabela tiptoed toward the bed. 'What did a Calvinist prayer sound like?' she asked herself. Don't Calvinists speak directly to God? They don't need an intermediary—a priest, Mary, or Jesus? They don't even have saints? She had never asked God for anything. If Pieter were still alive, she did not want to insult him further using Catholic language, yet that was all she knew. As she stood near him, gripped by

271

fear and uncertainty, trying not to let the sobs escape, she heard a weak, but familiar voice.

"Did you miss me?"

She moved closer. She saw tiny red welts on Pieter's cheeks and chin—on both his upper and lower lips too.

"Stop sniveling, silly girl. Lift up this cloth. I want to look at you."

Terrified of what she might find, Isabela slowly peeled back the cloth covering Pieter's upper face. She nearly threw her arms around him when she saw those familiar teasing eyes, those adoring eyes that never seemed to tire of studying her. It was as if the two of them were locked in a permanent state of artist and subject. Yet those welts surrounded his eyes too and peppered his damp forehead. She sat beside him. If she was looking at a contagious disease, she didn't care. She'd die right here with him and be content.

"I did not want you to see me like this."

"What is it, my sweet friend? Measles? Small pox? Please tell me it is not."

"My sweet friend?" Pieter echoed. "Mmmm, I like that. Even though I'm feverish and have—momentarily I assure you—lost my strength, it's nothing so dire, my darling Isabela."

"What then?"

"Man of peace that I am, I seem to have accidentally invaded a village—more like a city actually. The residents were not happy with me."

Pieter stopped and took several deep breaths. "I think there's water on that table over there. Could you bring me some please?"

Isabela put her arm under Pieter's neck and lifted it so that he could drink. It was the closest she had been to him since they sat by the canal together in Amsterdam ten years ago—the day he gave her a drawing lesson on the role of perspective in art. She wanted to pull his head against her chest and hold it there forever, but she laid it back down gently.

Pieter seemed to draw strength from the liquid or perhaps from her presence. He continued his tale.

"Red ants. Vicious biting ants. I tried to convince them that I only wanted to draw them. I even offered to give them a drawing at no charge. They would have none of it. At first they thought my ankles were the enemy. They got inside my boots. When they discovered a whole body above the ankles, they brought out the cavalry, the cannons, the spears. Judging by my wounds, they even had muskets, the little critters."

"My poor darling."

"My poor darling? Sweet words to this would-be soldier's bitten-up old ears. I think I'll do battle more often. I'd like to be able to tell you I was a brave and strategic warrior, my lady. No. I went screaming and stomping through their little mounds of sand, arousing them further. My fellow travelers, observing my distress, made no effort to rescue me. I'm sure it must have looked to them exactly how it felt to me. I thought I had fallen into Hell. And all I had wanted was to relieve myself, for God's sake."

"Perhaps you should just rest, Pieter dear. Continue the story later."

"If my resting means you'll leave, I'll keep talking."

As if he wanted to hold her in place, Pieter tried to free his hand from under the blanket tied tightly onto the bed frame. He could not. He took a few more deep breaths and closed his eyes.

'Don't try to free your hands for a day or two,' is what the friar advised me. 'You must let the lesions be.'

"But, I repeat. Did you miss me?"

"Miss you? I hated you, you irritating man. Away far longer than you said you would be. I feared you were going to continue right up the coast, that I'd never see you again, that the natives would get you, the English, pirates, starvation. Then that scribbled little note."

"You were so mad you tore that note in little pieces and threw it away, didn't you?"

"If you must know, as irritating as it was—no news, no reassurance, no mention that you missed ME—well, it's tucked into my bosom right this moment," she finally admitted.

"Whooooo!" Pieter almost yelled in his hoarse whisper. "Interesting storage spot. Assuming your bosom isn't stuffed with notes from OTHER men, I do feel so very privileged. If I could free my hands, I'd write you dozens of notes right now. So, in other words, you did miss me."

"Since you insist. Yes. I did. I did miss you. I admit it."

"When did you miss me most?"

"Are you sure you shouldn't just rest?"

"Absolutely not. Talking to you distracts me from this infernal itching. Those ants wanted to be sure I never returned. They've left me with plenty of memories of their attack. That's why the friar tied my hands. So I won't scratch."

"My poor darling. But what have I been thinking? I have the perfect remedy."

Isabela kissed Pieter's dotted forehead and replaced the cloth. "I'll be right back."

"Quick. Come back quick. I'll be here. I'm not going anywhere."

Isabela had lost her self-consciousness about running through the streets of San Agustín. She ignored the stares, the curiosity, the calls, "Hey, what's your hurry, Lady? Somebody dyin?" She threw open the door to the Governor's house, lifted her skirts and bounded up the stairs. She found what she needed arranged in neat pots on the two windowsills of her room. And if these weren't enough, she'd dig up the ones she had planted in the garden.

One of the few items she brought with her to the New World was Cook's healing plant. The one that healed the Frenchman's wounds long ago. Gérard. The same one that healed Angel's slashed wrist after the pirate attack. When they ran out of fresh water during the voyage, she watered the plant with salt water. It almost died. Once they arrived in this town one of the first things she did was give that plant fresh water and change the soil. It had shrunk to a lonely floppy single stalk, but tenuous little shoots began to spring up.

Cook had told her she could cut a stalk at any point and soak the end in water. Once she saw roots, she planted it in soil. She never again wanted to lose the precious plant. Soon she had multiple pots. She gave them as gifts. To Maria Luisa to soothe her hands damaged from being immersed in water all day, from the lye in the laundry soap, from the abrasiveness of rubbing cloth again cloth. Soon Maria Luisa's hands, if not as smooth (and certainly not as delicately white) as Cook's, lost their ancient-lady look. Fewer wrinkles, knuckles less red.

She gave a pot to the cook and the maid at the Governor's house and to all the women in his family—even the Governor's arrogant sister-in-law. Angel took a plant with him on the maiden voyage of the new El Oviedo. She gave one to Big Owl. Although Big Owl had grown up observing the healing power of plants—thanks to the skill of his tribe's shaman, he too was impressed with the "fingers of magic" as he quickly named it. Isabela hated herself right now for never having given a "magic fingers" plant to Pieter. If he had had it with him after the attack, it would have saved him so much suffering. He might have been healed by now. When she thought of how those welts could have become infected, how the infection could have spread throughout his body, how he might have died, she was furious with herself.

She grabbed three of the largest, most mature plants, the ones with the thickest, longest stalks. Hugging the pots to her chest, she ran down the stairs, out the door, and through the town to the boarding house. The streets never seemed so long.

'This is what I can do for Pieter,' she thought. 'Cut open these stalks and spread the healing salve. Care for him, see that he gets water and food, clean the bites and replenish the balm every day, read to him. When he's well, then I'll tell what I can NOT do. But at least I will have done this.'

Five more houses to the boarding house. The pots were heavy. 'I must look a sweaty mess,' she thought, 'but Pieter won't care. He'll just be pleased to see me.' Three more houses. Two. One. She was there. The landlady stood in the doorway.

"If you're planning on visiting Mr. Hals, I must inform you that this is a respectable establishment, Missy. For gentlemen only. No women are allowed in the rooms."

* * *

Isabela had not run all that way with the burdensome pots only to be turned away.

"Hello, Señora Varragoza. I'm pleased to meet you. My name is Isabela Calderón. I've heard so much about your establishment since I arrived here from Spain six months ago. My neighbors. My friends. The Governor himself in whose house I reside. Friar Alonzo too. They all speak so well of you. You know I am just so grateful to the friar for caring for my betrothed. It's because of the Governor and the friar that I'm here to continue Mr. Hals' care. Nothing contagious. Don't worry about that.

"While Mr. Hals and I make plans for our wedding, Mr. Hals and the Governor have become great friends. And I really must mention that my betrothed himself has been grateful to call your home HIS home since arriving in San Agustín. 'Such a clean, quiet, well-run business,' he's told me. Perhaps you've seen Mr. Hals' works of art? Once he is well, it is his intention to make a drawing of your attractive sitting room."

Isabela's voice became lower and conspiratorial.

"In fact, Mr. Hals told me he will make TWO drawings. One to leave with you. The other to show on his travels. You must have noticed how the town is growing. More and more visitors can be expected. Your excellent reputation will be spread far and wide."

While her impatience was growing and her worry too, Isabela acted as if she had all the time in the world to stand there chatting with Señora Varragoza.

"I see you've noticed these plants. They came all the way from Spain. Perhaps you've had a rash at some point in your life? You've had a little cut? An irritation? Just between us women, the sap of this plant can be used on any part of the body at any time of the month. It soothes, but it does more. It heals. Faster than anything any physician has ever recommended. Here, please take one, Señora Varragoza. The friar told me he must spend the next few days administering to the sick in a nearby mission. After examining Pieter, he said to me, 'Doña Isabela, stay by your betrothed. See that he eats and drinks and takes the medicine. I'm leaving you in charge. I expect to see a healthier patient when I return.'"

"Well all right then. But I don't like the precedent. Don't tell anyone I gave you permission. One hour. And leave the door unlocked."

"Thank you, Señora Varragoza and good day to you."

With all the patience she could muster, Isabela entered the boarding house, climbed the stairs clutching the two remaining pots, tiptoed down the hallway, and knocked on Pieter's door. When there was no answer, she entered to find him much as she had found him earlier—minus the cloth on his head. Not moving. She closed the door. As she approached him, she could see that he was breathing and he was asleep. She had been away from him perhaps twenty minutes, but it felt like days. She had such a short time to administer the salve and to tell him all that was in her heart.

Chapter Thirty-Nine
Treatment

Isabela pulled a chair to Pieter's bedside. She did not take time to search for a knife. She broke off the sturdiest, thickest stalk and slit it down the middle with her fingernail. With all four fingers, she scooped out a generous amount of the stalk's sticky substance. Starting just below his hairline, she dabbed it on every spot on his head and face, behind his ears. Dozens of spots. She lifted his head and dabbed the back of his neck. With that familiar, subtle, amused smile, Pieter turned himself over to her.

"It's my feet that suffered the worst of it," Pieter said.

Isabela gasped in horror when she lifted the blanket at the bottom of the bed to reveal swollen feet and ankles. She broke off a second stalk and rubbed until both feet were covered with stickiness.

"Yes, I see. Your feet must be bothering you terribly."

"Not as much as they were a few seconds ago. I had no idea that in addition to your many appealing qualities, you are also a skilled nurse."

"Frankly, I had no idea either. I just believe in this plant."

She took a third "finger of magic" and used it like an applicator to spread the salve directly onto Pieter's skin. She lifted each foot so she could reach all around it. While she worked she told him the story of how Cook saved the Compostela pilgrim with this very plant. She was so intent on what she was doing and on sharing Cook's story, she was halfway up Pieter's lower legs when he said,

"Uh, Isabela, I think I should warn you. The friar felt the fresh air would be good for my wounds. He stripped me of all my clothing. You may want to stop where you are. The friar tied my hands to the bed . . . and though it's torture, I think it was for a good reason. If my hands were free, I would be scratching every inch of myself. I can't apply your salve to my own body . . . not for now. If he agrees, I'll ask him to apply your remedy to the rest of me."

"Just a little further," Isabela said working on Pieter's knees and starting on his lower thighs.

"How can I abandon the rest of these welts? The friar may not return for a couple of days. You'll need a fresh application every day."

"I won't argue. I can feel the cooling effect already. These damnable bites are finally calming somewhat . . . at least where you've touched them."

So without really thinking, just determined to give Pieter relief, she continued up his thighs. She felt maternal as if she were carrying for her own child. In some places, it looked as if he had been lashed. Pieter's appreciative moans encouraged her. She stopped once when she told Pieter about the gifts—at least one of them—that Gérard gave Cook. She showed him the double cross.

"I only wish I had given it to YOU before you left for that cursed trip."

'And why did I NOT give Pieter the cross?' she asked herself. Because Cook said it should be given to someone you love and she had never allowed herself to admit that she did love Pieter?

"Now where was I?" she asked.

"Halfway up my left thigh, I believe."

"Oh yes, I can see. The salve is shiny. I'll continue here."

And continue she did until she stopped abruptly, stunned by a purple, pulsating bulge. 'The size of it! No wonder Diego caused me so much pain.'

"I warned you, Señora. But for ten years you were a married woman. Surely you've seen one of these before. Plenty of times, I suspect. You're a mother."

Isabela covered Pieter's body with the blanket and leaned back in the chair. She took a deep breath. She recalled the landlady's voice. "One hour. And leave the door unlocked." 'How much time has gone by?' Isabela wondered. 'She might come barging in at any moment. And here I sit with a naked man, green ointment up to my elbows, greasy spots on my apron, probably my face too, my hair hanging loose from my bonnet.'

She poured water from the pitcher on the nightstand. She cleaned herself up as best she could. She lifted Pieter's head and gave him a drink. She sat back down again.

"Actually not. Not once. Yes, Pieter. Married ten years, mother of two, and yet in some ways I am still the innocent girl you knew in Amsterdam. I haven't wanted to tell you. I knew you'd be angry, not with me, but with Diego. Diego was not like you. I imagine with you it would have been different. Diego was not a gentle man. He was rough. Fast. Inconsiderate. He never loved me. Never really cared for me at all. I rarely saw him and for that I was grateful. His abandonment was difficult for my children, however."

She was right. When Pieter saw that she was trembling, that sharing the memories made her tear up, his easy-going nature abandoned him. He was furious. If Diego were to walk through that door at that moment, he had no doubt he would pull free from the straps that bound him to that bed, put his hands around Diego's neck, and choke him for as long as it took—until the last breath left his body.

"For ten years you endured that, my darling? What an insidious idiot! The bastard!"

Still trembling, Isabela said,

"So you see Pieter, I am a ruined woman. I am damaged. I am so filled with fear of the marital act that I can never respond to any man. I am going to do everything in my power to cure you, Pieter. Then this is my wish. That you return to your country and marry a woman you deserve. Find yourself a loving Dutch woman—no religious conflicts, no cultural differences, someone untainted, someone free to love you fully. And there is more. Something about me that might put you in danger."

The boarding house owner opened the door abruptly.

"Time's up, people. Say your good-bye's."

And she stood there as they did just that.

"Angel will bring you fresh water and food later, Pieter. I will see you tomorrow."

Seeing her tears as she brushed by, Señora Varragoza said,

"I don't want anybody dying in my establishment. Are you sure he ain't gonna give us all some disease?"

"Ant bites, Señora Varragoza," Pieter called out in as healthy a voice as he could fake. "Curable. Nothing I can pass on."

* * *

That same evening Angel was a dinner guest at the Governor's house. The Governor himself was travelling and the women always enjoyed some male company. Angel was wearing the suit of clothes Isabela had made for him for just such an occasion. He no longer had the rumpled look of a carpenter sailor. He presented himself as a gentleman.

"Do tell us about the maiden voyage of your boat, Señor de Vega. El Oviedo, is it?" Fania asked with batting eyelashes.

But Angel had recently met another young woman who apparently impressed him.

"Petal."

"They named Big Owl's little sister Petal?"

"I do so love the way they choose names, don't you Captain de Vega? Not after a saint. Not after one's mother," Fania said glancing at Estefania. "But something that reflects who the child is. Something unique. Something clever. But Petal? Why, Captain?"

"When you think of a flower petal, what other words come to mind?"

"Fragile, I would say. Delicate. Soft. Pretty."

"Exactly. You've got it. And what might happen to something that is delicate?"

"It might not last too long. The wind might take it away. It might fall off."

"You are describing exactly the fears Big Owl's parents felt when Petal was born. She was undersized and weak—often too weak to seek nourishment at the breast. She was so pretty and sweet, they did not want to lose her. Big Owl's father asked his workers to grind fish bones into a fine powder. They ran the powder through their fingers repeatedly to be sure it contained no graininess, certainly no pieces of bone. Eventually only a light powder remained. Big Owl's mother dipped her little finger into a dish of pig's blood and then into the powder. The fish powder stuck to the sticky blood. She placed her finger on Petal's tiny tongue. She did this for days until Petal became strong enough to suck at the breast. Meanwhile villagers gathered around the tent chanting.

They built fires to drive out whatever threatened Petal's life. They played solemn music. They danced. The incantations worked.

"What does Petal look like now, may I ask?"

"Today, fifteen years later, Petal is only a little bit shorter than her older brother, if you can believe it. The muscles in her arms and legs are amazingly strong."

The women, all covered from toe to neck, lowered their gaze uncomfortably. They had never ceased to be scandalized by how much of their bodies native women revealed.

"I didn't see this myself, but I'd like to. Big Owl told me that one time Petal spotted strawberries growing on the other side of a stream. She was caring for her baby sister. She placed the infant in one palm and used her other arm to propel herself all the way across that deep stream. The baby wasn't even wet when she reached the island. Petal had herself a berry feast and swam back with the baby again raised high above the water. Now that's a strong woman!"

"And would you say your trip was a success, Captain de Vega?" Estefania inquired.

"I would say so, Señora. We stopped in native villages and small settlements. We invited people to visit the boat. We told them we carried people and small goods up and down the riverways. By the time we had travelled two weeks, many people had asked us to stop for them on the return trip. They didn't pay us in gold, of course. Some had a few *maravedíes*. Others gave us woven cloth, a chicken, baskets—things we could trade. We dropped the passengers off at other villages or brought them all the way to San Agustín. Many of them had never seen the town and were just curious. I suspect we'll have passengers who want to return to their families, although some may want to stay here."

* * *

Pieter lay awake thinking of his beloved. He was still livid with Diego and with himself for not being clearer about his feelings for her when she was in Amsterdam. But would it have made any difference? How could she have resisted the two men who woke her, took her from her bed in the middle of the night and carried her off? Did she even want to protest? She believed she was being an obedient daughter, following her father's plan for her. She had met Diego only twice before. How could she have known what he was like, what lay ahead for her? And didn't she say she did not want to alarm the little girls? She did not call out? She allowed herself to be taken far away from him—to a country at war with his own.

'No wonder she always gets that downcast, tense look when I mention anything about a future together,' he thought. 'Even a light, fleeting comment drives her away.'

He assumed those tight pressed lips were an expression of her negative reaction to the idea of being with him, maybe even of disgust. Now he knew that every time he spoke of becoming a couple, she was feeling the pain from her marriage. He wished she had been able to express that sooner. His thoughts turned to what he could say to convince her to accompany him back to his home. That large empty house on the Heerengracht just sitting there. Waiting empty for her for ten whole years. He couldn't bear to be there long without her. 'And what was that last comment about anyway?' 'Something about me that might put you in danger.' 'Is that what she said? What could that be about? Oh the mystery of the woman! Whether she becomes mine or not, I will never know her fully.'

* * *

Isabela rose early and prepared foods that could be eaten in a prone position. She prepared a double portion of cold squash soup and sprinkled it with well-chopped hazelnuts. Soft bread to dip in it. Orange segments.

Fania treated Nelita like the little sister she never had and would take good care of her. Besides, the girls had watched the cat give birth the day before. Afterwards, Nelita begged to sleep on the kitchen floor. She wanted to be there the minute the first kitten opened its tightly shut eyes. She would probably stay in that same spot for as long as Isabela was gone today.

Isabela hurried out, miserable at the thought of her darling Pieter tied to that bed, his skin itching and aching all over. And she would not go directly to his room. Now that she had begun, there was so much to say. She wanted to tell him everything before he left forever. They needed more than an hour a day together in that room.

Isabela greeted Señora Varragoza in the same friendly relaxed tone she had tried to use the previous day.

"Señora, how are you this morning?"

"Quiet night," the woman said. "No crying out in pain or anything like that. Just hope your betrothed ain't dead."

"Mr. Hals just needs rest, Señora. He'll be fine soon. Up and ready to make those drawings of your establishment if you wish it. I've brought some things from the Governor's kitchen for you. May I come in?"

Isabela followed Señora Varragoza to the parlor and lifted from her basket the items she had packed. "I know you're a busy woman, Señora Varragoza, but I wonder if you might have time to chat before you begin your day's tasks. Women are scarce in this town and I do sometimes hunger for a good talk. May I sit down?"

"Well if you're making yourself at home, I might as well make you a cup of tea."

Isabela waited, jiggling in her chair and tapping her toes up and down, then forcing herself to sit back, stop fiddling, and relax while she sipped her tea.

"So what brought you here, Señora?"

"Same thing brought you here, Señora Calderón. A foolish husband. I've heard about yours. Sorry you lost him before you even landed. In my case we did land, but when he discovered there was no gold to be had here, he brooded and drank himself to death. So how did I end up in one of the largest and nicest houses in this god-forsaken town, you might ask? My father and uncle took pity on me. They sent me enough money for my return trip and then some.

"My husband had already purchased one house. I used my acquired money to buy another and combined them. At first I had a low-level clientele. I couldn't offer much. But I saved my money. I traded for nice furniture, solid beds, clean quilts. Gradually I was able to attract a better-paying clientele. Now I allow only officers, visiting government officials, and priests into my house. Your betrothed is none of those, but he pays in cash. That's rare and I like it. Nice fella too. You certainly wasted no time finding yourself another man, Missy."

"It's not the way it seems, Señora. Mr. Hals and I first met ten years ago in Amsterdam. I nearly died with my Captain father when his ship was downed in a storm. I was working in an orphanage and Pieter painted my portrait as a gift for the orphanage. When he learned I had come to San Agustín, he happened to be in New Netherland. He came for a visit. Upon learning I was a widow, he asked me to be his wife."

"So we're both survivors, ain't we? In our own way? Would you like more tea?"

"Yes, I would. You're right. Besides being Spanish women, we do have other experiences in common. This tea is delicious, by the way. And this cinnamon cake! Did you make it yourself?"

"I certainly did. I do it all here. The marketing, the baking, the cooking. I do have a woman who cleans. Gave that up several years ago. Too hard on the back."

"You are so right. It's worth paying someone else to do the most physically demanding tasks. I grew up with servants, but since you know so much about me, you may know that I earn my living as a seamstress now. Excuse me, but would you mind if I play a tune on your harpsichord over there in the corner?"

"Oh you noticed it. Myself, I can't play a note, but when a past governor determined he had no room for it when he returned to Spain, he offered it to me. I thought it would add a touch of finery and class."

"I agree with you. It adds to the elegance of this room. Growing up I played frequently. My mother and aunts taught me. I had hopes of teaching my children, but my husband sold the instrument before they were born. Now I've been pleased these past months to be able to play my favorite music again in the Governor's house. I'm teaching his daughters along with my own."

"That's right. I forgot. Your son was snatched by buccaneers, wasn't he? At least you have a daughter. I never had children. Yes, please do play. It must be terribly out of tune, though."

"Oh, I know how to fix that."

Isabela fiddled with the keys and the strings until they sounded right to her. Then she sat down on the harpsichord stool and ran her fingers up and down the keyboard. She stopped and turned to Señora Varagosa.

"I do so love a melodious Cavalli aria, don't you? It just feels good for the soul. I only wish I knew the words and could sing this piece like Romero did. Romero was the Italian who taught my aunts and me to play. We could have listened to him perform all day long but, with our limited Italian, we were not successful in memorizing the lyrics."

Isabela played one aria after another. When she broke out into a lively *conzonanze stravaganze*—also from Italy, joy filled every room. Although she was wrestling with how soon she could terminate the visit with the Señora, she stopped abruptly as if remembering her purpose for being there."

"I really must check on Mr. Hals. Thank you for this lovely visit. I hope we can repeat it soon."

"Come as often as you like, Señora Calderón, and take as long as you need to mend that young man."

Isabela gathered Pieter's breakfast and rapidly ascended the stairs to his room. His hopeful voice invited her in. She put down the food and hurried to him.

"How is the patient today?"

Even as she asked, she could see that the spots on his face and neck had changed from fiery red to pink. The magic fingers were working.

"And the itching? Is it better?"

"Everywhere you applied the innards of that plant, my dear. Every place you touched. Better. I think there are only two areas that are still suffering badly. My back which you couldn't reach and my wrists which are bound. I think I can control myself now. If I don't recover the use of my hands soon, I may go mad. Can you remove the binding please?"

Isabela had brought a pair of strong scissors for that very purpose and a second smaller pair to cut Pieter's fingernails down to the quick. She did not want him to scratch and undo the healing. Pieter put his head back and moved his head from side to side. He twisted life back into his wrists. Shook out his fingers.

"Do you think I'll remember how to draw?"

"You'll never forget that. But let me see your nails. Now that's done, can you turn over so I can apply the sap to your back and wrists? You're right they are red and inflamed. Turn over again. Let me see your face. Oh, how wonderful you can sit up now."

Isabela hovered over Pieter and patted the still-visible bites with fresh sap.

"Now that you can move, you can open the shoots and apply the juice to your own legs and stomach."

"Too bad. I liked it when you did it. Almost makes me want to be bound again. Was that YOU playing? Señora Varragoza doesn't strike me as the type. The more I learn about you, the more I realize I don't know about you and the more I want to know. That last piece brought me back to Italy. I danced to it so many times."

"Italy was your favorite, wasn't it Pieter. I think you miss your Lucietta. While you were dancing and making love with HER, I was stuck in that fishing village. Every time Diego motioned me to join him on the cot in his room, usually after I heard his parents pressuring him to conceive another grandchild for them, I felt like a cow, a mother pig. Good for nothing but having babies."

"A woman's body is not just for birthing and feeding, Isabela. It is designed for loving. Every inch of it. If touched in a certain way, kissed gently in special places, it responds in ways—well you can't imagine it. You have to experience it. Lucietta had a tremendous capacity for experiencing pleasure. She never tired. Nine years younger than she and I would eventually need to rest. She never did. She could continue all night long. I can show you my darling. Unrushed. Slowly. It's not too late."

"You told me you loved her. Wasn't it difficult to leave her, Pieter?"

"I considered asking her to marry me, of course. But it would not have worked. I faced the same issue with her religion. My mother was dying. I had to return home quickly. My father was grieving. It was never the right time to ask his permission. He would never have consented and I wasn't ready to leave my homeland forever and move permanently to Rome. Besides, I think she enjoyed her freedom."

"Her freedom. You mean she had many lovers then?"

"Quite a few. Yes. It was a totally different way of life from my strict Calvinist upbringing—living in the art community in Rome. I was young, away from home, exploring, trying to find my way as an artist. I was still that upright boy, though. I was careful."

"Careful. I don't understand what that means in the context you're describing. Lucietta—she never bore a child? She didn't become diseased?"

"Do you really want to know such details?"

"Yes, I do. I need to."

"Somehow I don't see you taking a leap into the free life yourself."

"I'll explain. Just tell me."

Chapter forty
Protection

"*Un petit linge.*"

"*Un petit linge?*"

"Yes. Excuse my accent. It sounds better when you say it. It means "a little piece of cloth." In a leather bag tied to her waist, Lucietta kept her *petits linges* cut just the right size along with slender ribbons. I think she once told me they were made out of animal bladder. They were stretchy."

"Big Owl told me those big round startling ear pieces he stretches over bone are made from fish bladder. But I'm confused. What did Lucietta do with her stock of *petits linges?*"

"The first time we were together in bed, she introduced me to the idea in such a charming, but firm way, I didn't question her. Wrapping *un petit linge* around a man's member and tying it with a ribbon was for her part of lovemaking. Both serious and amusing at the same time. And stimulating! She would say, '*Pas de petit linge. Pas d'amour.*' That was the deal. And that is how she protected herself. Using French—the language of romance—just made it more appealing."

Feeling utterly naïve compared to the experienced Lucietta, Isabela let out a big sigh.

"I haven't even served you your breakfast, Pieter dear."

Pieter did not yet seem strong enough to walk. She pulled over a table and arranged the food for him.

"Sometimes I find my unworldliness disgusting. I've travelled more than most women from a Spanish fishing village. I know something of music and art. I've been studying poetry, literature, and philosophy. I haven't told you about that yet either. Yet I know so little that's practical. What you're telling me—about those little pieces of cloth—might have saved the life of a dear friend."

Isabela stopped. This was so difficult, so sad, but she must continue, she must explain, she must warn him.

"The danger I referred to yesterday, Pieter? I think there's a possibility I may have a serious disease. I think I may have the *mal francés*."

When Isabela used the expression "Something about me might put you in danger" yesterday, he wondered, 'Wait. Is that bastard husband of hers alive after all? Is he jealous? Coming after me?' But *mal francés*? That was the last thing Pieter expected to hear. With that irresponsible husband, rarely at home, carousing—it makes sense.'

Hungry as he was, Pieter could not touch another bite of breakfast.

"Diego had a long-term mistress—Leonor, the mother of Angel and two daughters—all Diego's children I'm convinced, although he didn't necessarily claim them. He was no more attentive to her family than he was to mine. He stole from both of us. Stole and sold all my father had accumulated in a lifetime. Yet for reasons I don't fully understand, Leonor always welcomed him back. Angel is convinced that his father passed on the disease to Leonor—one of the loveliest, serene and motherly women I've ever known. Our five children—half siblings—adored each other. Angel suffered when his little brother—his only living brother—my Pedro—was kidnapped.

"Leonor died shortly after our departure to the New World. Diego was always careless, lazy, and impetuous. But during the last months of his life, preparing, if you can call it that, for our voyage to San Agustín, oh such lethargy. He was always curt and defensive, but he let Angel and the rest of the crew take over the ship. He slept most of the time. He was sleeping below deck when the pirates came on board. He must have heard the tromping, fighting, and shouting. He had two sons up there on deck, yet he made no attempt to save them. I think he may have known that he too had the disease, that he didn't want to live anymore. That and possibly some shame—if he was capable of such an emotion—maybe that's why he threw himself overboard in the middle of the night."

"But you said you rarely had relations with him."

"True. But I've researched the disease. I saw people wandering the streets of Santos Gemelos with distorted features, sores. One contact can be enough. But I may have contracted the disease from someone else too."

Pieter's eyes grew wide. Did he know this woman at all? Could her loneliness have driven her to lie with other men?

"Leonor. I noticed lesions on her arm and on the back of one of her hands. This was after I had spent the night in her bed. She calmed me after Cook was killed. After the tailor and his family escaped. I collapsed and Angel carried me all the way to her house. It was the only night in my life that I was away from my children. It was the last time I ever saw Leonor. You can contract the disease from coming in contact with lesions like that."

"Your cook was killed? Who would kill a cook?"

"Aurelia. I like to call her by her name now—out of respect. The Church killed her. I loved her dearly. She was like a second mother—to me and to many people. I don't think I'm a Catholic any more, Pieter, but I feel unanchored."

'A murdered cook? An escaping tailor? The threat of a deadly disease? The challenge of their different religions perhaps no longer an issue? How permanent was her alienation from the Catholic Church, though? What caused it?' Pieter felt overwhelmed. 'Perhaps Isabela was right. I should do what she suggested—return to Amsterdam and create a family with a Dutch woman.'

* * *

Isabela rose early to prepare a day's worth of meals for Pieter. She stepped over Nelita and Fania who had spent a second night stretched out on blankets on the kitchen floor. The kittens looked like furry balls with tiny ears and eye slits still glued shut. It looked as if their eyes would not open today. Perhaps not for many days, maybe weeks. She needed to lure her daughter away, clean her up, and divert her, but for now she left her sleeping in Fania's arms. She made as little noise as possible and slipped out with a basket full of food and an unused pot of "magic fingers."

To her relief, Isabela found that the boarding house owner was apparently still away on her morning marketing jaunt. She slipped up the stairs and knocked on Pieter's door. Friar Alonzo opened the door. After the slimmest of greetings, he said,

"Your betrothed here tells me that, unbeknownst to him, you are a skilled nurse, Señora Calderón. I can see that for myself. I've seen the result of ant attacks before. But never have I seen a recovery as rapid as Mr. Hals's. Do share with me your remedy. I am most anxious to replicate it."

Pieter was up, dressed, sitting in a chair by the window. Behind the friar's back he greeted her with that twinkle that made her feel so treasured,

"Good morning."

When he saw her glance at the slate and charcoal that lay on the floor next to him, he said,

"I attempted to draw for the first time in days. To my dismay, I discovered that I have not yet regained sufficient strength to dedicate myself to that activity."

'Or is it dealing with this woman,' he thought, 'that has drained me of energy? How long will it take for me to sort out all she's experienced in the past decade? What of the young woman I loved still remains?'

Yet even as these questions occurred to him, he felt the familiar tug growing rapidly now into the desire to envelope her, lift her, twirl her. Delighted to see him slowly returning to normal, Isabela smiled and laid out his first meal of the day.

Oblivious to the couple's struggles and confusion, the friar talked about his own challenges in the mission he had just visited.

"For the most part, they've accepted Jesus Christ as their Lord. They attend my services. Yet they will not give up their own bizarre beliefs and practices. Their shamans still maintain a hold on their daily lives. Signs of the devil is what they are. They spend their time making charms from herbs or snake skins, white feathers, owl eyes.

"Their belief in omens is particularly vexing. Take lightening for instance, or even the popping of a fire. These predict something to come, but I don't always understand what that might be. Even if one of them observes a neighbor twitching his eyes, mouth, or eyebrows, he reads meaning into those harmless gestures.

"During confession, I try to dispel these ridiculous notions. I think they're harmful. I ask them,

'Before hunting deer, did you take the antlers from another deer and pray to those antlers the ceremony of the devil?

'Yes,' they'll say innocently 'and I easily found a deer to bring back to my family. A plump, healthy one too.'

"I ask, 'Have you ever made an attempt to bewitch someone else?'

"'Yes,' they may say, 'the boy who stole the arrowheads I had worked on for days. I took the skin of a poisonous snake and mixed it with black guano. I placed the mix in front of his family's hut. It worked. The lad returned the arrow heads to me.'

"And then there's that Black Drink they prepare. They drink it to excess and enter some kind of trance. It's the devil's work. I'm sure of it."

Isabela could see that the friar might keep talking all day. She wrapped some food in a napkin and gave him the plant she had brought.

"I understand that your work in the colony is very demanding, friar. You must feel a great sense of satisfaction doing your part to bring the natives to our Lord."

As soon as she said the words, she felt a sense of guilt. She didn't believe what she was saying. She had grown to admire Big Owl and his disappearing way of life. But she wanted the friar gone. She wanted to be alone with Pieter. She placed the healing plant in the friar's arms and ushered him to the door of Pieter's room. She shut the door. She lugged a table over to where Pieter was sitting and laid out his breakfast.

"I assume you're not so weak that you can't feed yourself?"

Pieter lifted a spoon and placed it back down again.

"Actually, I can hardly hold this spoon up and I'm ever so hungry. Might you be willing to feed me again, dear Isabela?"

"You tease. You're looking awfully well today. The friar had your clothes washed didn't he? And he helped you dress?"

"He's a good fellow. Doing his best to provide care in this demanding environment."

"I find the Timucuan beliefs fascinating. These beliefs are centuries old. They seem to work. Why should Europeans have all the answers?"

"I agree. But let's talk about OUR beliefs, Isabela. You hinted that you're no longer a devout Catholic? How did that happen?"

He soon found himself once again wanting desperately to comfort her, but knowing that he should not interrupt. She turned somber as soon as she began telling about Cook. Then she kept breaking down, holding her head in her hands for long periods, unable to continue. He reached out to her and gently caressed her hand, waiting. Each time she would eventually move to the next part of Cook's story. He knew the ending must be something horrific. It was causing her so much grieving. 'Didn't she say the church had killed Cook?' He held her hand and waited. The food sat uneaten before him.

When she arrived at the part where the soldier strangled Aurelia and set fire to her body, she did not cry. She described it quickly. She was finished.

"That's when you collapsed then? Right in the middle of the plaza? That's when Angel carried you to his mother's house?"

"No not exactly then. I ran to the tailor's. I was desperate. But . . ."

She stopped. She looked at Pieter with eyes brimming again, head moving side to side as if to shake away the memories.

"I can't share that with you just yet, Pieter."

"While we're on the subject, shall I tell you something about my religion, then?"

"Yes, Pieter. I would like to hear that. Please eat first, though."

She picked up the spoon, dipped it into corn mush mixed with honey, and brought it to his lips. He closed his eyes and savored it.

"In all my travels, nothing I've ever eaten has tasted so delicious," he said.

"You are so dramatically ridiculous," she said as she continued to feed her recovering patient, her Pieter.

When he had had his fill, he said,

"By the way, I owe you an apology. I told the friar we were engaged to be married. Please forgive me for the deception. I thought your presence here might be more acceptable."

"I did exactly the same with Señora Varragoza. In an attempt to lend my visits some respectability in HER eyes."

"It doesn't mean anything. It's a practical lie."

"Exactly. Misleading, of course, but necessary."

"I don't plan to mix the skin of a poisonous snake with black guano in order to atone for the lie."

"Nor do I. Drink the pomegranate juice. I added a little orange pulp to it."

"So. Calvinism."

"Yes. Tell me."

"Take the concept of free will."

"Free will? Your religion allows you to make your own choices? I am accustomed to being told what to do and what not to do, not to ponder and think. Playing chess did that for me, though. It's a game. It's not a religion, but I think I can relate to the concept of free will because of chess."

"Who taught you to play chess?"

"The tailor's family. Go on. Tell me more about free will. In some ways it's probably easier to let the Church tell us what to do, but the Church is fallible, it is not as perfect and divine as it portrays itself."

"That's probably heresy you're speaking."

Automatically they lowered their voices. They moved their heads slightly closer. The discussion was serious, but it became another of their games.

"So. Free will," Pieter whispered as if being overheard might cause thunder and lightning. Her intelligent, expectant eyes made him want to stop the discussion. He wanted to reach over, gently close those still-damp eyelids and cover them with kisses. She was waiting for an explanation. This was his chance, wasn't it?

"It's the idea that an individual can make his or her own choices in life. The Church provides guidelines of course, and they can be very strict, but ultimately we each decide. It's related to another concept. Predestination."

"Predestination. Sounds serious. What is it?"

"It's the idea that God gives us life, places us on earth, each of us with a particular purpose. We only need to discover that purpose to fulfill it."

"Are predestination and free will both tenets of your religion? The two concepts seem to conflict."

Pieter had not predicted that he would be having this conversation with Isabela. He felt ill prepared. He had never analyzed the religion of his birth. He had never questioned it much. He just followed it. Since the time he was a small boy old enough to not cry in church, he had gone to Sunday services at the Nieuwe Kerk, sat between his parents in the stern but majestic environment, and allowed his mind to wander. The only time he gave much thought to his religion was when it seemed to be a barrier to marrying the woman he loved. This woman. The woman before him.

"It has to do with God's plan. You're right. The two concepts do seem to be in conflict. To resolve the conflicts, our church leaders turn to the Bible. That is the source of their truth. They interpret the Bible for us, the ordinary folk. We aren't the specialists who try to figure it all out. I'm certainly not."

Isabela was confused. 'At first,' she thought to herself, 'Pieter seemed to be saying that Calvinists believed they had leeway to interpret the

Bible themselves. Yet Pieter just said the Church leaders interpret the Bible for 'the ordinary folk.' This too seems contradictory.'

Suddenly Isabela missed the tailor acutely. He would be able to explain this seeming conflict. And if it were true that he was of a different religion altogether, he would be able to integrate these conflicting concepts into his own beliefs. He would be able to explain it to her in a way that made sense.

Chapter Forty-One
Packing Once More

Aknock on the door sent them moving apart. Angel. He was so busy these days. Isabela did not realize how much she had missed him. His sudden appearance in this room reinforced her impressions from the night before when he dined at the Governor's house. Now sixteen, he seemed to have moved from youth to manhood overnight. His beard was full and dark. He still had those gentle, aware, sensitive qualities, but he walked with larger, firmer steps. He was more assertive.

"My friend, how are you faring?" he asked with a gentle pat on Pieter's back. Pieter made an attempt, but was still too weak to rise. "My mother Isabela is taking good care of you, I see. I wanted to tell you both something. I have no idea what your plans are, but you should know that I have a list of passengers waiting for another trip up the river. Most of them wish to go all the way to New Amsterdam. If you're ready to return home, Pieter, New Amsterdam is the best place for you to set sail."

That night Elizabeth and her new husband came to dinner at the Governor's house. 'Did God deliberately set this couple at the table tonight to taunt me?' Isabela wondered. 'Are they unwittingly sending me a message about my destiny? Am I predestined to sit here and observe this newly married couple smiling and laughing? Their shoulders pressed against each other? As if they could never get quite close enough for long enough? What is my jealousy telling me? That I have the free will to make a choice about my future?'

* * *

15 February 1652
Dear Friend,

    I do believe that Pieter has ceased to woo me. Perhaps he's realized that I am not the innocent castaway he knew years ago. Perhaps I've exhausted him with my fears and my doubts. Since he has fully regained his health, I feel I have no excuse for lingering in his room at the boarding house. The only time we are alone is in the garden of the Governor's house with that silent parrot between us. But the garden is a favorite after-dinner gathering spot for the Governor's guests so even that space is often denied us.

    Pieter continues to spend his time as he always does wherever he is. Today I believe he's down at the docks sketching Angel as Angel prepares for the journey to New Amsterdam. Labeling a passage on El Oviedo 'luxurious' may be an exaggeration, Angel says, 'but my goal is to make it the most comfortable passenger boat to ever set sail from San Agustín.' Soldiers, housewives, and children know about the planned journey. They gather on the dock during the day to watch the progress.

    Lately though, Pieter has been sketching Nelita. He always asks her permission first. Since neither speaks the other's language, they've been communicating with gestures. He spreads parchment over his board, picks up a piece of charcoal and makes drawing gestures with a questioning look asking her permission to proceed. "Sí," she'll say, "Porqué no?" She stops to arrange her skirts and straighten her bonnet.

    But Pieter indicates that he doesn't really want her to pose. It's as if he wants to remember her as she goes through the activities that consume her small life. I never allow her to go beyond the palisade, of course. Too many stories of wild boar attacks. Once a Spanish child was snatched by a hostile native, they say.

    Pieter has quite a collection now of Nelita surrounded by the kittens or holding only Suavita, the orange kitten, her favorite. Angel made a swing for her from a cast-off board. He smoothed it down, cut holes on either side, passed strong ropes through the holes, and hung it from the sassafras tree in the Governor's garden. Pieter's drawings show my Nelita sitting demurely on the unmoving swing holding a flower or kicking the ground with both feet to make herself go up and up. In one sketch she's even standing on the swing, but I put a stop to that.

    What surprised me today was that they've begun to have verbal exchanges in a mixture of their languages. She's been listening to me speak to Pieter in Dutch for months now. The language, so different from her native Spanish, seems to come naturally for her. I watched them from my upstairs window today and had a sudden vision. I saw Pieter drawing Nelita as a ten-year-old, a fourteen-year-old, a young woman. The vision shook me, it seemed so real. I tried to erase the images from my mind. She will miss him when he goes.

When he goes! I am not ready. I am not ready. Neither to say good-bye to him nor to join my life to his.

I think of you often, of Reza, Bernardo, and little Briana. I pray that you are safe, that you are thriving.

Your loving and confused friend,
Isabela

* * *

One week after composing the latest fantasy letter to the tailor, Isabela returned to the Governor's home to find a little Chinese man preening in front of the gilded mirror that dominated the front hallway. The costume was too large and dragged on the stone floor. The broad black sleeves drooped over and hid the wearer's hands. The red circular collar hung loose as did the long thick hair of the model.

"From Father's collection," Tania explained. "He's an expert on clothing from the Ming Dynasty you know. He gave us permission to try on these costumes. This is Nelita's favorite."

"Mama, do you think Tío Pieter will draw me wearing this?"

"I'm sure he will if you ask him," Isabela answered, but she was thinking, 'When did Nelita begin calling Pieter uncle? She's lost a father, a brother, the two half sisters left behind in Spain. She has only Angel and me. She's creating a family for herself. She will be so unhappy when Pieter, Tío Pieter, leaves.'

And he did seem to be preparing to leave San Agustín. Pieter hired the carver to make frames for some of his drawings. 'Departing gifts?' Isabela wondered. 'Is this what he always does when he's about to leave a town?' One for each member of the Governor's family. One for the boarding house owner. One for Angel. One for the carver himself.

As Nelita continued to stand in front of the mirror and examine her outfit from every angle, trying not to trip on the over-sized hem, a messenger knocked on the door and left a note for Isabela.

If at all possible, please meet me at the Chapel today at half past four.

She noted that while SHE always referred to that special spot as "Our Lady of La Leche," Pieter called it simply "the Chapel." Was this another indication of the difference in their religions?

It was the only time she could remember that he had summoned her. She hadn't been alone with him for several weeks. After putting on a fresh blouse and apron, she hurried toward "the Chapel." So as not to appear too eager, she slowed down when she heard him whistling. The sun was low in the sky and she could not see him through the trees. But he must have seen her approaching in the distance.

Yes, there he was, her Pieter, leaning casually against the outside wall of the chapel. Legs crossed at the ankles. Arms hanging casually at his sides. Fingers tapping his legs in time to the tune. As if he had nothing much on his mind. As if he had nothing better to do than whistle away alone in that isolated spot.

'Is this how I'll remember him?' she wondered.

She felt certain, though, that the tune she heard was meant to welcome her. Like Briana who never sang a song the same way twice, Pieter lured her forward with a tune that was new to her. A melody that reflected . . . what? A guarded cheerfulness perhaps? He watched her approach and continued whistling until she was standing right in front of him.

He maintained the same position, but stopped whistling and, as always, took a silent moment to regard her. Admiring her? Assessing her mood? Getting up the courage to explain why he had invited her here? Fixing her in his mind before he left never to set eyes on her again?

She expected that they would enter the chapel and converse in reverent whispers and semi-darkness as they had several times in the past. Instead he took her arm and led her on a stone path around the chapel to the back of it. A bench sheltered under the eaves provided shade. They sat there for awhile saying nothing, admiring the inlet in the distance, the verdant island beyond it, and the sea still further out.

He reached for her chin and turned it toward him. There's something I've wanted to do ever since I set eyes on you in that jail cell. She expected him to kiss her, but he moved away from her slightly, and raised his hand. Gently with two fingers he reached over and traced the silver stripe in her hair.

"Do I look terribly older to you? Older than you expected?"

"For as long as I may know you, you will never look old to me."

Pieter took a deep breath and let the air out slowly. He swallowed. He looked away. He looked back directly into her eyes. He spoke.

"We still have conflicts, you and I. We may always. Life is never perfect. Here is the plan.

"I will leave on Angel's passenger boat in approximately three weeks. You and Nelita will accompany me to New Amsterdam."

Pieter did not stop for acquiescence or objection. He continued matter-of-factly.

"We will consult a physician about your disease concerns. From what you have told me—no signs, no fatigue, healthy in every way—I do not believe you are ill. I suggest the consultation only to put your mind at ease. I do not trust the friars here to make such a judgment. They care more about saving souls for a supposed future life than saving lives in this one.

"We will also meet with the clergyman at the church in New Amsterdam. He will explain to us both what is required for you to convert. We will be married in the church there. We will wait until we are able to buy passage on the safest, most comfortable Dutch vessel available. We will set sail for Amsterdam. I have every confidence that with a loving husband your dread of intimacy will eventually disappear. I am a patient man.

"If you choose to stay here, I will return to Amsterdam alone. I don't think I need to tell you how very sad that would make me. I believe you would also be unhappy. The choice is yours. After all, you do have free will," he added in a cheerier tone.

"Do you play chess?" she asked.

"Are you trying to divert me from what I've just said? Do you have any idea how many times I've rehearsed my little speech?"

"I appreciate all the effort you've put into the 'plan' as you call it. I ask about chess because more than advice from others, certainly better than guidance offered by my religion, I've found chess to be helpful in exercising what I now understand is my free will. For my part, I've considered my possibilities. I've analyzed my options. I'm ready to make a move. If it doesn't work out, you can always divorce me—Timucuan style."

"Oh, and what is that? I should like to be prepared just in case."

"The hut belongs to the woman. If she wants the marriage to end, she gathers up her husband's clothing, bows and arrows—all his belongings—and places them in front of the hut. That's the signal to him and to the community. They are no longer a couple. They're both free to marry someone else. Your hut is a large house you've told me. It would take me a long time to gather all your belongings and pile them up on the Heerengracht."

She reached over to take his hand—that hand with the permanently charcoal-stained fingertips that she loved. She held that hand in both of hers.

"Besides," she said, her voice breaking, "I'd rather live in Maria Luisa's shack WITH you than in a mansion WITHOUT you."

* * *

'Is life but a series of preparations for the next phase?' Isabela thought as she emptied, packed, emptied and repacked her few belongings. 'Childhood prepares us for adulthood. Betrothal for marriage. Pregnancy for child rearing. A full circle. Learning letters that eventually become words, then sentences, then paragraphs. Training and apprenticing for a hoped-for career—if you're a man, anyway. According to the Church, life is pure preparation. We live obediently now so that our souls can live forever after we die.'

She thought of Nelleke's fascination with numbers, how she pestered everyone, even strangers to help her count higher and higher. How stumped Nelleke was when she first learned that no matter how high she learned to count, she would never reach 'the highest number ever.' She would never reach her goal. She would never be able to say, "I now know every number that exists." When she learned about infinity, Nelleke stopped counting higher and higher. She moved on to studying insects.

'Is that where I am? I've stopped trying, at least for now, to figure it all out? I've reached a level of acceptance?'

She took a deep, satisfying breath and once again packed that familiar old trunk. Books on the bottom. Reza's wedding gown folded on books. On top of the gown, the cushions, their hidden treasure known only to her. Personal items resting on cushions. So few belongings and she was about to become the mistress of a large home full of objects.

Pieter told her that his father, a silver merchant who also served in the lucrative and mostly ceremonial position of postmaster for the city of Amsterdam, was a collector. A collector of what exactly she did not know yet. She had the rest of her life to explore whatever had at one time attracted her father-in-law.

To "prepare"—oh that word again—to prepare Nelita for moving into his house, her Tío Pieter first drew the front door for her.

"My house is a double canal house," he explained. "It has two front doors with seven steps leading to the entrances. We use only one of those entrances for going in and out. The first thing you'll notice as you arrive is a man's large hand."

"A real hand?" Nelita asked in dismay. "Will it try to grab me?"

"Definitely not. If it could talk, the hand would say,

'Welcome to 319 Heerengracht, little girl. I am made of brass. See how Adriana keeps me shiny and polished? Just pick me up and drop me a few times. Adriana will hear the dinging sound I make. She'll come running from the kitchen and let you in. She'll give you a slice of warm bread spread with butter.'"

Next he drew the entranceway.

"It's the only dark part of the house because it's the only place without its own window. Still, you'll be able to see the rug for your shoes and the coat rack for your warm wool shawl. It's colder in Amsterdam than it is here. There's a small bureau for your gloves and your scarf. Adriana likes everything put in its place—from the very moment you enter the house. She's what I would call 'meticulous.'"

Nelita struggled to repeat the long Dutch word. "Meticulous."

"You'll see a mirror in the entranceway," Pieter continued as he drew. "That's so just before you leave the house to go out again, you can check to be sure you're presentable."

"Presentable?" Nelita asked.

"Yes. Presentable means your bonnet's on straight and you don't have any gooseberry jam stuck to your teeth."

Nelita laughed when Pieter drew on a second piece of paper a little girl making a face, jam dribbling down her chin.

"This will never be you," he said. "Adriana will not let you leave unless you appear to be dressed in a way that 'befits your station' as she likes to say."

"Adriana is strict," Nelita said with some wariness.

"Yes, but she'll tell you 'it's for your own good, Nelita.' And she's going to just love having a little girl in the house again.

"Where shall I take you next?" he asked as he stretched out a fresh piece of paper. "To the library on the left? To the sitting room on the right? To the kitchen straight back? We'll pass through the dining room on the way there."

* * *

20 July 1652
Question: What is a DRONE?
Dear Isabela,

I am almost eighteen so you are almost twenty-eight. I try to imagine you at that age.

I was happy to read just now that your days in that tiny cottage sewing and mending were short-lived. The Governor's house must suit you and Nelita better. I hope you are meeting some suitable men there. Do you think about remarrying? Or do you, dear Isabela, still mourn the loss of your husband?

My cousin, Willem, bought me a beehive. It comes with directions on how to care for the bees and collect the honey. I didn't ask Mama and Papa. I just set it up in the shed way in the back of the garden. Eventually, of course, Mama followed me, wondering why I was spending so much time there. "It keeps her busy, Jos. She always needs a project," I heard her say to Papa afterwards. Their fears about angry stinging invaders have subsided.

I cover myself with netting, but I think the bees know me. Either that or they're just too busy to take notice of me sitting there, observing and recording their activities. Like the ants I've written about before, the bees are highly social, focused on their families and working together. I wish I could communicate to them my admiration for their industriousness and commitment.

I must confess to you the other reason I spend so much time there, Isabela. Willem and I can visit on the other side of the hive unobserved. The side away from the house. He enters the garden through the alley in the back. I've placed two chairs there so we can talk all afternoon if we want. He's such a patient dear. He listens while I describe how the bees build nests, how they all have the same mother—the queen—who is the only bee who lays eggs. A queen can live for five years, I tell him. She might lay as many as 1500 eggs each day. Her only duties are to mate and lay eggs. She doesn't have to care for all those offspring. Her workers feed and raise the young bees.

Today Willem helped me scrape the first of the honey from those amazing cones the bees construct. I brought bread from the kitchen and we feasted. I did get stung once—right through my sleeve. It hurt terribly. Willem was worried for me. He rolled up my sleeve. He always carries a small magnifying glass. He could see the stinger still stuck in my flesh. He removed it with his teeth. Can you imagine? I feel sorry for the poor bee that attacked me, though. Once a honeybee stings, it dies.

Anneliese is frantic. She has not heard from Pieter for months and does not know where he is.

Your loving Nelleke

Answer: A DRONE is a male bee that develops from an unfertilized egg. Its one and only job is to mate with new queens.

By the way, I hope your travels keep you in the New World for a while longer. We in the Dutch Republic are quite upset about two recent events: On the 7ᵗʰ of July, our City Hall burned to the ground. There did not seem to be enough water in this entire watery city to put out that raging fire. From my garden perch, I could see the flames rising above the Dam. Even the bees seemed upset.

Also, just when our long war with your country finally came to an end, only four days after the fire, England declared war on our dear young Republic. I hope life in the New World is calmer and not so chaotic.

Nelleke's letter arrived the day before Isabela's departure. Isabela sent off a quick note saying only that she was leaving San Agustín and would write from her new destination, that she was happy, that Nelleke should not worry about her.

Isabela read Nelleke's letter to Pieter. "Why have you not written your sister?" she asked him.

"I wanted to wait until I had something positive to report," he replied. "I'll write Anneliese a letter now and send it as soon as we arrive in New Amsterdam. Something reassuring, but with no details. She'll learn my happy news soon when she discovers her lovely friend living nearby."

They stood and smiled at each other, saying nothing, imagining a future together, feeling blessed.

* * *

10 April 1652
Dearest Friend,

It is with hope in my heart mixed with great sadness that I write what may be my final communication to you ever. As I am soon to become once again a married woman, I can no longer justify these secret letters. Reading through them I feel rather embarrassed. It is clear to me that no eyes but mine must ever see the thoughts I have "shared" with you. Destroying them does not mean I will forget you. I will carry you in my heart on the journeys I am about to embark upon. I will think of you as I walk through the city I am returning to—a city where I believe you and your family would feel free and would thrive. I will remember you every time I ponder a move on the board of chess. Pieter tells me that, although he himself never learned to play, his father always kept a game current in the parlor at 319 Heerengracht.

As for your diamond, it has offered me great comfort, not only because I knew Nelita and I would never starve but because of your kindness in giving it to me. You seemed to know the challenges I would face before I myself had any inkling. And your books, Señor Valverde, that have kept me company every night, that have taken me to imaginary worlds, that have kept my mind and spirit alive—I will continue to treasure and enjoy them.

What can I say about the gown? Shall I follow your example and put it on display in my new home? It is too beautiful to waste away in a dark trunk. Thank you. Thank you for everything. The flames are waiting. I must say good-bye.

Your loving Isabela

While the letters burned, Isabela wrote a final note and then watched as it too disappeared among the ashes.

The words
Want out.
They pound

From inside my skull.
They drill
Holes through my head,
Get tangled in my hair,
Swing from my curls,
Launch themselves
Into the air.
Tiny arrows
Headed straight for you
Wherever you are.
The words cover you with pinpricks
Vying for your attention.
Tailor. Señor Valverde. I love you.
I do so love you, love you, love you.

PART III
Amsterdam
New And Old

Chapter forty-Two
Wind, Wishes, and Warnings

⌒

The crowd parted to allow the Governor's entourage to pass through. Estefania, sheltered by her ever-present parasol, her free hand resting on the arm of her husband. Their two daughters behind their parents. Pieter, Nelita, and Isabela following just in front of the four soldiers that guarded the Governor wherever he went.

As they reached the ship, Isabela said good-bye for the third time that day to the family that had given her and her daughter not just shelter, work, and companionship, but the opportunity to be part of a family in what was possibly the safest house in all of New Spain. Fania clung to Nelita as if she would not let her go. In fact, Fania had asked if Nelita might stay with them. Pieter and Isabela could send for Nelita once they were settled in Amsterdam, she suggested. Of course, Pieter and Isabela gently refused. "You will soon have a niece or nephew, sweet Fania. What a wonderful aunt you will be. My aunts helped raise me and I loved them dearly," Isabela said.

Pieter bid the family good-bye too and thanked them once more for the care they had shown for his beloved. Once on board, the future family of three waved at their hosts and the large crowd of villagers gathered to see them off, and then turned their attention to the ship's Captain.

* * *

As his passengers and crew gathered round, Captain Angel de Vega held up a map that Pieter had drawn.

"Good morning. Welcome aboard El Oviedo," Angel said. "In order to lessen the possibility of encountering storms, we begin our trip north on the inland waterway. Once the waterway meets the Rio de San Juan, we will stop for the night.

"Many of you know Big Owl, the son of Chief Standup Bear. Big Owl has kin up and down the waterway. He has arranged for us to stay as the guests of a Timucuan village friendly to white men and will accompany us to our final destination. There are few men who know water travel better than he. His perfect aim with a bow and arrow will astound you and assure that we never lack for fresh game.

"Day and night, mosquitoes abound. However, they are considered quite tasty by dragonflies and damselflies. So swat a mosquito, yes, but learn to identify their predators and leave those alone. You may also spot salamanders, snakes, turtles, and alligators.

"I apologize in advance if the competing frog choruses rob you of sleep. Some of you are expert at identifying the tens of thousands of birds you'll see. Both wading and water birds like the white ibis, wood stork, and purple gallinule. On our maiden voyage two months ago we saw limpkins and owls. Again, they can be quite noisy. Think of the rowdiest drunken tavern party you've ever heard and multiply it by 100.

"The ladies have been instructed to bring parasols to guard against the elements, but also to avoid the prolific bird droppings we are likely to encounter. This trip is an adventure for all of us. For the especially curious among you who wish to take a small side trip, we have a dugout canoe onboard—meticulously carved by our Timucuan friends who have thrived along these waterways for thousands of years."

Pointing to various points on the map, Angel continued,

"After Rio de San Juan empties us into the Atlantic Ocean, the remainder of our journey will be by sea. Soon we will have left Spanish Florida behind. Approximately three-quarters of our trip will remain. Although we may not always be able to see these settlements, we will pass the English-controlled colonies in Virginia and Maryland and a tiny swath of New Sweden. Approximately ten days after setting sail from San Agustín, we will arrive at our destination.

"The Dutch colony of New Amsterdam is located on the southern part of the island of Manhattan. In an attempt to keep out marauding natives and English invaders, we hear the Dutch are constructing a wall across the northern part of the entire town. The English maintain control of areas north and east of New Netherland as far north as Massachusetts Bay. They and hostile natives are a constant threat.

"How will we repel attacks if necessary? We have weapons on board and a crew trained to use them. We have constructed a shelter for the women and children. Every woman knows to carry a knife in a sheath at her waist. Hopefully our female passengers will use their knives only for scaling fish, skinning small animals, and chopping fresh vegetables for as long as the supply lasts but, if need be, they can use the knives to defend themselves.

"May I introduce the ship's musicians who I'm certain will entertain and delight us. Also the expert carver, Señor Manolo Manchego, and the artist, Pieter Hals, who will lend his drawing skill to both amuse us and document our trip.

"Friar Alonzo, I call upon you to ask God's blessing on El Oviedo, its passengers and this voyage."

All on board stood and bowed their heads. Those watching from the shore did the same.

"Harken, O Lord, to our supplications," prayed the friar. All on board except Pieter made the sign of the cross. Isabela made the sign of the cross with one hand and clutched her double cross with the other. The friar continued.

"Bless this boat and all who travel in it, as Thou hast vouchsafed to bless Noah's ark carried upon the waves of the flood. Stretch forth to them, O Lord, Thy right hand, as Thou hast done to Blessed Peter when walking upon the sea, and send Thy holy angel from Heaven, who may deliver and protect this boat from all dangers, with all who will be therein. And, repelling all adversities, grant Thy servants a calm voyage and the always-wished-for haven, let them carry out and rightly finish their business, and when the time comes again, call them back to their home with all joy. Through Our Lord, Jesus Christ we pray. Amen."

Captain de Vega placed a mallet in the hand of his little sister, lifted her and nodded. When Nelita gave the ship's bell a hardy whack, the passengers let out a communal whoop. The crew pushed the ship away from its moorings. The wind whooshed and greeted the sails as if they were long-separated partners. The musicians played a jolly, hopeful tune. The gathered villagers cried out good wishes, broke into song, watched and waved until the ship disappeared around the first bend in the waterway.

* * *

The passengers introduced themselves to one another: a Dutch family, Mr. and Mrs. Visscher and their three children, Jan, Liesje, and Juliana. Five young Spanish soldiers, their swords dangling at their sides. A frightened Spanish mother and her small son, Doña Mariela and Carlos, hoping to find their lost Dutch husband/father who had disappeared months ago on a ship north. A pair of serious Spanish historians/writers documenting the culture of Native Americans. Two jaunty Spanish brothers with no particular goal other than exploring the New World. With Pieter, Nelita, and herself that made nineteen passengers. Big Owl would make twenty.

Pieter set about drawing them one by one or in groups. The five female passengers arranged the sleeping quarters built for them. Carlos, too young to be separated from his mother, would sleep there also. With his usual thoughtfulness, Angel had directed that area be built in the stern where the ship's motion was less pronounced.

Except for the soldiers, this was a wealthy group who had paid for a well-stocked larder and the most comfortable passage available. Pieter had his own cabin. Although the size of a wardrobe cabinet, it afforded him privacy, a small cot, and a place to store his belongings. Mr. Visscher shared a cabin with his son. Each historian had a cabin of his own. The brothers shared a cabin. Angel, Big Owl, the soldiers, and the crew slept on hammocks on the deck.

Pens held one goat, three chickens, one pig, and one sheep, thus ensuring the passengers would enjoy fresh milk, eggs, and an occasional meat dish. Strong winds moved the ship along quickly. Before nightfall, they arrived at the Timucuan village where Big Owl awaited them. Immediately, he rowed out to the ship where he and Angel greeted each other warmly.

More natives followed behind Big Owl and soon a dozen rowboats and canoes carrying the ship's passengers landed in the village. Doña Mariela, fearful of all natives, remained on board with Carlos as did most of the crew and two of the five soldiers. Angel left his First Officer in charge of the ship. As they came closer to the village, Angel stood up in the canoe nearly toppling it. 'That is so unlike him,' Isabela thought.

'What is he searching for on the shore? Is he concerned we may be in danger?'

As the villagers lined the marshy beach to welcome the passengers, Isabela's question was answered. In fact perhaps the purpose of this stop might be nothing more than an excuse on Angel's part. A girl his age but half a head taller than he smiled directly at him and flicked from side to side the dark hair that reached her waist. Her tawny, high-cheeked beauty made Isabela think of the laundress—of the way Isabela imagined Maria Luisa in her youth. Indeed, the girl was introduced as Maria Luisa's niece—Petal—Big Owl's younger sister.

Isabela was unsure how Angel knew the girl had muscular arms and legs since she, like most of the women, was dressed in the typical colonial long skirt and blouse. Isabela felt a stab of sadness seeing the lithe beauty in European clothing.

'It must inhibit her freedom of movement,' she thought. 'Had the native women been warned by a passing priest not to "parade your heathen nakedness before the distinguished guests?"'

Yet Petal had not rejected all of her native attire. Over the modest blouse, she wore a rough gray wrap of Spanish moss draped across one shoulder and wrapped around the opposite hip. She also wore around her neck layers of shells in various colors, sizes, and shapes. Shark teeth woven through string fell from her ears. The tinkling sound of the brass ornaments on her bare feet beckoned them as they followed her.

Native guides led the group around the clean and well-ordered village. The smell of fresh pine, burning embers, roasting meat and herbs rose from every hut. The native men demonstrated their weapons and tools. Petal, followed by a trail of curious children, led the female passengers to her own space in the communal garden.

"We do not cultivate corn, beans, and squash in separate plots as you do," she said. "We place seeds from each of the three in the same hole in the ground."

She pointed proudly to the healthy growth.

"The corn plant is the tallest. It provides a stalk for the bean to climb up. See how happily the bean plant winds affectionately around the corn plant? Yet it does not impede the corn's growth. The low squash plant protects all three crops by holding moisture in the soil. We call this arrangement 'The Three Sisters.' They support and care for each other. To help them flourish, I place a piece of fish at their roots. I myself owe my life to fish bones."

Mrs. Visscher asked Isabela to translate a question which she hoped would not be too impertinent.

"Why, when most of the women have very long hair, do two of the village women we've passed have short hair?"

"Their husbands died recently," Petal explained. "Our widows chop off their hair and cast it over their husbands' burial mounds. It is a sign of respect, but it is also a way of feeling connected to their husbands, you see—while grieving them. Only when her hair grows out fully may a widow remarry. My grandmother explained why. It allows the widow time to recover from her loss and helps her avoid leaping into an ill-conceived marriage just to assuage her longing and loneliness. It also protects her. Men know to leave her alone while her hair is still short."

Petal and Big Owl led their guests to a long, large hut in the village center.

"This is a communal meeting space," Big Owl explained, "and the home of the Chief, my father, Standup Bear. This hut also houses our granary—the grain we all share."

The imposing man Isabela had seen at the Governor's house sat cross-legged on a pile of soft animal furs at one end of the hut. All around him were bowls filled with meats and fruits. A boy fanned him with turkey feathers. He nodded, but did not rise to greet them.

"This is where I will live when I myself become Chief," Big Owl added.

The smoke from a small fire in a hole dug into the hut's center escaped through an opening in the roof. The dirt floor was swept free of debris. The native women invited the visitors to sit on benches built around the periphery of the meeting place. The women disappeared and returned with individual palm leaves covered with fish, squash, beans, and corn. The banquet began. The final course included roasted snake and alligator. The children served bird eggs they had gathered, on clay plates they themselves had decorated. A corn-based drink was served to all. Gourds of cool, sweet water circulated.

Oil lamps were lit to illuminate the entertainment. To everyone's amusement, several children reenacted a hunt. One played an unaware duck or rabbit going about its business, while another snuck up quietly and grabbed it. Youths took turns arm wrestling while their friends cheered and encouraged their favorites.

Adult entertainment followed with chants, flute music, men and women dancing separately, mock wrestling and battles. When all the children, native and white, had fallen asleep, the women brought blankets. Most of the passengers accepted the natives' invitation to stretch out on the benches and spend the night. With both native men and colonial men uneasily together guarding the hut, the passengers spent what would be for many days, their last night on land.

Dawn arrived too soon. As they were preparing to leave, two of his assistants helped Chief Standup Bear to his feet. He spoke no Spanish, but he held out to Angel a large quantity of yellowish powder. Petal explained that the powder was a journey drink.

"The women ground up the flours of nuts, corn, dried persimmons, and blueberries for you. Whenever one of you is thirsty, you need only add fresh water to the dry mix. It's quite refreshing and it relieves some of the fatigue and stress of travelling. We hope you enjoy it."

After good-byes and gift exchanges, the natives rowed the passengers to the ship so they could resume their journey. Angel lingered until he was able to find a moment to give Petal a wooden sculpture of a beautiful Timucuan woman made by San Agustín's famous carver.

Chapter Forty-Three
Terror Aboard

ook's healing legacy lived on in the rocky seas along the eastern coast of the Americas. On any given afternoon, queasy passengers on El Oviedo could be seen gathered on the deck, sipping tea made with the anti-seasickness herbs Isabela had carefully guarded while on land. Between the herbs and the yellow powder from Chief Standup Bear all stomachs were calm and receptive to the plentiful meals served on board. Beer and wine flowed. Musicians entertained.

Isabela was reminded of what Anneliese once wrote,

"My children adore their Uncle Pieter."

The ship's five children gathered round him every minute he would allow it.

At first he drew just for Nelita as he continued the visual tour of the home that would soon be hers.

"After your mother and I marry, this will be YOUR house," he explained.

"You are marrying my mama?" she asked.

Apparently Isabela had not yet informed Nelita of their plans. Pieter hoped he was not overstepping by informing Nelita himself.

"Yes. When we arrive in New Amsterdam before we sail to your new home."

"That means you will be my Papa?"

"That's right, little girl—and I am thrilled about that," Pieter said smiling up from the drawing he was making of her in the front hall of 319 Heerengracht.

"You'll need a warm cloak. Let's give it a fox-fur collar. And how about . . . Pieter continued as the children gathered round . . . a warm wool bonnet with trim to match the cloak . . . . oh, and a muff."

"A muff?" Nelita asked.

"It's to keep your hands extra warm. Even if you're wearing gloves, you still might be cold. It's open so your hands fit in . . . like this . . . and it's all furry."

"I want a muff," Liesje said.

"Me too!" demanded Juliana.

Pieter spent the day drawing each child with a personal hand warmer.

"Thank you, Papa Nuevo," Nelita said when he placed her drawing in her hands. He was no longer "Uncle Pieter." Nelita had now dubbed him "New Papa."

It was not easy to contain the energy of five children in a small space. The adults took turns leading them in active songs and games. They all became horses.

Hop-hop-hop	Hop-hop-hop
Paardje in gallop	Little galloping horse
Over plassen, over stenen.	Over puddles, over rocks.
Maar pas op, breek niet je benen	But watch out, don't break a leg
Paardje in gallop!	Little galloping horse!
Hop-hop-hop-hop-hop	Hop-hop-hop-hop-hop

They became flying birds and jumping jacks. They imitated the sneak-up hunting games they learned from the Indian children.

Pieter drew a fountain with a fish spouting water from a pedestal in the middle. He led the children in drawing various kinds of birds. The children cut them out. One at a time Pieter blindfolded each child, stuck a tack through the child's bird, and turned the child around three times. The passengers yelled directions as the child tried to find its way to the fountain to give its fish a "drink."

Big Owl blindfolded the children and imitated bird calls. The children had to guess: turkey or parakeet? Duck or goose? Cardinal or canary? After the second or third time playing this game, they didn't need choices. They competed to see who would be the first to call out the correct name. "Nightingale!" "Woodpecker!"

Each day, Isabela and Mr. and Mrs. Visscher joined by Liesje, set aside some time for the children's reading and numbers lessons.

"Look, Mama. Listen, Papa Nuevo. See what Liesje taught me?"

Nelita's written Dutch word collection had already reached one hundred. After a week she could count to twenty in Dutch, name body parts, clothing, animals . . . and had learned a vocabulary from another category Isabela hoped Nelita would not need often in her life—ship lingo.

By early evening, prayers and lullabies in Spanish and Dutch could be heard coming from inside the various cabins. Sometimes the parents sang themselves to sleep along with their children. Other times, they snuck out for one more glass of beer or wine and some adult conversation.

Doña Mariela kept Carlos close to her and did not mix with the others. Mrs. Visscher, on the other hand, delighted in describing the family's life in Maastricht—"the oldest settlement in the country," she said, "and so lovely stretching out on both sides of the River Meuse. You must come visit."

Her excitement about returning to her native Dutch Republic was infectious. Between Mrs. Visscher's descriptions and Pieter's visual house tours, Isabela found herself growing impatient to begin her new life. She had almost lost count of how many times she had started over in a new situation. She thought of all the people she already knew in Amsterdam.

"I'll be the corn sister," she told Pieter, "because even though I'm the smallest, I'm the oldest. Nelleke will be the bean sister because she's always striving and reaching. Anneliese will be the maternal squash patiently looking out for all of us. The three sisters."

A pleasant but curious woman, Mrs. Visscher urged Isabela to share the story of her life.

"Now do tell me, Doña Isabela, how does a young Spanish woman meet a handsome eligible Dutch bachelor? And such an appealing one as your betrothed?"

One week into the trip the passengers and crew were operating like a tiny village. Even Carlos's attempts to interrupt the games and the loud arguments between the explorer brothers did not disrupt the positive mood. It was exactly what Angel hoped for—not just a trip to take people from one location to another, but an interesting and enjoyable experience in its own right. To the relief of all, they had just about passed by the English settlements without incident. In consultation with his

First Officer, Angel had decided to take the ship away from the shore where he hoped they would encounter no or at least fewer foreign ships.

Each night before the children's bedtime, Pieter pointed out a constellation. He was delighted to discover that his betrothed could not only identify many of them, she could recount the Greek legends that accompanied them. By now the children were taking turns. They would delay bedtime by pointing out a constellation and dragging out their stories. The mothers limited the children to one turn, one legend per night. Otherwise they would compete, interrupt, and want to tell story after story. They each had their favorites. Carlos—The Lion because, as he said, it was fierce and fearless. Liesje—The Lyre because it not only played beautiful music, it resembled her name. Nelita—The Seven Sisters because she had no sisters of her own.

Jan looked up into the sky. When it was his turn, he usually retold the legend of Orion—The Great Hunter—but tonight he wanted to share the one about Andromeda—The Chained Lady. He looked up, but he could not see her. In fact he saw no stars at all. Only thick fog above, in front . . . all around them.

"It's as if we ourselves move through the night sky tonight," Jan said, "As if this very ship is itself a constellation."

Nonetheless, Jan insisted on telling Andromeda's story. Knowing they would have a turn another night, the drowsy children sat on their mothers' laps and listened. At age twelve, Jan was the oldest of the five children and on the verge of manhood. The children knew all the stories by heart. They found the Andromeda story scary and thrilling. Told by Jan, though, in multiple registers, sometimes deep, sometimes in an unintentional squeak, the story sounded comical and made the children laugh.

"Andromeda's mother proclaimed that . . ." Jan hesitated trying to control his unpredictable voice.

"She was the most beautiful girl in the world," Liesje said.

"Yes, the most beautiful girl, but one of the gods . . ."

"Poseidon," chimed in Nelita.

"Poseidon said, 'No, MY sea nymphs are the most beautiful.'"

"Poseidon chained Andromeda to a rock so that the sea monster would come kill her."

"But he didn't," said Juliana.

"I wish he had killed her," said Carlos.

"Well, he did not kill her. Perseus turned him to stone. What happened next? I don't remember."

"Perseus made her his bride," all three girls said together.

"She's a Queen now," added Juliana.

The women and children bid the men goodnight, shut the door to their cabin and settled onto their cots. The men lingered a while longer for a final smoke, another beer. Then they too retired.

Only the night crew remained awake. Guided by a new, shiny brass compass, the ship continued its smooth route north until suddenly a sharp blow to the bow followed by scraping and splashing sounds shook everyone awake. The terrified animals, some of whom had been knocked from one side of their pens to the other, sounded like a chorus in a mock opera. At the top of their lungs, they bleated, cackled, snorted, and screeched.

Pieter was the first to grab a lantern and arrive at the door of the women's cabin. After he had taken three steps, he realized his stockings were damp. Mr. Visscher and Jan, holding a cloth over a bloody nose, arrived a second later. Without taking time to knock, they pulled open the door and then took a step back. Doña Mariela blocked the way. Carlos peeked out from behind her. Standing in the doorway, she wore a fierce, threatening expression. In her right hand above her head, she held a knife.

"It's all right, Doña Mariela," Pieter coaxed. "I don't know what happened yet, but I do know there are no strangers onboard. No pirates. No natives. No English. Just the crew and passengers of El Oviedo."

Doña Mariela did not budge. She looked at the two anxious men sternly as if she did not recognize them, as if they were enemies.

Behind Pieter, Mr. Visscher spoke up. Pieter stepped aside so that Doña Mariela could see him clearly.

"Are you and Carlos all right, Doña Mariela? Please put down the knife. I want to see my family."

In an attempt to communicate with her husband while keeping an eye on the knife, Mrs. Visscher peeked cautiously over Doña Mariela's shoulder.

"My darling husband," she said in a loud whisper. "Liesje bumped her head. I see no open wound, but it requires a cold cloth. Juliana is frightened, but unhurt. Are you all right?"

"Yes, dear, I'm fine," he answered through chattering teeth. "With the sudden rattling of the ship, Jan's face slammed into the wall of our cabin. He has a small gash above his eye and a mild nosebleed, but is otherwise unhurt."

Pieter had not seen or heard any movement from Isabela or Nelita and he was becoming frantic. He did not want to have to wrestle the knife from Mariela.

"Return the knife to its sheath, Doña Mariela."

He moved aside so that the distraught woman had a clear view of the deck. The soldiers and crew had congregated at the bow.

"You see, there's Captain Angel, his First Officer, the cook, the carpenter. You know them all. You recognize the Spanish soldiers."

Doña Mariela took a step forward out of the cabin. Behind her, Carlos clung to her skirts. She took a long, thorough look around the deck. Slowly, she lowered the knife. Even as she stood clutching the knife's handle before she returned it to its sheath hanging from her belt, the Visscher girls rushed into the arms of their father. Mrs. Visscher followed. Pieter entered the women's cabin. He held the lantern high, filling the small space with flickering light. He saw the mussed bed of his loved ones, but he did not see them. He saw neither Isabela nor Nelita. The room looked empty. Panicked, he turned to leave, when he heard whimpering.

Relieved but still frightened, he knelt down to help them where they were pinned after taking refuge under the low cot. He reached under the cot which was bolted to the deck and pulled them to their feet. Nelita embraced him as if she would never let go. Isabela fell back down on the cot. She sat trembling and babbling incoherently. He caught some of the Spanish words.

"Lightening. Thunder. No, no, no. Father, no," she kept repeating as she shook her lowered head rapidly from side to side. With both hands she clung to the double cross digging into her palm.

Pieter had often imagined his betrothed on their wedding night with her luscious black hair loosened from its tight bonnet and falling over her shoulders. Seeing her now with freed, tousled hair in her nightdress, he felt a surge of lust followed by shame. Isabela was reliving the shipwreck in which her father perished. She was terrified. He sat beside her. Nelita, still clinging to him, sat on his other side.

During the ten days of the voyage, Pieter had not touched Isabela—not once. The eyes of the crew and passengers were often focused on the attractive couple and there was nowhere they could be alone. Holding her now even under these frightening circumstances, trying to calm her he felt an immense relief. Yet he could only mumble soothing phrases.

"It's all right, Isabela. Nelita is here. She is unhurt."

He took Nelita's hand and reached it across him. He took Isabela's hand and placed the child's hand in hers. He tried to bring Isabela into the present, although that was difficult when he did not yet know the extent of the damage to the vessel.

"You're on El Oviedo. You're with Captain Angel, my darling. You're with me, Pieter Hals. You are with the man who loves you. You are with your betrothed."

Anxious to join the others and learn what happened, he slipped Isabela's somewhat soggy felt slippers on her stockinged feet, wrapped her in a blanket, and led her to the deck. She still trembled and occasionally moaned, but she had stopped babbling. Nelita put her arm around her mother's waist. As they approached the gathering, they could see the crew and passengers hovered around a life-size piece of wood dripping sea water. Pieter stood on tiptoe and found himself looking at a replica of the woman beside him.

"A large ship burst out of the fog headed east," a soldier explained. "It clipped off the figurehead, scraped the front of our ship and kept going. We don't think it ever saw us."

"If that's the worst that happened, we are fortunate," Pieter replied.

"It ain't the worst, man," another soldier said. "The carver leapt into the sea. Guess he wanted to save that sculpture. The figurehead bobbed and floated. The crew was able to pull it up with a fishing net. The carver sank. What's more, there's a hole in the bow where the thing was attached."

Angel stood on a bench. Looking out at the frightened assembly, he tried to calm himself before speaking.

"By now you all know that a large vessel clipped the front of our ship. We're assuming it was not an aggressive act, that it was an accident. The vessel may not have realized it hit a smaller ship. We've seen no sign of it. It was coming from our left and just kept going. We have recovered the figurehead, but not our talented and valued friend, the carver, who made the work of art. Angel stopped to control himself before continuing. 'Each new loss brings back feelings of previous losses' he thought.

"We will have a service to honor his life, but first we have urgent business. We have managed to plug the hole where the figurehead was attached. The epoxy is temporary, however. We must repair it properly before we continue our journey. We must turn west and seek land."

"Seek land." Everyone knew what that meant. Delays for one thing. But also the specter of encounters with the English colonists or the Indians. Big Owl had been clear.

"Should we come upon any hostile natives beyond my tribe, I cannot guarantee that my presence will help soothe them. It could even increase tensions. White men tend to think an Indian is an Indian, that we're all the same. Actually we are highly diverse, with our own languages and customs. We have often been at war with one another. They may distrust me just as much as they distrust you."

The passengers had also heard stories about conflicts between New Netherland and English leaders. More and more citizens of both countries were coming to the New World, vying for land and control. The Dutch and the English were now officially at war.

For his part, Angel was furious with himself. He had made sure there was an ample supply of epoxy. He had brought excellent tools for caulking. He had not brought any lumber. He would not make that mistake again. He was a novice Captain. He thought he knew everything. He believed he would be the opposite of his lazy, incompetent, disengaged Captain father. Yet here they were perhaps only one-and-a-half days from their destination with three holes in the ship's hull and no wood to repair them. He could take a chance that the epoxy would hold, but more likely it would have to be changed regularly. The holes might increase in size. He had nightmares of seeing New Amsterdam Harbor just ahead and the entire ship going down. Harbors everywhere were littered with sunken wrecks.

So even in the fog, even though it was still dark, the crew adjusted the sails. They turned the ship away from its northern route and sailed west. The passengers had retreated to their cabins after learning the explanation for the loud bang, scrape, and rocking. Lying in their cots, they felt the boat swoop as it turned. The men rose and dressed.

As dawn broke and the sun shined through the early morning fog, they spotted land. They slowed down, positioned the telescope and tried to decide what to do next. If they were seen bearing the Spanish flag, they might be fired upon and have to turn back. Taking turns with the telescope, Captain Angel and his First Officer agreed. They were not looking at a shoreline. They were looking at a tiny island. A forested one. They saw huge numbers of birds, but no humans. Were the people still asleep or was the island uninhabited?

Crew members were taking turns keeping an eye on the openings. "The epoxy is loosening I believe, Captain," one of them called. The carpenter ran to replace the epoxy, but sea water seeped in during the process. The crew had managed to mop up and remove most of the water during the night. Now they started over.

The decision was made. If no one lived on the island and if they remained on the eastern side of it, they might not be detected. Even given the flexibility of the caravel, they did not want to risk running aground. They had one dugout that held three people. They lowered the boat and off it went with Big Owl rowing, one crew member with some building skills, and the carpenter holding his bag of tools on his lap. As the threesome approached, the sound of birds became deafening—singing, cackling, hooting, calling, whooping.

"They must be sun worshippers," the carpenter yelled above the din. "Either that or they have a huge party every day as the first ray comes over the horizon."

Big Owl easily recognized twenty or so different bird calls, but he did not know their Spanish or Dutch names.

Angel wanted to split the soldiers—some on land, some aboard ship. It took only five minutes to reach the island's beach. Big Owl helped the other two men climb out of the boat, watched them trudge through the surf with the tools held over their heads, and immediately rowed back to El Oviedo to bring two soldiers to the island. Captain Angel dropped anchor and remained on the ship.

Five men on the island now. Communicating with whispers and gestures, the carpenter and his assistant searched for a suitable branch. The soldiers followed close behind, muskets drawn and ready. They left deep prints in the wet sand as they walked. The forest was equally damp and marshy. They saw a few felled trees, but their trunks and branches were mired in the swamp. They would have to cut down a branch and that would add more time to their task. Ideally they would arrive back at the ship with two possible planks. The planks did not have to be large. The challenge was to turn a piece of raw timber into a block that bent just so in order to fit the curve of the boat's bow. Even if it fit well, it would be very green. The makeshift patch would last only a few days.

Big Owl explored on his own. He knew that the proliferation of birds probably meant they had few predators, including humans. Just in case, he did not share his opinion with the soldiers. 'Best they remain alert,' he thought. He also surmised that this piece of land was what his tribe referred to as a "sometimes island." It was not on Angel's map. It might disappear and reappear with the seasons, the tides, storms.

He had hoped for some game. The passengers were hungry for meat. 'No deer. No rabbits. Not even squirrels,' he noticed. 'It appears this island may have never been attached to the mainland.' He saw no abandoned shelters. No footprints. No weapons. No hidden stash of corn.

His arrows downed twenty of the plumpest birds. After placing them in a satchel, he returned to the beach where he dug up and washed off scores of juicy oysters. Still the carpenters worked on. Big Owl had hoped to find berries growing, but the land was just too watery to support them.

Cheers went up when at dusk Big Owl arrived back at the ship with the carpenter and one soldier. He promptly returned for the carpenter's assistant and the second soldier. It was difficult to determine which was more popular—Big Owl's stash of fresh food or the simple blocks of wood, one of which they all fervently hoped would stop up the openings long enough for them to reach Manhattan. The strong odor of pine tar did not distract from the smell of roasting fowl in oyster sauce. With their bellies full and the holes temporarily blocked, the passengers and crew broke out in song, drank and feasted.

"I know you're waiting until we arrive in New Amsterdam to reattach the figurehead, Captain Angel," said the First Officer but, if I was you, I'd abandon it right here. Its likeness to that Spanish woman—the artist's betrothed—is uncanny and it almost got us all killed."

"What are you saying?" Angel responded. "Yes, Isabela Calderón is the model for the figurehead. Apparently you are unaware that she is like a second mother to me. Far from endangering us, that figurehead, SAVED our lives. Whatever it was on that passing ship that hit it and tore it off might have gouged the ship beyond repair. We could have sunk right then and there. The figurehead protected the ship. Yet there's only a small scratch on the left side of it. Otherwise it's intact. It's infused with some kind of magic—I'm convinced of it."

Angel turned and bellowed the order.

"Pull anchor. Northeast."

Wood creaked. Ropes twanged with tension. Wind whipped the sails. The deafening bird calls faded.

Chapter forty-four
New Amsterdam

hirty-six hours later at 3:00 in the morning, the ship stopped at Staten Island where the Visscher family would stay with relatives before sailing back to their homeland. The passengers pulled on day clothes over their night clothes and stood on the deck to bid the family good-bye. Although they immediately sent a message to Mr. Visscher's brother, it took another hour to fetch rowboats and unload the five of them and all their belongings. Mrs. Visscher insisted on saying good-bye to each crew member, soldier and passenger individually.

"Now don't forget, Isabela," she called over her shoulder as she was helped into a rowboat, "Mr. Visscher and I want to be among your official witnesses."

"Such a marvelous couple!" she said to the rower as he sat her down.

Anxious for their first glimpse of the southern tip of the island of Manhattan, the passengers set sail once again. During the trip, Pieter had made a drawing of the island for the children.

"Imagine a giant. One day, he was walking from north to south. On his way to the ocean, he stepped down with his right foot and left behind his huge footprint. Up here at the northern point is the giant's heel. Under his heel and the sole of his foot were rocks, streams, and dense forest. Giant pines and oaks tickled him and made him laugh. Right where the widest part of his foot stepped is where New Amsterdam begins. First with outlying farms and pastures. Next the area we'll catch sight of first—streets, houses, and shops. Finally, down here on the southern tip of the island are the imprints of the giant's toes. His little toe lined up along the North River. His big toe stuck out into the Hudson River. The left side of his foot rests along the East River. That's where we will dock."

* * *

"Leave it to the Dutch to cross the ocean and find the perfect harbor," one of the Spanish sailors said as the ship slid easily to shore and gently came to a halt.

From his perch in the crow's nest, Captain Angel called down the order that all lamps be extinguished.

"Watch this," he said. "You're about to be blessed with one of nature's best shows."

For a moment the group huddled together in total darkness. Children shivered beneath blankets parents had dragged from their cots. Pieter stood with one arm around Nelita, the other around Isabela. No one moved or spoke. The only sounds were raucous gulls overhead and the waves delivering gentle welcoming kisses to the sides of the ship. Nearly in unison everyone looked up where stars still twinkled.

"I see the Big Dipper," Carlos said.

Carlos and Nelita—the only children left on the ship—chanted in unison the name of each of the seven stars in the constellation. Dubhe. Merak. Phecda. Megrez. Alioth. Mizar and . . . Alkaid!

On the eastern horizon a tiny sliver of light drew their attention—a promise of the sun's reappearance after a night of nurturing the other side of the earth. Every head turned eastward. All eyes watched in wonder as the orange globe—magnificent and commanding—gradually rose to its full size.

Like a host proudly presenting the town to new arrivals, the light crept right to left slowly illuminating the town. First it lightly touched the highest point in the town's center—the church steeple. Gliding along the tops of tiled roofs, it ended on another raised structure—a windmill on the west side right on the North River.

"Grain!" said Pieter. "Am I ever looking forward to a breakfast of bread and cheese!"

The light showed off the four towers of the Fort and kept going across the North River. As if that same giant Pieter talked about had raised an invisible curtain, the light eventually infused the entire town.

A few "players" could be seen moving on the ground in the distance. A woman with her toddler trailing behind her carried a bucket, sat down on a stool, and began milking a lone cow. Chickens gathered around a child who scattered grain. Shopkeepers opened their doors, stepped out into the street, stretched, hung signs, and drank their morning beer waiting for their first customers. Tavern owners, moving slowly, swept out onto the street the mounds of refuse left by the previous evening's patrons.

Then shouts.

"A new ship!"

"A Spanish one!"

"Be careful!"

"What do they want?"

Curiosity overcame the residents. Families, farmers, and craftsmen ran to the dock. Town officials, including the sheriff and his assistant, pushed their way through.

Chapter forty-five
Nagging Doubt

O n the narrow, uneven mattress in a room in the back of a tavern, Pieter twisted, turned onto his back and sat boldly upright in the dark.

'Could her melancholy be due to something we haven't discussed? Something so distressing she hasn't been able to share it?'

The thought of what that might be paralyzed him. Of course, it made perfect sense. An unfeeling husband. A critical mother-in-law. Isolated on that bluff. She could see the harbor from her bedroom window, she had told him. She always knew when Diego was in town, even though he might not come by the house for days after arriving. How could a warm, attractive woman in her twenties decade go without love? It would have been relatively easy to hide from Diego the fact that she had a lover.

She had asked him outright, "Did you love Lucietta?" But he never thought to ask HER if SHE had loved someone all those years. He thought of her, not as a virgin, but as virginal-like. He looked forward to a long seduction, to introducing her slowly to pleasures he believed she had never experienced. Now he felt deflated—even ridiculous. He was consumed with jealousy and confusion.

'I want to marry her as much as ever,' he thought, 'but I don't know how to proceed.'

After a night of imagining and rejecting images of his beloved in the arms of another, he had worked himself into a frenzy.

'I must learn the truth. I must know who he was.'

As early as he dared the following morning he sent her a note.

"Meet me at the church today, my darling. Name the time. Soon please."

He knew that Isabela was occupied most of the day at the town's orphanage. She seemed to have thrown herself into volunteering as if she were a fully-paid staff person just as she was at the orphanage in Amsterdam. Yet in her terse, scribbled reply—"4:00"—he read only rejection and lack of enthusiasm.

He waited and paced. 4:00. 4:15. 4:18. His pocket watch was getting a workout. Finally he saw her. She had obviously made an effort to freshen herself up. How nice to see her in a new practical clean dress, shoes, bonnet. He watched her approach as he always did. Today, though, he felt almost shy as if he were still courting her.

She smiled a greeting, but he could not read her mood. He had a vision of a lifetime of trying to understand this woman who seemed more complex by the day. He made an exaggerated swooping motion to indicate that she should enter the church before him. They sat in the first pew they came to where at this hour they could talk in low tones and not be overheard. Isabela had to stop herself from genuflecting. Her hand went automatically to her chest to make the sign of the cross but dropped down into her lap when she remembered that within days she would no longer be Catholic. Her hand lay listlessly in her lap.

She knew that promptness was important to the Dutch and apologized for being late.

"The young women staying in the orphanage face one problem after another," she said. "I was comforting one of them. She was terribly upset and frightened. After she refused the overtures of the tavern owner where she was working, he accused her of stealing and fired her. Now she has no paid work and no way to support herself. He won't even give her back wages."

"That's too bad, Isabela, but you can't get so involved in all their problems. Women are in demand here. They'll all marry eventually. They'll be all right."

Isabela looked at Pieter sternly as if she were thinking,

'Marriage solves all problems? Really?'

"Isabela, I've noticed that ever since the ship's accident, you've been melancholy and withdrawn. This is frightening for me. I must ask you something. YOU asked ME if I loved Lucietta. I confessed to you that I did love her at the time. I told you all about her."

He hesitated. Their arms had been touching. Their heads were bent toward each other. Now she moved away from him slightly. She did not look at him. He braced himself.

'She certainly did not love that Diego. Who could it have been?'

A new thought occurred to him, 'Could Nelita be the child of her lover?'

Suddenly he saw Isabela in an entirely other light. He felt as if he were betrothed to a stranger.

"Now I'm asking you something I should have asked sooner. Now I find myself needing to know. During those long years you lived in Santos Gemelos and then in San Agustín, was there a man you loved?"

"I suppose I did love someone," she began slowly. "A man who was kind and generous. He made me feel cared for. He loaned me books. We corresponded. But he was more like a father, Pieter, really."

She looked directly at him for what felt like the first time since they arrived in New Amsterdam. The tears in her eyes alarmed him.

'Was she missing this man so terribly that she would call off their plans? Where was this man? WHO was he?'

A parade of all the men he met in San Agustín passed through his mind. He had seen no indication of a love affair. It must have been in her village back in Spain.

"It was an entirely chaste relationship, Pieter. You needn't worry yourself about that. He was married, the father of two children. I was lonely. I was grateful for the attention."

Since the first time it occurred to him in the middle of the night that he might have a serious, unknown rival, Pieter felt his body relax somewhat.

"And are you still corresponding?" he asked.

"No. I don't know where the family is." She began to weep softly. "They were driven out of town. It was immediately after Cook was killed in the public square. I don't even know if they are alive."

She gave him all the details—the attacks on the tailor's home. The fallen cross. The discovery of the tunnel. The tiny rolled piece of paper Angel found with words in an alphabet she had never seen with the initials "I.J.V." on the top.

"They were Conversos then," he said.

"Yes. Probably. But they attended church regularly. I didn't understand at the time. Day and night. Trying to protect their children. Never knowing when soldiers will knock on the door and take them away. I've learned since that the Church tortures not only men and women, but children too—to make them confess. Briana was so full of life. She wanted to burst forth, to sing her joy, to interact with people. Her parents would not allow it. She escaped them long enough to sing at my wedding. I was utterly charmed by her impromptu song. Later I heard them reprimand her for it. I thought they were overly strict. I had no idea then of the constant fear they lived under."

Isabela continued. "The tailor may have been taking risks loaning me those books. I'm not sure. I may have put myself in danger by accepting the books. By even associating with their family. I was naïve. I still have some of the books. They are a comfort for me. A connection. They give me hope that the family has found a place where they can live without fear. Where they're free to be their true selves."

It occurred to Pieter that Amsterdam might be the perfect place for the tailor family, but he did not want to raise such a hope. He certainly did not want her to marry him only because he was taking her to Amsterdam where she might re-engage with this tailor, where their relationship might intensify. At the same time, he felt a growing sense of gratitude to the man and to his family for caring for his beloved in the limited way available to them.

"They may have moved to the orient or perhaps to somewhere in New Spain where they could use the language they knew," Pieter suggested.

"But missing that family and worrying about them does not explain the melancholy you referred to Pieter. Since the accident on the ship . . . Oh, Pieter. On my first voyage, I lost my father. On my second I nearly starved. On my third I lost my son. On my fourth an unseen ship clipped off the figurehead and tossed it into the sea. When I saw my likeness lying on the deck, dripping sea water nearly drowned . . . I fear all this is a sign. How many times can I sail and survive? I have survived four voyages, but I don't believe I can survive another. I don't want to take down with me the two people I love most in the world."

Pieter let her continue.

"I survived the first thanks to my father who delayed the voyage in order to build a hiding place for the rowboat on which I escaped with Cornelius. I survived the second possibly only because Diego wanted to keep me alive long enough to marry me and sell all my possessions. I survived the third and the fourth, I'm convinced, because I was wearing Cook's double cross."

Pieter thought this was nonsense, but he asked, "So why wouldn't the double cross afford you the same protection when we sail to Amsterdam?"

"Because I won't be wearing it anymore."

"Why would you not wear it when you believe in it so strongly?" he asked, his irritation growing.

"Because it will no longer be in my possession. Because I'm giving it away. Gérard said not to hold onto the cross forever. 'Give it to a younger adult,' he instructed. 'Someone you care deeply about. Someone who may be in danger.' That someone is Angel. He has been like a son to me. His ship is almost repaired. In a few days he will sail back to San Agustín. Sailing has become his life. There will be constant threats. We will probably never see each other again. I feel strongly that the cross's protection belongs to HIM now."

She stopped a moment and then added, "This town is still primitive, but I will be all right here. I have work. I have resources—enough to live on for the rest of my life."

Pieter was incredulous. He loved this woman. He intended to marry her as soon as the minister returned. He had offered her everything he thought any woman wanted. He did not want to begin courting her all over again. He felt his alarm turning to fury, but he knew he must hear her out. The two sat in silence. A dog barked repeatedly. It must have been tied up on the street just outside the church. The sound of a cart being pushed over the rough, uneven streets reached their ears. A baby's crying swelled and passed. Still they sat without talking.

Finally, with head bowed, Isabela continued. "Nelita adores you. Dubbing you her *Nuevo Papa* is so exactly right. In Amsterdam—with Anneliese and her children—like cousins to Nelita. Playmates. Opportunities to learn. The excitement of the city. Your love. She would thrive. I will give you enough money to pay for her upkeep and for a dowry."

"What are you saying? Nelita WOULD. Nelita WOULD. Not Nelita WILL? Nelita WILL? Where is this leading, Isabela? And my nieces and nephews will not be LIKE cousins—they WILL be her cousins."

'And what am I to make of her offering me money?' he thought. 'I believed she was penniless.'

Pieter knew that no matter what the outcome of this discussion, he was finished with travelling. He had found what he had been looking for all those years even if he couldn't hold onto it. He imagined himself taking one last lonely journey, returning to his empty house—a house that cried out to be filled with children, laughter, feasts, lively gatherings and discussions.

He imagined himself married to a solid, dependable young Dutch woman—a Femke, a Margriet, a Saskia. She would take charge of his household. It would be well ordered and clean at all times. She would give him the healthy children he desperately wanted. He would be okay with all of it.

He was so wrapped up in his joy and his plans with Isabela that it had not occurred to him that leaving Angel represented one more loss for her. Angel was her last tie to her homeland and to Pedro. He thought about inviting Angel to come live with them. He was a fine young man. 'After an initial adjustment, after learning the language, he would thrive in my city,' Pieter thought. 'But he is well on his way to establishing himself in the New World. Everything about it excites him. He belongs on this side of the ocean.'

'As for the tailor,' he thought, 'I sense what Isabela has told me is only a beginning, that there is more I'll learn in due time—when she's ready to share it. Isabela has assured me there was no affair. I feel rather ridiculous for letting that possibility become an obsession.'

Ignoring everything else she had just said, Pieter seized on the words, "I don't want to take the two people I love most in the world down with me." "The two people I love most." She was referring to Nelita and to him. He clung to those words. They gave him courage. He scooted over toward Isabela. He put his arm around her. Slowly he pulled her toward him. She collapsed on his shoulder. After holding her for several minutes he said softly, "A child belongs with her mother. We never know what lies ahead. We can only ask for God's blessing and live each moment. But my darling Isabela, life is best lived with those we love."

She lifted her head and looked directly at him. Her smile seemed to lift the fog of doubt surrounding both of them.

"You know, Pieter, even though I lived in the center of Amsterdam, I rarely left the orphanage. I have impressions, but I did not really experience the city. Tell me what you love about it."

"Where shall I begin? It's more than just the familiar city where I was born and raised. The most ordinary of citizens has the freedom to choose a religion. We've rejected the concept that a ruler is imbued with some God-given power. We govern ourselves. We have a large class of educated and prosperous merchants. We've talked about this a little already. We reject the idea of God's will being imposed on us. We believe in a God who allows us to make choices, even if our choices are not always wise. We are allowed to interpret the Bible for ourselves."

Isabela took a deep breath. She was beginning to grasp for the first time what the repercussions of such freedom might mean for her, Nelita, and her future children. How different such a life would be from the constant control and dominance of Spain's Church and Crown.

"Go on. Tell me more."

"The city feels modern. I'll walk you through every corner of it. You'll feel part of the excitement. Every day ships sail to and return from the farthest continents. Yet discoveries of a different nature take place every day too—just by looking into a microscope."

"Go back to what you said about how your country is governed."

Pieter had never thought to talk to Isabela about such topics. Their conversations were mostly personal. Were these the kinds of discussions she had with the tailor? He realized that once again he had underestimated her.

"Seven separate provinces." Pieter explained. "Together they form The Dutch Republic. Amsterdam is the commercial center and the heart of The Dutch Republic. The Republic was born out of our rebellion against your country. As you know, it was a long, violent conflict. The anti-Spanish sentiment was part of what made it difficult for me to declare my love for you so many years ago. The mutual mistrust remains still, of course," Pieter said with one of the expressions Isabela loved. She could not always distinguish between his serious statements and his frequent light, teasing attitude.

"Mutual mistrust?" he said with eyebrows raised and a slight, amused smile.

She knew what he was referring to—how they reconnected after a decade—in a jail cell. They gazed at each other, both remembering that tense, threatening incident, but also thinking in their separate ways how different their lives might have been if their countries had not been at war.

"You describe a society that has a high level of tolerance, correct?"

"That is something that distinguishes us, yes. And we are very proud of it."

He believed that in this rare instance, he might be able to read her thoughts.

"Tolerance is an idea. We still struggle. We're not perfect."

"Yes, I'm confused. Catholics are not allowed to worship openly. That doesn't sound tolerant."

"You're right. But it's certainly far better than butchering people who don't follow an official imposed religion."

Pieter saw Isabela wince, probably thinking of her dear friend Cook's violent end. He immediately regretted his choice of words.

"It's true that life can be difficult for Catholics—and there are many. But they are not persecuted. Although it hasn't happened yet in Amsterdam, some cities, Protestant and Catholic churches stand side by side," he said in an upbeat tone.

"I understand the attitudes and I respect them, but I still don't understand how your country is governed, Pieter."

The dog was no longer barking. The bells rang out. It was 17:00.

Isabela jumped up.

"I promised to help with dinner at the orphanage tonight."

Pieter kissed her lightly on the cheek. They walked out of the church into a bright low beam of afternoon sun and walked briskly to the orphanage steps.

'My betrothed is like a fine wine,' he thought on his way back to the tavern. 'She continually gives off small wisps of herself. I can never gulp her down all at once and I'll never be able to get enough sips. I must admit to myself that I don't feel capable of responding to all her queries, though. The Dutch have a certain fascination with genius. We will surround ourselves with lively, informed friends. He imagined Isabela's face alternately frowning with concentration and lighting up with insight during discussions of the philosophies of Descartes, Francis Bacon, or perhaps Hugo Grotius.

'I fear, though, that the orphanage and its problems are dragging down her spirits. I must find a better place for her. When is that damned minister returning anyway?'

When he arrived at the tavern, he found a note waiting for him.

Dear Mr. Hals,

It has been brought to my attention that we have an excellent artist visiting our humble town. A student of the great Rembrandt no less. My husband, Peter Stuyvesant, the Director General, is away. I am hoping that you, your betrothed, and her daughter will be my guests for dinner tomorrow night at 19:00.

Yours sincerely,
Judith Bayard

Chapter Forty-Six
Remembrance and Reminiscence

After a week in dry dock, El Oviedo was fully prepared for its return to San Agustín. New Amsterdam's excellent shipwrights repaired the three holes in the bow. The new wooden planks were barely distinguishable from the originals. They also sanded down and repainted the small scrape on the left cheek of the figurehead. The master ship builder suggested bolting it back in place in such a way that the lower portion did not reach the waterline. The sculpture raised now above the waterline was more visible than before.

Angel had a list of passengers waiting impatiently for the trip. But he was aware that Pieter and Isabela's love for one another was fraught with challenges. He would not leave until he saw Isabela married to Pieter and sailing to Amsterdam. He also had another serious matter to attend to.

After several inquiries, Angel concluded that no Rabbi was present on the island of Manhattan. No synagogue either. But there was a very small Jewish community. Two or three families at the most. Perhaps an unmarried Jewish man or two. On the morning after Isabela and Pieter's talk in the church, the two of them along with Nelita joined Angel, Big Owl, the crew of El Oviedo and several of the passengers from its most recent trip. By pre-arrangement, the group passed through the leather shop and into the home of Ezekiel Levy, a serious man with the gnarled and stained hands of a life-long craftsman.

A striking young woman whose auburn hair spilled out from her head shawl greeted them in Dutch and invited them to sit in chairs arranged in a circle.

'Briana may grow up to look like this woman,' Isabela thought with a stab of longing.

"My daughter, Rebekkah," Ezekiel said.

Rebekkah brought a silver candelabra and placed it on a table in the middle of the circle. All were silent as she lit the candles one by one. A worn, but friendly-faced older woman appeared with a large heavy carafe. She poured a cup of wine for each guest. When Ezekiel introduced her as his wife, she nodded but did not speak. Angel handed Ezekiel a piece of paper on which the carver's name was written.

Ezekiel who, like the carver, had emigrated from Brazil, spoke in halting Dutch.

"We join together today to honor the memory of Manolo Manchego who left his native Portugal not willingly, but because he was . . ."

Ezekiel looked at his daughter and said a word in Hebrew.

"Persecuted," his daughter offered.

"Yes, persecuted," Ezekiel said. "He hoped to find a new home in Brazil, but there too he was not allowed to follow his own religion. He was not permitted to be a Jew."

"We know little of how he developed his great gift—his gift for . . ."

"Carving," Rebekkah said.

"Yes, his gift as a master carver. And gifted he was. We believe, do we not?" he continued, looking to Angel for confirmation, "that Manolo Manchego had two wives both of whom died in childbirth. One child left this world with its mother. The second child—a son—lived only to succumb to disease at the age of fifteen. It was at this point that Manolo decided to leave Brazil and seek solace in other lands. What a pity he did not make it as far as Manhattan where we would have welcomed him into our little community with open arms."

"He died trying to save his last and, so I'm told, most artistically sensitive and accurate likeness—that of the lovely Isabela Calderón who sits with us here today."

Ezekiel and Isabela nodded at each other.

"In our religion," he explained to the mixed group of Catholics, Calvinists, doubters, nonbelievers, and one shaman-follower before him, "the prayers we say for the dead are called 'Mourners Kaddish.' My daughter will translate."

Ezekiel, his wife who stood off to one side, and his daughter bowed their heads. The others followed and listened to the alternating Hebrew/ Dutch, male/female voices. Ezekiel, unaccustomed to praying in front of a group, mumbled at first, but gained strength. Rebekkah spoke in slow, clear Dutch. The Spanish made the sign of the cross and waited for the prayers to end.

"God, filled with mercy, dwelling in the Heavens' heights, bring proper rest beneath the wings of your Shechinah, amid the ranks of the holy and the pure, illuminating like the brilliance of the skies the souls of our beloved and our blameless who went to their eternal place of rest. May You who are the source of mercy shelter them beneath Your wings eternally, and bind their souls among the living, that they may rest in peace. And let us say: Amen."

"Amen," echoed the others.

Ezekiel continued, "Oh God of Abraham and Jacob, have mercy upon Manolo Manchego. Pardon all his transgressions. Shelter his soul in the shadow of Thy wings. Make known to him the path of eternal life."

Ezekiel, his wife, and daughter sang a sad and haunting song in Hebrew. "Amen," they said when the song was finished. "Amen," said the group.

Rebekkah and her mother poured more wine for the mourners. After they had sipped for several minutes Angel stood and said,

"Ezekiel Levy, Mrs. Levy, Rebekkah Levy, we thank you for your hospitality, for welcoming us into your home. Most of all we thank you for leading us in honoring our friend, Manolo Manchego, with prayers and praise in the language denied him for much of his life."

* * *

Isabela and Nelita returned to the orphanage to help with the younger orphans' lessons. Pieter and Angel left for a pre-arranged meeting with the Magistrate. An hour later the pair knocked at the orphanage and asked to speak with Isabela. It was unusual for anyone to call on her there without prior arrangement as there was no space in which to sit and visit. A tiny reception office with a desk and one chair led directly to the kitchen, then through the dining area and to the bare rooms that served as sleeping quarters for the residents. These included children of both sexes as young as four and young women ages sixteen to twenty with no family and no means of support. Isabela had learned recently, but did not share with Pieter, that at least two of those women had been prostitutes in Amsterdam.

As she took a step into the street she was greeted by the two smiling faces of her men.

"You tell her first," Angel said to Pieter.

Pieter cleared his throat as if he were about to deliver a speech to a large audience. Isabela could be unpredictable and he so wanted this brief meeting to go well.

"Isabela, my darling." He hesitated while Isabela waited.

'What could this be about?' she wondered. 'Perhaps the minister has returned? But we've expected that. Something else must have happened. Something Pieter's somewhat uncertain about.'

Since Pieter seemed to be having trouble continuing, Angel took over,

"Pieter and I have just been to see the Magistrate. We wanted to confirm and indeed did confirm . . . in the absence of clergy, a certified ship's Captain may legally conduct a wedding ceremony."

With Angel having delivered that news, Pieter seemed to regain his courage.

"Angel has all the words necessary to guide us in repeating our vows, Isabela. AND . . ." he continued, removing several papers to show her.

"Once you, I, and Angel sign these, we return them to the Magistrate for his official seal. After arriving in Amsterdam we register the papers with the proper authorities there. Because I . . . and I believe you too . . . wish to be married in the eyes of God, we will repeat our vows led by a clergyman in the Nieuw Kerk."

"But that's not all," Angel said. He nodded at Pieter to encourage him to continue. "We have two more bits of news."

"True. That's not all," Pieter repeated holding back his glee. He was tempted to say, "I know you fear and dread another sea voyage," but he decided instead to emphasize the positives of their situation.

"The ship from Amsterdam that arrived two weeks ago is loaded and nearly ready. It will set sail the day after tomorrow. Angel and I have been working with the Captain to make the passage as comfortable for you, Nelita, and the Visscher family as we possibly can."

"There's more," Angel said.

"Yes. There is more news. You seem to have a way of attracting the attention of Governors' wives wherever you go, my dear. If this keeps up, when we return to Holland, we'll be travelling to a different province every week as guests of the Stadtholders' families."

Pieter reached into his pants pocket and removed the note from Judith Bayard Stuyvesant. He knew Isabela well enough by now not to expect an outpouring of joyous emotion at any of this news. She always needed time to ponder before reacting. Even so he was vexed by her look of concern. He might even, if he allowed himself to, call her expression a frown.

"Angel. Pieter," Isabela said, reaching out to touch each on the arm and draw him closer. "This is indeed all wonderful news. Do we need witnesses for the signing? Shall I accompany you to the Magistrate and sign there?"

Pieter sighed his relief. So she was not only agreeing, she was thinking clearly about how to facilitate it all. Still that frown remained. She took a step back and bit her lip.

Angel, the only male raised by a mother in a home with two sisters, guessed at what might be bothering her. He was right.

"I couldn't help noticing in church, Pieter dear," Isabela said, "that Mrs. Stuyvesant's manner of dress is quite elegant. Her four children too—even the toddler—are dressed in expensive fabric in what I can only assume are the latest Dutch fashions. What on earth will I wear?"

"You must have something, Darling. The drabbest of gowns does not detract from your loveliness."

"I do have one magnificent gown, but it's really too exquisite even for an evening at the Director-General's house inside Fort New Amsterdam. I'm thinking of a future occasion when I might show off THAT gown. In any case, I think of it as more of a loan. The gown doesn't really belong to me.

* * *

When early the following day a large box arrived at the orphanage addressed to Isabela Calderón, Isabela could not imagine what it might be. She doubted the box was from Pieter. Pieter had said she should pack lightly for this voyage, that she could purchase whatever she needed once they arrived "home." Not that she had many possessions anyway. From Angel? Probably not. 'An overflow from the Visschers,' she guessed. 'The family of five probably had too much to fit into the small boat they would travel in from Staten Island to New Amsterdam the day of the voyage.'

Isabela set the box on top of her bed and went to assist with the orphans' breakfast. When she returned to her bed, she saw that the box had been discovered. The young women who, like Isabela, paid board to share the multi-bed room, were speculating on its contents. They gathered around as Isabela tore off the packaging. She reached in, pulled out and laid flat garment after garment wrapped in brown paper. After five minutes both her bed and three others were completely covered. A red-velvet dress with a black-lace collar. A matching black-and-red shawl. A low-cut green linen. A playful yellow cotton with billowing sleeves. A gold with empire waist. The number and variety were staggering.

Oohs and ahhs accompanied the appearance of each dress, pair of shoes and leather boots. At the bottom of the box was a note.

Dear Isabela Calderón,

I look forward to meeting you, your betrothed, and your daughter for dinner at my home this evening. When I was selecting a gown for our event together, I realized that after four births in four years time and now expecting a fifth child, I will never again fit into any of the enclosed garments. Please select whatever you wish for yourself if you would like and distribute the others among the other female boarders.

Sincerely yours,
Judith Bayard Stuyvesant

The four women could wait no longer. They stripped to their undergarments and began trying on the dresses. With no mirror in which to admire themselves, they depended on each other's opinions.

"Look, there are four shades of purple in this one dress. What do you think?"

"Not a suitable color for you. Let me try it."

"What about this green silk?"

"Too tight around the bodice. Looks ridiculous on you. It would be better for me."

After an hour of wrangling and arguing, each woman had a new dress. Isabela took the one remaining garment for herself. Brown velvet with beige insets in the sleeves and bodice. Not her favorite perhaps, but it would do. She spent the rest of the day adapting one of her own gowns for Nelita.

* * *

Early that evening Pieter, Isabela, and Nelita walked past the already bustling and noisy taverns and approached Fort Amsterdam—a large rectangular space with four lookout towers toward the tip of lower Manhattan. The fort's administrative offices served all of New Netherland. Like San Agustín, the fort was designed to be surrounded by an imposing palisade of tightly spaced logs.

The fledgling colony, less than thirty years old, faced fierce competition from the British and French for beaver skins and land, plus a history of attacks from hostile Mohican and Mohawk tribes. Strong and alert protection was necessary. Funds were scarce, however, and in reality Pieter noted, the poles were often topsy-turvy and rotted, leaving unprotected gaps.

The fort's strategic location at the junction of the North and Hudson Rivers did afford the military a wide range of visibility though. The West India Company garrisoned the company soldiers' in the fort. The Director-General met there with his council. Isabela, Pieter, and Nelita passed the office of the colony's secretary, reputed to be a keeper of meticulous records. After passing a nondescript building with an imposing name—Court of Justice—they arrived at the two-story home of the Director-General.

The soldiers at the entrance had been alerted to expect guests. One of them accompanied the threesome to the front door of the home and knocked. Soon they were greeted by an African servant. 'Is the man a servant or a slave?' Isabela wondered. The idea that a human being could "own" another was so disturbing to her that she felt sick. Isabela had overheard an African servant at the orphanage say that her people were hopeful about their future in New Netherland because of their freedom to secure both skilled jobs and church membership through baptism. Yet their situation seemed so tenuous.

She shut her mind to the specter of whole families being loaded on ships and sold like cattle or timber. Surely, with its reputation for tolerance, The Dutch Republic would not engage in such a cruel practice. When the black man bowed slightly, said in perfect Dutch,

"Good evening. Right this way please. Mrs. Bayard Stuyvesant is looking forward to your visit," she felt that familiar longing, that pressing need to discuss the whole sordid topic with the tailor. Then she chastised herself. 'Why not discuss it with Pieter?' she asked herself. 'It's HIS country I'm wondering about.' For the moment, though, she could give the matter no more attention.

As they approached the main room of the house, the noise of shouting, running children made further pondering of that upsetting topic impossible. Although the activities of the children in the Amsterdam City Orphanage were highly regulated and discipline was enforced, Isabela had heard that Dutch families had a reputation among the English and other foreigners for spoiling their children utterly.

"A rowdy bunch of little hooligans," one English tourist reported.

Interrupting an adult conversation might be met with a fond, amused squeeze and a kiss, not a reprimand.

Here before them were four children—two girls and two boys each only half a head taller than its next younger sibling. Isabela estimated that they were two, three, four, and five years old and they were engaged in a lively game of tag. When the toddler was unable to keep up, he sat in the middle of the room and bellowed at the top of his lungs. The other three ignored him. They continued chasing each other and arguing.

"You're it, Nicholas," the oldest girl said.

"I am not, Rebecca. You did not tap me."

"I most certainly did, you little pumpkin head."

When Nicholas and his older sister fell onto the ground in a scuffle, they knocked over the younger sister who added her wailing to the mix.

After the three guests stood watching the scene for several minutes, the children's mother appeared with two maidservants who picked up all four protesting children one by one and carted them out.

"A treat before bed!" Judith called after the maids before moving to greet her guests.

With no apologies for the chaos or for keeping them waiting, she bid them to follow her directly to the dining room. Once they were seated around the long oak table, the same black man poured them each a glass of wine.

Judith obviously relished the opportunity for adult conversation. As platter after platter was placed on the table, she first launched into her own life story.

"Petrus and I met in Breda when he was recovering from that terrible wound. Lost a leg, you know. The pain was excruciating—still sometimes is—and he was so brave. He's never let it interfere with anything he's felt needed doing. We affectionately call his artificial leg 'Silver.' 'How is Silver feeling today, Dear?' I might ask. "It's decorated with silver bands you see.

"His sister, Adriana, introduced us. My sister-in-law. She is married to my brother, Samuel. Petrus is sixteen years older than I am. He took one look and just had to have me. We were married on August 13, 1645 in the Walloon Church in Breda—a church my father had served as minister. We were immigrants. French Huguenots. I guess Petrus liked my dark looks and wide hips. He certainly has made use of them. Four children in four years and now expecting again. Finally after a long and brutal voyage—I swear I'll die here in the New World rather than undergo another trip like that—we arrived here in May 1647 just in time for Rebecca's birth. Now tell me about YOUR origins. Mr. Hals, I know you've been charming the residents of our town with your charcoal portraits. Are you related to the painter, Frans Hals, by any chance?"

"I am distantly related, Mrs. Bayard, and I certainly admire his work. I remember vaguely meeting him as a child when my family took a trip to visit relatives in his town of Haarlem. I was raised in Amsterdam, however, and I look forward to returning there with my new wife and her daughter. My father, now deceased, was a silver merchant. He also served as postmaster for the city."

"A mostly ceremonial position as I understand it? Appointed? Well-paid with few responsibilities? By the way, Petrus has relatives in Haarlem also. Perhaps yours and his know each other? Now do tell me about that rascal, Rembrandt. Is it true you studied with him?"

"True, Mrs. Bayard. In fact some ten years ago on the wall surrounding Amsterdam I met the woman I am about to marry."

Pieter reached over to pat Isabela's hand. They smiled at each other knowing they were silently sharing the same memory.

"Ever inventive, Rembrandt had led his students OUTSIDE the studio into the natural light. Most unusual. Some may regard him as a 'rascal' as you say. It is true he can be irascible and unpredictable. But he is always brilliant. Anyone who hires him to do a portrait must be prepared to see in the final work emotions which they didn't even acknowledge to themselves they felt. Rembrandt goes beyond the surface. He has an uncanny ability to see into the mind and heart of a subject. And that goes for his large number of self-portraits as well. He looks in the mirror. He paints. He hides nothing.

"Many say, and I would agree, that Rembrandt is the most magnificent painter the world has yet produced. Not all experts are of the same mind, but his painting of the urban militia that hangs in Amsterdam's Musketeer Hall is a work of genius. It's far more than a portrait of the militia members. It's a vibrant scene of the group gathering together and preparing to march. Yet some observers of the painting see only chaos. They do not understand his vision. Perhaps you have seen the painting? Isabela knows the model for the little girl walking through it—the one in the golden dress with a chicken dangling from her dress."

"I must confess I've never been to your city. Nor have I seen the painting I believe you refer to. The Shooting Company of Frans Banning Cocq isn't it? And I've heard people speculate about the model for that strange child determinedly moving among all those men. Who was she then?"

Isabela explained how when she and Pieter met, Rembrandt had been charmed by Nelleke, the orphan who accompanied Isabela to the butter market that day.

"I've since learned that he had lost two daughters. Perhaps that had something to do with it," she said, "but Nelleke made a strong impression on him. He drew a spontaneous portrait of her. She had no idea that she was talking to a famous artist, of course. They had a playful exchange and he announced right then that he was working on a major commission that would be his largest painting to date. He declared that he wanted her to be in it. Two years later she appeared on that canvas. Her parents are protective and asked Rembrandt not to reveal her identity. Few people know who the model for the child in the painting really was."

"The secret will remain with me," Judith said.

"You may be aware, Mrs. Bayard," Pieter added, "that Rembrandt has fallen on hard times since completing the militia painting. He's fallen into serious debt. When I was last in Amsterdam rumors were circulating. He may lose his large home and studio on the Joodenbreestraat."

"How sad," Mrs. Stuyvesant said. "Before you go tonight, though, may I make a request, Mr. Hals? Giving birth year after year is aging me. I'd like a portrait of me before I become an old lady. Might you oblige?"

"Mrs. Bayard, I am indeed flattered to be asked and might I add that the trials of giving birth aside, your appearance is that of a girl. Your old age is decades ahead of you and I suspect that even then your looks will favor you. I regret that I cannot accept your offer. This is our last evening in your town. Tomorrow, after being married by the Captain of El Oviedo, our friend Captain Angel de Vega, we sail for Amsterdam on The Dolphin."

Chapter Forty-Seven
First Night

Isabela had not set foot on El Oviedo since she moved into the town. She was not prepared for the tide of emotions that washed over her when she stepped onto the deck. The flopping and killing of the enormous sea creature. Diego's indifference and eventual disappearance. Pedro's capture. She shook away the memories and concentrated on repeating the vows after Captain Angel. She experienced a moment of disbelief when she heard the words,

"I now pronounce you husband and wife."

'I am a married woman again?' she thought. 'How did that happen?'

Then she remembered the good-bye she had prepared.

She asked Angel to lower his head. Thinking her request had something to do with the brief wedding ceremony, that perhaps she wanted to pray with him as they had prayed together several times before, he obeyed. Isabela pulled the chain over her own head and placed it over Angel's. Before he understood what had happened, she kissed the double cross dangling from his chest, placed her palm against it, and held it steady so that he could not grip it himself.

"I offered this to you once before and you refused to accept it. Now it is I who refuse to accept your rejection of this gift. When Gérard gave it to Aurelia and when Aurelia gave it to me, they explained that the cross should not be kept by one person indefinitely. It should be given to someone younger, someone loved, someone who may face danger. That someone is you, Angel.

"Twelve years younger than I am, dearly loved by me and others. Plus, just by living in San Agustín and with every voyage you take, you face threats. Take the double cross, Angel. Wear it until you feel compelled to pass it on. It has protected me through two voyages and protected me against my own foolishness. You have just blessed my new marriage. I have a wonderful husband now. He will take care of me."

Isabela glanced at Pieter who smiled back with sympathy. He knew how difficult this good-bye was for her. When he put his arm around her waist, she felt that familiar sharp sting behind her eyes that told her she would not be able to hold back her emotions. How wonderful after all these years to have someone at her side who understood what she was feeling.

"I have a home in that city. A home in a city that does its best to take care of its citizens—all of them."

Isabela was sure she spoke for Pieter as well as herself when she added,

"We would help you a make a new start there any time you wish."

She fell forward and embraced the young man, the brave young man she had often referred to as "my son." They both realized that this good-bye might be final.

"You will be very busy, Angel. And needed. But do take time to write from time to time. Promise me."

"I promise, Isabela," he said, his own eyes dampening.

"I love you. I will never forget you. And," he said, reaching for the double cross for the first time and holding it in his fist, "I will honor your wishes. I will honor the tradition of your gift. When you think of me from time to time . . ."

Isabela shook her head at the words "from time to time."

"Often, Angel. Very often," she insisted.

"When you think of me OFTEN, you must picture me wearing this magical icon. You must conjure up an image of me as safe. Safe and content."

* * *

'No wonder Pieter was so adamant about waiting to sail on a Dutch passenger ship and only a Dutch ship.' Although all ships carried some goods and at least a few passengers, Isabela's previous trips had all been on Spanish ships. This was a totally different experience. With a country built on and surrounded by water, the Dutch were as comfortable on water as they were on land. A Dutch vessel was regarded as an extension of The Dutch Republic. Regardless of their nationality, all crew members on a Dutch ship were treated as if they were Dutch citizens. Provisions were ample and regulated. No ship left harbor without a defined amount of dried peas and beans, meat, bread, cheese, butter, vinegar, and beer on board. "Defined" meant an exact quantity per seaman and passenger.

'Even with all his knowledge about sea travel, Angel may have been tutored by Pieter in one respect,' thought Isabela.

All sea voyages were arduous, smelly, dangerous, yes, but this Dutch passenger ship had made an effort to provide as clean, pleasant and safe an experience as possible—for those who could pay high prices for their passage at least. Two crew members were assigned the task of continual sweeping and mopping—not a pleasant way to spend one's time, given the inevitable seasickness and other stomach upsets—but much appreciated by all aboard.

Refusing to be separated at night from the woman he had longed for during the past decade, Pieter hired a New Amsterdam seamstress to design a double hammock with a removable mattress—a set that could be tucked away or propped up during the day.

Mrs. Visscher was aware that in their tiny cabin, the newly married couple would have no privacy. She knew that although Nelita had a separate hammock, the rocking of the ship would probably cause it to sway right against the larger hammock throughout the night. Ever gracious, Mrs. Visscher made an offer.

"Nelita dear, I know my Liesje would so enjoy it if you spent your nights with us in our cabin. What's one more child to us after all? What do you say, Nelita?"

With a meaningful look at Isabela and Pieter, she added, "If your parents do not object, of course."

* * *

Pieter, bare-chested, lay on his back on the hammock mattress. Isabela, in the pale-blue ankle-length, long-sleeved nightdress she had made for this occasion lay beside him. A single candle illuminated their faces.

"You begin," he said.

"I begin? How? What do I do?"

"OK. Here's some guidance. Do you remember when I kissed you along the canal?"

"You mean a decade ago? On the way back to the orphanage after Saskia's wedding party?"

"Yes. After we had talked and laughed and danced for hours. I found a magical space. A handsome linden tree full on top, but with an arched opening underneath. It was as if it had been waiting just for us. It seemed so old, knowing, wise, and welcoming. It was poised just close enough to one of those front door candles to light up your face, yet we were not so well lit that an insomniac looking out a window could clearly perceive us."

"Until that night, I thought a kiss was just a kiss. You taught me otherwise."

"Oh? So what did you learn about kissing that night, my little pupil. Show me now."

"You took my face in your hands," Isabela said. She turned on her side and demonstrated on Pieter.

"You kissed my forehead, my temples, my cheeks, my chin, the corners of my mouth."

With each word she pronounced, Isabela planted a tender kiss on Pieter just as he had done on her face so many years ago.

"Your memory is excellent, Isabela darling," Pieter said with his eyes closed.

He could recall that night quite well himself and lay anticipating what might come next.

"I remember every detail. I'm not finished."

"Oh, sorry. Continue."

"You kissed the corners of my mouth, back and forth, one corner and then the other, back and forth slowly and sort of rhythmically."

"Mmmm. Did you like that as much as I'm enjoying it now?"

"While you were doing that you brushed the tip of my nose as if you were playing with, it moving it from one side to the other and back again."

"Don't smash mine. I'm ugly enough as it is," Pieter said from his dreamy state.

"You are not. You kissed each side of my nose, then you kissed me directly ON my nose and on my eyelids."

"I certainly found a lot of kissing spots on your dainty countenance. What happened next?"

"You pulled away from me. I thought we were finished, that we would continue walking."

"And . . ."

"You looked into my eyes. I'm not sure what you saw."

"Acquiescence maybe? Encouragement?"

"Apparently so. You kissed my mouth several times very lightly. By the time my lips parted, I just wanted to press myself against you."

"And did you?"

"I did. Oh, Pieter," she sighed, "I felt totally cared for, completely trusting, desired. I believed I could remain there in that exact position until daybreak—no, for days, weeks, months. It felt as if I needed nothing else from life. I've never felt that way again, not even for a moment."

Pieter felt a surge of deep sadness and disbelief at her next comment.

"In fact," she added, "I've never been kissed since then—not by anyone."

"It was so long ago, my darling. You've re-enacted that sweet encounter very well—in reverse. Would you like to relive it?"

"Oh, Pieter, yes, please." Isabela lay on her back, smiling, her eyes closed, waiting.

Pieter took her head in his hands and kissed her exactly as she remembered, exactly as she had just kissed him. Slowly, tenderly. Stopping to look at her occasionally. When the memory came to an end, he stopped. She opened her eyes.

"Is that all?"

Although it was excruciatingly difficult for him to move away from her even slightly, he was determined to follow his plan.

"That's all for tonight, my darling."

But you told me that a woman's body is made for pleasure—every inch, you said."

"Every inch. That's true. But not EVERY inch EVERY night. We have tomorrow night, the night after that, and the next night. We have the rest of our lives. We're not rushing."

Delighting in her curiosity and impatience, Pieter blew out the small candle, took her in his arms, and caressed her hair until she fell asleep.

* * *

After a week of encouraging her, patiently helping her to be comfortable with advancing intimacy, using all his determination to control himself so as not to frighten her or reverse their progress, once again he felt her tensing up, resisting. Once more he stopped, just held her and inquired about what was on her mind.

"Cook gave me some ointment. 'To smooth the path,' she said. She must have understood how painful and unpleasant my encounters with Diego were for me. It helped somewhat. But that was long ago now. The ointment has evaporated. I no longer have it. I don't feel prepared."

"Darling, you don't need to be concerned. Nature takes care of that challenge too. She endows women with their own ointment. You needed Cook's help because Diego was abrupt, inept, careless, and uncaring. You have a very different husband now. I ask you to have faith in me, in us together, and in your body. When it's treated lovingly, it knows what to do."

An hour later nestled beside her sleeping husband, the call of the ship's Watch—"twenty-two hours and all's well"—sent Isabela's thoughts back to Amsterdam where she had fallen asleep each night listening to the reassuring call of the city's wandering night watchman. She sometimes lay awake then, listening to the gentle breathing of her twenty little six-year-olds and wondering what her future looked like. Although as Pieter said—"We never know what lies in the future"—she felt that at last she now had the outlines of an answer. The next morning as the Visscher and Hals families shared breakfast, Mrs. Visscher observed that her friend, Isabela, seemed enveloped in a distracted, dreamy glow.

Chapter Forty-Eight
Home

⁂

Inspired by a mouse sighting, Isabela spent time each day of the two-month trip gathering the four children around her to write a series of stories about Moeder Muis and her adventures onboard an Amsterdam-bound ship with her little mice children, one girl, one boy. Juli became entangled in a coil of rope. Joost got stuck in a vat of lard. Juli tried to climb up the masthead and had to be rescued. Joost delighted in running under the ladies' skirts and hearing them scream. Juli mouse had a craving for almond cake, tried to make it herself and made a mess in the kitchen.

With the help of Mrs. Visscher, Isabela and the children wrote, rewrote, edited, and perfected the stories. Isabela could see Nelita's comfort with the Dutch language growing daily. Pieter illustrated each story according to the children's vision. The children drew their own mouse pictures. His exaggerated expressions on the mouse faces when they found themselves in treacherous circumstances provided endless amusement.

Earlier, Pieter had described and drawn in detail for Nelita the entrance to his home. Now as each day brought them closer, he drew a different room and told them about some of the objects they would find there. He told stories of growing up in the house, including an alarming one.

As children, Pieter and Anneliese loved playing in the out-of-the way attic. They could play make-believe, paint, glue to their hearts' content and never have to clean up.

One hot day they were joined by one of Anneliese's friends, Janneke. Seeking relief from the attic's sweltering temperature, they opened a window. It happened to be the window that overlooked the street four stories below. Like all canal houses, just above the window, sticking out like the raised nose of an elephant, was a horizontal wooden beam. Because the interior stairs were so narrow, the bar was used to hoist large chests, beds, and other wide furniture up through the window and into the house.

Free of parental observation, feeling daring and wanting to show off for Janneke, Pieter had climbed out the window. He wrapped his legs around the beam and pulled himself up onto it. He placed both feet on it and slowly stood, one foot in front of the other. At first he tried to be brave, but when he looked down, he felt such terror that he almost lost his footing. With no way to turn around, he had to kneel and crawl backwards in an undignified manner. His bottom was the first part of him to re-enter the window.

"I remember the pounding of my heart," Pieter said. "How hard it was to force myself to concentrate. How slowly I had to move. Plus my knees were beginning to hurt from rubbing that hard beam. I didn't want to lift them, so I scooted.

"Anneliese opened the attic door and screamed.

'Mama. Adriana. Pieter's about to fall down onto the street.'

"When the two women ran up two flights of stairs and burst into the room, they bent down to embrace me where I lay splayed and panting on the floor. As if I'd been gone for years—away on a dangerous mission.

"Dutch parents are pretty forgiving of their children's misbehaviors, but Anneliese and I were not permitted to play in the attic for an entire month and then only after repeated promises to NEVER again walk out on that bar. They needn't have worried."

As if he were that seven-year-old again, Pieter seemed shaken at the memory. As if she were the parent, Nelita threw her arms around him. Isabela felt limp hearing this story. 'What if Pieter HAD fallen and crushed his skull?' she thought. 'Where would I be now?' She felt a surge of gratitude to his mother for saving him and sadness that she would never meet her. 'I WILL thank Adriana, though,' she promised herself.

Although this was by far the least frightening sea voyage Isabela had ever taken, with each lurch, each sudden loud sound, each ship sighting, she reached for the double cross. When she remembered it was no longer there, she would begin to cross herself and stop. Searching for some repetitive, comforting gesture, she often ended up in prayer pose, palms pressed together, head slightly bowed, praying to Mary.

'That is one thing I will not change,' she said to herself. 'A prayer offered to Mary is comforting. A prayer to God is too intimidating. It offers no reassurance. But perhaps as I become more comfortable with my new religion, I will not find God so unapproachable? So distant? I assume the tailor prays directly to God. If so, I hope God is listening.'

Aware that Mary played no part in the tailor's religion, she nonetheless offered up a prayer for the Valverde family.

"Dear Mary, Mother of us all, please look after my friends. Please intercede on their behalf that they may find a new, welcoming home."

Isabela knew by now that the first two weeks of a voyage were the toughest on her stomach. Every morning she drank a cup of tea made with the dwindling herbs from Cook's cottage. By the third week the herbs were gone, but her system had adapted to the constant motion. Early in the eighth and final week, she woke up and wondered.

'What is this? The sea is relatively calm. Why after all these weeks with no heaving, am I suddenly feeling sick again?'

She noted, though, that this sickness was not like the earlier seasickness. It did not tug at her insides constantly. She experienced nausea mostly in the morning. It was brief.

'Could it be?' she thought, with a sense of fear, wonder, and delight. 'I will wait another month to tell Pieter. I won't tell him until I'm sure.'

* * *

The few memories Isabela had of Amsterdam's port a decade ago were erased with one glance. She was looking at ten times the number of ships and hearing twenty times the noise from before. Every seaman, every passenger, every tradesman, seemed to be moving and shouting at once. Nelita stood gawking, clinging to her mother. Isabela pointed out flags from fifteen different countries, although she could not name them all. Anxious families pushed through the crowds. Joyful shouts arose when someone spotted a returned husband, a brother, a son.

Men unloaded goods, took them to the weigh-station, and carted them off to warehouses. Inspectors circulated, making notes. Investors traded information. Merchants stood on tiptoe to determine what new enticing items they might purchase for resale. The demand for luxury foreign goods was high. Competition rife. After being shown a few samples of porcelain from a ship recently returned from China, one merchant purchased the ship's entire stock.

While they were waiting for their luggage to be unloaded, Pieter presented Isabela with a thin, narrow box. "Welcome back, my darling. The wind can be nippy at times in my city. I thought you might like these. Our New Amsterdam craftsman friend, Ezekiel Levy, made them."

The beauty of the box's contents took Isabela's breath away. She picked up one of the gloves, caressed it, and held it to her cheek. "It's as soft as you were the day you were born, Nelita. Here. See?" Nelita took a glove, imitated her mother's gestures exactly, and nodded her head.

Pieter had not thought of it when he chose the color, but now he noted that the beige matched perfectly the skin tone of his new wife and daughter.

Anticipating further expressions of delight when he placed the gloves on Isabela's hands, gently fitting each finger into place, he was dismayed and disappointed to see that familiar shadow pass over her face instead. He recognized the signs. A detachment. A tightening just below her left eye as if she were attempting to keep a tear from falling.

"How Aurelia would have loved these," Isabela said, stretching out her hands to admire the gift in place.

"She had dozens of gloves, you see. But none like these."

Isabela forced herself to recognize only briefly what she knew would be a longing that would never leave her. To have Aurelia here with her—not as a cook certainly, but as her companion and confidante, as a grandmother to her children.

Then she smiled at Pieter. Not the indulgent, mildly amused smile he sometimes observed when he had said something amusing, but a large smile coming from those full, sensuous lips he adored, accompanied by a long gaze directly in his eyes.

"Thank you, My Darling. They are perfect," she said above the din and shouts.

* * *

Pieter sent a note to his housekeeper, Adriana, and hired a sleigh to take his new family and their possessions to 319 Heerengracht. If Isabela had not been so weary, she would have leapt down from the cart to take Nelita on a walking tour of the Dam. The new city hall was complete, she noted. She pointed out the *pannekoeken* ladies, the boys running by pushing hoops that reached their shoulders, the stock exchange where Pieter had said you could trade in thirty different currencies.

When she caught site of a woman selling spices, the memory of trying to control a seven-year-old Nelleke on the busy dam twelve years ago came rushing full force into her mind.

"That could be the same woman who placed spices in Nelleke's sweaty little hand," she told Pieter. "Remember? She showed them to Rembrandt and he incorporated them into the spontaneous drawing he made of her. A cinnamon stick, one tiny clove, and a nutmeg. That was after she chased your escaped dog, Runt, up to the city wall and I came puffing after her. What's Nelleke like now, Pieter?"

"Much the same, really. Still impetuous, forceful, constantly searching for new experiences. I find her tiring actually. I'm sorry, Darling, I know you've been corresponding and that you loved each other dearly, but being in her presence can be daunting. You have been warned."

As they continued through the Dam, red, green, and orange parrots squawked in protest of their caged confinement. A crowd gathered around a monkey chained by the neck and performing its antics under a large parasol. Flapping flags with the city's symbol—a red shield with three silver Saint Andrew's Crosses in the shape of X's arranged vertically on a black strip—reminded Isabela of the Amsterdam City uniform she had worn nearly every day of her eighteen-month stay in the orphanage. A man with a heavy beer belly leaned against a post. Cheeses, artichokes, and carrots were mixed in among large cabbages arranged on a cloth on the street before him. A dog stood guard over the merchandise. A barefoot child held onto his father's shirt and munched on a slender carrot.

The wide space of the Dam gave way to a narrow street on one side of a canal. "Pavement!" Isabela said to Pieter as she listened to the click click of horses' hooves.

"Stone," Pieter corrected.

"No more mud?" Isabela asked.

"Well occasional puddles, but you're right. No more sinking in mud up to your ankles."

Again that broad smile. Two smiles within such a short time. "No more sinking in mud up to my ankles," Isabela repeated as if that summed up all the excitement she was feeling about returning to the city.

Rows of slender houses, their walls touching companionably, temporarily blocked out the sun. Pieter pointed out the symmetrical gables framing the gray sky. Each a different color and unique shape. They passed wheelbarrows straining under loads of bricks. Women in billowing skirts scrubbed stoops. Children and dogs ran alongside their cart.

Nelita sat quietly looking to the left and right, overwhelmed by all the activity and the mixture of smells she could not identify.

"Go around back through the alley," Pieter told the driver.

Adriana was waiting by the gate. She had been with the Hals family ever since Pieter could remember. She fell into his embrace and then looked at him for a long time. With each trip he took, she prayed constantly for his safe return. Once she was convinced that her boy was safe and healthy, she turned to greet his new wife and daughter, surprised to see that they were not Dutch.

Whenever a trading ship had left New Amsterdam laden with lumber or beaver pelts, Pieter had made sure the ship carried a note to Adriana. Like Pieter's sister, Anneliese, and all of Pieter's neighbors and friends, Adriana had assumed he met the widow in New Amsterdam and that he was returning with her to their shared homeland.

"Hello, Adriana," Isabela said. "We've actually seen each other before, although we were not formally introduced. Ten years ago, the day Pieter and I met. You may recall seeing him in front of this house with me and my little friend, Nelleke, both in our black-and-red orphan uniforms. Pieter was accompanying us back to the orphanage. He had just purchased hot buns for us from a pushcart. When the bun-maker knocked on the door, you answered. You said, 'Aren't you supposed to be working with the master?' You were referring to Rembrandt, of course. 'Out gallivanting with pretty girls instead, eh? Will we see you for dinner tonight?'

"Nelleke and I had been gaping at the large house and at the complex process of cleaning the tumbling façade with water tumbling from the upper floor windows. Not until you appeared and we overheard the playful exchange between you and Pieter, Adriana, did we have any inkling that he lived there . . . here. Pieter called up an answer to you. 'I'll be home tonight. Would I miss one of your meals? Now get back to work yourself, Miss.'"

Adriana brought both hands to her cheeks and sucked in her breath. "I do remember. That was you, Mrs. Calderón? Yes," she said peering more closely at Isabela, "And now you are mistress of this house. What the Lord has in store for us we can never know. Welcome home."

"Thank you. Please call me Isabela."

After a few steps, Adriana stopped and stared at Isabela again.

"And that's you in that portrait, isn't it? I've kept the back of it dusted all these years. Pieter insists it remain facing the wall. I've certainly been tempted to take a peek, but he won't let anyone look at it. I just remember he told me once he was painting someone who worked at the orphanage."

"Isabela will see the portrait soon enough." Pieter said. "If she approves, we'll share it with you, Adriana, at last."

Isabela added, "Thank you, Adriana, for taking such good care of the portrait. I'm impatient to see what Pieter saw in me twelve years ago."

"You're welcome, Mistress. Not easy moving around that rat's nest of a studio. Pieter works a little and then takes off leaving a mess behind in the attic."

Pieter put his arm around his loyal housekeeper as she shooed away some demanding chickens and the group approached a small wooden gate. The gate led to a private outdoor area with a stone floor and stone walls—"the interior garden," Adriana called it. Isabela suspected it was often hung with laundry and scattered with onion and potato peelings, but today it was scrubbed clean.

As Pieter had predicted, Adriana was bursting with information she was itching to share with the neighborhood house servants. She thought about the instructions in her master's most recent note sent two hours ago from the Amsterdam dock. His words were explicit, but also puzzling.

"Dear Adriana,

We have arrived and will appear at the back gate soon. I trust the house is ready. I look forward to introducing my new family to all my friends. BUT NOT FOR A FEW DAYS. We all need rest. During this week please DO NOT mention the names or nationality of my wife and daughter to anyone.

Your Pieter

Curiosity infused the neighborhood. It would be difficult to keep the secrets Pieter insisted upon.

* * *

When Adriana opened the kitchen door, Isabela had an impression of scrubbed cleanliness and order punctuated by blue-and-white Delft tiles. She had no time to study this important room, however. Pieter covered her eyes and led her and Nelita to the front door of the dwelling.

"Pretend you've just entered the door on the canal side," he said. "I want your first views of your new home to be from this vantage point."

"Papa. It's just like the drawings you made," Nelita said.

She opened the drawer in the small, familiar-looking bureau at the entrance.

Holding up a pair of soft leather child gloves, she asked, "Are these for me?"

"Well, let's see if they fit," suggested Nelita's Papa Nuevo.

The child was so pleased and satisfied with the surprise gift that she wore the gloves the rest of the day and night. Yet there was more.

"Did you not see this, Nelita?" Pieter asked her.

When she looked up at the coat stand, she gasped with delight.

"The cape you drew, Papa. Is this it? With the fox-fur collar?"

Pieter wrapped the cape around her shoulders, tied it under her chin and lifted her up so she could see herself in the mirror. As he set her down again, she caught site of more fox fur. As if it were curled up around itself cat-like. She smiled up at Pieter, trying to remember what he had called it. He smiled down waiting for her to say it.

"M. It starts with 'M., she said.

"Correct." Isabela stood by enjoying the exchange.

"M . . . U, I think?"

"Keep going."

"M . . . U . . . F . . . F. I have it! Muff! It's a muff, isn't it Papa?"

With Nelita contentedly dressed for winter, Pieter led her and her mother into the main sitting room. A low fire burned in the chimney. Through the canal-side windows afternoon light illuminated the scene. Isabela caught sight of a large globe on a raised platform. She noticed a scroll, two long, white clay pipes, several busts, colorful fans, an hour glass, an array of candlestick holders. Her first overall impression, though, was a feeling of being surrounded by Turkish carpets and silver—silver molded into every form imaginable.

A tall oak cabinet with a glass front housed silver pitchers and decorated goblets in various sizes. A smaller matching cabinet caught Nelita's eye.

"What are those?" she asked peering through the glass.

Pieter opened the smaller cabinet, reached in and placed in Nelita's open hand a silver sculpture that just covered her small palm.

"It's a monkey, I think?"

"Exactly. Fifty animal sculptures in all. Anneliese and I played with them endlessly. We took turns hiding one behind our backs while the other tried to identify it. 'Does it live in the desert? In the mountains? In the water? Does it hop? Slither? Run fast? Is it dangerous? Can you eat it?' Now it's your turn to enjoy these silver creatures. Shall we play the game after you've rested?"

Isabela was focused on the carpets. Wool ones. Thick. Decorated. Varied. Rugs on the walls. Rugs covering tables. Small rugs in front of chairs—apparently to warm the feet. The gleaming black-and-white floor tiles were bare. And in the corner? What was that rug covering up? Another table? Some other piece of furniture? She looked at Pieter as if asking permission. He nodded his encouragement. She walked through the room, barely registering the many objects. Later she would explore the china sets, the paintings, the silver and bronze art pieces, the collections.

She went directly to the mystery object. She could see now that it had two legs in front. Slowly, starting with the part of the rug covering the one leg in back, Pieter rolled the rug forward until the black-and-white keys were revealed. He brought over a matching stool and motioned for Isabela to sit. Instead she threw her arms around him and clung to him. Nelita, unwilling to remove her gloved hands from her new furry accessory, leaned against them both. The little family stood there in a tight unit until Isabela composed herself. She sat down, lifted her hands above the keys, and launched into a lively tarantella. Pieter removed Nelita's muff, took her little gloved hands in his, and twirled her around the room, her cape flying up behind her. When Adriana left the kitchen to watch and listen, Pieter reached out to her and the three of them danced while Isabela played on.

A clock in the room chimed fourteen times. It was two o'clock in the afternoon. Too excited to sleep, the family spent the rest of that

Wednesday taking turns bathing in a wooden tub in Adriana's "interior garden," and gorging on fruit, fresh bread with butter, and mutton stew. That night Isabela tucked an exhausted Nelita into what used to be Anneliese's bed. She was still holding the silver monkey.

In what had been his parents' room, Pieter pulled back the heavy curtain and helped Isabela up the two steps and into the box bed. He pulled back the quilt to reveal fresh white linen sheets.

"These were my mother's pride," he said. "She used white linen for all the beds but also for tablecloths and napkins—'Les serviettes,' she called them. She had a preferred special bleach-works shop. Twice a year, though, she and Adriana hung them in the sun in the garden."

Pieter brought the linen up to his nose and took a deep whiff. Surrounded by the clean welcoming fragrance he associated with his childhood, he marveled at the wonderful turn his adult life had recently taken.

Chapter Forty-Nine
Two Baptisms and a Wedding

ying in Pieter's arms in his parents' bed, Isabela regretted that she had never met Pieter's mother. In addition to the clean scent of bleach, she could smell cologne—'perhaps splashed on the sheets and pillows this very day by Adriana while we were in the cart approaching the house,' she thought. As she had every night for the past two months, before remembering where she was, she braced herself for being bumped and lifted by waves.

"I am so grateful for the steadiness," she told Pieter. "As long as I live, I never again want to sleep in a hammock. I don't even want to see one from a distance."

Before Isabela fell asleep, Pieter brought up something that had been worrying him.

"I know you're concerned about attire for our party, Darling, and there's really too little time to have a new gown made. I have a suggestion. Anneliese went through my mother's dresses after she died and took some of them, but there are still a few left in her wardrobe. Perhaps tomorrow you could look at what remains and adapt one for yourself."

As so often happened, Pieter was surprised by her response. He thought that after her preoccupation with what to wear for the Judith Bayard Stuyvesant visit and the importance of the upcoming occasion, she would want to give careful attention to her outfit. She smiled her thank-you for his suggestion, yawned, and said casually,

"I've already chosen a gown, Pieter. Don't worry about that anymore."

Pieter had deliberately left the bed curtain open enough to let in a small amount of light from the front-door candles across the canal. Just enough so he could see Isabela's face. As tired as he was, he lay awake a long time gazing at her. Several times he woke up startled and amazed that she was still there.

* * *

The family rose for an early breakfast the next morning. Hoping to avoid seeing anyone they knew, they took winding narrow streets before crossing the round, crowded Dam Square and entering the Nieuwe Kerk for a prearranged meeting with the Rector. Isabela recalled from one of Nelleke's 1645 letters that due to the carelessness of a craftsman making repairs, the church roof had been destroyed and the rest of the church had suffered much damage. The newly restored church was reconsecrated three years later, Pieter told her, timed to give thanks for the end of the Dutch Republic's eighty-year war with her own country.

This was the second time Isabela had stepped into a non-Catholic church. She had passed this one often and was curious, but as the good Catholic girl she was at age sixteen in 1641, she was forbidden by her own church to enter "foreign" territory. She knew its history, though. Originally built by Catholics in the mid 1400s, the church was taken over by Calvinists during the reformation. Isabela cringed thinking of the how the nuns, priests, monks, and clinging worshipers were driven out, of the shredding and burning of Catholic icons.

Yes, it did seem plain compared even to the small-town Catholic churches of Santos Gemelos and San Agustín, yet she was captivated by her first sight of the church's interior. Nelita and Isabela bent their heads back to observe the height of the magnificent thick white columns on either side of arch after arch. She was overcome with the same mix of feelings she experienced looking up at the stars—insignificance, mystery, gratitude, awe.

As they walked along the side aisle, Isabela asked about and Pieter pointed toward, the orphan gallery where she knew Nelleke had worshipped every Sunday until the Broekhofs took her as one of their own.

"Later I will show you the magnificent baroque carved pulpit, the ten chapels that ring the sanctuary, the tombs of some of our heroes. For now let's get to our business," he said.

* * *

"I must ask you, Mrs. Calderón. Immigrants are pouring into our city these days. Are you asking to be baptized as a Calvinist because your husband is pressuring you to do so?"

Seated across a plain wooden desk from the family of three was an unsmiling man dressed entirely in black. She had anticipated that the Rector would be of stern countenance and the business of converting was serious, of course. Isabela suppressed the image of the warm, fatherly, smiling Friar Fernando in Santos Gemelos. She cleared her throat, looked directly at the Reverend and ventured a slight smile. He sat rigid waiting for her answer.

Ever since she and Pieter had begun discussing her conversion, she carried in her mind a vision of sitting in church—this church—every Sunday with Pieter and their children by her side. It had never occurred to her that her request might be rejected.

"Absolutely not," she said. "The decision is mine. If there had been an alternative while I still lived in Spain—before meeting Pieter for the second time—I would have left the Catholic Church then."

She described the tight control, the paranoia and the violence she witnessed. She hesitated, but not wanting to upset Nelita and without using their names, she hinted at Cook's killing and the attacks on the Valverde family.

"I love my husband, yes. But aside from that, I wish to raise my children in—a tolerant community."

Pieter sat attentively during the Minister's questioning, but he reacted most to her use of the word "children." He had been so focused on winning her, they hadn't discussed that topic much. For a moment he indulged in a daydream—running after an active little boy—a miniature of himself—and somehow convincing the child to sit long enough for a drawing.

"Follow me," the Rector said. He rose from his desk and led them to the front of the majestic church. People were milling around the sanctuary. Foreigners perhaps visiting the city. A widow praying alone. One man walked with his head Heavenward, apparently lost in the magnificent heights of the ceiling. He was so transfixed, he bumped into a pew and let out a little cry.

"You did not bring witnesses?" the minister said over his shoulder as they approached the baptismal font.

"I'm sorry, Reverend. I did not realize witnesses were required."

The Reverend turned and looked at Pieter.

"Apparently you have never attended a baptism."

"Oh, yes, of course, the baptisms of my nieces and nephews, the infants of my friends. I believed we were there to support the parents, to celebrate with them. I now remember I did sign papers at some of those baptisms."

Pieter feared they would be turned away, that they would be required to return another day. They needed the baptisms completed in order to register with City Hall. He wanted no delays.

Pieter turned and approached the well-dressed man who had so rudely been returned to earth when he bumped his knee. Having recovered, the man stood gazing upward at a stained-glass window so distant and untouchable it might have been in Heaven.

"Excuse me, Sir, might you have a few minutes to serve as a witness to two baptism ceremonies?"

The man seemed confused. He answered in a language Pieter did not understand.

"The witnesses must be Calvinists themselves, Mr. Hals, preferably members of this very church," the minister called out in his deep, commanding voice.

Pieter looked at the widow, but she was praying fervently and crying quietly. He did not want to disturb her. Then, as if God has placed them there, way at the back of the sanctuary, he saw a family of five enter the church. The Visschers. Hadn't they mentioned they were staying with Amsterdam relatives for a few days of rest before making their way to Maastricht? 'They must be touring,' Pieter thought, 'taking advantage of their short stay to get to know the city.'

While the Reverend grew impatient, Pieter walked the length of the church. He returned with the family, who were delighted to see their travelling friends and be called into service. Pieter made the introductions, explained the connection and added,

"Both Mr. and Mrs. Visscher were baptized as infants. They are active members of the St. John's Church in Maastricht. Perhaps you know that church, Reverend? It's named after St. John the Baptist."

When the minister observed the expensive clothing of the family and the commanding demeanor of Mr. Visscher, he waived his requirement that witnesses be members of the Nieuwe Kerk.

"Let us begin," he said.

Thrilled to see each other so soon and so unexpectedly, but controlling their excitement, Liesje Visscher and Nelita held hands.

Before conducting the formalities of the baptism, the minister could not resist a bit of educational preaching to his captive audience.

"God is all powerful and all knowing. God is outside of time. He exists in the past, the present, and the future. God has predestined all of us to join him in Heaven. Yet in His greatness and wisdom, God has given man what we call free will."

He stopped and looked sternly at the group.

"It is up to each of us to obey His laws and to define our own unique path—the road that will lead us to the Heaven God has prepared for us."

He waited a minute as if to allow the group to absorb his words then turned to Pieter. "What name shall I give this woman?" he asked.

After the woman spoke for herself, the Reverend dipped his hand three times into the font and said, letting droplets fall on the top of her bonnet, "In the name of the Father, Son, and Holy Ghost, I baptize you, Isabela Maria Lucia Calderón and welcome you into the Calvinist faith."

"And the little girl?" he asked again looking at Pieter.

The little girl spoke for herself as well.

"Nelita Anacleta Hals," she pronounced as if that had been her name since birth.

"In the name of the Father, Son, and Holy Ghost, I baptize you, Nelita Anacleta Hals and welcome you into the Calvinist faith." He then turned to the adult members of the Visscher family who chorused "We do" to his question—"Do you as devout Christians swear that you have seen and heard today, the second October in the year of our Lord 1652, the baptism and blessing of both Isabela Maria Lucia Calderón and Nelita Anacleta Hals?"

The minister motioned for all of them to follow him back to his office.

"To sign the official papers," he said.

Pieter reminded the minister that he and Isabela, although already legally married, wished to be married in the eyes of God. The minister turned around and conducted a brief ceremony. He led the couple in repeating their vows of devotion and ended by saying, "In the name of our Lord, Jesus Christ, I pronounce you, Pieter Johannes Hals and Isabela Maria Lucia Calderón, husband and wife. May the Lord bless you and your children, may you live long, fruitful lives on this earth until such time as you together join our Lord in his Heavenly palace. Amen."

The Hals and Visscher families followed the minister back to his office where the adults all signed two copies of documents—one for the church records and one to take on their next stop to the temporary city hall nearby. After the clerk had registered the marriage and Isabela and Nelita had become legal citizens of Amsterdam, the two families once again took leave of each other with promises to visit soon. Nelita and Liesje clung to each other and kissed each other good-bye.

Next Pieter and Isabela went directly to a shop on the Singelgracht. Outside hung a large symbol of an ornate bracelet—probably made of wood but painted with silver geometric patterns and deep green "gems" that probably represented emeralds. The letters curved around the bottom and sides of the bracelet and read "Van de Venne. Jewelers."

"Good afternoon, Mattheus," Pieter said as they entered the shop.

"Pieter Hals, how are you? It's been a long time. Your most recent travels were successful, I've heard," he said smiling at Isabela and Nelita.

He moved around the glass cabinet in front of him in order to approach the potential customers.

"A wedding ring for your bride, perhaps, Pieter? She is lovely. I congratulate you." Placing his hands on Pieter's shoulders, he added, "You are well aware, I'm sure, that for many years your father was my most reliable supplier of pure silver. Tell me what type of ring you're thinking of."

The jeweler returned to his perch behind the cabinet and brought out samples. "Something like this for the lady? The best quality silver— all the way from Peru. A thick silver band, embossed with a design of small crosses. One large ruby with two smaller rubies on each side. Let me take the lady's measurements. We can have the ring ready for you early next week."

"I'd like to see something simpler, please, Mr. Van de Venne," Isabela said. "A smaller band. A single small ruby perhaps. That would please me most."

After trying to suggest alternative, but still elaborate designs, the jeweler finally relented.

"She knows what she wants, your wife. If you agree, Pieter, we will follow her wishes."

The jeweler was beginning to write out a bill of sale, when Isabela said, "I wish to purchase a ring for my husband as well . . . using this."

She reached into her skirt pocket and unwrapped the jewel she had freed from her petticoat only that morning. She held it out on her open palm, showed it to Pieter, to Nelita and then the jeweler.

"Using this diamond," she said.

"Darling," a startled Pieter said, "Where did you get that stone? Not that it makes any difference to me and thank you for offering to have a ring made for me, Isabela, but are you sure it's truly a diamond?"

"Shall we test it?" the jeweler said. "As you can imagine, people come to me with all kinds of stones to sell. Frankly, most of them are fakes."

He placed a microscope atop the counter. While he was bent over the instrument and examining the stone from all sides he explained,

"What an expert looks for is imperfections. A true diamond is not clear. You cannot see through it. I should be able to see tiny inclusions within—intricacies unique to each stone. Light cannot pass all the way through a gem that is genuine.

"I have formed an opinion, but before I share it, let's give your stone what I call 'the sparkle test.'"

He placed Isabela's stone on a piece of brown paper and reached into his pocket for another stone—a much larger one. He invited Isabela and Pieter to view both stones from the side and the top.

'Does the dealer wish to persuade me to trade diamonds and ask me to pay the difference?' Isabela wondered.

The jeweler continued his lecture.

"Compare these two stones now. You see how both shine and reflect light when viewed from a side angle. Only YOURS shines and reflects from EVERY angle. As the microscope confirmed, only YOURS is imperfect. Only YOURS is unique. What you have here is a small, but quite beautiful and genuine diamond," the expert pronounced with satisfaction.

The jeweler returned the large, fake stone to his pocket.

"How shall I mount your diamond? A simple silver band to match the ruby ring perhaps? Or a more manly heavier, wider band?"

Pieter answered by looking directly at Isabela for her approval.

"I am an artist. My hands are integral to my work. I should not wear a piece of jewelry that interferes in any way with the relationship of brush, pen, or charcoal with paper. Were it up to me, I would choose the more slender band that matches yours, Darling. The slender band also seems more suitable for that size diamond. What do you think?"

"I agree, Pieter."

Can you have the rings ready by Friday afternoon?" Pieter asked.

"Oh my, that's very soon. Next week would be better."

"We've recently arrived from the New World and we would like to show off your handiwork at our Saturday afternoon event. I'm happy to pay a surcharge if you can guarantee they'll be ready by then."

The hefty surcharge made up for the fact that the jeweler was not able to convince the couple to purchase more ostentatious pieces. What's more, the shiny new rings would alert Saturday's guests to his excellent craftsmanship.

After taking leave of his father's former business associate, the couple returned home—again, taking a circuitous route.

"I know you must be wondering, Pieter. The source is not important. It was a gift—probably one meant to protect me at a time when I might have been perceived as vulnerable—when I was, in fact, more vulnerable than I knew. I am certain the bearer of the gift would be pleased to know I am using it this way."

Pieter certainly was curious.

'Definitely not Diego,' he thought to himself. The Director-General in San Agustín perhaps? If it had been her father's and she had somehow managed to save it from Diego's clutches, she would have said so. That tailor? But where would a poor, immigrant tailor have acquired such a gem and why would he give it away?'

Chapter Fifty
Portrait of a Young Woman

D ay three in Isabela's new home. Thursday.

"I'd like to see your studio, Pieter. May I?"

"But of course you may. Just be prepared, Isabela. It's a most untidy space."

Isabela followed Pieter up the narrow stairs leading from the second floor to the garret where, since leaving Rembrandt's tutelage, whenever he was not travelling, Pieter worked.

With each step the odors became sharper. When Pieter opened the door, the smells engulfed her. He had warned her, but she could not have imagined the disarray. How did he practice such a visual craft with so little light? Three small windows tucked under the eaves, smeared with dampness and dust. He did not permit Adriana to enter this space often obviously. It may have been years since it was cleaned. Paint cans knocked over, their contents long ago dried up. Splashes of every color on the floor, the walls, the tables. Cast-aside brushes, their bristles twisted, useless. Old opened cans of oil. With each step, she felt and heard the crunching of charcoal.

But mostly she saw parchment. Rolls of it. Some unopened. Some hanging from the rafters. And what must be hundreds of individual sheets. 'How long has it been since he even stepped foot in here?' she wondered. The opening of the door had curled some papers into a corner, adding to the untidiness of the cast-offs scattered throughout.

Pieter stood in the doorway. Seeing his studio through Isabela's eyes made him feel rather ashamed. Even shocked.

'How could I have expected to create anything worthwhile from such careless disorder?' he asked himself.

Isabela reached down and gathered an armful of drawings. She picked up more sketches that Pieter had thrown on the room's only chair—how long ago? Ten years? Six months? She sat on the chair and began to peruse the drawings in her lap.

Studying this initial stack, she noticed that on most, although not all, he had scribbled the name of a place and a date. He had given a title to some. Seized by a desire to establish some order, she attempted to separate the drawings she was holding. She placed "Rome" in a pile on the floor by her right foot. "Antwerp" on the left.

Of the roughly twenty drawings she held, five of the titles began with the word "Woman."

"Woman at her handiwork. 1646."

"Woman in Gypsy costume. 1643"

"Woman praying. 1642."

Drawn with black-and-white chalk on blue paper, this woman held her hands clasped tightly together. She posed on her knees, facing upward, pleading.

'Did this woman reflect Pieter's emotions at that time?' she worried. 'Was he desperate? Filled with longing? Grief?'

Isabela was particularly drawn to "Woman with jug. 1644." Viewed from behind, the woman carried a large earthen container under her right arm. The fingers of her left hand circled the jug's narrow neck. A slice of her profile was visible as she looked down at the heavy object.

"Woman pouring. 1644." The same woman in the same layered skirt, now drawn from the front. She knelt down and tipped the jug over. Water spilled into a pitcher. Her curls escaped the band around her head. Small mounds of breast showed above her bodice. Her sleeves pushed up to the elbows revealed slender arms, straining. A seductive curl wrapped itself around her one visible ear.

Isabela kept on. 'Pieter's determination. His striving. His fascination,' she thought. 'Yet there is a loneliness that pervades these works.'

Pieter kicked the drawings aside and made a path to the opposite wall.

"So, are you ready?" he asked.

Isabela had not noticed what must be a painting resting on an easel. Or was it an empty canvas turned around facing backward?

"Ready?" she asked, aware that her heart was beating in little skips and starts. "Ready for what?"

"Ready to be the first person ever to view Pieter Hals's portrait of Isabela Calderón."

He stood with a hand on each side of the canvas, ready to turn it forward, waiting for her acquiescence.

'Perhaps she does not want to see it,' he thought. 'Perhaps she fears it will bring back too many memories she doesn't want to deal with.'

"You don't have to. It's been here in this position for ten years. It can sit here another ten."

"Of course, Pieter. Of course I want to see the portrait, but are you sure? 'No one is allowed to look at it until it is finished,' you said. You were quite emphatic."

Isabela put down the pile of drawings and drew closer to the easel. She signaled to him that she was ready to give it her full attention.

When he turned the portrait around, she wished she had dragged the chair with her. Viewing herself from a decade ago might be easier if she were sitting down. She stared and stared. She looked at Pieter who waited patiently for a reaction. She stared some more. Forget the face and the expression for a moment. The uniform. She hadn't thought about it much since. But now she remembered every day stepping into the same long wool skirt, red on one side, black on the other; pulling over her head the same long-sleeved white blouse, then the vest that matched the skirt, same fabric, same colors. On Sundays only, depending on the season—and this must have been late summer—she was permitted to drape a thin white shawl over her shoulders and tuck it into the cinched waist. How thin she was!

She remembered growing tired of the same head-covering day after day—a tight white cap down over her ears, a bulgy spot at the top in back for tucking in her hair followed by more tight cap all the way to her neck. This was a Sunday outfit, though, with subtle changes. An almost sheer cap with rows of narrow lace on each side, it was held in place with metal clamps. Right in front of her ears, the clamps seemed almost like pieces of jewelry. She used to hope they gave her a touch of glamour.

Her dark hair—with no silver strip, of course—was barely visible under the cap, but Pieter did capture its thick, curly texture in the exposed area starting at the hairline above her forehead and continuing backwards a few inches until the cap took over. Her twenty-eight-year-old eyes tried to judge the look in the eyes of the seventeen-year-old before her. Shy probably since Pieter was staring at her so intensely. Curiosity too—wondering what he saw as he studied her. Yet she looked so calm, so poised—sweet was the word that came to mind. And that Bible she was holding in her dainty hands. So naïve. Except for the horror of the shipwreck, what did she know of the world then?

She studied the smile. Lips together loosely. Corners turned up slightly. She tried to imitate that smile now and, when she did, she recognized it. She probably laughed and smiled with her children, and with Leonor but THIS smile was one she had returned to only recently. She was first aware of it under the most ugly conditions—when she recognized Pieter in that jail cell. Risking the jealousy and viciousness of the Lieutenant, she couldn't resist smiling that way even then no matter how brief. It was a Pieter smile—the amused, playful, and now she realized thoroughly loving smile they used just for each other.

'Even back then?' she thought, 'when we'd known each other only a short time? No wonder we've both suffered apart.'

She knew she would study the painting many times. She was on the verge of asking where in the house they might place it, when she suddenly realized something unexpected.

"Pieter, it's complete, isn't it? What more could you add? My small nose, my narrow face, my thin eyebrows, the thick lashes—it's all there. Did you finish it AFTER I left?"

"My darling, I completed the painting after two weeks of sittings. I told Mrs. Heijn and I led you and everyone else to believe that I needed a few more weeks. I said that so that I would have more time to be in your company, you see. It was stolen time in a sense. Mrs. Heijn would never otherwise have allowed you to be free of your duties for that period. I had promised to donate the completed painting to the orphanage so she allowed us that extra time. For the last two weeks I faked the entire process. I made a big show of mixing colors, dabbing, looking back and forth between you and the portrait, cleaning up afterwards, but I never touched the canvas."

"So until now, only that irritating maidservant scrubbing and rescrubbing the area around your feet has known the truth?"

"If she thought the painting was finished, she apparently kept it to herself. By the way, it was very nice of you to keep that adorable nose all these years."

"I'm glad you like it."

"That nose is immortal, you know. It will live forever in this portrait. I've been worried all these years that I didn't quite capture it. Now I see that I did."

Wiggling her nose and batting her eyelashes, Isabela said, "Well, I hope you're proud of yourself. I'm so pleased, Pieter—and flattered. It's lovely."

They stared at each other as they often did since they found each other eight months ago. Pieter came and stood by her and they looked at the portrait together arm in arm. Isabela looked up at Pieter and they shared that same amused, mildly disbelieving smile that smiled out at them from the canvas. They both felt as if they had tricked fate. Once again, they were together.

* * *

While Pieter happily played endless games with Nelita below, Isabela continued to organize Pieter's decade of work in the attic. Eventually, Nelita climbed the stairs to see what was occupying her mother. She enjoyed order and playing mother's helper.

"Mama, these are all Papa's, aren't they? You're organizing."

"What a big word for a little girl, Nelita. You are correct. I am organizing. I'll tell you what. These are what I've called 'city piles.' You can pick up any stray paper that's not already in a pile. When you read the name of a city, you put it in the proper pile."

"A city. Like Amsterdam?"

"Yes, what else?"

"New Amsterdam?"

"That's really just a town, but, yes."

"San Agustín?"

"Correct."

Nelita began picking up drawings and putting them down again.

"How about Santos Gemelos?"

"Not that one. Your Papa was never there."

"Only first Papa right?"

'What about Diego will she remember when she grows up?' Isabela wondered. 'Hopefully, very little.'

"Florence. Is that the name of a woman or a city?"

"A city. In Italy. Like Rome."

Nelita let out a cry and threw a drawing face down on the floor.

"Mama, who is that woman in Papa's drawing? Is she a friend of his? She has no clothes on, Mama. She should not be taking a bath in front of him."

"Come here, Sweetheart. Let me explain something about artists."

Isabela put her arm around her pouting daughter.

"Two things. In order to draw people even when they're covered with clothes, artists need to understand what is below the clothes. They need to be able to portray skin. They even need to understand our bones. Like your pretty cheek bones, knees, elbows, even the bones in our fingers."

As she talked, Isabela tapped gently on Nelita's own checks, knees, elbows and fingers.

"They also need to understand how bodies move and bend. That's why they sometimes practice drawing people with no clothes on. Those drawings are called 'nudes.' If you find more and you don't like looking at them, just put them facedown in that pile there."

"Well, I think they're disgusting," Nelita responded.

She continued working for another quarter of an hour. Each time she found a sheet with a city name, she said the name out loud and placed it where it belonged. Whenever she found a drawing of a naked woman, she acted as if she had found a snake. "NUDE!" she cried and threw it facedown.

After the midday meal, Isabela continued to organize the drawings. She really had not seen much of Pieter's work. The more she saw the more she admired his skill, the more she wanted to see.

* * *

While Isabela sifted through drawings in the attic, below in the sitting room Pieter rummaged through some old books from his childhood. Although they were dusty and decades old, Nelita was intrigued.

"Read me one, Papa."

They sat side by side in one of the cushioned chairs near the harpsichord in the main room. Nelita seemed to be involved in the story about a misbehaving little farm boy who knocked over milk cans and chased piglets with a stick and made them squeal.

Suddenly she looked up at Pieter and asked, "Who are the women in the nudes you draw, Papa? Are they your friends?"

"They are called artist models."

"But why do they agree to let you draw them like that?"

"It's a job. I pay them. They're mostly poor women and they need the money. They don't seem to mind."

"Well that one woman stepping out of the bath—the one looking directly at you, Papa—she didn't seem poor. I'm never going to let an artist paint ME like that."

"No, darling, you never will. You won't ever need to. You don't need to do anything you don't want to do."

Nelita thought for a minute. "Are some artist models men?"

"Yes." One of the world's most famous artists ever—an Italian. His name was Michelangelo. He made a sculpture of a man and named it 'David.' I saw it. It's beautiful. It's said to be the perfect male body. I can find a drawing of it in my art books if you like."

"No thank you, Papa," Nelita said emphatically. "Please finish this book. Does the naughty boy get punished?"

* * *

That night as Isabela and Pieter lay in each other's arms, Isabela said, "May I ask you two questions, Pieter?"

The way she asked made him nervous. He could not imagine what she was going to say.

"Of course, my love," he responded.

He pushed up the long sleeve of her nightdress and caressed her lower arm.

"The nude drawing that Nelita found."

"Yes, she wanted to know if the women were my friends."

"As a matter of fact, so do I, Pieter. I assume most of them were paid models. They're involved in some activity. Brushing their hair. Dipping a jug into a stream. Cuddling a newborn. They're concentrating on what they're doing. But THAT drawing, Pieter. The woman is stepping out of her bath. She has a cloth wrapped around her shoulders like a shawl, but it's a long piece of cloth and it's wound around her lower body too—at least around her waist. It appears as if the artist spent considerable time getting the drape just right. He probably tried all kinds of different arrangements. Her breasts and even the darkness between her legs are visible. What's truly shocking, though, is that she looks directly at the artist. Her expression is quite bold as if she's taunting him."

Pieter waited for the question, although he thought he knew.

"My question," Isabela said, "is this. Is that Lucietta I was looking at?"

"Yes," Pieter answered simply.

Isabela seemed to have grasped everything about the drawing, what happened before the scene and what happened after.

'Does she expect some sort of apology?' he wondered.

"You saw many drawings today," he said.

"Yes, I did Pieter. Thank you for sharing them with me. They're truly outstanding. I've seen some of the work you did in San Agustín and in New Amsterdam, but to get a sense of what you've done over the past ten years, that huge body of work, to see the way you changed and grew as an artist . . . it was invigorating."

Pieter was not sure if this was the end of the discussion.

'Was she just curious? Did she merely want to confirm that nude was Lucietta? Was she jealous?'

He waited.

"My second question," Isabela said.

Pieter braced himself. He pulled the sleeve of the nightdress down to her wrist. He placed her arm on the mattress.

"My second question is this. Do you think I'll have time to run this large household, continue to organize and possibly publish your drawings, and care for a newborn all at the same time?"

She rolled over on her side then, put her arm around him and gave him that special teasing look. This time that look had an air of triumph about it.

He had expected more questions about his relationship with Lucietta. He had his answers ready. He would have said, "Did you look at the date on that drawing, Isabela? 1643 probably? It was a long time ago. Nine years ago. Lucietta is no longer part of my life. Nor is she even in my thoughts."

Instead he tried to figure out what exactly was behind this three-part question number two. Yes the house was large and would require her attention. How nice she was suggesting that his drawings reach a larger audience. But a newborn? She didn't refer to a "future child" or even a "baby." She used the word "newborn" as if its arrival were a certainty. As if she had already imagined them both holding the infant, exclaiming over it, counting its fingers and toes, arguing over who it resembled. "My father's nose. MY mother's eyes. YOUR hair. YOUR skin."

When he held her against him, she felt the dampness on his cheeks.

All the loneliness. The wandering. The longing. All he ever wanted was this. To hold this beautiful woman in his arms. To hear her gently announce that she was expecting a child. His child.

"I may be thirty-four, but I feel as if I've waited decades to hear you say those words. From now on, call me Abraham."

Understanding Pieter's Biblical reference to Isaac's elderly parents, Isabela said, "I'm no Sarah, though, am I?"

"Most assuredly not, my youthful darling. Do you think we'll ever stop making each other cry . . . about one thing or another?"

"No. Never. There may just be longer periods between weeps."

"Tomorrow will definitely NOT be a no-crying day."

"I hardly know what to expect. I'm all nerves and tingles."

Chapter Fifty-One
Speculation and Surprise

'Saturday. My fifth day in my new home' thought Isabela. 'And what a day it's going to be. Not as fancy as Saskia Comfrij's celebration long ago certainly, but small and cozy befitting our situation. Not a huge crowd, but a gathering of a few close friends. Not a formal dinner that lasts until the next morning, but an afternoon party.'

When Isabela and Pieter wrote out the invitations months ago before they left New Amsterdam and sent them to Adriana to deliver, it was hard to believe this day would actually arrive. They agreed they wanted an intimate gathering and wrote out a guest list of approximately twenty-two adults and five children.

Given that Pieter abruptly quit his apprenticeship with Rembrandt, the two were not on good terms. Pieter did not feel comfortable including him on the list. Isabela, on the other hand, felt grateful to Rembrandt for bringing the couple together in the first place.

"If you had never been his pupil, if he were not an experimental artist who led you OUT of the studio and into the fresh air, we would never have met, Pieter. I also admire the way he adores and relates to children, the fun he and Nelleke had on that first meeting, his immediate grasp of how spirited she was, and his instant assuredness that he would include her in a major painting. Plus, after what you've told me about the problems he's facing, well, I feel some concern for him, Pieter. I would like to include him."

Isabela won. He was added to the list. Rembrandt. That would make twenty-three adult guests, five children. Guest list settled, they launched into an endless discussion of the wording of the invitation. Knowing that they would need time to rest and adjust after the two-month trip, and fearing that if Isabela were identified as his bride they would be deluged with attention, after much word shuffling Pieter wrote out nine invitations in a playful script that read:

Neighbors, family, and friends,
Please join me at a reception to celebrate my recent marriage.
It will be a great pleasure to introduce to you
    my new wife and her daughter.
Saturday, 28 October 1652
15:00-18:00
In our home
Children of all ages welcome

Only later did they realize the further implications of not identifying Pieter's bride by name. They had not taken into consideration the curiosity they were creating. The friends understood the couple's need to be alone in their new home for a while. They maintained a respectful if impatient distance. The servants and delivery folks did not. They all knew Pieter and felt affection for him. All week long they strode through the back alley and snuck up to the kitchen door to pester Adriana for information.

Loyal to "her boy," Adriana shared nothing. One time, however, Nelita was sitting in the kitchen with Adriana helping her knead bread. The two of them were happily chatting away when three people using various excuses poked their heads in.

"Felt like bringing you a bunch of tulips today, Adriana, my sweet lady."

"I'm sure you've got your hands full. I'll be glad to help. Put me to work."

"Had an important question to ask you, but now I forget what it was."

When they caught sight of Nelita, they knew from the way she was dressed that she was sprinkling that mixture of cinnamon and sugar onto the rolled-out bread dough for her own amusement and not because she was being paid to do it.

"Aha, who's this?" one of the curious said, "Might this be the daughter of the new missus? Now I have to say you don't look like a Dutch little girl. Where might you be from, Miss?"

"I'm not supposed to answer that question, Sir," said the demure child as she folded one end of the rolled dough over the other. "Not yet anyway."

"Scat now, all of you," Adriana told the intruders.

"It's a surprise," Nelita added.

But the word was out. Speculation reigned.

"That Pieter Hals is an unpredictable lad, you know."

"Beautiful, but that child had a Mediterranean look to her. Hint of an accent too."

"You don't suppose he's gone and married that model after all, do you? That woman he met in Rome?"

"Or he's found himself a Gypsy like Nelleke's father did?"

"The native people in the New World. Aren't THEY sort of dark?"

"Don't even think of it. He wouldn't . . . would he?"

"That child might be foreign, but she's no savage."

* * *

Since Isabela was not familiar with what foods were available in the city, it was Pieter who sat down with Adriana to plan the menu. Adriana hired two servant girls for the day plus a young woman, Aletta, to watch the children. Everything was ready. Almost.

The day after Isabela arrived, she unpacked her trunk. She dug down to the bottom, removed the tailor's gown, and hung it in the back of the wardrobe in the one room they were not yet using—Pieter's childhood bedroom and the room that would eventually belong to their child. She would deal with the cushion money later. She had never mentioned the hidden coins to Pieter.

Among the few pieces of jewelry and other personal items that Anneliese had left behind in the house after her mother's death, Isabela found a wide clothes brush with an engraved silver handle that fit into her palm. Its design and soft bristles made it perfect for fabric.

Beginning with the V-shaped delicate lace at the top and working slowly, using light tiny strokes, Isabela brushed the entire gown—front, back, sides. She marveled again at its allure and beauty, especially the billowing folds in the crimson skirt. She had forgotten how intricate the layered sleeves were. She lifted each layer and brushed under it. She brushed each individual ruffle at the wrist.

She assumed she would remove the slim side panels she had added when Elizabeth, daughter of San Agustín's Governor, borrowed the dress, but was surprised to find that she needed those panels. Apparently to accommodate the child growing in her belly, she had already added some width.

She thought of the first time she met the tailor and his family when she hired him to add panels to her skirts before Pedro was born. The way he measured her belly with nothing but a glance. She reached into the tiny, hidden pocket and felt the miniature scroll. She didn't need to look at it to be able to see perfectly in her mind the initials I.J.V. in a clear script before the undecipherable words in the unknown alphabet began.

Other than the new ring she had put on for the first time that morning, Isabela had no jewelry. She had hoped for earrings or a bracelet or two, but a search of the drawers in her bedroom resulted in nothing. The new ring with its sweet ruby that matched the dress—that would be fine. The dress was decorative enough.

She slipped out of the dress and hung it up again in the wardrobe. Closing the door behind her, she called Nelita upstairs to get dressed. Per her request, Pieter had asked the Broekhofs the favor of loaning them the complete outfit Mrs. Comfrij sent for Nelleke to wear to their daughter's wedding years ago. They sent it immediately—as clean and fresh as the evening Nelleke wore it.

Isabela slipped the pale-blue gown over her daughter's head and tied the slippers with blue silk bows. She stood Nelita in front of the mirror and pulled the lace bonnet over her ears. It covered only the back of her head, leaving her thick dark curly locks exposed on top and falling softly to her shoulders. Shiny silver clips brought out the sunny yellow flecks in Nelita's dark-brown eyes. Around her soft little-girl neck Nelita placed a simple necklace of small pearls.

Nelita had already seen the outfit and was thrilled to be able to wear it. "Really wear it," she said, "not just look at it."

"If this were not all a surprise," Isabela said, "I would have sent a note to Nelleke asking her to wear the matching outfit I wore to Saskia's wedding. That is if she still has it."

As for Pieter, Isabela had made a feeble attempt to convince him to dress as she knew their male guests would—in something dapper like the small-of-stature but fashion-conscious Jos Broekhof. Pieter would have none of it.

"Those tight vests and jackets that fall to the knees. Those matching pants. I can't BREATHE in them. Those broad-brimmed hats. I can't SEE wearing one of them. I'm an artist. My fingers are permanently stained and my boots too. A gentlemen's suit does not fit me. I WILL promise you a clean, unstained shirt and pants, though."

* * *

"Mama, I don't agree with you. On several occasions since the orphanage delivered this dress to me years ago with the note from Isabela all the way from Spain instructing Mrs. Heijn to deliver it to me, Pieter has seen me wearing it. He always comments. He always admires it. He's a dear friend. We're celebrating his marriage today. I want to wear something I know will please him."

"But, Nelleke, please listen. This is why I'm not comfortable with it. That dress is lovely, of course, and you do look wonderful wearing it. Pieter is right. But that is the dress Isabela was wearing at the celebration of Saskia Comfrij's wedding ten years ago. You were too young to notice. Pieter and Isabela spent that entire evening practically ignoring everyone else, they were so involved with one another.

"Seeing them together like that, well, everyone assumed they would soon be celebrating their own wedding. Then she disappeared. You know the rest. Now here's Pieter ten years later, at last married to,——we all assume—a Dutch woman he met in New Amsterdam. I don't think it's appropriate to remind him of that evening long ago. In fact, I think it would be disrespectful."

Myriam removed several gowns from Nelleke's ample wardrobe.

"How about one of these? The purple one with lavender lace around the bodice? Or this one—wine red with red-and-black embroidered sleeves? Or . . . oh, yes, this is my favorite. It's gorgeous on you, Nelleke," Myriam continued, holding up a gold dress with matching shawl. "It highlights your blonde hair."

"Mama, I'm sorry. I understand what you're saying, but Pieter's surely forgotten all about Isabela by now. And she's been married to someone else all these years. She has never once mentioned Pieter in any of her letters. I expect any day now I'll get a letter from San Agustín telling me she's married another Spaniard."

Myriam Broekhof knew it was useless to argue further with Nelleke on this topic. She would save her breath and energy for one of the many other issues on which they disagreed. She sat on her daughter's bed and watched as Nelleke slipped into the pale—blue gown and then the slippers tied with blue silk bows. Nelleke pulled the lace bonnet over her ears. It covered only the back of her head, leaving her thick curly locks exposed on top and falling softly to her shoulders. Shiny silver clips brought out the sparkling black of Nelleke's eyes. Around her neck she placed a simple necklace of small pearls.

"Oh and I forgot the most fun part of all this, Mama. The little girl—the daughter of Pieter's wife. The unnamed child. She will be wearing the exact outfit—right down to the pearls and the bows on the slippers. I do hope it all fits her. I believe Pieter wrote that she's seven. That's the age I was when I wore it. Thank you for sending it to Pieter after he requested it, Mama. I guess you're right. He does remember that evening awfully well. At least he remembers what Isabela and I were wearing, that we shed our orphan uniforms that night and arrived in the matching outfits the mother of the bride supplied. I suspect Mrs. Comfrij wanted us to look good for her daughter's wedding and hoped we'd blend in with all those elegantly dressed guests."

* * *

Nelita and Isabela descended the stairs just as the knocker announced that the first guests were at the front door. Pieter gasped when he saw Isabela in the gown. His artist eyes took it all in quickly.

"The tailor? He made it, didn't he?" he asked.

"Yes."

"He made it for you?"

"No, for Reza, his wife. It was her wedding dress."

"But he gave it to YOU?"

"Yes. When the family fled. I suspect they left with few of their belongings. The dress would have been too bulky. I know how precious it was to them both. I feel utterly blessed to have it. I consider myself the caretaker of the dress, not its owner. I think they would be pleased if they knew I were wearing it on this occasion. I know that everyone in town understood what a scoundrel Diego was. I think of their gift as a wish—a wish that I might some day, somehow, marry a good man."

Pieter could see that Isabela was becoming upset, as she always did when she talked about the tailor. Or were those tears of gratitude that she was now married to that "good man?" 'Will I ever know everything that passed between them?' he wondered.

The brass hand on the front door sounded again. Sometimes after seeing Isabela upset, Pieter held her and she would break down altogether. He did not want their guests to arrive for a celebration only to see a sobbing bride. He had caught a glimpse of Adriana approaching the front door. He cursed himself for rarely keeping a handkerchief handy.

Nelita noticed her mother's upset. She was familiar with the tone of voice she was using—that tentativeness. It was Nelita who came to the rescue. She reached into the pocket of her pale-blue dress and pulled out a matching cloth bordered with sky-blue lace.

"Here, Mama. Dry your eyes. Three people have just arrived."

* * *

The three members of the Molenair family stepped tentatively into the foyer. A humble couple who lived in the Jordaan, they had never heard of Pieter Hals and were confused by the invitation to a fancy address on the Heerengracht. Yet clearly their names appeared on the invitation: Jan, Griet, and Sophia Molenair. They half expected to be put to work when they arrived, but just in case the invitation was correct and they were being invited as guests, they dressed in the only set of Sunday best they owned.

"We are the Molenair family," they said to Adriana when she opened the front door to greet them.

Half expecting there had been an error, they showed Adriana the invitation.

"We received this invitation?" Jan said more as a question than a statement.

"But we really don't know why Mr. Hals invited us," Griet added, still giving the maid an opportunity to send them back home or assign them a task.

"Welcome and do come in," Adriana said to the hesitant couple. "You are the guests of Pieter and his new wife. They will explain the connection."

Looking to their left and right, trying to take in the opulence all around them, the three Molenairs followed Adriana into the sitting room. For the present, Isabela had regained her composure. She walked right to them and reached out her arms.

"How perfectly appropriate that you should be the first to arrive," she said. "Jan, Griet, Sophia, how are you?"

When Isabela saw that they did not seem to have any idea who she was, she explained.

"It's Isabela. You remember. Over a decade ago your son, Cornelius, brought me to you. He saved my life. For two days while I alternately bailed water and slept, Cornelius rowed me to Amsterdam. By then I was a sodden, unconscious mess. I'll always be grateful for the care you gave me. For six weeks you fed and bathed and clothed me. I had nothing. When I was well enough, you took me to the orphanage where I worked with the youngest girls as a Big Sister. That's when I met my husband, Pieter Hals."

"Isabela? Is that you?" Griet said.

She was having trouble reconciling the elegant woman before her with her memory of the emaciated sixteen-year-old she brought back to life. That girl spoke no Dutch, but this woman spoke the language with only a slight accent. The family stood looking at Isabela. They seemed speechless.

Finally, Sophia asked, "My brother. Have you had word of him? Cornelius wrote us that he was in some kind of trouble. He's not sure he can ever return here."

This was not the time to go into the story of their son's poor judgment, of how he had stolen the uniforms of Spanish soldiers and broken into the orphanage to take her back to Spain.

"I have heard that Cornelius is banned from the Republic," Isabela said. "You must miss him terribly."

When the bronze hand announced more guests, Isabela led the Molenairs to the buffet, gave them each a pewter plate and invited them to serve themselves. Delving into the cherries, plums, pears, and figs spilling out of several large straw cornucopias in the table's center, they next turned to the steaming platters of venison wrapped in pastry, roasted pheasant, sliced beef, and every manner of fish. For a while, they forgot their wayward son.

Chapter Fifty-Two
Uninvited Guest

$\mathcal{A}$driana was showing six people into the room. Isabela had met the elaborately dressed and bejeweled Mrs. Comfrij at the orphanage where she volunteered as a Regentess. For several weeks while she taught embroidery to the little girls, speaking in dramatic changes of cadence, imitating voices, occasionally laughing heartily, Mrs. Comfrij told the story of her daughter Saskia's courtship. How Saskia refused the suitors her parents presented to her and eventually announced that she wanted to marry a man she had first noticed in church, Philip Hoogstraten. Isabela, who had just turned seventeen at the time, and was curious about how one found a mate in the Dutch culture that was so foreign to her, hung on every word. She was impressed that Saskia was able to choose the man she married whereas she, Isabela, had been betrothed to a virtual stranger while still an infant.

Now here was Saskia with her husband, Philip, and their two children. It was at their wedding that Isabela and Pieter never left each other's side, feasting, dancing, conversing—the only evening they spent together before meeting in the San Agustín jail.

After five days of seclusion, Nelita was pleased to see children arrive. For the amusement of the youngest guests, Pieter hired Aletta, a young woman known for being able to entertain children for hours. Taking Nelita's hand, Aletta introduced herself and the child hostess to arriving families.

"This is Nelita. She lives here. Would you like to join us to blow bubbles? I'll bet some of you are terrific at spinning tops. Choose your color. We're having a contest. Which one of you can keep your top spinning the longest? I've got a whole basketful of knucklebones too. And whirly-gigs!"

Aletta led the children to the library. Pieter greeted the four adults.

"Dear friends," he said putting his arm around Isabela's waist, "if you had not given that long, lavish, and entertaining wedding celebration, we might not be here, Isabela and I, to invite you to our own party."

While the men peered into the silver cupboards and examined the paintings and sculptures, the women shared memories of that night.

All of a sudden the house was filling up. A former Big Sister Isabela had worked with, Catharina Terborch, her husband and child.

Maira Elsevier, owner of the home where Isabel used to worship with other Catholics in the hidden attic chapel, Our Lord in the Attic.

Another student of Rembrandt and one whose talent Pieter especially admired, Carel Fabritius, who came all the way from Delft.

The jeweler, Mattheus Van de Venne and his wife, Lysbeth.

Daieman Raynier, current manager of Stradwijk and Son, the print shop founded by Nelleke's grandfather where Pieter was a frequent customer.

Anneliese had struggled to control her curiosity and concerns for five days. She was somewhat resentful that she had not been introduced to Pieter's new wife and daughter earlier. For the past ten years, enjoying her status as the wife of prominent merchant, Johannes Steen, busy raising two daughters and a son, she had worried and stewed over her older brother and only sibling. Each time he returned home after a long period away, she hoped he would return with a wife. She saw how he loved his nieces and nephew, how patiently he entertained them for hours, how they adored their Uncle Pieter. She knew he would make a wonderful father.

Pieter never spoke of Isabela, but Anneliese remembered clearly the day the letter from Isabela arrived saying she was married and expecting a child. Pieter alternately hung his head and paced as Anneliese read each English sentence silently and translated it into Dutch. At one point, holding the letter in one hand, she tried to pat Pieter on the back and calm him. But he rose and continued to pace. She had never seen her easy-going brother so tense.

She and Isabela corresponded about twice a year during this intervening decade. Isabela wrote about her children, about life in her village, but she never asked about Pieter. Anneliese assumed Isabela led a life as contented as her own. Yet as soon as Anneliese learned that Isabela's husband had died and that she was living in the New World in a place called San Agustín, she wrote her brother, hoping the letter would reach him in New Amsterdam, hoping he hadn't already moved on. For the next five months, she heard nothing.

Now suddenly Anneliese was holding both hands of the new mistress of her childhood home, her sister-in-law, older but still beautiful with that same reserved sweetness. They held onto each other, shaking their heads in disbelief, smiling through tears.

"It was destiny wasn't it?" Anneliese said. Not now but soon, I want to hear everything. Every detail. Welcome home, Isabela Calderón."

* * *

A loud shriek caused everyone to stop talking for a moment and turn toward a new arrival. A young woman came running up to the sisters-in-law, grabbed Isabela, put her arms around her, and held her so tight that for a few seconds Isabela could not breathe. When the young woman finally let go and stepped back, Isabela did not recognize her until she saw the light-blue dress, the familiar pearls, the shiny clasps that contrasted with the nearly black eyes. It was the blonde hair spilling out of the lace bonnet that convinced her.

"Nelleke? I didn't recognize you, my darling girl. You're all grown up. And you're wearing my dress!"

"Of course I am grown up, Isabela. I'm eighteen. You're twenty-eight. Will you be my Big Sister again? As for this dress, you wrote Housemother and told her to give it to me, remember?"

"Do you know that Nelita is wearing the dress you wore to Saskia's wedding? Ten years ago was it? The very dress that matches the one you're wearing? Oh, I must introduce you to one another.

"Nelleke, I read and reread every one of your letters. I think I have them memorized. Yet I have so many questions. There's so much more I want to know."

'What was I thinking?' Isabela asked herself. 'That I could meet all these people and chat casually with them at a party? As if I hadn't missed them all this while? As if hours and hours of mutual stories weren't pressing to be shared? How will I ever catch up?'

Isabela needn't have worried. She had forgotten how Nelleke could launch into any topic, how she lived a life of excitement and wonder.

Everything she saw and touched and smelled and heard was cause for exploration. The intensity that sometimes wore on Isabela when Nelleke was a child was quickly tiring her now. Being the center of attention could be exhausting, she realized.

'I need to sit down. I need to eat something,' she thought.

"I want to talk to you seriously," Nelleke whispered forcefully into Isabela's ear.

"I need to leave here. I need to find someone to travel with. But I need travel money too. Papa won't release my inheritance from my first father. He controls my investments. He insists that inheritance is part of my dowry. He tells me he has grown my funds considerably. Yours too, Isabela. The last week's salary you left behind. I believe you instructed Mrs. Heijn to give it to Papa to invest on your behalf."

Since corresponding with the orphanage Housemother on that topic, Isabela had not given a thought to those few guilders she had earned a decade ago.

Nelleke stepped back to take a breath and then continued whispering in Isabela's other ear. "And Mama. When I was little and kept running and falling and skinning my nose and my chin, she would say, 'What's your hurry, Nelleke? Walk. If you scratch that nose one more time, it will be so deformed that no man will marry you.' But I don't want to marry, Isabela. I want to study. I have to get out of Amsterdam. It's stifling me.

"Rembrandt believes life is too short NOT to take risks," Nelleke continued. "'Risks provide the most exciting times, even if they sometimes result in failure,'" he says. "'Routine deadens the mind.'"

"I may be able to help dear. We will set aside time later—soon—to discuss this."

Nelleke was pulling Isabela to a corner where apparently she hoped to hear what help Isabela could offer when the buzz of conversation in the room seemed to lift for a moment. A man wearing a flowing yellow turban, loose cream-colored shirt, and a wide leather belt over an expansive belly strolled into the room leaning on a crude wooden walking stick. The past tumultuous decade combined with the pull of gravity showed in his jowls and the wrinkled folds of his fleshy cheeks and chin. Yet he entered the room steadily, stoically, in a dignified manner.

He spotted Nelleke in the corner and approached her.

"My little firefly," he said kissing her on both cheeks. "I haven't seen you for such a long time. You don't visit me anymore."

Turning to Isabela, he introduced himself. "Rembrandt here. Are you a guest? A visitor?"

"Hello, Rembrandt. We've met before, you and I. Up on the wall that surrounds the city. You and several of your pupils. My husband, Pieter Hals, among them. That was the first time Pieter and I ever set eyes on one another."

With a nod to Isabela, Myriam Broekhof approached the group, took her daughter's arm and led her away.

"A most appealing young man by the buffet table would like to meet you, Nelleke," Myriam said.

Nelleke looked back over her shoulder at Isabela and rolled her eyes.

"You're not Isabela Calderón by any chance, are you?" Rembrandt asked. "The subject of that portrait Pieter worked on at the orphanage? Pieter was supposed to submit that portrait to the guild. Part of the requirement for becoming certified as a legitimate artist. I never saw that portrait," he said with dismay.

"Where is Pieter by the way?" Rembrandt asked. "I've taken some liberty with his invitation. I've brought an uninvited friend. Someone I met recently. On the street where I live. I frequently take my walks on the Joodenbreestraat. Yesterday a man approached me.

"'Might you be Rembrandt?' the man asked, squinting up at me. 'I've seen several of your self-portraits. Just now I'm coming from the Musketeers' Meeting Hall. I stood for an hour studying your militia portrait. I know it's controversial,' he said, 'but I find it utterly brilliant.' He went on to point out quite precisely what he admired about the painting. I liked the man immediately.

"Then he startled me by asking, 'That little girl in the yellow dress . . . is her name Nelleke?' Although the Broekhofs permitted Nelleke to pose for me several times for that one painting, they do not want it known that she was the model. They are quite protective of her and they need to be as she has always been a bit of what I would call 'a wild child.' Her name is indeed Nelleke." I told him. "Do you know her?"

"'No,'" he said. "'A friend of mine knew her when she was a child.'"

"In this case I answered truthfully. I was so curious to learn how this man with the heavy accent knew Nelleke's name. This man dressed as all men from that quarter are—in a black wool suit with white shirt, a skull cap, fringed tassels visible from beneath his jacket. They must all have the same hatter, the same tailor. I enjoy their company. They're wonderful conversationalists and very well educated and they've posed for me several times, especially for my paintings that deal with the Old Testament.

"Well, if you wish, I could introduce you to the adult Nelleke," I offered. "I'm attending a party tomorrow to celebrate the recent marriage of a former pupil of mine. Nelleke Broekhof is a neighbor of Pieter's. The Broekhofs will surely be there. Of course, I should ask the host first."

While he told the story, Rembrandt gazed at Isabela's gown. By the time he said, "Isaak is waiting just inside the door," he had bent over her so closely she feared he would bury his face in the fabric.

"This is a magnificent gown. I've never seen anything quite like it. I should like to paint it. I know exactly what mixes I need to capture the varieties of red . . . oh and that subtle gold that runs throughout the bodice."

Rembrandt reached out with both hands now. "May I?" he asked. Without waiting for an answer he examined the sleeves. Starting at her shoulder, he caressed each layer, raised it up, felt it and put it back in place.

"Moon gold," he mumbled to himself. "That's the color I would use as a base."

'He may run his fingers over the skirt next,' Isabela thought, 'or kneel at my feet. All the better to sniff the dye and finger the texture.'

Pieter caught Isabela's eye from across the room.

'I know exactly what Pieter is asking me with that glance,' she realized. 'Are you okay? Is he bothering you? Shall I rescue you?'

She was equally certain that Pieter would interpret correctly the slight shake of her head, the momentary piercing of her lips together.

'I'm fine. I can handle him.'

'This is like those moments of communication I observed between the tailor and his wife, how they sometimes made decisions without saying a word.'

The silent intimacy and assuredness of her communication with her new husband sent a thrill through her.

Isabela was curious, though, as to how this Isaak knew Nelleke's name. Jews and Calvinists did not mix much except for business. But she could see that the story told in Rembrandt's rambling style might take quite awhile and really, she must stop him from exploring the gown.

Pieter had told her that, although he was falling out of fashion and having difficulty attracting clients, one of his admirers described Rembrandt as a "man of deep empathy for the human condition."

Yet Isabela understood why others found the brilliant painter difficult. Here he was taking up her time telling stories and attempting to examine every inch of the fabric covering her body when she had a houseful of friends she hadn't seen in a decade and there was an uninvited guest standing alone by the front door. She took his arm and guided him toward the entrance way.

"I'd like to meet your friend," she said. "Let's invite him to join us."

* * *

Her body knew before her consciousness. Her heart began to palpitate wildly. Her knees gave way and she reached for a surprised Rembrandt's hand to steady herself. With each step, she became infused with a multi-sense of awareness and increasing intensity. She feared she might faint. 'Perhaps I should just suggest that Rembrandt accompany the guest into the parlor by himself. I must be fatigued and overexcited. I need to rest,' she thought.

But they were already there. During the eighteen months she spent in Amsterdam's orphanage, she had seen only one family from this tribe. They mostly kept to themselves. She recognized the style of dress which Rembrandt had just described and the way the beard reached to the man's chest. She smiled a vague welcome, still trying to manage the sudden onslaught of emotions. To steady her trembling hand, she reached into the hidden pocket of the gown. She felt the tiny scroll.

It was the man's spectacles resting low on his nose, though, that made her stop and stare at him. The bow of the spectacles was wrapped in black silk. The intense dark eyes behind the spectacles gazed at her directly. Were they watery from the dust outside? Or were those tears? Tears that were beginning to run down his cheeks. Tears, she now realized, like the ones she herself had been shedding for some moments now.

"Isabela Calderón, may I introduce my friend, Isaak Jonah Valverde?" Rembrandt said.

Then perhaps as a way to explain his friend's display of emotion, Rembrandt offered, "Mr. Valverde arrived recently in Amsterdam after a long difficult journey. I too lost a wife I loved deeply. I understand his sadness."

Epilogue

Angel and Petal are married twice. First in a Timucuan ceremony in Petal's village that begins with two gestures symbolizing their pledge to care for each other. With the help of his brother-in-law, Big Owl, Angel kills and skins a deer and presents it to Petal. Petal prepares a tasty corn-and-cherry dish and places it in Angel's hands.

Their second wedding ceremony takes place in the San Agustín church immediately following Petal's required conversion to the Catholic faith. Friar Alonzo leads both the conversion and Christian wedding rituals.

As a wedding present, Angel explains Gérard's instructions and places around Petal's neck the Caravaca Cross.

"This I give to you, my wife, Petal, as a sign of my devotion with the hope that it will protect you from danger for many years to come," he tells her before leading her to the bed he has recently constructed.

Petal prefers her native necklaces. She never fully grasps the meaning or symbolism of the cross. Words like "died for your sins" are meaningless to her. For Petal, the main value of the cross is that it was a gift from her husband on her wedding night. The bronze sometimes irritates her skin. Once Angel finds the cross mixed in with the laundry. Another time he finds it dangling from a rafter. Yet during some of his favorite times when Petal reaches out to him invitingly under the colorful woven Indian blanket they share, he discovers that the only thing on her strong body is the double cross playfully hidden between her bronze-colored breasts.

* * *

During a grain shortage in 1656 Florida Governor Diego de Rebolledo sends out an order that every male Timucuan must bring all the way to San Agustín a large quantity of corn from his own storage. The deliveries threaten the food supply the natives had set aside for the winter. The Timucuan have no beasts of burden. The order requires them to walk carrying a seventy-five-pound sack on their backs. The order applies to ALL males, including Chiefs. Furious at the indignity of being treated as common laborers and fearing an undermining of the authority and respect they had maintained for millennia, the Chiefs rebel. Although few people are killed in the rebellion itself, the Governor orders that all Chiefs be publicly hung. **Big Owl** is among them.

By 1700, the Timucuan population is reduced to 1000 from the 200,000 when the Spanish first landed. In 1752 only twenty-six remain. A short time later the last known Timucuan dies.

* * *

After the rebellion, the de Vega family packs up their belongings in preparation for a permanent move away from San Agustín. Petal hurriedly prepares some food for the trip. Perspiring in the heat, she removes from her neck the cross which she had looped through a long reed, and places it on the kitchen table. She scoops up unusable fish bones, inedible vegetable peelings, pieces of broken crockery, a bent spoon, and a few unneeded buttons. She places it all in the deep trash pit in the garden and covers it with a wooden plank. Later as she, Angel, and their children sail to their new home, she realizes she is no longer the keeper of the double cross.

'Perhaps someone else—someone else who needs the protection more than I do, will find it,' she thinks.

Petal could not have imagined that the double cross would remain in that refuse pile for the next 350 years.

* * *

Well into his fourth decade of life, **Angel de Vega** continues to run his passenger transport business. Often Petal and their children accompany him. One afternoon a river boat flying a Spanish flag pulls up beside them.

"Permission to board, Sir," one of the crew from the Spanish boat calls up. "Only myself. A friendly visit."

"Permission granted, Sir—with the understanding that you leave all weapons behind," Angel calls down.

The heavily bearded man scrambles aboard. Until Petal turns them away, the children stare at the long, slim, jagged scar on the man's face. The scar begins just under the man's hat on the far right, cuts across his eyebrow, through his eye which surely is no longer of much use, across the top of his nose and left cheek. It ends just as it reaches his left ear.

"What is your business, Sir? How may I be of assistance?" Angel asks the stranger.

"It's about that carving, Sir. The one at the front of your boat. The figurehead."

"Do you wish to know the name of the carver? He was a most talented artist. Now deceased, I regret to say."

"If he is half as talented as his model apparently was beautiful, he must be gifted indeed."

"At my request, my mother served as the model, Sir."

"Interesting. The figure reminds me of my own mother. May I ask her name?"

"Her name is Isabela Calderón."

"YOUR mother? MY mother had that very same name. At the time we were separated, I was her only son. Any sons born after me would have been younger than either me or you, Sir."

Angel is distracted by the scar. Now in the afternoon sun he notices that in the man's intact dark-brown left eyebrow, he can detect hints of red. His eyes move to the man's shoulders. Just like Angel's own, this man's left shoulder is visibly lower than the one on the right. The two men stand staring at each other.

"If I am not mistaken, Sir . . . might your name be . . . Angel de Vega?"

"The very same, Sir. And might YOUR name be that of my long-lost brother? Might you be **Pedro de Vega?**"

"The very same, Sir."

Once Petal has determined that the man is not a threat, she turns her attention back to her tasks and to her children. She has not heard any of the men's discourse. She is quite taken aback when, curious as to why the men have ceased speaking, she turns around to see her husband locked in a tight embrace with the stranger.

* * *

Isabela arranges **Pieter's** stockpile of drawings chronologically by town into separate albums—Rome, Florence, Brussels, San Agustín, and Amsterdam, New Amsterdam. Stradwijk and Son prints the publications with appealing covers. Collecting the entire set becomes a sign of status among wealthy Amsterdam residents. When the fad spreads to other cities, customers purchase them at such a pace that the printer can barely keep up with demand. Because he never completes the requirements for becoming a member of the artist guild, Pieter cannot benefit financially from the books' earnings. He donates the profits to The Amsterdam City Orphanage.

Isabela and **Nelita** continue the *Mouse Onboard* series. When the mouse discovers books on the ship, the mouse realizes how limited his life is. He reads voraciously. Nelleke and others contribute to the books' content on mathematics, insects, and constellations. Each new version of the series is highly anticipated by Dutch families.

* * *

Living only two houses apart, **Isabela** and **Anneliese** are each other's closest confidante. Their five children are both cousins and best friends. At age eighteen, **Nelita** marries her cousin, Ludolf Steen. The young couple settles nearby. **Anneliese** and **Philip**, **Isabela** and **Pieter** are all grandparents to the same children.

* * *

Nelleke Broekhof and her cousin, **Willem van Randen,** who have adored one another since childhood, learn the surprising and upsetting reason why they can never marry. **Nelleke** grapples with her parents' unwanted attempts to find proper suitors for her and her own determination to explore the world beyond the city of Amsterdam.

* * *

Radiant in her mother's wedding dress, **Briana Valverde** marries a fellow Portuguese immigrant, Jakob da Fonseca. Isabela and Nelita sit in the balcony of the synagogue with the women. Pieter sits below with the men. At the feast following the ceremony, men dance with men, women with women. When the Klezmorim musicians take a break, Briana first delights and then mesmerizes the guests when she spontaneously breaks into song. In a voice now transformed into a crystalline soprano, she pours out her joy in a variation of the very piece she performed at Isabela's wedding party years ago. This time the bird does not disappear into the sky. It does not seek to escape, but it does explore. After its wings come close to being singed by the sun, the curious bird returns to earth and lands in a nest where its mate is waiting.

* * *

In 1665, more than a decade after first becoming entranced with it, **Rembrandt** borrows the bridal gown from Isaak Valverde for one of his final works—a tender portrayal of Jewish newlyweds. Rembrandt dies in 1669 at the age of 63. Centuries later artist Vincent van Gogh, speaking of the painting which was by then titled "The Jewish Bride," declares,

"I should be happy to give ten years of my life if I could go on sitting here in front of this picture for a fortnight, with only a crust of dry bread for food."

* * *

Isaak Jonah Valverde becomes a partner in his brother's diamond-cutting business. He also assists the Rabbi in preparing young men for becoming a Bar Mitzvah. Isaak's real joy is tutoring young Jews and non-Jews alike in a variety of subjects. He is in such demand that he is able to choose among Amsterdam's most gifted students of all religions, including **Hendrik Hals,** the son of Isabela and Pieter. While attending the University of Leiden, Isaak's own son, **Bernardo,** dies in the plague of 1653.

Isaak is a frequent visitor to the Hals household. He never remarries. Each night after three hours of reading in his home on Joodenbreestraat, just before he puts out the lamp, the last objects his eyes rest upon are a pair of framed paintings on the wall opposite his bed. In one painting a man and a woman sit on either side of a chess board. The woman's hand is raised as if she is about to pick up a piece and move it. The man leans back and observes her.

In the second painting the same man and woman sit in separate chairs on either side of another small table. Each holds an open book. Both rest an arm on the table and lean toward each other intently. The table is narrow, but their arms do not quite touch. The man wears the typical garb of a wealthy Jewish Amsterdam businessman. The most striking feature of the attractive woman is the swath of silver hair on one side of her still—dark widow's peak. The signature of the artist is visible in the lower right corner of both paintings. **Pieter Hals**.

* * * *

Acknowledgements

I wish to thank Maarten de Haan, Jacob GunderKline, Barbara Gorney, Howard Gorney, Martha Kline, Judy Slight, and Allen White, early readers of the manuscript for their thoughtful reactions and suggestions that helped shape this work; Lodewijk J. Wagenaar of the University of Amsterdam for keeping my characters firmly in the 17th century; Faye Camardo for her encouragement and sharp editor's eye; the Ximenez-Fatio House; the helpful staffs at both the St. Augustine Historical Society Research Library and the Holland Society of New York for steering me toward crucial seventeenth-century historical documents; and the dozens of published novelists, historians, and researchers whose writings plunged me into the worlds of Golden Age Amsterdam, small Spanish villages, the Inquisition, and struggling New World towns St. Augustine and New Amsterdam.

Resources

Barnes, Donna R. and Peter G. Rose. (2012) *Childhood Pleasures: Dutch Children in the Seventeenth Century.* Syracuse, NY: Syracuse University Press.

Barnes, Donna R. (Curator) (2004) *Playing, Learning, Working in Amsterdam's Golden Age: Jan Luyken's Mirrors of Daily Life.* Hofstra Museum. Hempstead, N.Y.: Hofstra University.

Berlin, Irving. (1954) "Sisters," from the musical, *"White Christmas."*

Brook, Timothy. (2008) *Vermeer's Hat: The Seventeenth Century and the Dawn of the Global World.* New York: Bloomsbury Press.

Carvajal, Doreen. (2012) *The Forgetting River: A Modern Tale of Survival, Identity, and the Inquisition.* Riverhead Books. de Bie, Ceciel and Martijn Leenen. (2001) *Rembrandt: See and Do Children's Book.* Los Angeles, CA: J. Paul Getty Museum. de Cervantes, Miguel. (2001) *Don Quixote: The History and Adventures of the Renowned.* Translated by Tobias Smollett. New York University: The Modern Library Classics.

Defourneaux, Marcelin. (1979) *Daily Life in Spain in the Golden Age.* Stanford University Press.

Dewhurst, William W. (1885) *The History of St. Augustine, Florida.* New York: G.P. Putnam's Sons.

Else, George (ed.) (2003) *Discovery Series: Insects & Spiders.* Barnes & Noble.

Florida Humanities Council. (2012) "The View From the Shore: Florida Before the Conquest." *Forum.* Vol. 3, Fall.

Greer, Bill. (2009) *The Mevrouw Who Saved Manhattan: A novel of New Amsterdam.* Brooklyn, NY: Manhattan View Press.

Hatcher, Patricia Law. (2007) *De Halve Maen Index, Volumes 52-79, 1977-2006*. New York: The Holland Society of New York.

Hird, Henry E. (ed.) (2008) *Handbook of 50 Pirates: Ships, Weapons, Flags, Maps, Treasure & Stories*. St. Augustine, FL: Historic Print and Map Company.

Jacobs, Jaap. (2009) *The Colony of New Netherland: A Dutch Settlement in Seventeenth-Century America*. Cornell University Press.

Mak, Geert. (1999) *Amsterdam: A Brief Life of the City*. The Harvill Press.

McFarlane, Jim. (2012) *Penelope: A Novel of New Amsterdam*. Greer, S.C.: Twisted Cedar Press.

Platt, Donald Michael. (2008 and 2011) *Rocamora: Man of Masks*. Peterborough, N.H.: Raven's Wing Books.

Resnick, Seymour and Jeanne Pasmantier (eds.) (1958) *An Anthology of Spanish Literature In English Translation: Volume I*. Frederick Ungar Publishing Company.

Sappington, Drew. (2011) *Hidden History of St. Augustine*. The History Press.

Sarti, Raffaella. (2002) *Europe at Home: Family and Material Culture 1500-1800*. New Haven, CT: Yale University Press.

Schama, Simon. (1987) *The Embarrassment of Riches: An Interpretation of Dutch Culture in the Golden Age*. Vintage Publishing.

Scheltema, Gajus and Heleen Westerhuijs (eds.) (2011) *Exploring Historic Dutch New York: New York City, Hudson Valley, New Jersey, Delaware*. Dover Publications.

Shorto, Russell. (2005) *The Island at the Center of the World: The Epic Story of Dutch Manhattan and the Forgotten Colony that Shaped America*. Vintage.

Weitzel, Kelley G. (2000) *The Timucua Indians: A Native American Detective Story*. University Press of Florida.

Wikipedia.org.

Winkel, Raphaël. (1998) *Liedjes Van Vroeger: Samengesteld en Getekend*. Lisse: Rebo Productions.

Discussion Questions for Readers of
The New Worlds of Isabela Calderón

Part I. Spain

1) A young Spanish ship captain poses as a Dutch soldier, breaks into an Amsterdam institution, locates his betrothed, wraps her in a blanket and carries her in his arms to his ship temporarily and illegally flying a Dutch flag before returning with her to their native village. This daring deed seems to have romantic overtones, but does it? What motivates Diego de Vega to take such risks? What does his behavior on this trip say about his character? What adjectives would you use to describe him?

2) Some readers find it odd that Isabela does not protest when Diego comes for her. What reasons does she give for her compliance? Given the situation and her relationship with the orphans, do you think her explanation is understandable? What might have happened if she had resisted?

3) How does Isabela learn the reasons for Diego's act? How does the realization of his true intentions change her and shape her future?

4) The villagers of Santos Gemelos sometimes refer to Isabela as "la princesa." Her child friend, Briana Valverde, calls her "the princess in the castle on the hill." What do they

407

mean by this? How does her perceived status affect her relationships within the village?

5) Arriving back home after two years away, Isabela finds a situation totally different from that of her childhood. Expecting the secure haven she remembers, she instead experiences shock, fear, loss, and threats. Elaborate the ways she copes and adapts over the next ten years.

6) Cook/Aurelia, the Valverde family, and Leonor's brood all play a significant role. How does each contribute to and challenge Isabela's life? How does she do the same for them?

7) The Valverde family is closed and self-protective. Why are they upset when they learn that Briana has escaped for a brief period in order to sing at Isabela's wedding? What is it they fear?

Part II. New Spain

8) Isabela is forced to start life over once more in San Agustín – an isolated and dangerous colony. How is she a different person at twenty-eight than she was at eighteen when she arrived back in Santos Gemelos? What has she learned during her twenties decade that helps her adapt?

9) Discuss the letters from Nelleke. Do they add to the narrative or distract from it? What does it mean to Isabela to maintain that connection with Nelleke as Nelleke grows from a child to a young woman?

10) Freed from all judgment but her own self-judgment when Isabela writes letters to the tailor that will never be read, what does she reveal about herself? Why does she write a final letter and destroy all her fantasy correspondence? Why does the tailor continue to occupy her thoughts?

11) Discuss Angel's character and his deepening relationship with Isabela. Do you think such a seemingly good person is capable of murder? Given that he is a mere youth, do you think his sensitivities and his ability to take charge and forge a new life for himself are realistic?

Part III. Amsterdam—New and Old

12) While in New Amsterdam, Isabela is in a kind of holding pattern. What must still be resolved before she and Pieter can marry and return to Amsterdam? How does Isabela busy herself during this period? How do you react to her last-minute doubts and fears? To Pieter's handling of her continued uncertainty?

13) During their visits and correspondence while both were in Santos Gemelos, the tailor's comments are limited to business transactions or intellectual discussions. Why do he and Reza give Isabela the diamond? What does that gesture reveal about the feelings they have for her? What is your reaction to the way Isabela ultimately uses the diamond?

14) Were you surprised by the ending or did you suspect this reunion would take place at some point? Rembrandt gives an explanation for Isaak Valverde's unusual display of emotion. What do you think Isaak is feeling? Comment on the role of Reza's bridal gown in his relationship with Isabela.

15) Do you find the wrap-up stories in the Epilogue believable? Satisfying? We never witness the initial meeting between Isaak Valverde and Pieter Hals which assuredly takes place during Pieter and Isabela's wedding celebration. Given the final description in the Epilogue of the paintings by Pieter Hals, how do you suppose the relationship among Isabela, Pieter, and Isaak evolves?

General

16) Which character do you think undergoes the most change? Discuss the arc of that change. What influences the alteration? The words "New Worlds" in the title refer to physical places, states of mind, and new experiences. How many "new worlds" does Isabela encounter?

17) One of the themes of Isabela's story is protection. How many different kinds of protection appear in the book? How effective are they? Why was protection such an issue in the seventeenth century? Is protection still an issue in today's world? Is the protection we seek similar or different?

18) Beginning when she was a little girl and adored her often-absent father, Isabela has intense relationships with several men. Name these men. How does each relate to her? How do they lead her to both question and define her own self-image? How do they change her?

19) When asked, "Who is your favorite character?" readers seem to choose a character that reflects their own age and gender. Do you have a favorite? If so, what is it about that character that appeals to you?

20) What do the Timucuans add to Isabela's story? Trace the evolvement of her attitude toward the Timucuan characters beginning with the first time she sees Big Owl on the streets of San Agustín.

Excerpt from The Seventh Etching

Book One of Amsterdam Trilogy

onkey brain. That is his affliction. Creatures arrive from every direction and insist that he give them life. A black lion stands on its hind feet, its large front paws reaching forward ready to grab. A horned one-eyed reptile gazes with a menace that won't let go. A wizard with horizontal hair focuses his tiny eyes on the end of a long nose so sharp it could cut a slice of morning cheese.

After two rushed days of drawing, painting, cutting, and rolling the heavy presses back and forth, Nicolaas tried desperately to ban the haunting images that drove him. 'Surely there is a comforting thought I can conjure up to calm my spirit and my aching body,' he thought.

And then there it was. His mother. Her long dark skirt on wide hips. The mussed faded white apron. The cap tight around her face. Her usual expression—straight, thin lips, grim and determined. The full sleeves of her blouse rolled up above the elbows. Her arms covered in suds, she massages the shoulders of her husband. Father. Sitting in the wooden laundry tub. His back to her, head bent forward, the tips of his long hair touching the surface of the water, hiding his face. His chest naked, glistening.

No. Wait. This couple is young, playful. The girl pulls the young man's head against her belly, reaches down, cups her hand under his chin, pulls his head backwards, bites his lip. The man reaches up toward the woman's turban, unwinds it, tosses it in the water. Her thick hair cascades.

Lying on his narrow, wooden bed, hoping for a few hours of deep sleep, Nicolaas moves one hand instinctively toward his groin. To unbuckle and unbutton, though—that would require the work of both hands. His breathing slows. He collapses. His inky fingers rest on his thigh. His dreams continue without him.

Excerpt from Book Three of Amsterdam Trilogy—
Working Title: The Rise of Dirck Becker
Expected publication date: 2016

"Miss Broekhof, I feel certain that we have met before."

"Oh, really? Where might that have been, Mr. Becker?"

"I know exactly where and when and how, but I'm not going to tell you."

"Not going to tell me? Was it that horrid a meeting?"

"It was quite wonderful really—at least for me. I wouldn't expect you to recall it. It was many years ago. How about if I try to lead you back into the memory of that meeting? This will be a long voyage. Only one month past. Two more months before we land in New Amsterdam. How about this, Miss Broekhof? Every day I'll give you a hint—a one-word hint?"

"Like a puzzle then? All the words will eventually fit together and I'll see in my mind the time we met? Do you think I'll remember it exactly?"

"I certainly hope so. Are you ready for the first hint?"

"Yes, please."

"Hint number one is . . . breakdown."

"Breakdown? Breakdown of what? A bridge? Communication? A whole system of some sort?"

"OK, here's the second part of the . . . the game, if you will. You may ask me one question each day about our meeting. One question that can be answered yes or no. You already have your first hint. So what is your first question—your question for today, Miss Broekhof? Is your chosen question 'Was it a bridge that broke down?' or will you pose a different question?"

"Are you finished with making up rules now?"

"I'm finished. Only two rules. One hint a day from ME. One yes or no question a day from YOU."

"All right then. Where were we?"

"That is not a question that can be answered yes or no. Rephrase the question."

"This is quite irritating, you know. Why don't you just tell me where and how we met. And, by the way, are you SURE we've met or are you just making that up?"

"Is that your question?"

"No, that is not my question. It does not relate directly to our supposed meeting."

"Agreed. I'll answer that one then. No, I am not making this up. You get another question – a REAL yes or no question."

"I have too many questions. How can I choose?"

"Only you can choose. I just answer with 'yes' or 'no.'"

"All right then. Forget the breakdown for a moment. Where did we meet? Rather, I suppose I should ask, in order to phrase my questions as you require . . . did we meet in Amsterdam?"

"The answer to your question, 'Did we meet in Amsterdam?' is no."

"But to have met elsewhere is unlikely. I've lived nearly every year of my life in that city."

"For tomorrow's question, I suggest you focus on one word in your last statement."

"And what might that word be?"

"That one word is 'nearly.' You've lived NEARLY every year of your life in Amsterdam."

About the Author

Judith Kline White came of age in rural Ohio and earned degrees at both Oberlin College and Ohio State University. Her adult life includes extended periods with her husband in Central and South America, Amsterdam and Boston. A lifelong lover of language, Judith is fluent in French and Spanish and conversant in Dutch which she regularly refreshes during visits to the Netherlands. Her careers span linguist, educator, entrepreneur and nonprofit fundraiser, including Peace Corps volunteer and trainer; Founder of Foreign Language for Young Children; Co-Founder/Co-Director of Global Child, Inc., and Director of Development of Latin American Health Institute. Her previous publications include *Phrase-a-Day Series for Children in*

French, Spanish and English. The New Worlds of Isabela Calderón is her second novel and sequel to *The Seventh Etching* (iUniverse, 2012). She is currently writing the third historic novel of *Amsterdam Trilogy* as well as a memoir, *Life in a Plastic Pouch: A Tale of Romance, Stem Cells and Rebirth*. Mother of three grown children and grandmother of three, Judith lives with her husband in the Boston area and Ponte Vedra Beach, Florida.

CPSIA information can be obtained at www.ICGtesting.com
Printed in the USA
BVOW03*1501280514

354457BV00001B/2/P